# THE
# OATHWARDEN

EPIC ONE

## PATH OF BLOOD

# THE
# OATHWARDEN

EPIC ONE

## PATH OF BLOOD

*by*

## JAMES D. CONRAD

This is a work of fiction. While it draws inspiration from mythological traditions, all characters, places, and events are products of the author's imagination. Any resemblance to actual persons, living or dead, is purely coincidental.

Hardback ISBN: 979-8-9936099-0-4
Paperback ISBN: 979-8-9936099-1-1

Cover design by Deborah Conrad.

Printed in the United States.

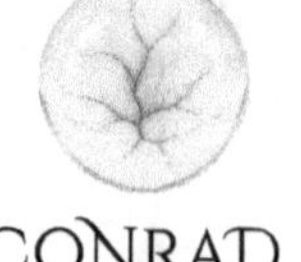

CONRAD
PUBLISHING


Website: JamesDConrad.com

*My love,*
*My life,*
*My heart,*
*To my wife*

# TABLE OF CONTENTS

# CHAPTER 1
## *Survive the Night*

Thomas woke standing.

He was on the side of a hill, surrounded by trees. Darkness pressed in from all sides. He turned his head but couldn't see more than a few feet in any direction. There was no sound: no wind, no voices, nothing familiar. Just his pounding heart.

It was cold, and a mist hung in the air, clinging to his skin. The area smelled of earth and leaves, with the faint scent of something sweet and rotten.

His head pounded with pain. His world spun with exhaustion and fear. He was breathing hard, like he'd been jogging. He shivered, whether from cold or shock, he couldn't tell. He didn't know where he was or how he'd gotten there.

He shifted his weight; his legs felt sluggish. As he tried to move his foot, it caught on something—a root or a rock. He couldn't tell in the dark, but he nearly pitched forward down the slope. Panic surged. He thought about sitting down, but the darkness felt too heavy, too wrong. The ground was too foreign. He didn't trust it or his surroundings. He didn't trust his perceptions or his own mind.

This wasn't just unfamiliar. It was hostile.

The last thing he remembered was going to bed in his own house. He fell asleep quickly, and then he was there. Alone. Hurt. Lost in unknown woods.

Pain burned across his palms. They were raw and stinging. He squinted down at his hands and could see scratches. Maybe blood—probably his. But as his mind began to clear, a deeper unease crept in.

**Snap.**

A twig broke behind him.

Thomas froze. His eyes widened.

He didn't know what was happening, but every instinct screamed: Don't be seen. Don't be heard.

His thoughts steadied, narrowing to a single idea:

*Survive the night.*

He crouched slowly, trying to reduce his profile until his fingers rested on the damp ground. His breath came fast, too fast. He hadn't even realized he was holding it, but now he needed air.

*Focus, Thomas.*

*I don't know why I'm here, but I want to live through it.*

*Someone's here with me, and I need to hear them before they hear me.*

Something moved in the dark. Quiet, but not silent. Not random. It was heading in the direction he'd been facing when he woke.

*Is that even the right word? Woke? Was I asleep?*

*I don't sleepwalk. Never have.*

*Control your breathing.*

*Deep and slow. In through the nose. Out through the mouth. He'll hear you if you panic.*

He scanned through the black of night, straining. Almost nothing was visible beyond a few nearby trees. One stood a foot away. It was solid, rough-barked. He pressed against it, grateful for something to hide behind, a refuge in the black. Somehow, just touching it made him feel safer.

Then came a sound. It was low and distant, but it was growing closer. His mind was foggy, struggling to process the situation—to contain the terror and focus on the moment. He recognized the sound, but his mind was filled with questions. He pushed them out except for that sound.

*A car.*

*Don't get too excited.*

*A car just means people, but not necessarily the kind you want to meet.*

*I still don't know what's happening or why I'm here.*

The light from the car started to drift through the trees. The car was going to pass nearby.

*Okay, Thomas, a car means a road, and a road means civilization.*

*That means a way home.*

*Escaping from this nightmare.*

He watched, waiting to see where it would pass. That's when he saw it.

A silhouette.

Not the car, but a person. It stood between Thomas and the road. The figure slowly crouched, hunched awkwardly, his head partially obscured by branches. Between the fear and the fog in his head, details were hard to pinpoint—but the figure looked big.

Thomas wished he could see it better, but was grateful the branches masked the figure's head. If they hid the shadow's face, maybe they hid his too.

*Okay, I woke up facing downhill. I turned and looked behind me when I heard the twig snap.*

*The silhouette is to my left now, which means it is facing the same way I was when I woke.*

*When it turned, it wasn't a coincidence. He's looking for me.*

*Chasing me or traveling with me?*

*Don't move. Don't breathe too loud. Lean into the tree. Sink. Disappear.*

*Think thin thoughts.*

The figure's head turned. It was slow, deliberate. Searching.

Thomas didn't need confirmation. He knew.

It was hunting him.

The car continued on; the light faded, and the figure faded back into the shadows of the woods. Thomas knew that to reach the road, he would need to go straight past the stranger. He was certain that it would lead to a confrontation with an opponent who could be armed. Instead, he just had to remember the route and go later.

For now: pause, wait, watch.

*Okay, the big guy hasn't moved. I can't see him anymore, but there are leaves everywhere. I'd hear him.*

*Just stay calm. Be steady. Listen.*

*If he charges, don't run. You'll trip, and he'll be on you.*

*If he charges… fight!*

*You got this—you got in that one fight in high school. You did great.*

*Confidence. Keep a calm head. Eye of the tiger, Thomas.*

**Snap. Snap.**

*It's moving—I mean, he's moving! It can't be an "it."*

*My hands are shaking. It's the adrenaline.*

*Breathe.*

**Snap. Snap.**

With a slight sigh, Thomas realized the snapping twigs were getting fainter. The silhouette was moving away. It was heading down the hill and toward the road.

Thomas wanted to go to the road too, but not now. He had to plan his next move. He was tired and hurt, though he didn't know why. He didn't know how he would fare in a fight right now, but probably not as well as in high school.

*Let's think this through. If I move now, I could be heard. If I can hear him, he could hear me.*

*If I wait, then head for the road later, he might already be there—waiting. I'd never know, and he would have the advantage.*

*I could wait until sunrise. Vision could really help in a situation like this… but I assume the other guy can see too.*

*I could move away from the road, give this whole place a wide berth, and try to find a road or a house somewhere else.*

*Thomas looked around again, startled.*

*Where am I anyway?*

*When I went to bed, it was cold. There was snow on the ground.*

*There's no snow here.*

*So how far did I travel?*

*Is "travel" the right word? Was I kidnapped? Drugged?*

He turned his head. Listening. Straining for any sound.

*Wait… no more snapping twigs or crinkling leaves.*

*Either he stopped, or he stepped onto a different ground layer. If it's rock or hard dirt, I've lost him.*

*If he just stopped, then he's listening again. He knows I didn't make it to the road.*

*At least this isn't the worst thing I've ever been through.*

*No—it is. It absolutely is the worst thing I have ever been through.*

Thomas began creeping as quietly as he could, moving away from the last place he heard the silhouette's footsteps. That meant moving away from the promise of safety the road provided. He decided to give the whole area a wide berth and try to pick up the road later. He'd made some distance through the woods when—

**Snap.**

He froze. His breath caught in his throat.

He messed up. He knew he had messed up. The person chasing him had stopped to listen, and Thomas had given him exactly what he wanted.

Proof that Thomas was still here.

**Snap.**

The other person was moving slowly, too, trying to creep. Thomas almost laughed. It would be comical if he didn't feel his life hung in the balance.

*Here we are—two people in the woods in the dark, creeping around and trying not to be heard by the other.*

*The silly part is, I have no idea why. I suddenly want to yell, "Marco."*

*Yeah, don't. That's the irrational fear, Thomas. Maybe ignore that part.*

*Maybe the person following me is my friend? Maybe I'm hunting him? Maybe—*

His mind was starting to reel again. He could feel it spinning out of control. He was an engineer. He liked spreadsheets. The most adventurous thing he did on an average day was eating the older leftovers in the fridge.

*NO! Calm down. Don't speculate.*

*Survive the night and get therapy in the morning.*

The snaps stopped again. He strained his eyes between the trees, but there was nothing.

He waited. What felt like hours passed, but it was only minutes. His knees ached from crouching in his awkward, sneaking position.

Another car in the distance. Thomas watched the shadows. No silhouette this time as it passed. They had wandered too far from the road; the light didn't reach them anymore. The woods remained dim, indifferent.

*He knows I'm here. I know he's here.*

*If I wait until daylight, we'll see each other—I'll have to fight.*

*If I'm reckless, he'll get the upper hand.*

*I'm in good shape. If I head deeper into the woods, maybe I can outpace him and circle back to the road.*

*If so, I need to do it before my nerves and knees give out altogether.*

Thomas stood and began to walk. He walked away from the road and civilization, but most importantly, he walked away from the other person. He wasn't trying to be noisy but knew he would be heard no matter what he did. So, he walked steadily, hoping the other person would continue creeping and fall behind.

**Snap. Snap. Snap.**

Apparently, the other guy had the same idea, but maybe he was walking faster.

Thomas picked up his pace. Brisk walk... no good. The snaps were getting closer.

He shifted to a jog, crouching as he moved, shielding his face from branches with his left hand. The slaps against his skin were starting to sting, but he didn't care. He didn't dare slow down.

**Snap. Snap. Snap.**

Up ahead—light. An opening in the trees. Moonlight streamed through. He pushed harder. If he could just see where to plant his feet, he could keep going. He could outrun the danger chasing him. The snaps were right behind him, but as he cleared the trees, he broke into a full sprint, confident in his speed.

His feet suddenly had nothing beneath them. He sailed through the air as he fell off a cliff.

The trees had opened up for a good reason. There was no ground beyond them. He dropped eighteen feet, landing hard on a steep bank, tumbling through brush, and slamming into a rock with his ribs.

He came to a breathless, stunned stop. His mouth was filled with dust, but he fought the urge to cough. He blinked back the grit in his eyes.

Everything hurt; each breath cost him pain.

He lay still, forcing back a moan. The impact had knocked the wind out of him and lit a fire in his side. He'd moved fast, fallen fast, and hopefully avoided severe injury, but he'd pay for it if he had to run again.

He looked back toward the edge. After a few seconds, the shadowy figure appeared, still cloaked in shadows from the trees. Thomas could see it peering down, head turning, scanning the ground for signs of him.

Thomas didn't move. When he landed, if that could be called a landing, he slid right into a patch of weeds and brush. He was hidden. He hoped playing opossum would work.

*Control the breathing… yeah, it hurts. Get over it.*

*Survive the night. Go to the hospital in the morning.*

*Why isn't that guy breathing hard? I can barely control my breath, and he's just standing there. Barely moving.*

Thomas watched him. The silhouette didn't seem winded. It seemed almost inhuman. But it apparently didn't want to jump off a cliff to continue the chase.

It moved back into the trees. The snapping sounds picked up again, drifting off to Thomas's left, moving along the top of the cliff. That was the direction he'd been heading when he first woke up, parallel to the direction of the road.

He had decided that left was "south," though he didn't have a good reason why. It just helped him sort out the directions in his mind. That meant "west" was the path back to the road.

Thomas allowed himself to breathe again. He slowly stretched out, one hand pushing him up from the dirt, the other pressing against his ribs. Pain coursed through his whole body. Some parts had already hurt when he woke up, but more of him hurt now.

He crawled slowly and quietly to the edge of the brush and listened.

No more sounds.

*Okay, Thomas. Decision time.*

*Climb the cliff and head toward the road? No—that's stupid. "It" is up there.*

*Head left? That's where that figure is going.*

*No point running from that shadow just to walk back into it.*

*Continue into the woods, away from the road, become lost, grow a beard, become a mountain man?*

*Hard pass.*
*Head right? That's the direction I was leaving when I woke up.*
*It's opposite to where "it" went and might run parallel to the road.*
*Hopefully, "it" won't expect me to double back.*
*All right, Thomas. Let's hobble back to society.*

# CHAPTER 2
## *Climbing Through Darkness*

Thomas made slow progress, but it was still progress. He half-crawled, half-slithered across the ground, careful not to make a sound or rise above the brush.

He paused often to listen. He was starting to feel safer. There were no sounds of pursuit. No signs of the figure that had haunted him since he woke in this nightmare.

He had no idea how far he'd come, but one thing was clear: he needed to start working toward civilization.

*Okay, Thomas. Time to find the road. That means climbing the cliff. It's a small cliff. You got this.*

He scanned for an easier route. He was in good shape, but he wasn't an athlete. He wanted to find a spot with plenty of handholds he could feel in the dark.

*You're in luck, Thomas—why do I keep saying my own name when I think?*

*Not important. Moving on.*

*You're in luck, Thomas—there's more light now.*

Earlier, it had been terrifyingly dark. Now, it was only frighteningly dark. The moonlight would help him find handholds.

*Things are looking up. Now all you have to do is climb a cliff in the dark, navigate the terrifying woods, avoid the silhouette of doom, find civilization, and figure out what happened.*

With a calmer mind and renewed focus, he began to climb. He picked a spot where a channel in the rock let him brace his hands to one side and his back to the other. After a deep breath, he inched upward. His palms burned from being pressed against the rock, and his ribs ached with every breath, but he pushed forward.

At the top, he paused and listened.

Someone, or something, was still out there in the dark. Maybe one day he would want answers, but for tonight, he just wanted to live.

He crept through the dark for over an hour, moving toward where he hoped the road would be. He didn't return to the spot where he had woken. That felt like a mistake. His new friend might still be there... and might not be feeling friendly.

*Okay, roads usually keep going. It feels like I should've found it by now, but roads curve. Plus, the darkness and adrenaline are messing with my sense of time.*

*I'll assume it's ahead of me.*

Then, finally, he heard it.

Faint, but unmistakable: the sound of a car.

Thomas nearly sobbed. He wasn't the kind of man who cried, but tonight had been strange. A blur of adrenaline, fear, pain, and confusion. Emotions welled up, sharp and sudden, but just as suddenly, they were gone. It was like a jump scare in reverse—a joy sob.

Pushed down by focused will.

*Survive the night and cry in the morning.*

He moved quickly and crouched beside a tree, pressing into the cold, damp bark.

He watched the shadows, straining to see any signs of his new, unwanted companion.

Would the car's headlights reveal something again?

*I know he's not here. He can't be. But I'm still alive because I've kept my cool.*

Nothing. He smiled when he saw only darkness. No figures. No shapes. No boogeyman.

With renewed effort and hope, Thomas moved on, keeping to the trees beside the road. He avoided open space when cars passed and kept moving, farther and farther from where it had all started, and hopefully away from what was stalking him.

As the time passed, the sky began to brighten. Dawn. Thomas gave a small, quiet laugh. He was going to make it.

Light brought hope.

Doggedly trudging along through the edge of the woods, he finally stumbled into a gas station parking lot. It was a large open gravel area that was often host to locals, passing truckers, and the occasional tractor. It wasn't pretty, but it held the promise of safety.

Every step had drained him—physically and mentally, but he was here. Alive. Almost safe. He could go home.

He leaned forward, hands on his knees, to relieve his aching back and catch his breath. That's when he saw his pants.

Blood.

He saw the pants first, then his hands. He reflexively pulled his shirt forward and saw that it too was completely covered.

Not from his own wounds. This was too much blood. His wounds were shallow. But this? He was covered in someone else's blood.

He let out a strangled gasp. Of all the horrors he'd faced, somehow this was worse.

*Okay, Thomas. Hold it together. Being chased is one thing, but... this...*

Panic surged. His mind scrambled to make sense of it.

*This is someone else's blood. A lot of someone else's blood.*

*Breathe. In through the nose. Out through the mouth.*

*Maybe you tried to help someone. Maybe you hit your head.*

*Focus. You're at the edge of a parking lot, and you're soaked in blood. That's a bad thing.*

*Back to the trees. Now.*

Thomas limped back into the woods and checked his surroundings. No one was around, not in the trees or the parking lot.

His hands were trembling. He looked at them and forced them to stop. To obey. They didn't want to listen.

*Now what?*

*You need a phone. You need help. But you can't go in like this.*

*Alright, Thomas, old boy—dripping with blood is a social faux pas.*

*Clean up in the restroom? No. Too much blood. Steal a car? Tempting. Still no, plus I don't know how.*

*Walk in covered in blood and ask for a phone? That feels like a death sentence.*

*I can't remember what happened, but every fiber of my being says to stay out of that building.*

*So—find another place. A phone booth. A pile of clean laundry.*

*Anything. Nope.*

*Out of options.*

Thomas sat just beyond the tree line, eyes locked on the gas station. Panic simmered again, but he forced it down.

He wasn't the meditating type, but now felt like the right time to try. He passed the time calming himself, focusing on understanding what had happened, and planning what to do next.

He waited.

An hour passed before he saw an opportunity.

A tractor-trailer pulled into the lot. One of the long-range rigs with a sleeper cab, where a trucker lived. It was black and had a snub nose. He knew it was just his mind, but he would swear the windshield slightly dipped in the center, and it looked mad. It didn't matter. Mad truck or not, it had a living space for the driver, and that meant clothes.

It wasn't right. He knew that. But he didn't see an option. He needed to get out of his bloody clothes before he could figure out a way home.

Thomas watched the trucker go inside. Then he ran—stumbling, limping, arms pumping like a broken marionette.

He reached the truck and clambered in, covering his face as he crawled past the steering wheel to avoid the driver-facing camera. They might see a bloody figure crawl by, but at least they couldn't make a positive ID on him.

He slipped into the living area. Inside, he found a basket of clothes. Dirty, smelly, too big. It wasn't a great option, but it also wasn't soaked in blood.

In a cupboard, he found a case of water bottles. He grabbed two.

His heart pounded with the fear of being caught. On the way out, he covered his face again and jumped down—a mistake. His legs buckled, dropping him to his knees, but he caught himself by landing on the clothes. He gathered them, along with the water, and hobbled back into the woods.

Thomas hastily gulped one of the bottles but saved the other.

He stripped off the bloody clothes and used the remaining water to wash his hands and face, then changed into the trucker's clothes.

A quick search of the area turned up a hollowed-out stump. He shoved the old clothes deep inside, covering the opening with leaves.

Evidence. For him or against him, he didn't know, but truth matters.

*If it is evidence, I want to know where to find it.*

*Things are looking up, Thomas. You're alive. You're not covered in blood. Now, just get home.*

Thomas sat at the edge of the trees and watched. He was a planner. He didn't like to take rash actions. Sometimes rash actions lead to consequences like flying off cliffs. So, he watched.

Several locals stopped, but occasionally other commercial trucks pulled in as well. That was when his plan took shape.

*I don't know what happened last night, but I'd rather not meet any locals just yet.*

*I don't know who to trust.*

*But I distrust the truck drivers less than I distrust the locals. Yeah, that makes sense.*

*Truckers understand car troubles. I just need one to park on this side of the lot.*

He waited. Twenty-five minutes later—give or take, he didn't have a watch—a driver pulled in and parked near the edge.

Thomas waited until the man went inside, then casually approached the truck, timing it so they crossed paths on the trucker's return.

Thomas put on his most friendly, slightly pathetic face and gestured to get the driver's attention. "Excuse me, sir. Hey, I'm sorry to bother you. I wrecked my car last night and had to walk through the woods. I just got here. My wallet was in my jacket, and when I crashed, my phone must've bounced somewhere. Can I make one quick call from your phone?"

The driver hesitated. He looked like he felt awkward, torn between kindness and caution. The trucker shifted his weight before replying, "They've got a phone inside."

"I know, I know, and I hate to ask, but like I said—my wallet's in my car. They'll want me to buy something if I ask to use a phone. I'm not asking for money or anything. I just need to call my girlfriend and ask for a ride, that's it. I know it was a bonehead move to leave my wallet behind, but it's miles away. It'll just take a minute. Please?"

Reluctantly, the man handed over his phone, then looked around to make sure there was no one else walking up behind him. He had heard stories of one person asking for help while another clubbed the Samaritan with a tire iron.

"This might sound strange, but it was a long trip and I'm a little lost... what town is this?" Thomas asked.

"Greene."

Thomas immediately dialed Rebecca. He smiled awkwardly while it rang.

Her voice came through the phone, "Hello?"

"Hey," Thomas said, working to keep his voice calm after the events he'd experienced. Hearing her voice gave him hope. He almost laughed with relief, but he held it together because of the trucker. "My car broke down. Can you come pick me up?"

Her sobs came through the line. They were sudden, uncontrolled, ragged.

Thomas's heart dropped, but he forced a smile for the trucker. "Yeah, I'm at a gas station with an ice cream stand called the Lickity-Split, in Greene. I've had a rough day. Can you come get me?"

"That's it? That's all you have to say?" Her voice cracked.

"I know. I'm sorry. I had to borrow this phone to call you, and he needs to be on his way. I'll explain everything when you get here. Please, just come. That's the Lickity-Split in Greene."

He hung up before she could respond. Something was wrong, but he couldn't discuss it without exposing his strange situation to the trucker standing by him. He smiled and handed the phone back with a polite nod. "Thank you so much for that. I really appreciate it. There are still good people in the world. Stay safe out there."

The driver, clearly relieved, smiled back. "Yeah, you too, buddy. Take care." He walked away, quietly pleased to have helped someone.

Thomas wandered toward the store until the trucker pulled away, then he doubled back and slipped into the woods, sinking to the ground.

*Okay, Thomas. Each time I think, "At least it couldn't get worse"— guess what?*

*Rebecca was crying. Why? She doesn't know what I went through last night. I haven't even seen her in two days.*

*So all that blood I was covered in... was she crying because she knows who it belongs to? Did I hurt someone? What did I do?*

His eyes burned. It was a bad day.

Thomas waited, alone at the edge of the woods, with nothing but his thoughts—afraid to know why she cried.

# CHAPTER 3
## *So Much Has Changed*

Thomas sat quietly in the woods, tucked into the best spot he could find for his current task: waiting. Surrounded by trees, shrubs, and vines. The natural enclosure gave him a clear view through a narrow gap in the foliage, but nothing could see inside. Nothing could see him. If anything tried to approach, he was confident he'd hear it coming.

He waited. His thoughts spiraled and jumbled as the hours crawled by.

*Why was Rebecca crying? She shouldn't even know something happened. I went to bed last night and woke up in the woods.*

*Something bad happened. Bad enough for her to already know about it.*

*Did I hurt someone? Are the police looking for me?*

*Why would I hurt someone? I'm a nice guy… I'll stand up for myself if someone else starts it, but I wouldn't—well, I was going to say I wouldn't cross the line… like somehow end up covered in someone else's blood.*

He looked at his hands. His knuckles were torn. It was the kind of skin damage you get from hitting someone.

His legs were bruised. His back felt like a punching bag.

There were cuts on his arms, too. They were shallow, surface wounds, like scratches from fingernails. He couldn't tell how many came from the cliff or how many were already there.

Thomas started to question how far he had traveled. He didn't know where Greene actually was, but how many towns named Greene could have a place called the Lickity-Split? She should be able to find him. He couldn't be that far away. Then again… the snow was gone. He must have traveled south. Still, it couldn't have been that far.

She couldn't exactly call back and tell him how long it would be.

So, he waited, slowly going crazy with his thoughts, replaying the night.

For a second, he thought he saw the silhouette again, across the parking lot. But by now, he'd seen that figure in every direction, always out of the corner of his eye. Always gone when he turned his head.

*There!*

*No, nothing. Is that the same tree I thought was moving earlier?*

*Why yes, Thomas, it is.*

*Did it actually move?*

*No, Thomas—it's a tree.*

*Hold it together. Rebecca is on her way.*

He felt like he needed to do something, but he couldn't. And that's the hardest thing about action. Sometimes, the action you need to take is waiting, and it feels like inaction… but it's not.

Finally, Rebecca's blue hatchback with a black fender pulled into the lot. His heart pounded in his chest. His legs barely worked as he tried to stand and fell back down. He shifted to his hands and knees and used a tree to pull himself up.

She got out quickly and started toward the store, but Thomas emerged from his hiding spot and hobbled to meet her.

Seeing her finally gave him hope. Her light brown curls lifted in the breeze as she turned, catching the sunlight and flaring gold at the edges. She was beautiful, she was hope, and she made the world feel a little more normal.

"Rebecca," he called, much hoarser than he expected. He hadn't spoken or had anything to drink for hours. He coughed to clear his throat. "I know you want answers. I do too. But we have to leave. Right now. Please trust me."

Rebecca stared at him for a moment, wide-eyed as his words sank in. Her eyes were red; she had clearly been crying. His heart felt like it was breaking to see her in this state. He needed to be strong—for her, for both of them—to figure out what was really going on.

"You drive," she said. Her voice was ragged, and her hands were trembling as she handed him the keys.

Thomas gave one last glance at his hiding spot, scanning the trees. Still no sign of a threat. But he didn't feel safe. That building meant something, and he didn't know why. He just wanted to be gone.

They got in, and Thomas pulled onto the road. He'd had hours to plan how he would drive: slow, signal every turn, stay under the limit. He wouldn't do anything to draw attention. As much as he enjoyed speeding, today, he would be the perfect citizen.

Thomas spoke first. "I am so happy to see you. Are you okay?"

Rebecca said nothing at first. Her lips trembled. She blinked fast, trying not to cry. She was in shock, struggling to find the right words to say. Finally, she blurted out, "What happened? Where have you been?"

Thomas checked his mirrors. No silhouette running behind them. No movement in the woods.

He kept his voice calm. "Last night… I don't know what happened, but somehow, I woke up in the woods. I don't sleepwalk. Or at least not that I know of. I-I don't know what happened. But when I woke up, I was standing. Someone was out there. He was looking for me." He took a shaky breath. "I just want to go home. I'm sorry you were worried, and I—"

Rebecca cut him off. "What about the rest of the time?"

Thomas blinked. "What time?"

Her voice shook, but it wasn't fear or panic. It wasn't anger or pain. It was a storm of emotions that didn't have a name—the kind that makes the throat close up and the body tremble.

"You've been gone for two months." Her voice broke as she blurted it out.

Thomas froze. He didn't stop driving—his body kept going—but his mind slammed to a halt.

*No snow… there's no snow.*

*There was snow when I went to sleep. I didn't even think about how long it had been.*

*I questioned how far I traveled… but never how long.*

*Two months. Two months of life gone.*

*Two months of memories, of work, of Rebecca. Gone.*

His heart was pounding. He knew it was a panic attack and not a heart attack, but he felt like he couldn't breathe. It wasn't possible. What had he done? He was in a tailspin, but he was also driving. He had to stay in control, so he did. He focused on the road ahead and keeping the car between the lines.

Finally, he whispered, "Two months?" He already believed her. He knew she wouldn't lie, but saying it out loud made it real. "The last thing I remember is going to bed on March third. We had that meeting about the new product launch. What's today?"

Rebecca broke. She placed her hands over her face and finally sobbed.

Thomas reached over and rested a hand on her leg. It was hard to focus on driving while someone he cared about was falling apart beside him. But they weren't safe yet. He had to hold it together for both of them.

She choked out the words through tears.

"May 14th."

*Over two months.*

*How?*

*That's a long time to sleepwalk. Or be drugged.*

*That's a lot of blood to be covered in…*

Thomas started to question his sanity again. He was running out of reasonable explanations.

One dark thought fluttered around the edge of his mind— uninvited, unwelcome. *Could I be one of those split personality murderers?*

*It happens, right?*

*Do they know? Before they do it?*

*No. That can't be right.*

*There's no way to not know.*

They rode in silence for an hour. Rebecca tried to gather herself. Thomas tried not to unravel.

Eventually, she broke the silence. "We need to call the police. Something happened to you. You wouldn't just disappear for two months. Someone had to take you. You should go to the hospital too. To get checked out." She was trying to control something, trying to make sense of everything.

Thomas hesitated. "Someone was stalking me last night. He followed me for hours. I got lucky—I fell off a cliff and he didn't follow. If I go to the police or the hospital, he might find out who I am. I don't know what is going on, but I know I'm not safe."

"He might already know," she replied.

They drove in silence a bit longer.

Thomas offered a compromise. "Let's go home. I'll shower. We'll eat. Tomorrow, I'll go to the police. I probably have to prove I'm alive anyway… though I'm sure I don't have a job anymore. Two months of no-shows. I'm probably unemployed."

"After everything, you're worried about your job?" Rebecca stared at him, stunned.

Thomas laughed—not because it was funny, but because it felt good. Because he needed it. A release valve. A tiny bit of normal after a night that didn't have any.

Rebecca joined in. It was mostly laughter, with a hint of tears, but at least she smiled.

"I didn't like that job anyway," he added.

She smiled again.

They pulled into the driveway. The house looked off. It felt like his home belonged to someone else.

His lawn was unkempt, there were flyers in the doorframe, and his mailbox hung open. It didn't feel like his home.

Inside, things were slightly disturbed. Not destroyed, but everything felt touched. Drawers stood open, a picture frame tilted, the bed rumpled.

"The police searched it?" Thomas asked. "Looking for clues about my disappearance, right?"

Rebecca nodded. "They said it was a potential crime scene. I didn't touch anything. I didn't want to mess it up."

He gave her a hug, placing his hand in the small of her back, pulling her firmly to his chest. She rested her head on his shoulder as he said, "I'm back now."

She hugged back and didn't want to let go. The last two months had been a nightmare, but now, having him back felt like waking from the nightmare into a dream.

They let each other go and walked to the kitchen.

Thomas walked to the fridge and paused. On his long wait by the gas station, he'd thought about what he'd eat. He had imagined leftover Chinese food, Kung Pao chicken, fried rice, and an egg roll.

That would have been his reward for surviving.

He opened the fridge. The smell hit him immediately.

He shut it fast.

Rebecca quickly stepped forward and said, "I'm sorry, I should have cleaned it out."

He gave her a quiet smile and pulled her into another hug. "You didn't do anything wrong. It's just food. We're together. We'll be okay."

They heated some cans of tomato soup. It wasn't Kung Pao, but it was comforting and delicious.

Thomas showered. They lay on the bed in silence, just being close. Thomas was on his back, and Rebecca placed her head on his shoulder, happy to have him home.

Finally, Thomas relaxed. His eyes drifted closed. He could finally have peace.

# CHAPTER 4
## *Rebecca's Nightmare*

Rebecca woke with a start, panicked by the fear that Thomas's return had only been a dream.

She turned her head quickly, looking beside her in the bed. She sighed with relief; he was still there.

It had been a hard two months without Thomas. He had vanished without a trace, but now he was back. She wanted to start crying all over again, but there was nothing left to give.

She believed him. She knew he was a good man who wouldn't just disappear without a reason. And if, for some reason, he had needed to leave, he would have explained it when he returned. She knew he was as confused and hurt as she was, even more so, with his wounds and trauma. But she would help him heal. They would get through this together.

His beard was shaggier now. He normally kept it trimmed, but now he looked like a wild man. She liked it. It added a ruggedness to his kind nature. Not that he wasn't a bit rugged. He was tall and had his grandfather's coal mining shoulders, but they hid a gentle heart. His hair was shorter now as well, a dark brown bordering on black, like his eyes. They were kind as ever, but now they carried weariness.

She watched him sleep for several minutes. It wasn't restful; he twitched and moved from time to time. But she did not want to wake him. He needed rest, even if it wasn't peaceful. She needed him to sleep so he could regain his strength.

*I will help you be strong. I will help you heal.*

*I am just happy to have you back.*

Quietly, she slipped from the bed. Her mind was a jumble and wouldn't let her rest. Her eyes refused to stay closed. She needed tea. Somehow, tea would help.

She carefully closed the bedroom door behind her, twisting the knob to avoid the usual clunk.

She heard a *clunk* anyway—or a *click... a clop?*

Her heart pounded. That sound came from behind her. It wasn't the door. Her breath caught in her throat as she turned.

The hallway was dark. Darker than usual. The electronics in the kitchen at the end of the hall weren't aligned with the hallway, so she normally could not see them directly, but at night their clocks and timers cast a faint glow that spilled into the hall.

Now, something was blocking that glow.

Rebecca quickly flicked on the hallway light. She couldn't stand the dark; she had to know what made the sound. She almost regretted it.

Something stood in the hallway before her. Not a human. A nightmare. It was hunched over, but when the light came on, they locked eyes. It smiled and slowly straightened to its full height. Eight feet tall, maybe more.

Its hands were furred and clawed, but not sleek like a predator's. They were rough, gnarled things made of splintered bone fused with blackened iron. Each claw curved unevenly, as if broken and regrown incorrectly. Dirt and dried blood caked their edges.

The creature untied the rope at its waist that held its cloak and let it drop behind it with a heavy thump. It stood before her naked. Proud. Its legs bent the wrong way. Something animal, not human. It had hooves for feet, and its body was covered in coarse, shaggy brown hair. Muscles rippled beneath it. But the face—

The face was the most terrifying. It wasn't a mask. It was real. A snout, a snarling mouth with tusks or fangs. Deep sunken eyes that expressed joy in pain. Malevolence. Intent. Atop its head: two long, dark horns, arcing forward, then twisted into a slicked back curve like a ram's horn.

It smiled. A nightmare's smile, the kind you see just before it overwhelms you.

Rebecca's eyes looked at its face, its rippling wall of muscle that barely fit in the hallway, and at its excitement—proudly displayed— showing it was looking forward to more than just violence. It was evil incarnate.

She squeaked. She meant to scream, but nothing worked. Her lungs wouldn't cooperate.

The creature bent its head forward, then reared back, howling like a wolf, but worse. The sound was like an elk's bugle, but pure anger. It was the sound of hatred and joy mixed together—a battle-cry.

It charged.

Rebecca barely managed to raise her arms, shielding her chest and face. It didn't stop the attack, but the gesture saved her life.

The beast slammed into her with its horns, smashing through the bedroom door.

It skidded to a stop on its hooves; she crashed into the dresser with a splintered thud. The frame cracked. Items on top jumped. Drawers split open, spilling their contents. The room erupted in chaos as items crashed to the ground, wood splintered, and a painting fell from the wall.

She was stunned. Pain radiated through every fiber of her being. She fought to stay conscious.

The creature loomed, ready to inflict more pain—

Thomas launched himself off the chest at the foot of the bed. His fist slammed into the creature's face. It was driven by weight, momentum, and unshakable will. The impact was brutal. He overextended and crashed to the floor, but the blow had landed.

He was already scrambling back to his feet as the creature staggered sideways into the wall, bracing itself awkwardly.

Thomas pressed the attack, striking the creature's face again and again. Blood sprayed with every blow—some from the beast, some from his own torn knuckles. He didn't stop.

The creature fought back, shoving Thomas away in a clumsy attempt to regain its footing. They both stumbled on the uneven debris-strewn floor.

Thomas crouched, panting, waiting for its next move.

The beast turned its head to Rebecca. She saw it look right into her eyes and smile. Its face was dripping with blood, but it looked happy. It liked pain. Even its own pain.

Rebecca was terrified, but at least she was recovering. She half-stumbled, half-crawled upright, bracing herself against the splintered dresser, trying to steady her breath beneath the creature's stare.

Thomas grabbed a broken piece of the door and swung at the creature, catching it in the chest. It shrugged the blow off. Thomas swung again.

It caught the board mid-air and turned its head. It smiled at Thomas and slowly forced him to lower the board. It leaned in and locked eyes with Thomas to let him know that he was weak. The smile widened as it yanked the board effortlessly from his grasp. Thomas yelped as his hands were left bleeding and with splinters of wood in them. The creature casually tossed the board aside. It didn't need a weapon. It was the weapon.

Thomas staggered back, gasping as he yanked the larger shards from his palms. He tried another flying punch, but the creature caught his wrist mid-air and slammed him down.

Thomas stumbled, but he did not quit. He would not quit. He fought like a man possessed.

The pain and fear of the last twenty-four hours, the lost months, the need to protect Rebecca—they all fueled him. He punched with his free hand, swinging again and again.

The creature caught that hand, too.

Thomas used it. He jumped, pulling with both arms for leverage, and slammed his forehead into the beast's face.

He headbutted the goat-man.

The creature lifted him, spreading his arms apart, suspending his legs in the air. The goat-man was going to show him what a real headbutt felt like.

But Thomas wasn't feeling fear anymore. Right then, he didn't want answers or safety. It was primal—he just wanted to win.

Sure, he wanted to protect Rebecca and survive, but in that moment, he only wanted to kill the creature that invaded his home. To destroy the silhouette that haunted him through the woods. To reclaim his fear and to conquer it.

Rebecca watched in horror. Thomas was losing. But he wouldn't quit.

Then—he kicked.

The creature was strong, naked, muscles like iron—but it was still a man, and it wasn't shy about exposing its most vulnerable spot.

Thomas kicked it as if he meant to drive his foot through the creature.

Rebecca gasped. The creature felt pain. It dropped Thomas and doubled over.

He grabbed its horns, twisted it aside, and shoved it into the bathroom. The beast scrambled for footing, its hooves skidding across the tile.

Thomas ran and rammed it backward into the clawfoot tub. It flailed in the tub, limbs sticking out awkwardly. It let out angry bleats, struggling, hooves slipping against the slick ceramic.

Thomas grabbed the broken board. "Run!" he yelled.

Barefoot, she sprinted across the broken door. Splinters bit into her feet, but adrenaline drowned the pain. She charged across the hall and down the stairs.

Halfway down the stairs, she stopped and looked back, torn. Then she heard a loud crash of broken glass.

*If Thomas is going to lose this fight… then he won't lose alone.*

She ran back to the bedroom.

The fight had shifted. Thomas was on his back. The creature sat on his chest, pinning his arms.

Rebecca couldn't take it anymore. She ripped the towel rack from the wall and swung it into the back of the creature's head.

*TWANG.*

The bar bent from the force.

Cool, she thought—a strange reaction to a strange moment. She was a woman reclaiming her power.

She swung again. And again. The creature's skin split open. It turned with an angry growl and caught the bar mid-swing.

It released one of Thomas's hands in the process.

Thomas reached for the dagger on the creature's belt. The one it refused to use, insulted by the idea that it might need a weapon to kill weak humans.

That arrogance was its undoing. It felt the dagger come free, and its head turned, eyes wide, but too late.

It knew. The moment had passed. The human couldn't be

stopped.

Rebecca stood beside it, her hands still on the bar, watching.

Thomas thrust the dagger up—under the chin, into the creature's brain.

Blood poured over him, thick and rancid, with a sickly-sweet stench like rotting fruit.

Thomas gagged, struggling to shove the massive creature off. Rebecca helped, and together they toppled the beast onto the bathroom floor.

He slid across the tile and placed his back against the wall. Rebecca stepped around the blood pooling on the floor and collapsed beside him. Her brain hadn't processed what just happened. She was in shock, numb from the horror of every second since she entered the hallway.

It had worked. They had fought. They survived, but she didn't know if it was real. Shock made her cold. She started shivering as she leaned on Thomas for support, for grounding.

*This can't be real. I'll wait here until I wake up. This can't be real.*

Suddenly, Thomas stood, pulling her up with him.

"There could be more. We have to go," he said, yanking the dagger free from the corpse.

Thomas stripped off his bloody shirt and donned a clean one, then grabbed her clothing and shoes. He took the creature's sheath and slid the dagger into it. They crept through the house without turning on any lights. He didn't want any signs of change or a reason for anyone outside to notice.

At the front door, Thomas gestured. "That's your car. It can't be here. If anyone asks about me, you haven't seen me. Go to your mom's house tonight."

Rebecca turned toward him in disbelief. "You can't stay!"

He ran his fingers along her cheek. "I can't let these things come after you. I'm going to disappear so I can investigate what's going on—but you need to be safe."

Her breath caught as she fought back tears. "You need to be safe."

"But I'm not. That thing hunted me in the woods and tracked

us here. I need to learn what happened to me. I need to stop them. If I stay, they'll keep coming and I couldn't live with myself if they hurt you."

"Thomas… I can't do this again. I can't mourn you and wonder if you're alive."

He didn't answer. There was nothing left to say.

He kissed her, a desperate kiss of passion and pain in the same breath. They had no time for it, but that didn't matter, as time itself seemed to freeze in their embrace. They stole that moment for themselves.

She had just gotten him back. Her heart ached, but her mind agreed. He couldn't survive in her world; they were already hunting him here. And she couldn't survive in the world he was about to enter. She loved him, but she couldn't face a life of this kind of danger. She was a nurse who healed sick children, not a warrior.

She touched his face. "I will never forget you."

He looked in her car to make sure it was empty, then opened the door for her.

As she sat behind the wheel, she grabbed his hand.

She looked into his eyes through the haze of mist and tears. Thomas flexed his jaw and barely managed to whisper, "Go."

As she drove away, she looked in her mirror and saw him standing in the driveway, watching her go. She gripped the steering wheel as hard as she could. Her chest tightened as if each breath pressed on a wound she couldn't reach. It burned at what the powers that be had made of their lives.

Thomas looked down at the dagger tucked into his waistband, at what it represented.

He would hold those powers to account.

# CHAPTER 5
## *Freedom*

Thomas watched Rebecca's taillights disappear into the night. He knew it wasn't safe outside, but he would not go back until she was out of sight.

He felt hollow, but he was still practical. He needed to act quickly and get away from this area in case the thing had friends.

Every word he said to her was true.

*There could be more of them.*

*I am going to figure out what is happening.*

*You need to be safe.*

He scanned the darkness but saw nothing.

Thomas limped back into the house with grim resolve. He had to get out of there quickly, but intelligently.

The garage door creaked open slowly. Thomas still wasn't sure he was alone. With dagger in hand, he flicked the light switch and scanned for massive goat-men, relieved to find none. For a moment, Thomas just stood there—still bleeding, still shaking—and stared at the bike.

It sat in the corner, exactly where he had left it.

His trusty Thunder Black Indian Springfield had way too much chrome, but it was what he had. The polished tank reflected the fluorescent lights overhead, and the pipes sparkled from the flickering bulbs.

Rebecca had named it *Freedom* the day he brought it home. She said it wasn't about horsepower or chrome, just the promise of the open road.

Before she decided on the name, he had suggested they call it the *Go-mobile.* She was not amused.

He used to take her on camping trips with that bike. It was a bagger, fitted with a trunk and armrests so Rebecca could travel in what felt like a rumbly recliner. Freedom was built for weekend getaways and relaxing. Tonight, it would be used for escape and survival. He loved the bike and all the memories it had given him, but tonight he wished he had another option. It wasn't exactly low-profile, but it didn't have GPS, and he could wear a helmet to obscure his face.

Thomas went back to his closet and grabbed his camping gear. He shuffled through what he needed and what he could take on a motorcycle. His hands throbbed as he packed, knuckles shredded from the goat-man's fangs, palms splintered from the plank that was ripped from his grasp.

He quickly stuffed some gear into a backpack for his new life.

*You're probably never coming back here, Thomas, so don't leave anything you can't live without.*

He loaded a warm-weather sleeping bag, a multi-tool, a few lighters, emergency blankets, a first-aid kit, a mess kit, and a canteen. He wanted simple items, only what was necessary.

Thomas looked around his closet. It was a large walk-in with things organized perfectly on the shelves. He wasn't compulsive, but he liked to keep things neat. Shoes were on the lower level, sweaters on the middle level. Suits hung to the right, other clothes on the left. Everything was perfect.

He ripped the shelves off the wall and scattered everything on the floor.

*The police searched the house when you were missing.*

*They'll notice changes—like the massive corpse and the missing motorcycle.*

*Make it look like a robbery... or something else that would produce a giant goat-man. Just make it look like you weren't involved.*

He opened the small fireproof safe tucked in the back. It was meant to protect important documents in an emergency. He didn't need those anymore. Thomas was going to disappear until he figured out what was happening. But he did need the cash inside. It was only two thousand dollars. Not enough to start a new life, but hopefully enough to escape his old one.

Everything he had built in his life until now was gone: his house, car, and career. They didn't matter. Rebecca mattered. Keeping her safe was his new life. That meant leaving the worldly things behind.

Thomas moved into the bedroom, still cautious as he entered. The room already looked trashed, so he didn't worry about messing it up further. He grabbed a few clothes and stuffed them into the bag. He was about to leave when he paused, his attention drawn to a book on the nightstand: *Grimm's Complete Fairy Tales*.

It had an eerie cover with a scene of a terrifying forest. Black with red ink, the trees' leaves formed a twisted frame around half the cover, and faces glared from the trunks. He'd given it to Rebecca for her birthday. He told her part of the gift was that she didn't need to ask. If she handed him the book, he'd start reading it to her immediately. She'd bring it on camping trips, but sometimes she liked hearing him read it to her before bed.

He smiled darkly. It was a smile of pain, but also of happy memories. He grabbed the book and slipped it into a side compartment of the bag. He considered bringing a photo of her, but decided against it; if he didn't survive, he didn't want to put a target on her. The book, though, was just a book to anyone else, yet to him, it was a memory worth carrying.

He hobbled down the stairs, still attentive, cautious. He moved to the kitchen. Turning on the lights could alert someone outside, but he was relying on speed instead of stealth now.

*Don't worry about the lights, Thomas. Move fast.*

*Besides, no more goats have broken in yet… what a strange string of words to put together.*

*Food. You need food. Noodles are light and easy. Grab some cans, too. They're heavier, but you need more than just carbs.*

*Clif bars—yes! I have two boxes of them. Costco shopping triumphs again.*

*Okay, I have wh—*

He stopped cold.

*The goat didn't actually break in, though.*

The doors were closed and locked. He had scanned the entire house while packing. All the doors were shut, and he had checked them before going to bed. He knew he had. After the previous night, he'd made sure no one could get in.

*Was it already inside?*

*Is it the same shadow that chased me through the woods?*

*How did it get here ahead of me? Someone would have seen a goat driving down the road.*

His heart started pounding. He had told Rebecca there could be more because it was the smart, practical thing to say. It was better to assume the worst and try to outmaneuver it. But now it felt real.

Were they already here?

Did they already know who he was?

Panic crept in.

What if the creature had been hiding in the guest bedroom or the garage the whole time—just waiting until they fell asleep?

*Move, Thomas. Get what you need and go.*

It had been easier to be brave with Rebecca here. He'd been strong for her, protecting her. But honestly, she gave him strength. She made him feel more powerful.

Now he was alone, and he started to shake. He didn't have any strength left. He had barely survived the last one. If another one came at him now, he would be powerless, and it didn't just want to kill them. It was having fun.

He moved with renewed purpose. He stumbled into the hallway, hobbling as fast as his injuries would let him, and grabbed the cloak the creature had left behind. It reeked, but it might help with his research. He stuffed it into a trash bag to help with the smell and headed to the garage.

He took his riding gear out of the side bags to make room for the few things he could take with him. He filled the saddlebags with whatever fit and strapped the primary pack to the back seat, Rebecca's seat.

His hands were trembling from pain, adrenaline, terror—he wasn't even sure. But every second that passed was making it worse. He recognized a panic attack setting in. He looked at his shaking hands.

*In through the nose, out through the mouth.*

*Control the panic, or don't drive a motorcycle.*

He took a few deep breaths and looked at his hands again.

Steady… enough for now, anyway.

He put on his leathers and swung his aching leg over the bike. He sat for just a moment longer than he meant to while he listened.

For what, he wasn't sure, but he knew he was afraid to open the garage door and face the darkness.

Once underway, it would be different. He would have speed on his side. But the transition—moving from dead stop to accelerating into the night—was terrifying.

Something could be on the other side of that door, and he wouldn't have a chance.

He hoped Rebecca hadn't felt that way when she left.

He felt guilty. He felt like, somehow, he should have found a way to make everything better instead of sending her out into the night.

He knew she would be safer at her mother's house, but that didn't make it better.

*Stop it, Thomas. You can't see if you're crying, and seeing is important for driving.*

*Survive the night, cry tomorrow.*

*Now, open the door.*

The engine started up as soon as he hit the button. It was a good bike. It had never let him down. Hopefully, tonight would be no different.

His hands throbbed with pain as he wrapped his fingers around the handgrips. Now wasn't the time for splinters. Now was the time to move.

He pressed the button on the handlebars. The garage door rose. Slowly. It felt much slower than normal, but he knew that wasn't true.

He looked under the edge as it rose. He couldn't see hooves, but his heart pounded with every slow inch of movement.

When it finally opened, there was no goat-man waiting on the other side.

*Go, Thomas.*

It was real. He was leaving his life behind. Just twenty-four hours ago, he woke up in the woods and couldn't wait to get home.

Now he was leaving forever, saying goodbye to Rebecca.

He accelerated into the night.

It was a bad day.

It was a bad day.

# CHAPTER 6
## *Strong Body, Strong Mind*

Thomas drove for a little over twenty miles. He watched his mirrors. Nothing was on the road behind him. His paranoia was starting to get to him, though. He began to wonder how fast those creatures could run. Then he started wondering what else might be out there.

If half-goat, half-man creatures exist, was there something flying after him? He was in the Appalachian area. Was Mothman up there? Could there be a man-cheetah sprinting through the woods? He didn't believe it, not really. He knew it was fear talking, irrational paranoia. But it still made him want to drive until sunrise.

Logic won out. He hadn't truly slept in two nights. A few hours of restless sleep last night before the creature attacked wasn't enough. His whole body ached from everything he'd endured. He couldn't go indefinitely. He needed rest, time to remove splinters from his vibrating hands, and think about what to do next. He was an engineer, not an action star.

He rode to a place where he used to take Rebecca for picnics. It was quiet, right on the water, and far from the main roads.

Gravel popped beneath his tires as he turned off the asphalt. The sound was comforting. Familiar. It took him back to better days: road trips and fishing.

The dirt road opened into a peaceful clearing beside the river. It was a gravel pullout, unchanged, untouched. Not monster-infested. It was a refuge from the horrors he had faced. Then again, so was his house. Once.

He killed the engine and coasted to a stop, then wheeled the bike behind a wide oak, hidden from casual eyes.

*I'm back in the woods again.*

*I can't see them coming in the dark, but they can't see me either. The*

*creature that stalked me had just as much trouble with the dark as I did…
goat-men have poor night vision. You learn something new every day.*

*It looks like I'll be shivering tonight.*

*No fire.*

Thomas stank. The smell clung to him like oil: thick and pungent. The creature's blood wasn't normal. He had smelled his own blood before, but this stuff was sickening. Putrid. It was impossible to ignore and would draw attention if he stopped anywhere. The creature's blood was greasy and foul, like rotting fruit.

*I didn't think something could bleed rotten blood.*

*Then again, I didn't think goat-men existed either.*

He checked the first-aid kit strapped to the bike and found a bottle of pine-scented camp soap.

*Good,* he thought as he looked around at the trees. *Now I'll blend in.*

He stripped off his clothes and walked to the river.

*No time for modesty, Thomas. It's just you and the mosquitoes.*

With a bracing breath, he stepped into the cold, fast-moving water. It curled around his toes, numbing them instantly. He splashed water on his face, then poured soap into his palms and scrubbed hard. The blood came off in greasy red clouds. He cleaned every open wound and every spot of blood. His knuckles throbbed, split open and raw. Tiny splinters from the plank poked from his fingers and palms like needles, burning while he scrubbed, but he didn't stop until the worst of the blood was gone.

Shivering back at the bike, he toweled off, dropped the towel on the ground, sat on it, and opened the kit again. He used a USB-powered headlamp. He didn't like using light, but he needed to assess the damage. He was bruised everywhere, but nothing that wouldn't heal. Hard to tell what was from an hour ago and what was from the night he woke up.

*Has it even been twenty-four hours?*

Thomas wrapped his sleeping bag around himself to keep the chill off.

It was time for the tweezers. One by one, he pulled the splinters free. His jaw clenched, hands trembling. Each tug sent a new jolt of pain up his arms. He didn't flinch. He didn't groan. He just worked. When finished, he wrapped his knuckles and palms in clean gauze, methodically covering every open wound. He didn't know how to handle his ribs; his right side was black, but he couldn't tell if anything was broken.

The river murmured behind him, comforting like a friend. The woods, though, whispered of terror.

Fully dressed again, Thomas laid out his tent and sleeping bag. At first, he considered sleeping under the stars to save energy. But the thin tarp wall felt safer somehow. He knew it was irrational. If anything, the tent made him more visible. But he didn't care. He'd take fake comfort over dark woods and open skies.

He knew he wouldn't sleep, knew he'd toss and turn all night from imagined sounds and shifting shadows.

Thomas woke with a headache.

He wasn't surprised by the pain. He was only surprised that he didn't remember falling asleep. One moment, he rested his head on his leather jacket. The next, it was daylight.

It was the kind of ache born of too little sleep and too much everything else. Between the fatigue, the injuries, the tension, and the raw terror, he was drained.

But he had work to do.

*Get up, Thomas,* he told himself, *before someone sees you and calls in a homeless guy camping by the river.*

*All you have to do is figure out what happened, who did it, how to stop them, and how to keep Rebecca safe—and I swear, I'll get you a king-sized bed and a pizza.*

It wasn't much of a plan. Really, it was just a direction: pick a path and start walking. Typically, he made big decisions with flowcharts, research, and sleepless nights of second-guessing. But how do you prepare for the kind of day he had just lived?

He rode into a neighboring town and stopped for fuel, a bottle of water, and directions.

No fire last night meant no boiled water. A bottle of water was once a mindless purchase. Now it was a luxury.

*All right, Thomas. You've survived a lot, including a fight with a monster that shouldn't exist.*

*So where does a hardcore goat-man killer go?*

*The library.*

*Nothing can stop me now.*

The public library sat on the edge of town, between a post office and a shuttered diner. Its plain brick façade was exactly what Thomas needed. It was a quiet place with internet access.

He tried to look unremarkable as he stepped inside.

*Don't draw attention, Thomas.*

*You're just a regular guy who needs a computer.*

*Happens every day.*

Warm air greeted him, carrying the scent of old paper and carpet cleaner. A woman sat behind the desk, typing slowly. She wore a pink knitted sweater and glasses. The only thing missing was the pencil in the bun.

He hesitated, then crossed the lobby.

"Sorry," he said, voice rougher than expected. "Do I need a card to use the computers?"

She looked up with a practiced smile. "Nope, you're fine. Just use any that says 'Guest Access.' First-come, first-served."

He nodded. "Thanks."

"Printing's 15 cents a page," she added without looking up again.

He gave a polite nod. She didn't notice.

*Step one: enter—check.*

*Step two: be completely unnoticeable to women—check.*

The computers were tucked behind low shelves. Six terminals. Two occupied. He took the one farthest from the others, woke it up, and clicked "Guest Session."

The desktop loaded slowly. He kept his eyes low, only glancing around once to clock exits and people. No one was watching him. It was probably just paranoia.

Then again, it's not paranoia if they really are after you.

He opened a browser and pulled up maps. He searched "Lickity-Split." He would recreate the night and go back, but this time he would be there on purpose. He scanned the road visually, searching for landmarks. Then he found it. The cliff. It was burned into his memory.

*Thomas… I thought you were better than this.*
*You didn't pack a notebook or a pencil?*
*Seriously? You're an engineer.*
*Always have a book to record notes.*

He looked around and spotted some pencils and scrap paper on a nearby table. Grabbing what he needed, he shoved a few extra slips into his pocket for the future. He scribbled down directions and distances to help locate the area from the road. He also noted a nearby pullout where he might hide the motorcycle while exploring. Then he printed two pages: one satellite view, one terrain map.

Hopefully, it would be enough to get him back.

*Thirty cents for printing?*
*Wow. That's expensive.*
*Funny how one day can change your entire perspective.*
*What else do I need? A gun… a few guns. Lots of bullets.*
*Calm down, Dirty Harry—that's not going to happen.*
*You can't use your ID, and you don't know any friendly criminals.*

He considered other options, but he didn't have experience with bows, and he definitely wasn't a ninja. All he had was the old dagger. The one that killed the creature.

It worked well enough that time. So be it.

He moved the pin on the digital map to another location and then cleared it entirely.

Paranoia, it seemed, was becoming his new way of life.

Thomas drove back to Greene. He wasn't happy about it, but it was the only lead he had. He parked at the Lickity-Split, but on the side by his old hiding spot. Stepping back into the trees, he found the hollowed-out stump. The clothes were still there. He grabbed them and brought them back to his bike. It wouldn't pay to have them lingering longer than necessary. He needed to cover his tracks or find out who was responsible, but he didn't trust the clothes in someone else's hands.

Next, he drove to the spot near the cliff marked on the map, where he thought he could hide Freedom. Pulling off the road onto the grass, he coasted back to the tree line. He slid the bike into the tall brush.

He swung his leg off and struggled to make his body respond

appropriately. The long ride felt like it would shake his splintered hands apart. His legs barely held the bike upright.

Thomas looked down at the chrome gleaming through the leaves. He cut a few branches and tucked them into the bushes and over the bike, covering the exposed parts. Despite everything that had gone wrong, despite everything he'd lost, he took pains to avoid scratching the chrome. His practical side said, *"Protect the bike's value in case you need to sell it to keep going."* But he knew the truth: he didn't want to lose anything else. What little he had left was becoming special, and this motorcycle represented happy rides with Rebecca.

*Don't let your emotions cloud you, Thomas.*

*Solve the puzzle now, get a new bike tomorrow… or, well, at some point.*

He sat behind his makeshift motorcycle-blind and pulled the cloak and dagger out. He wanted to study them before venturing into the woods so that he would recognize anything related. Then again, if he found anything other than trees, he should probably look at it.

He leaned his back against a tree, a series of cracking sounds traveling along his spine. He pulled the cloak from the bag; the rancid smell hit him immediately. That was the same smell as the creature's blood, but it hadn't been wearing the cloak when it died. Was this blood from another of its kind? The cloak was stained. Some of it was blood; other stains might have been wine. The stench was so pungent, Thomas couldn't tell for sure. He couldn't pick up any wine scent through the cloud of rot.

It was well-worn, with frayed edges and cuts. It didn't have any noticeable holes or rips. It just had a couple of tiny tears, the kind you get chasing someone through the woods at night. He turned it over slowly, tracing the seams.

*This is when someone in a movie would find a secret pocket with all the answers to the bad guys' plans… but I guess I'm not that lucky.*

The outside was rough, weatherproof, stitched for travel. The lining was different. It felt soft, expensive, and threaded with a faint pattern. It looked like leaves. They were common enough. Thomas knew nothing about plants. But the more he looked, the more the pattern twisted in on itself. The vines didn't wrap; they writhed. In the negative space, he could almost see faces. Laughing or screaming? Both equally disturbing thoughts, but it made him think of the creature's smile—an evil smile that looked forward to seeing the pain it inflicted on others.

He folded the fabric over and shoved it back in the trash bag. He was thankful to be rid of it and the smell that came with it.

The dagger felt too deliberate. It was more ornate than he expected. The blade showed a lot of use. It was notched and chipped, but sharp, well-oiled. It was a blade meant to kill, not hang on a wall. The handle, wrapped in dark leather, was smooth from use. Suddenly, Thomas wondered if it could be human skin. *You've seen too many fantasy movies. Don't add details you can't back up.*

The pommel was worn and scratched, but he could make out a shallow carving: grapevines knotted into a circle. Inside that circle, just barely visible beneath the grime, there was a small theatrical mask. Tragedy or comedy? He couldn't tell, but it seemed similar to the cloak.

*So, I found leaves, grapes in a circle, and masks. Sure, why not? Now it is time to get to work.*

Thomas groaned as he stood. He attached the dagger to his belt. He'd been calling it a dagger, but it was more than that. It was too big to be just a dagger, but not quite a short sword. He wondered what a big dagger was called.

He heard a car coming down the road. He squatted behind the motorcycle and waited for it to pass. They probably wouldn't see him, but there was no point tempting fate. More paranoia or more practical thinking?

The car passed. Thomas strapped on his backpack and started walking into the woods.

*Thomas, you knew you were going to walk through the woods, and you didn't bring a walking stick.*

*You stopped at a gas station and only bought one bottle of water.*

*You need to step it up. Think more and think faster. Don't react to life—plan for life and make life react to you.*

*Whatever happened before, don't ever let it happen again.*

*Focus. Strong body. Strong mind.*

# CHAPTER 7
## *Sacrifice*

Thomas looked around and found a suitable fallen branch to serve as his walking stick. It was plain, knobby, and didn't fit his hand very well, but it would work for now. As he walked, he scanned for anything familiar and listened for sounds of monsters.

He also looked for a better stick.

It was something he and his friends used to do, something that felt instinctual in little boys: searching for the best wizard stick they could find. He didn't see anything that stood out, but he also knew he wasn't out here in the woods to find a nifty wizard stick. He was out there so he could track down whatever sent the creature after him. In the light of that quest, finding a nice-looking stick seemed less important, but not entirely unimportant.

*Okay. The monster's dagger. He carried it, but didn't use it. So why did he carry it?*

*It looked like it was meant for battle, not decoration. It was well-worn and had probably stabbed a lot of stuff.*

*I keep thinking "what sent the creature," but what if that dagger is a sign of its rank or importance?*

*The cloak seemed nicer than I expected. Thicker, more intricate.*

*Am I assuming it's just a henchman because it's a goat-man?*

*What if it were a priest and the dagger was used in sacrifices, but it didn't intend to sacrifice us, just kill us?*

*If the killing was just fun or to remove witnesses, then it didn't need the fancy-pantsed dagger.*

*I can't remember anything before waking up in the woods. Maybe I interfered with a ritual. Or maybe I witnessed something.*

He continued trying to solve the puzzle of his new life while trudging through the woods in search of the cliff where he'd fallen.

From there, he was sure he could find a few other locations from that night. He knew it was a long shot that he would find anything useful in the woods, but he really didn't know where else to go. So, Thomas kept thinking.

*Back to the priest idea, or leader… Maybe it was a solo creature.*

*I'm in West Virginia, after all. Family tree didn't fork?*

*Wouldn't that be nice? If it were the only one, then I could go back to my life—back to Rebecca.*

*Then I could actually use my ID and buy a gun. I could buy a big gun.*

Thomas recalled reading once about sai and how they were used. He tried to recall more, but it hadn't seemed relevant at the time, so it hadn't stuck in his mind. From what he could recall, a sai was a striking weapon, not a cutting one, about fifteen inches long with two prongs instead of a normal knife's crossguard. The prongs made a big "U" shape.

Mainly, he remembered them from the *Teenage Mutant Ninja Turtles*. Not that he would admit that. But what brought it to mind now was that Sai had once been used to show authority. He recalled that a person in law enforcement was supposed to hold up the Sai, and people would know that person was a cop. He was sure he was wrong about several details, possibly all of them—but the dagger from the beast could be a symbol of office, a badge.

The beast didn't use it. Almost like it forgot it was there, but the dagger isn't just about use. It looked nice for a goat-man's dagger. The pommel was engraved with an image.

Thomas pondered the implications of whether this creature had some kind of rank or station in life.

*It really is a nice cloak. Much nicer than I'd expect a normal goat to wear…*

*Yes. I actually just thought that. I actually said that to myself while wandering around in the woods.*

*He was a fancy goat.*

*But if he is a higher-ranking "person" in whatever evil social group is hunting me, and I assumed he was a henchman—am I prejudiced?*

*Wow. What a question. I'd like to think I'm open-minded, and if I met a goat-man under different circumstances, we could be friends…*

*I could have a Goat-Bro.*

*Okay, Thomas, I'll cross that bridge when I come to it.*

Thomas found a cliff. He wasn't sure it was the right one, but the map only showed one. He followed along at the base, scanning for landmarks he could recognize. He took his time. He was still in a lot of pain and didn't want to risk making things worse. He needed to heal so he could continue working, and that meant taking care. So, he moseyed along, staying alert to ensure he was still alone out there.

He came to an abrupt stop. He recognized a rock. This was where the creature that chased him stopped to look down, trying to find him. He looked at the brush and ground at the base of the cliff. He wasn't a tracker or hunter, but it was obvious from the signs that something large—roughly Thomas-sized—had crashed into the ground and slid into the bushes.

*Step one: Find the horrifying location where I almost died in the woods—check.*

It was getting later in the day, and Thomas didn't want to wander around after dark in these woods again. He consulted the map and found that a small creek ran by. He meandered over and filled his pot from the mess kit. It was very clean-looking water, most likely fed by a local spring. It was possible it was clean enough to drink straight from the creek, but he wasn't going to take a chance like that. His week was going bad enough without getting a parasite or spending the night throwing up.

He made his way back to the cliff and found a little spot that went under the rock. It had a natural covering, and it could help hide his fire. He wouldn't burn it at night. He just needed the fire long enough to boil his water and make dinner.

Gathering sticks and twigs for the fire almost seemed cathartic. It was a touch of everyday life. Thomas liked working with his hands. His job as an engineer was mostly brainwork, but his favorite part was building prototypes and testing them. What was in his mind— made manifest in the world. It was truly satisfying. So he worked at the mundane tasks of starting a fire, boiling noodles in creek water, laying out his sleeping bag, and getting ready for the night.

Once everything was laid out, he settled down onto his sleeping bag and picked up the pot of soup. It was a noodle pack, the kind that came with a seasoning packet. The smell of spicy chicken was unreal. He couldn't believe how much his mouth was watering for a bowl of basic noodles. It was one of the cheapest meals a person could purchase, but in that moment, it was Heaven. He dove in and enjoyed every slurp. He drank the seasoned creek water, smothered the fire with dirt, and took one last look around.

Whoa! Cool stick. The shaft was straight for most of its length, but it had a nice twist at about waist level that turned the stick ninety degrees. The whole thing was weathered smooth and fit right into Thomas's hand. It was like a tree decided he needed a cane, so it made one for him.

*Creek noodles and a nice stick. Things are looking up, Thomas. Don't you worry one bit about the dark woods…*

---

Thomas held the dagger in his hand. Moonlight filtered through the trees in pale shafts, soft and serene. He was smiling.

He looked down at the woman who lay bound to the stone before him. Without hesitation, he slid the dagger into her stomach and dragged it upward to her chest as she screamed. He smiled wider—this was his favorite part.

He reached into the open wound, pulled her intestines free, and lifted them to the sky. Tilting his head back, he let them drape over his face like a veil. They slid down slick and warm, and he inhaled deeply, savoring the smell, savoring the moment.

She was fading. It was always a shame when they died too quickly. He'd miss the screams. But there would be others.

He turned toward the round dais at the cave mouth. The runes carved into its surface shimmered. It was time.

---

Thomas woke with a start, heart pounding like it wanted out of his chest. He was soaked in sweat and gasping for air. Instinctively, he snatched the dagger and held it before him, eyes wide, scanning the dark as if he could cut the nightmare in half.

He blinked hard, then slid upright until his back hit the cold rock wall. Still clutching the blade, he tried to control his breathing, but his body wouldn't listen. He was making too much noise. If something were out there, it would have heard him.

His whole frame trembled. Part cold. Part terror. The dagger's tip wavered in the air, his hand jerking uncontrollably.

He pressed his free hand against the side of his head, as if trying to cage his own thoughts. The dagger hand kept twitching, no matter how hard he tried to still it.

*Breathe, Thomas. Strong body, strong mind. Control the body to calm the mind.*

*There's probably nothing out there. It was just a dream… probably brought on by the dagger. You spent all yesterday studying it. Staring at it. Thinking about what it meant.*

*Or maybe that's why you were covered in blood the night you woke up.*

*Maybe the goat-man was the good guy… and he was trying to stop you.*

*Breathe… it's not true… if the goat-man were a good guy, then he wouldn't have attacked Rebecca.*

*But it doesn't matter. Focus. Never lose yourself or control of your body again.*

The rest of the night went better than the dream, but still poorly. He shivered and stared at the darkness until the sun came up. He wanted to cry, but his practical mind told him no. *You don't have water at hand to rehydrate, and you don't want blurry vision if something is moving out there. Survive the night, cry in the morning.*

Daybreak was a welcome relief. Thomas was feeling better physically, but broken flashes of the dream kept popping into his head. At first, he fought them. But he realized he was missing over two months of memories, and if these dreams had anything to do with that, he needed to explore them.

If he had actually done those things, he had to know. He also started wondering if magical items could be real. His first thought was: *Don't be stupid, Thomas. Of course, magic isn't real… it is no more real than goat-men.* He sighed.

*What if the dagger put the dream in my head? What if someone else used it to kill someone, and I was freaking cuddling with the thing in my sleeping bag because it's the only weapon I have? Maybe it should be close to my sleeping bag, but not touching it. Maybe I should use my cool stick for defense instead.*

Thomas picked up his pot, made his way to the creek, and gathered more water. It wasn't like yesterday. He no longer felt that renewed sense of purpose and strength. He felt like a zombie going through the motions, but he did it. Showing true character isn't about what you do when things go well—it is about what you do when everything is against you. Thomas would show character. He would keep going, no matter what he learned, no matter how painful it was.

Thomas would have the truth.

He made another pot of creek noodles, as he liked to call it. Trying to raise his spirits, he repeated his new mantra—*strong body, strong mind*—redirecting his energy. He needed to stay sharp because of how heavily the nightmare weighed on him.

Thomas packed up his camp and continued along the cliff base, looking for the place he had climbed up before. It didn't take long. The night he found this spot, he was trying to hide, and he was hurt from the fall, so he had made bad time. He was still hurt now as well. It had only been two days. It felt like years. He actually had to stop and count the nights to make sure he was remembering it correctly.

*One, woke up in the woods.*

*Two, went to bed with Rebecca, woke up with a creature in the house.*

*Three, had creek noodles.*

It had only been a little over forty-eight hours since he regained his mind—or body—or whatever happened.

He climbed to the top the same way he had before, wedging himself into a channel in the rocks and sliding up. He hadn't had a backpack last time, so he tied his paracord to it before starting the climb. Once he reached the top, he looked around for anything alarming and then hauled his gear up once he was sure it was safe.

Using the map and compass, he laid out a course that should

roughly be the direction he was facing that night when he first woke up. He knew he'd been facing downhill, in the woods, but close enough to the road for light to reveal the silhouette of his stalker. He figured he would start there, face the same direction, then just turn around and walk forward.

It wasn't high-level detective work, but it's what he could do, so he did it.

He watched as he went, looking for any signs of disturbance in the leaves or brush. He scanned the ground for footprints. He glanced behind at his own freshly walked path and couldn't see anything there either. He knew he wasn't a tracker and didn't know what to look for, but he didn't give up. He continued walking in his estimated direction up the slope.

Thomas froze. He had a moment of recognition, but he couldn't tell what. His gaze drifted through the trees until it landed on a large rock. It jutted from the earth like the humped back of some ancient beast, half-buried, half-forgotten. Moss, soft and deep green, clung thick to its flanks except where rain had worn a smooth path down one side. There, the gray stone shone like an old piece of bone. It rose to the height of a man's chest and was as broad as a dining table. Its edges were rounded by time, but still stubborn and solid, immovable. A deep crack split its top corner; a jagged scar filled with fallen leaves and a tiny patch of fern.

Thomas *knew* that rock. There was no question. Some fragment of that night or perhaps the dream, he wasn't sure. But he knew it. He walked to it, placed his hand on the stone, and closed his eyes. Somehow, he knew which direction to go. Almost along his old path, but a little to the right. With renewed determination, he planted his cool stick on the ground and began hobbling forward to find his answers.

It was about two miles of rugged terrain for an injured man to cover. He didn't go quickly, but he went steadily. More landmarks were becoming familiar. Rocks. A tree that had been shattered by lightning. A crevasse in the mountain—things he shouldn't recognize but did. He started moving quietly, wary that he might actually find what he was looking for.

*Great job, Thomas. Seriously, you had a task, and it looks like you're going to accomplish it.*

*It might get you killed, but those are just details.*

*Be sneaky. Don't panic if you see another goat-man.*

*Use your mind.*

Thomas knew he was close. He half-crouched and crept between two chest-high rocks, easing toward a view of the hollow in the mountain. He had found what he was looking for, but now he wasn't sure if he was happy about it.

The ritual site lay in a natural clearing in a hollowed-out area in front of a cave. It was ringed by tall, ancient trees whose limbs arched overhead like watchful sentinels. At the entrance to the cave rose a low stone dais, half-swallowed by moss and dirt, but unmistakably shaped. It was circular, deliberate, and formed from the existing rocks. The ground around it was darker than the forest floor should've been, as if something had soaked deep into the soil long ago and never fully faded.

In the center of the area outside the cave was a flat altar of stone, cracked with age but stained at its center. It was dark, rust-red, like dried blood. A few totems made of bones and blackened wood still hung from the trees, spinning lazily in the breeze that didn't reach his skin.

The forest didn't seem to be making any sounds. There were no birds or insects. The only sound was Thomas's pounding heart.

Thomas knew that altar—it was where he had killed the woman.

# CHAPTER 8
### *No Light Inside*

Thomas scanned the area to make sure there was no one else around. If there were, he didn't really want to meet them just yet. He was afraid they would recognize him as an outsider, which meant they would try to kill him. He was more afraid they wouldn't recognize him as an outsider and would welcome him back.

He walked over to the altar, slow, nervous. He was afraid of what he would remember. He could see it in his mind—staring down at it… at her. His murder victim had been there, bound and helpless, crying for mercy. It was exactly what he dreamed. Every small detail matched what he remembered. He felt the panic begin to well from within. It made him nauseous, but he forced it down.

He needed answers, not emotions. He began walking the site, taking stock of the scene and looking for anything that could help him understand what had happened.

*You didn't think to bring a camera when you left your house, either.*

He didn't have his usual sarcastic tone with himself. This was too serious a moment, and he felt solemn. He killed someone here, and he enjoyed it. Or the dagger killed someone here and wanted him to see it. Thomas simply didn't know what to believe at the moment, so he would investigate instead, with his mind, not his heart.

*Don't add details you can't back up.*

*Do the work. Investigate the scene.*

*Force yourself to remember what you can since you didn't think to bring a camera.*

*Oh, good, my bitter, sarcastic side is back.*

The altar was a broad slab of stone with small channels in four places on the sides for the ropes that held the sacrifices. He ran his fingers along the grooves. They were smooth. No hope of fraying a rope. A central channel ran the length of the slab, growing deeper the further it went. It was a blood channel that let the blood run out at the end. The channel was rust-colored, like the blood had been absorbed and the stone could never forget it.

*Okay, altar first. There is a lot of blood, but it is dried, so hopefully nothing today.*

*No bodies. This much blood leads to bodies. There is a blood trail to the dais, and then it stops.*

*The altar has some engravings around the lip. Looks like runes… I guess. It's not English anyway.*

*When does something transition from a foreign language to a rune?*

The dais stood in front of the entrance to the cave. It was a circular stone with a flat top, ancient and weathered. Its edges softened by time and use. It was engraved with symbols he couldn't read, but they were partially obstructed by blood and moss.

*Dais next: also covered in runes, but a lot more.*

*In my nightmare, they glowed, but there was no electricity, no wires, no light bulbs, just light.*

*I hope that it was just some kind of nightmare flourish because if it actually glowed, then magic is real.*

*I am not happy with that thought at all.*

Thomas stopped at the entrance to the cave and studied it. Nothing was strange at the entrance, just a cave cradled in the rough rock face. The entrance was dark and still. It stood about nine feet tall with plenty of room to walk in, but Thomas really didn't want to go in. It looked like a typical cave, but Thomas felt something foreboding about the whole area. It seemed to scream that some nightmare from another world was waiting.

*Do the work, Thomas. Get out of your own head, strap on your light, and check it out.*

*Either there is nothing in there and nothing to fear—or your answers are in there.*

Thomas pulled out his headlamp and walked inside. The stench was almost overwhelming; it was so thick he could taste it. He had smelled it before; the clawing stench of rotten fruit smelled the same as the dead goat-man.

The cave walls were covered in drawings made of blood: vines, leaves, happy and sad face masks, and the circle of grapes on his dagger hilt. Thomas already knew the answer, but this confirmed it—this was where he was when he went missing. He was right here when Rebecca was calling hospitals looking for his body. He was right here with all this blood.

This didn't give answers, though, just more questions.

He had flashes. More memory fragments: He saw a woman enter the cave. She was running toward him, angry, violent.

She didn't look human, not quite. She was beautiful, but something else. She was a little taller than Rebecca, probably about five feet eight. She had long, dark hair that thrashed as she ran at him. One of her arms was made of metal, her left arm. She had a rope in her hand, and with a flick of her wrist, she threw it at him. But suddenly it wasn't a rope, it was a net. The vision was fuzzy and jarring. He saw a goat-man attack the woman as Thomas was falling to the floor, ensnared and screaming in pain. The pain stood out. It felt like it burned into his bones. That part was clear.

She killed the creature like it was nothing. No weapon, she just hit it in the head with her metal arm, and it sailed over Thomas's head into the back of the cave. Thomas remembered watching the creature fly past, and then he looked back at her. She stood over him, laughing, then squatted next to him and said something, but he couldn't hear the words. All he could hear was his own screams. He remembered trying to grab her sword to cut himself free from the net.

*Who carries a sword these days?* thought Thomas. Then he looked down at the long dagger on his belt.

She made no move to stop him as he reached for her weapon. She knew the pain had simply taken everything he had, and he wouldn't be able to reach her. She smiled, grabbed the net, and flicked it; suddenly, he saw a rope again, and he was free. She held out a glass mirror and broke it on his chest, covering him in shards and a silvery dust. The vision made no sense. She walked to the dais, and it glowed. She was no longer there.

He didn't know if she had vanished or if the memory jumped.

He had other flashes. This wasn't the first time he saw her. She had been there earlier in his mind.

He saw her questioning him, demanding to know where the veil was. He remembered defying her, and she beat him. She was not human. He remembered her picking him up with one hand before threatening to send him to Hades. The flash ended. He tried to hold it, but it was like trying to remember a dream. The more he tried, the more the details slipped. He lost it—the fragments were gone.

*Great, now I have memories of a goat-man and a cyborg-apothecary-siren.*

*At least they are memories that are not happening now.*

Thomas pulled the dagger from its sheath and continued into the cave. It didn't go deep into the mountain, which was good. Thomas had been through enough; there was no reason to add spelunking to the list. At the back of the cave, he found a few crates, trash bags, a stone chest, and a large stain of foul-smelling blood. *I guess the goat from the vision wasn't the same goat that attacked me.*

*All right, Thomas, normally you should start with the chest because the good stuff should always be in the chest, but in this case, I don't know.*

*I don't think it's trapped or anything, but let's be honest, these people have different priorities than I do, and that chest is probably filled with human hearts or something I don't really want to see.*

*I've been holding it together, but I'm man enough to admit the psychological trauma is really starting to build, and I am not ready for a chest of heads.*

He could feel the strain. He was masking it with jokes and sarcasm, but the dream last night had really put him on edge. He would look into the chest of horrors in a minute. First: the crate of horrors.

He found supplies: jerky, some kind of powder in jars, and bottles of ancient-looking, wax-sealed wine. He wasn't brave enough to try any of it. His first thought was that people were sacrificed, and he didn't know what the jerky was from. Once that thought crossed his mind, he decided he wasn't eating or drinking anything from this place. He did take one jar and one bottle, wrap them up, and put them in his bag in case he could learn something about what they were.

He looked at the chest and thought, *Nope, I'm still not ready for that one yet*, and moved to the trash bags of horror.

He opened them and saw personal belongings, wallets, keys, smashed phones, and purses. He wasn't a grave robber or a ghoul, but he needed answers. He needed resources and couldn't be too picky about the source. He flipped open a couple of wallets and pulled one from a purse. He scanned the names quickly in case he recognized something or someone. Then he saw the ID from the purse. It was her. She was the woman he killed.

Thomas broke down crying.

It was a hard cry. It had been building, pushing the limits of his mental barriers, but this was too much. A picture of the woman with her two children was across from her ID. He bawled like a child. It took several minutes before he even tried to gain control. His normal mantras did nothing.

*Search the cave, cry in the morning. Strong body. Strong mind.*

They were just words now. Useless. He dropped the dagger; it didn't feel right to hold it anymore. Then he collapsed, his back against the cave wall, and stared at the picture of his victim and her children.

*How do you recover from this?*

# CHAPTER 9
## *Impossibly Creamy*

Thomas cried for some time. He didn't know how long it had been, but his soul was frayed and raw. Every new horror he had faced in the past few days felt like the worst thing he had ever experienced or even imagined—but it just kept getting worse.

He fought to stay alive every step of the way, but now, he felt like walking off a cliff. If he had murdered this woman and taken a mother away from her children, then she deserved justice. Not vengeance, but an answer to the horror she suffered.

Thomas looked into the eyes of the woman in the picture and said, "Your murderer will answer for this. If it is me, so be it."

Thomas returned the wallet to the purse. He would go through the personal belongings later. For now, he just wanted to get out of this evil place. He consolidated the items from both bags into one and was about to toss the empty bag on the ground.

*I know you are hurting, Thomas, but you need to use your mind first, your emotions second.*

*Don't leave a bag with prints at a murder scene.*

*Plus, you haven't looked in the chest yet; you might need the bag.*

The stone chest had once been part of the wall and floor. It was hewn directly from the rock. It had rough tool marks and jagged edges; it wasn't made to be pretty, just permanent.

There were no visible hinges, handles, or locks. The same markings etched into the altar and dais flowed across its lid. Thomas knelt on the stone floor, studying it. He ran his hand over its surface, feeling the grooves of the runes. He had a quick flash—another memory fragment at the back of his mind. He saw his hand placing the pommel of the dagger on the front, under the lip. He thought it would do something, though he wasn't sure what. He just had an image that he had done it before.

Thomas walked back to where he dropped the dagger and picked it up. It was just a tool. It was a tool with a dark past, but it had saved his life once. It felt like a lifetime ago. He was fairly sure it was yesterday. He couldn't tell anymore. Thomas walked back and placed the pommel against the front, under the lip.

The runes flared to life. The lid slowly drifted back on its own along rails that were hidden inside.

Thomas sighed:

*Magic is real, Thomas…*

*Maybe it is actually good news.*

*Magic might clarify a few things.*

*It might explain why you lost over two months.*

Thomas slapped himself in the face. He was droning, and he knew it. He was in shock, and he needed his mind back.

Rather than drone, he worked to give himself a task, something to drown out the fear. He looked in the chest and found a number of books, scrolls, and papers. He picked one up, turning it over in his hands.

# Ὁδὸς Αἵματος

*The goat-people with ancient rituals and weapons don't speak English. You didn't see that coming, Thomas?*

Its cover was made of stretched, darkened hide. Human or animal, it was impossible to say. Stitched crudely at the seams with sinew that had stiffened into cords. The leather was brittle, and parts of it had peeled away, revealing a wooden board underneath, scorched with burns and inked in runes that still shimmered faintly when the light hit them just right.

The pages were thin, dark, and almost metallic-looking. Some bore the imprint of smeared fingerprints, possibly blood. Ritual diagrams filled the margins. There were scratches displaying rings of symbols, twisted figures, and annotations in scribbles he didn't understand. In several places, dried wax clung to the paper in dribbled patterns, mingling with dark reddish stains that had soaked into the fibers long ago.

He flipped through a few pages carefully. They were old, but felt solid, like the pages themselves didn't age. Thomas looked at a few other items, but there was nothing he could understand. He placed the first book in his backpack and stuffed the rest of the items in the spare trash bag. Hopefully, these texts would help him in his search for answers and to get justice for the people who died here.

In the bottom of the chest, he found a removable board with dark stains soaked into the surface. He lifted the board and stared into the hidden compartment. Nestled within the dust-lined hollow was a collection of unsettling relics. Bags of silver and gold coins bore the faces of long-dead Roman emperors and Greek deities, their edges worn smooth by centuries. Mixed among them were stranger pieces: blackened metal coins, etched with twisted, half-human creatures. Some looked like the creature on his bathroom floor, but not all.

*What other creatures actually exist?*

Scattered beside them were small bones, brittle and yellowed. Too delicate for any animal he could name. Two flat stones, each carved with unfamiliar runes, rested like sentinels on either side of what looked like ritual instruments: a narrow-hooked blade, iron tongs warped with rust, and something that might once have been a brand. There was no mistaking it; this wasn't a simple stash. It was an accompaniment to the altar, a secret hoard of dark purpose that he knew how to open.

He took it all. He didn't know what would be useful, but he didn't ever want to come back here. Thomas searched everything again, hunting for secrets and answers. The magic dagger and hidden compartment in the chest made him redouble his efforts. He walked around, placing the pommel of the dagger in various places, including the dais and altar. Nothing. He felt silly randomly touching a dagger to everything, but he gave up on understanding physics or using rational thought.

Thomas was preparing to head back to his bike, but his brain kicked in and started thinking again. Learning that magic is real could explain what happened to him. It could account for the visions and missing time. It helped knowing he might have been compelled. If that's true, then he isn't responsible. It could have been his body without being his mind. He was still fighting that shock, but now he had purpose again. Find the person who did this. Find the cyborg-apothecary-siren lady, translate the books, and get answers.

*Okay, Thomas, welcome back.*

*You need food, a bed, and a computer.*

*You need a Batcave. You don't have a Batcave.*

*Libraries will only go so far.*

Thomas set the trash bag of personal items on the altar and pulled out the wallets and IDs. He knew the woman had two children and probably had other people living at her house, but he wondered if they all did. Thomas flipped through a few and found one belonging to a 72-year-old man. The only pictures in the wallet were of adults, decades younger than him. Thomas looked at the address: 122 Silver Spur Trailer Court.

*Somewhere in this bag is a set of keys to the trailer at that address. If Rob Warren lives alone, then that trailer might be empty, and it might have a computer. It will probably be an old person's computer running Windows 98, but as long as it can access the internet, it'll do.*

*All right, Thomas, you have a solid plan now. All you need to do is drive around town with a bike full of personal items from murdered people, while you look for a home to break into.*

He packed what he could into his backpack, loaded the rest into the trash bags, and started the long walk back to his motorcycle. He thought about stopping at the creek again, but he didn't want to be out here for another night. He needed to be somewhere else.

His trek back continued to wreck his back and legs, but otherwise, it was uneventful. Thomas stopped short of going to the motorcycle. If someone had discovered it, he didn't want to be surprised. He circled around and crept up on the position. He was starting to get his strategic edge back. Fortunately, he didn't need it that time, but the time a person most needs that caution and strategic edge is right when they failed to use it.

Thomas packed the heavier items in the luggage bags on the bike so the weight would ride lower. He sorted his other items to fit his backpack, trunk, and luggage bar. The armrests on the passenger seat were great for keeping gear secure. He looked around, listened for cars, and prepared to leave.

*I need a local map so I can find this address. I definitely don't want to ask for directions to a missing person's house.*

*There is a gas station attached to the Lickety-Split, and I would love a banana split right now, but my instincts have kept me alive so far. The morning after I got out of the woods, I felt like there was a strong case of imminent death waiting inside. Maybe it was because of the day I was having, maybe they would recognize me… maybe the cyborg-apothecary-siren is the cone girl.*

Thomas had used the map program to look at the whole town while he was doing research at the library yesterday. He knew there was a gas station about two miles past the Lickity-Split. Now he had a plan. He carefully pulled the remaining branches from his bike, taking pains to save the chrome, swung a leg over, and fired the Springfield up.

It started immediately on the first tap of the button. Thomas smiled and patted the handlebars.

After the last few days, he was happy to be on his bike and on the road. The vibrations still made his joints hurt and his hands throb, but it was freedom. He was almost disappointed the gas station was so close, but it was getting late, and he didn't have time for a longer drive anyway. He filled the tank, bought two bottles of water, a map, and an ice cream sandwich. It wasn't a banana split, and it was a waste of money, but he earned it.

Thomas waited to unfold the map and look up the address. Instead, he looked at that ice cream sandwich. The edges slightly smushed, the wrapper torn open just enough to catch a glimpse of that perfect, pale slab of vanilla ice cream pressed between two soft, dark chocolate cookies. His life had turned into visions, dreams, goat-men, and general insanity, but this was real. This was cold. Delicious. Heaven.

The first bite hit like a memory—sweet, rich, impossibly creamy. The ice cream melted against his tongue, smooth as silk, while the cookie gave just enough, chewy and bittersweet. *Now, this is a dream worth having.*

Thomas had the strength to continue now.

He used the map to find the trailer park. It was close, but his motorcycle would draw attention. He looked for a place close to the address where he could stash it.

*Spots to hide Freedom where it will be safe?*

*I could check on local foreclosed homes and stash the bike on the abandoned property, but it's getting late, and I don't have time to find one before nightfall.*

*Leave it in a parking lot with all this stuff on it? I could lock the bags and take the pack.*

*It looks like I am parking it in the woods again.*

Thomas looked down at his chrome, patted the tank reassuringly, and said, "You keep taking care of me and I'll take care of you."

Thomas drove down a couple of back roads close to the trailer park. He was having a little trouble finding a spot to pull over because of the ditches along the road. They were too big for a bagger-style bike to get through.

He slowed when the fence posts came into view, with weathered wood, and a sagging chain strung between them, a plastic sign half-torn by wind: UTILITY ACCESS ONLY – NO PUBLIC ENTRY.

Thomas smiled.

He angled the bike off the shoulder and found a rut beside the post, just wide enough to squeeze through. The front wheel dipped, wobbled, then caught.

Twenty yards in, the trail curved behind a brushy hill. Power lines stretched overhead, buzzing with energy. No cameras. No lights. No reason for anyone to come looking.

He pushed the bike into the trees, covered the chrome with branches, and sorted all the items he needed for his research. He didn't want to leave anything from the cave behind, just in case the bike was discovered. There was a lot of stuff that would be hard to explain. He went through and found all the keys first; he just hoped that Rob Warren's keys were among them.

Once again, Thomas's poor back and legs groaned and cracked as he started hiking towards the trailer park. Fortunately, after fighting the goat-man, he felt prepared for the horrors of a retirement park. He was still cautious, but it was a pretty simple task coming up to the trailer from the woods. He saw there were no lights on in the trailer, but there were lights along the street. He scanned the path to the front door, making sure the coast was clear, then jog-hobbled as fast as he could muster to the door. The third key he tried spun in the lock; he was in.

Thomas quietly checked the house to ensure it was empty and that there would be no surprises. If his neighbors knew Rob was gone, they might notice a light turning on. Thomas used his headlamp, but he kept it pointed at the floor instead of the windows as he worked his way to the kitchen. Something other than creek noodles sounded like a treat. He opened the freezer, hoping for a frozen dinner.

Thomas needed a good night, which included food and sleep. He was still standing in front of the freezer, scanning the contents.

He smiled—ice cream sandwich. This time, with chocolate ice cream.

# CHAPTER 10
## *Rob's Chair*

With a full stomach of baked ziti and ice cream sandwich, Thomas was now ready to settle down for the night. He was still concerned about someone showing up in the morning, possibly a child or friend. He didn't want to get caught sleeping in Rob's bed.

He went to the guest room, which doubled as a storage space. There were several stacks of boxes on the floor and across the bed. Thomas arranged them to look natural, as if someone had simply stacked them for storage. Then he laid his sleeping bag on the floor behind the wall of boxes. If someone did come in, they shouldn't notice him unless they were specifically searching the house and not simply looking for Rob. Perhaps it was an overcautious approach, but he had had enough surprises lately. He would do whatever he reasonably could to stay ahead of what was happening and decide what to do next.

Thomas took the luxury of an actual shower before bed. It was not some water from a ditch thrown on his face, but water from a showerhead. He was quick about it. He did get undressed, but only after locking the door and hanging the dagger in its sheath from the shower curtain rod. Every sound, every light from a passing car made his heart race. Still, being clean made him feel human again.

Lather. Rinse. Repeat.

On his way to the guest bedroom, he stopped and walked to the recliner in the living room. He had Rob's ID, so he knew what the man looked like. He pictured him sitting in the recliner with a beer in hand and watching a football game.

Thomas felt the need to say something, though he didn't really know why. "Hey Rob, I'm sorry for what happened to you, and I am sorry to use your house like this. You deserved better in life than to meet the end you did. I am trying to get justice. I am going to respect your place and try to find the people who killed you. I guess, in a way, they took my life too." He bowed his head for a moment out of respect and then returned to the guest room.

He closed himself inside and settled down into his sleeping bag, fully dressed except for shoes. If another goat-man showed up, he would have his dagger under his jacket, which was also a makeshift pillow, and he would be ready to spring into action.

---

Thomas was running through the darkness. He thought he had escaped, but she found him. He looked back at the woman who was chasing him. She was running impossibly fast—easily three times his speed, and he was at an all-out sprint. He looked forward to make sure he didn't stumble. That was when he felt the impact. Her metal fist slammed into his back. He pitched forward into the dirt, hard. His face thudded into the ground, and he almost lost consciousness. He fought to stop from blacking out as she flipped him over handily, as though he were a child. She was massively stronger than him, and she wanted him to know it—to know that obeying was a better option than fighting.

She yelled at him in another language, but somehow, he knew what the words meant, "Oo DY-na-sai FEWG-ein me, KAHL-lis-teh. Ee seh ho-THON HE-mah-tos AH-kseis, ee HAI-dees hay-DEE-own eh-MOO fa-NAY-tai."

The words hit Thomas like a hammer; her metal hand punctuated them as it crushed his throat. He understood: "You cannot escape me, Callistos. You will lead me to the Path of Blood, or Hades will seem pleasant compared to me."

Thomas grabbed the metal arm holding his throat and used it to pull himself closer to her, unafraid. He locked his eyes on hers and, with every ounce of hatred and venom as he could muster between gasped breaths, replied, "KAH-lis-tos TETH-nay-ken. Eh-GO AY-mee ho Oh-meh-THAY-on, STO-ma theh-OO." Thomas didn't know where the words came from, but they were uttered by his mouth. It meant, "Callistos is dead. I am Ometheon, the mouthpiece of god."

The woman hit him with her free hand, and the dream ended.

---

Thomas was getting better at controlling his emotional responses. He didn't jump up, thrash, or cry out. His eyes opened, his breath steadied, and he listened—nothing.

He slid forward from the bag, grabbing his headlamp and backpack. From a side pocket, he pulled a pencil and scraps of paper from the library, writing the words as best he could remember. He didn't know how to spell them; he just sounded them out and wrote what seemed correct. He sat in silence, going over every detail of the dream. At this point, he knew it was another memory fragment. His last dream had been true. He was sure this was true as well.

He thought back to the woman's metal arm—not an arm— armor.

*Good, she's not a cyborg. I couldn't handle cyborgs and goat-men. She is too strong, though. She can't be human, can she? As much as I hate to admit it, magic is real. The dagger opened the chest; the runes on its surface glowed. That proved it. Maybe she had magic armor on her left arm. That would explain why it was only on one arm, right? Why would a person not have it on both arms? It's not like she's Michael Jackson.*

She was strong and confident. She wasn't military, or at least not United States military. The clothing was wrong. It looked old, like something out of time or myth.

Her armor was Greek or Roman, but worn not as a costume or relic. It matched her presence and seemed to be a part of her. Bronze gleamed along the curves of her chest plate, but the rest was too dark to see in the light of his dream.

The armor on her left arm was something out of a gladiator movie. It was a series of overlapping metal plates that ran from her shoulder to just above her elbow. Each plate gleamed faintly in the moonlight, layered like the scales of a dragon. Beneath it, supple leather wrapped tightly around the underside of her arm, holding the plates firm and shielding the vulnerable flesh beneath. It was a seamless blend of protection and flexibility, crafted to catch the blades that slipped past the metal.

Her right arm bore a bracer that matched the design of the left arm, but it didn't enclose her hand as the left did. Both were etched with sigils that caught the light when she choked him, but they didn't glow of their own accord. At least not that he had seen. Calf-high boots laced tight to her legs with metal plates along the front over the shins. They looked like something a tactical police team would use if they were in an ancient world.

Her hair was long and black, unbound, cascading freely down her back and around her shoulders. It was as wild as the anger in her eyes.

At each hip, she wore a sword: one had a straight blade, but the other was in a curved sheath, making it difficult to picture. It looked like it might even be an axe. She also had the rope on her hip. The one from the other vision. He remembered it well. Coiled at her belt like a serpent. It was a loop of dull silver, nearly translucent, as if woven from moonlight and smoke. It wasn't decorative. It brought great pain when she willed it. Somehow, it could become a net, and he had been trapped in it before.

*Okay, let's analyze this. It looks like a foreign presence possessed you. That is comforting and horrifying all at once.*

*This woman knows something. Is she an ally or an enemy? She certainly didn't like Callistos, so ally?*

Thomas tried to recover more details, but the dream was already fading. He kept replaying what he could to force it into his long-term memory.

As the sun came up, Thomas started moving. He still didn't want to turn on lights at night to draw attention, but now he could move around freely inside the trailer. He went straight to the computer in the living room.

An HP tower: it was old, dusty, and quiet.

He powered it on. Password protected. Of course. He tapped the keyboard. No hint. No guest account. Just the name: Rob.

He leaned back, thinking. Guessing a password could take forever. He tried "password," but it didn't work.

He dug into his backpack and pulled out a USB stick. He always kept one loaded with a bootable Windows installer and a few tools. This was his environment. Running through the woods, killing goat-men, and magic glowing rocks were not in his everyday life, but this was a computer. This was what he did in his old life. He was an engineer who liked thinking, planning, and overcoming electronic problems.

*There is nothing as satisfying as a perfectly built spreadsheet.*

He was the person who had fixed the machines, long after IT had given up on them.

The BIOS key was F9. He hit it at startup, navigating by memory.

The installer loaded slowly; the old machine chugged to life.

At the blue setup screen, he pressed Shift + F10. A black terminal window opened.

He looked back at the recliner, "I'm sorry, Rob. Whatever I find on your machine will stay between us."

He ran the commands like muscle memory:

move  c:\windows\system32\utilman.exe  c:\windows\system32\utilman.bak

copy     c:\windows\system32\cmd.exe     c:\windows\system32\utilman.exe

He ejected the USB and rebooted. He sat impatiently. It's funny how spoiled he got using his fast machines at work and home. After all the running and waiting, the time it took for this old machine to boot up seemed stifling. But it worked. This time at the lock screen, he went down to the bottom right corner and clicked the Accessibility icon—now a disguised command prompt with administrative access.

In the Command Prompt window, he entered:

net user Rob *

The machine asked for a new password. He tapped in something simple. Goatman. Something he'd remember.

He closed the window and typed the password into the login box.

The desktop loaded slowly. There were dozens of icons, outdated shortcuts, and a folder called "women" glowing at the center.

"Rob! You dog," Thomas muttered. "Don't worry, I'll delete that for you before I go. If you have kids, they won't find it."

He opened the folder to confirm what was there.

Yep.

Deleted. Empty Recycle Bin.

"There you go, buddy. Clean slate."

Thomas loaded the browser that was bookmarked, Edge. He

went through the settings and checked saved passwords: all the same. *This was going to be easy.*

First stop: Walmart.

He needed supplies. Things he could buy without showing his face, delivered to a porch he didn't own, paid for by a murdered man. He would do his best to make sure that man had justice for what was done to him.

He'd been assembling the list in his head for almost a day. Now it was time to click "Add to Cart" and pretend he was still a person with a shopping list and a plan.

He logged into Rob's account. Muttered under his breath as he worked:

- One cheap laptop, case, and scanner for translating the murder book.
- Five USB sticks, so I can lose four of them.
- Three cheap motion-detecting cameras and a smartphone, so I can detect motion… with a camera.
- Basic wristwatch. Notebook. Pencils. I am boring.
- Dumbphone to bypass smart systems that want to verify I exist.
- Maglite, batteries, disposable cameras, soldering kit, duct tape, and gloves. Because I am tired of running.
- Clif bars because I'm a growing boy.
- One variety pack of ice cream sandwiches, because the rest of the list is pointless without it.

He selected Express Delivery and clicked "Place Order."

It would be two hours before it was delivered. Since Thomas couldn't read the books as-is, it was time for breakfast. He did a quick scan of the fridge and pantry and decided to go with a bacon, egg, and cheese sandwich with shredded hash brown topper. His brother once showed him the "proper" way to eat a fast-food egg McMuffin. You place the hash brown on top and put ketchup on top of the hash brown.

It's tricky. The ketchup can't touch the egg itself because no self-respecting man would ever put ketchup on eggs. However, he could put ketchup on hash browns. Then put the hash browns on the eggs.

His brother had further explained that he didn't make the rules; the universe made the rules. He was just following them. Despite making fun of his brother, he had to admit: it was a good sandwich. He made it often.

He started with bacon because it was the slowest to cook, and he loved the smell. He settled into his morning breakfast routine and felt normal while he waited. It made him feel so normal that he thought about calling Rebecca for a second, but only a second. He quickly put that out of his mind. A murdered man's phone calls would be examined, plus it would potentially put Rebecca in danger. He wanted to let her know he was still alive and was making progress. He wanted her safe, more.

Thomas smiled, thinking about her, wondering if he would see her again. Part of him hoped he would find a way to wrap everything up, and they could be together. That wasn't going to happen unless he was absolutely certain of her safety.

So far, the mystery was just becoming stranger, and Thomas was becoming stranger with it.

# CHAPTER 11
## *No Remains*

"I'm telling you, Rob—hash browns on top of the eggs. Bonus points if there's peppers."

Thomas took another bite of his sandwich, bacon crisp, yolk still warm, the hot sauce soaking the toast. "You're missing out, buddy."

He sat at the computer desk while he ate, talking to the recliner as if it might answer. It didn't, of course.

He wiped his fingers on a napkin and clicked through a few tabs. The Walmart order was still out for delivery. Good. He had maybe an hour.

Curiosity pulled at him, a quiet gnawing he hadn't fed since this all started. He opened a new tab, paused, then searched his old address.

WHSV-3 News | Metro Briefs – Richmond Area

May 17, 2025

House Fire Leaves Questions, No Answers for Missing Engineer

He stopped chewing, the sandwich frozen in his hand as he read.

A house fire in the Greenbriar subdivision has left authorities with more questions than answers. No remains recovered. Accelerant used. Home belonged to Thomas [Last Name Withheld], 34. Missing since early March. Neighbors report that he always waved and kept the lawn mowed.

He had been reported missing over two months prior by Rebecca [Last Name Withheld], who described him as "deeply caring, the calm in a world of storms." According to the report, he was last seen in early March. Authorities had previously stated there was no sign of forced entry or suspicious activity at the time.

"This is an active investigation," said Fire Marshal Cynthia Darrow. "The absence of remains does not confirm or rule out any scenario."

No mention of a goat-headed body.

*My house burned down a few hours after I left. No remains were found. An accelerant was used.*

*The remains of an eight-foot-tall man with a goat head weren't found.*

*They cleaned up after themselves and burned the house down to cover the unexplainable part.*

*That's rude.*

He tossed the sandwich onto the plate and stood up. Pacing back and forth, he shoved the chair out of his way. He wanted to punch a wall or kick something. He didn't. He thought it would be rude to Rob's memory.

"How did they cover it up so quickly? What resources do they have?" he muttered.

He shook his head and let out a growl. He knew he was never planning on returning to that house, but seeing it burned down was somehow still emotional. Insulting. It felt like he lost something even though he had already lost it.

He looked down at the half-eaten sandwich. He decided he wasn't going to lose it, too, as he pulled it up for a big bite.

*Practical over emotional. Feed the body today. Write memoirs later.*

After finishing the sandwich, he felt like his old self again. He wasn't exactly okay, but sometimes, when you fake a smile, your body catches up later, so he focused on what he could do while he waited.

"I'm sorry if this seems rude, Rob, but if you have a gun, I'd like to find it." He glanced toward the hallway. "I'll look around, but I'll respect the place."

He didn't find a gun. He did find a duffel bag labeled *Timothy Warren.* A relative, maybe. A brother or son. He also found a backpack a child might use for school. It was in better shape, so he took it instead. Everything else was too bulky to carry.

But he also found pictures of Rob smiling with a woman and their arms around a few kids. A teenager holding up a catfish. Five young adults gathered around a Christmas tree—grandkids, most likely.

He smiled. "You had a good life and a family that loved you.

Good for you, buddy. Hopefully I'll have that too, when this is all over."

His life wasn't over yet; it was just taking a detour.

He glanced at the computer. Walmart order, out for delivery. The order had special instructions: "Leave on front porch." He didn't think he could pass for a seventy-two-year-old man, or he at least hoped he couldn't. He watched through a small opening in the blinds for the car to pull up. He expected a little compact car, but it was a raised pickup. He was initially surprised, but then considered that he was up in the Appalachian Mountains, not the city. They got more snow up here, and probably needed something that could handle the winters.

Every little detail that he did not expect had a bigger reaction than he felt it should. He pictured a car. A truck showed up. He started breathing hard. He knew it was the stress. If he were going to survive, he would need to learn to handle it better. Bluff better. React faster.

He watched closely—just one person, no horns. His fingers on the hilt of his dagger relaxed. He felt that nervous anticipation of someone trying to get away with something. Was it because people were looking for him, because he was anxious to get to work, and these were like gifts at Christmas, or because he was using someone else's credit card? He felt like a kid cutting class. Maybe a little bit of all of them, but it didn't matter. This was just a normal part of life now.

The driver stepped into view, just a regular guy doing a regular job. Thomas watched as the driver made several trips back and forth past the window. He followed the instructions and set everything on the front porch before getting back in his truck and driving away without incident.

Thomas watched to see if the neighbors had taken interest. He didn't see any blinds moving or doors opening. After a few minutes, he went to the front door and opened it slowly. The items were there, but were stacked against the storm door, blocking it from opening.

Thomas muttered, "I tipped, jerk. Plus, this is a retirement community. Show a little respect." He shook his head and shouldered the door to push the delivery back and make room. It opened just enough to start pulling bags inside.

As soon as the Walmart order was inside, he pulled out the gloves he had purchased. He slipped them on, then went through the trailer, wiping every surface he had touched. Every doorknob, counter, and light switch was wiped, just in case.

He spent his time setting everything up and getting organized. The cameras were placed in windows and linked to the smartphone, which didn't have any calling ability. He just needed the screen.

Setting the phone to vibrate would alert him to movement outside. Notifications were usually slow; he couldn't count on them to give advanced warning. He could, however, leave the phone on with a camera selected and see if anything was suspicious in the neighborhood in real time.

He was walking past Rob's chair as he was setting up the cameras. He stopped and placed a hand on the back of the chair. "I'm sorry, Rob. I've been thinking about this, and I know you have kids and grandkids—but I need your money. It should go to them under normal circumstances. The people who killed you are still out there, and I intend to stop them. I'm going to use your money to finance my investigation… I'm sorry." He squeezed the back of the chair where his hand was resting like he was squeezing a friend's shoulder. He didn't like some parts of his new life.

He set up the burner phone next, linking it to online accounts. He bought Bitcoin through Rob's bank accounts. Mapped out nearby towns with BTMs—Bitcoin ATMs—so he could withdraw untraceable cash. Fees didn't matter. It wasn't his money.

*The next step is a van. Yep, I'm going to be a van guy—who just ordered duct tape and disposable gloves.*

*I can't keep riding around on Freedom with this much stuff, especially in bad weather.*

*Assuming the bitcoin thing works, and I don't get arrested or shot, I'll have cash, and I can buy something through a private sale.*

He leaned back in the creaky chair and began the search. *Used cargo van. Pre-2006. No GPS. Minimal Windows. Fits motorcycle.*

*Goat-proof.*

Craigslist. Facebook Marketplace. AutoTempest.

He refined the search.

"Chevy Express or Ford Econoline cargo van, extended

wheelbase."

One van caught his eye: a 2003 Ford E-350, white, 210k miles, rust, but no electronics newer than a CD player. No questions asked. Two hundred miles away.

Another in the opposite direction: a 1999 Chevy Express 3500, decommissioned government fleet vehicle. Vinyl interior. No decals. Empty cargo bay.

He opened a spreadsheet and started logging them as he smiled. He loved spreadsheets. He had columns for make, model, mileage, condition, location, and seller notes. This wasn't just a van. It was his mobile investigation vehicle. It would give him the freedom to solve this mystery…

He stopped cold.

He was building the Mystery Machine.

The grown man and engineer in him winced. Then he chuckled and said, "Ruh-roh!" before continuing to type.

The van had to be forgettable, durable, and empty enough to carry Freedom without drawing eyes.

Once he had a few options, he took pictures of his spreadsheet and route directions with the smartphone so he could pull them up on the road.

Finally, after finishing with bitcoin set-ups and searching for vans, he turned his attention to the investigation itself. He put all the texts and books in the newer of his backpacks. As he scanned them, he moved them to his older backpack. His system: new books that hadn't been scanned went in the newer bag; old books that were already scanned went in the older one.

He loved having a system. It gave him control over something after spending days guessing and running. It was going to take a while to scan the books, but that was okay. It was tedious data entry, and that would lead to stored information. Stored information would let him see the bigger picture and make a plan—like a proper engineer. No more sprinting off cliffs in the dark. Just logic and data.

Things were finally looking up. He had control and a system. He would make a plan and call the shots. There would be no more surprises.

Thomas twisted in the chair, placed the most recent notes in the finished bag, and grabbed a few more pages from the to-do bag. As he was spinning back to the desk, movement on the phone caught his eye—a sheriff's car was pulling into the spot outside the trailer.

# CHAPTER 12
## *That's One*

Thomas quickly stood, packed his items, and grabbed his bags as he started walking toward the back of the trailer. He was prepared to leave quickly, and everything was packed except the three pages he was working on. It meant leaving the camera behind, but there were no prints on it, and he could get another. One hand was hovering over the doorknob at the back door, the other holding the smartphone with the video feed of the officer.

A woman wearing a floral shirt, green sun visor, and yellow pants was walking by when the officer stepped out of his cruiser.

"Officer," she called out. "Is something wrong?"

He glanced back as he said, "Nothing to worry about, ma'am. Mr. Warren witnessed a traffic incident last night, and I'm just following up."

"Oh, okay," replied the woman as she continued her elder strolls. It was like a slow-motion power walk with the elbows drastically swinging back and forth.

Thomas paused. Mr. Warren was dead. He had been dead for several days, so there was no way that he had called in a traffic incident last night. The cop was lying, but why? No one knew Rob was dead except Thomas and the people in the cult, which meant this guy wasn't what he appeared to be. Thomas had books and a few artifacts, but he didn't know if they had the answers he needed. This was the first time he had been a step ahead of them, and he needed those answers. He didn't open the door. Instead, he stepped into the guest room next to it and tossed his bags behind his makeshift wall. He turned off the audio on the phone and waited.

The cop fiddled with the lock for a couple of minutes before the door opened.

The sound of his footsteps was hesitant at first, then they crossed over to the computer desk.

The chair squeaked as the officer sat down.

Thomas had turned off Rob's computer once the laptop arrived, but now he heard the fans kick on.

The keyboard clicked, then a pause. They clicked again, followed by a whispered grunt of annoyance.

Then the sound of a cell phone being dialed:

"Yeah, the password didn't work. The old man lied."

"Of course, I'm sure. I typed in Timothy1, capital on the T."

"I don't care what kind of power Ometheon thinks he has to compel people, the password does—"

*Creak.*

Thomas had been standing weirdly, and when he shifted his weight to the other foot, the floor objected.

He heard a *beep* from the other room. The cop had stopped speaking and hung up.

He had heard the creak.

Thomas had had enough running. He decided to try a new tactic.

He opened the door to the living room and walked boldly forward.

The police officer pulled his gun and pointed it directly at Thomas's head.

The cop smiled as he said, "The one that got away."

Thomas sneered as he walked forward, using all his high school drama training to sell an air of confidence. He looked at the cop as though a master was disappointed in his slave. With all the arrogance he could muster, he said, "Eh-GO AY-mee ho Oh-meh-THAY-on, STO-ma theh-OO." The phrase he had learned during his dream. He knew it meant: I am Ometheon, the mouthpiece of god.

The officer instantly lowered his gun and dropped his gaze in obvious fear as he said, "ō-EE-thay-men seh eis TAR-ta-ron ek-se-STRAM-men-on EI-nai; ook Ē-day HO-tee DOO-na-sai loo-THAY-nai."

Thomas knew he had said his line perfectly. He could feel himself saying it in the dream. Unfortunately, that was the extent of his knowledge. He had no idea what the cop said in response, but the reaction was on the right track. He replied, "Your words sound like a pig sucking mud. Use the words you were born with."

The cop lowered his head further as he said, "M-my lord. We thought you had been banished to Tartarus. I didn't know you were able to be freed."

Thomas sauntered forward, voice filled with disdain. "I can't be contained so easily. My spirit was suppressed, not banished. Tell me what happened. I can't remember the time after my soul was quieted."

"Of course, my lord. Thaleia was waiting on the Path of Blood. When you opened the doorway, she stepped through and attacked. She cast the Threads of Ruin at you and destroyed the satyrs as though they were nothing. She killed them with her bare hands. Then she walked to you and threw something—a sheet of glass, I think. It broke on you. We thought that severed your spirit from that body."

Thomas leaned in and replied, "Is that when you killed her? Surely, you stopped her." He could remember that she stepped on the dais and vanished, but he didn't want to admit that he doubted the memory.

The police officer stammered, "N-no, sir. She stepped on the dais and traveled the Path of Blood. We couldn't follow. Her people must have taken the other side."

"Where is she now?" demanded Thomas.

"She's on the other side. We… we didn't follow," replied the cop, panic creeping into his voice. "One of the satyrs was still alive. It was in the woods and wasn't there at the altar when she attacked. Billy sent the satyr after your body to clean up the loose ends. We didn't know you could reclaim it. There aren't any other satyrs left in this area to send through. They are with Tearan."

*Satyr must be what they call the goat-man.*

Thomas slowly pulled the dagger from behind his back, under his shirt, and said, "It tried to kill me with this. It is dead now because it failed me. Because it didn't listen to me. And now you—you pointed your weapon at me? You still hold it in your hand as though it might keep you safe?" Thomas extended his free hand with his palm open.

The cop responded by immediately spinning the gun in his hand

and placing it into Thomas's waiting palm, "I'm sorry, my lord. I live to serve, and I will not fail you again."

Thomas looked down at the gun in his hand.

*This is going well.*

"How did Thaleia suppress my spirit?"

"I don't know, my lord. Since she is the one who arranged for your soul to be put in that body, I assumed she had the power to sever it. She is a goddess."

Thomas wished he had more time, but he was running out of material. It was time to end this. He set the dagger down on the computer desk, switched the gun to his right hand, slid the rack to confirm it had a bullet in the chamber, and flipped the safety off. Then coldly said, "Lie on your stomach, hands out to the sides."

Realization flashed over the cop's face. He was cowering in front of Thomas, the human—the one that got away and who now had his gun. Slowly, the cop started lowering himself to the floor. "You think you're going to live through this? You're a dead man. You can't escape what is coming for you."

"So, I should kill you now to make sure I take you with me? You'll answer questions or die. Who knows, you might do both. I'm already on borrowed time." Thomas responded as he knelt on the cop's back and secured his hands with his own cuffs. "I've had enough of this. Why did Thaleia have me possessed? Is she your leader?"

The cop started laughing, "You really have no idea what is going on? She had you possessed because Ometheon knew how to find the Path of Blood in our world. You were just a tool. You want more answers, let me go."

Thomas stood and stepped over to the desk. He looked at the gun for a moment, then placed it down. Then he reached over, wrapped his fingers around the hilt of the dagger, and dragged it so the tip scraped across the wood. With a metallic shing, he picked it up. He turned it over in his hand, watching the light glint along the blade.

"I have nothing holding me back. My life is over, and I am only alive as long as I stay a step ahead. My family and friends think I am dead. My career is over." Thomas paused and drew a deep breath. "The only thing I have left is this dagger… and what it does for me. You are going to answer my questions, or you will have no use to me."

He crouched down as he continued, "The Path of Blood, what is it?"

The cop demanded, "Guarantee you'll release me."

Thomas flipped the cop over, spun the knife in his hand, dropped a knee on his chest, and said, "Pick an eye!"

"No, no. The Path of Blood is a link between realms where the seal is weak. It's like a doorway," stammered the cop.

Thomas pressed for more: "Why is it called the Path of Blood?"

"I-it responds to blood. The divine can travel, b-but without the blood of the gods, we have to make a sacrifice. That's why you were— he—was brought here. Ometheon knows how. He had a book, okay?"

Thomas leaned in. "Tell me more about Thaleia. Why did she pick me?"

The cop stammered, "She's the daughter of Athena. She's a powerhouse, one of those half-gods that's been alive for hundreds of years. She's hunting my people in her realm. That's why they came here. They told me they would make me an immortal, so I joined them, but I learned my lesson. Just let me go, I won't come after you again."

Thomas asked, "Why did you come here? What were you looking for here? What did Rob have?"

The officer responded, "Nothing, I was just checking to ma—"

Thomas pressed the blade against the cultist's throat and started pulling—slowly.

With a strangled gasp, the officer answered, "He has a tape. He was investigating his friend's disappearance, and he recorded a few of us having a meeting."

"So, you killed him? You killed him for being a good man?" Thomas's voice took on a harsh, cold tone. He wasn't raising his voice. He just hardened it. "Did you think about the victims? About their families? About the children crying over their missing mothers?" The cop started to hyperventilate. He couldn't bear his captor's gaze.

He looked away.

"Look at me! You don't have the strength to face me? You are about to face the ghosts of your victims. You can't stand looking into my eyes? You are going to see the face of every person you failed, every person you killed—they will stand in judgment of your soul, I'm just sending you to meet them."

Thomas whipped the knife swiftly and stood up. There were tears in his eyes. He did not know what caused them. Pain. Justice. Empathy.

He had heard a debate when he was a kid. Someone had said that the Bible condemned killing. Another person pointed out that capital punishment was allowed. It was justified. The verse was supposed to say something like, "Their blood is on their own head." That brought him comfort about what he had to do. He was not murdering. He was introducing them to the fate they chose.

This wasn't vengeance or hate. It was justice.

Thomas walked over to the recliner and placed his hand on it, as if it were Rob's shoulder. He could hear the cultist thrashing and gurgling as he died. He gave the chair a little squeeze and said, "That's one."

# CHAPTER 13
## *Walk Away*

The cultist hung up quickly when he heard Thomas. That meant someone on the other end of that conversation was probably curious why. Police officers are supposed to check in regularly as well. Someone would come looking. He knew he had to move quickly.

He dashed to Rob's bedroom and grabbed the duffel bag he had discounted earlier. There was no time to be discreet; there was a dead cop on the floor. His presence here would be noted.

The cultist wanted a video on Rob's hard drive, but Thomas wanted it more. He set his smartphone on the desk next to the gun so he could monitor the camera feed while he worked.

He popped the side panel off the tower and pulled the hard drive. He turned his attention to the corpse. No body cam. No vest. He wiped the dagger on the cop's shirt and sheathed it. Then he removed the SIM card and stuffed the cuffs, phone, and utility belt in the duffel. A quick check of his pockets found a lockpicking set—unexpected. He tossed it into the duffel.

Knowing his time was limited, he sprinted through the house, grabbing his bags, cameras, and Rob's packed cooler from the refrigerator. With a ski mask on his face under a hat, a gun in his waistband, and keys in his hand, Thomas stopped beside Rob's chair. "I don't know what they did to you to get your password, but we're in this together. They didn't get the hard drive. I did. Whatever is on it makes them scared. You did good, buddy."

Thomas stepped outside. He kept his head low to obscure the mask as he walked around to the driver's side of the patrol car. His heart was pounding again. He knew people were probably on their way—and they had guns. He opened the door, tossed the duffel in the passenger seat, climbed in, and looked at the camera. Two quick smacks with the butt of the pistol disabled it before he started the car.

A man in a ski mask driving with the door cracked open was going to draw attention. He knew that some cars were used as bait cars by the police. They can lock the doors and shut off the engine remotely. After all the supernatural things he had survived, he, the engineer, was not going to be taken down by tech.

He pulled out and started driving as inconspicuously as he could, trying not to draw attention.

Taking a couple of turns placed him on the utility access road, where his motorcycle, Freedom, was stashed. It was a back road with no traffic, which was great for Thomas. He stopped in front of the chained-off entrance. He unhitched the shotgun mounted between the seats and shoved it in the duffel before making his way to the trunk. It was a treasure trove of new toys.

There was no time to inventory everything. He pulled the packs out of the duffel to make room and shoved everything from the trunk into it. There were several items, but in particular, Thomas noticed a rifle.

*People would call that an assault rifle… but all rifles can assault.*
*No time, leave now, inventory later.*

He used the strap to sling the duffel bag over his shoulder and lifted the other bags with his left hand. With his free hand, he put the car in gear and let it drift down the road. It would roll into the ditch at the turn, but he just wanted it far enough away that no mics would pick up the sound of his bike. To his knowledge, they didn't know about Freedom, and he wanted to keep it that way.

A quick glance around confirmed he had not been spotted. He headed up the path to his bike with his new gear weighing him down. He was panting by the time he got to Freedom. Adrenaline, injuries, and weight were stacking up against him. If he could just get the motorcycle on the road before reinforcements showed up, he would be in the clear. He tossed the branches aside. He didn't have time to care about the chrome right now. Gulping air, he packed his side cases and trunk. The big duffel got strapped onto the passenger seat between the armrests. He knew it would be heavy, but he didn't want to lose the options this gear represented.

Helmet on, he pressed the ignition. Freedom roared to life on the first tap, as dependable as always. He guided his bike down the utility path to the access chain and edged around it. He was back on the road, but paranoid. He kept glancing behind him and up at the sky, but he didn't see anyone. After an hour, he pulled over at a gas station to catch his breath.

He was starting to freak out. He knew he did the right thing, but it still got in his head. His uncle was a soldier and he had killed people in war. He had always said it was justified and necessary, but it follows you. It was following Thomas. He steered his bike around to a spot with fewer cars, removed his helmet, and quickly pulled off the ski mask that was under it. No one noticed it. His hair was matted and sweaty.

Thomas was not a pretty sight.

He wanted to go inside, but couldn't leave his bike, considering what he was hauling now. He pulled out his smartphone and used the free Wi-Fi to open a local map. He scanned around in satellite view until he found a local road with access to parkland. A place where he could stash something for a couple of days. He took a screenshot of the directions and headed back out.

His heart had slowed back down to a normal pace, and he was enjoying cruising down the road once again, simply a man and his machine—and cult books and magic and guns. He focused on the road so his mind couldn't focus on what had just happened.

The directions led him to a back road that would have been a pleasant place to take Rebecca if he weren't on the run.

The late afternoon sun poured golden light across the landscape, turning the dust kicked up by the motorcycle into a glowing veil behind him. The engine growled low and steady as he leaned into the handlebars, guiding the bike down a narrow dirt road that snaked between tall, weathered pines and patches of brush. The air was thick with the scent of leaves, warm soil, and the distant echo of cicadas humming somewhere deep in the trees.

He finally spotted the curve he had marked on the satellite map. He wanted an obvious landmark so he could find it easily in the future. As he reached the bend, he let off the throttle and coasted slightly, the tires crunching over loose gravel. A clearing opened just off the road, where the trees thinned for a short stretch. This was the spot.

He eased the bike off the road and killed the engine. It was a beautiful, quiet spot where the only human sound was the tick of his bike as it cooled. Birds chirped nearby. A breeze rustled the leaves, shaking sunlight down in flickering patches.

He swung his leg over the seat, unstrapped Rob's weathered duffel from the back, and slung it over one shoulder. With sore limping steps, he made his way into the trees. Not deep, just far enough to be hidden, and close enough to remember. He found a cluster of scrub oak and crouched, pulling a small collapsible spade from his pack. In a few quick movements, he dug a shallow hollow beneath the underbrush, dropped the bag in, and brushed dirt and leaves back over it. The books were in his locked side cases, safe from the weather. The handgun was in his waistband and close at hand. They were staying close, but the looted gear from the cop car would have to wait. Time—he always needed more time.

He set one of his motion-detecting cameras across from the stash and put a large leaf over the top. Even if someone found it, it would serve his purpose.

He stood, wiped his hands on his pants, and looked around once more. No one in sight. No sound but the wind and his own heartbeat, already settling down.

Then he turned, walked back to the bike, and pressed the ignition. He smiled when it roared back to life. The engine rumbled softly as he rolled forward, headed to the city. He needed money and a van.

He drove without stopping, but not without thinking. When the cultist was on the phone, he said Ometheon had compelled Rob to give up his password. That meant he was most likely tortured to death by Thomas's body. He was quite possibly the last thing Rob saw. He hoped one day, on the other side, he could explain to Rob that they were on the same team, but until then, he needed to keep fighting. So, he rode.

Once he arrived in the city, his first stop was the hospital, the engine idling just long enough to scan for anyone who followed him or helicopters overhead. Nothing obvious. Just civilians and hospital staff. He entered the main lobby, head low, the baseball cap obscuring part of his face.

At a folding table near the front, a nurse's station offered free surgical masks, hand sanitizer, and pamphlets about spring allergies. He grabbed a mask and moved on. Outside, he stopped behind a parked van, slipped on the mask, a plain charcoal ballcap, and glacier sunglasses. Anyone watching the CCTV footage would just see another cautious citizen. The getup wasn't for COVID—it was for discretion.

The sky was bleeding into amber when Thomas finally coasted into the edge of the city. His arms ached. His back burned. His hands throbbed. The day and the adrenaline were catching up to him.

He parked beneath a flickering streetlight outside a run-down liquor store. It was one of eight Bitcoin ATMs he mapped back at Rob's place, all picked for loose ID requirements, different operators, and private enough locations where he hoped he would go unnoticed.

The hospital mask itched against his skin, and the glacier glasses, with their leather side panels, looked goofy at night without the bike, but they masked his face from cameras. He walked past the rows of liquor on his way to the BTM. The clerk didn't even notice his strange-looking customer walking back to the machine and grabbing $780. Thomas followed his map, each withdrawal under the nine-hundred-dollar limit.

It took hours traveling around the city, but the time passed without incident. He got a few strange looks and was propositioned by a woman with a biting tic that kept saying, "Five dollars. Just five dollars. I'll blow your mind. Five dollars."

He passed.

It felt odd to him that the machine at the strip club was the cleanest. It was also the only one that drew attention. As he walked back to his bike, he noticed someone was following him. No one had followed him all day, so he figured it was just normal trash, not cult trash. He had been careful; they shouldn't have been able to intercept him at this stage.

He walked into an alley and turned. Two guys rounded the corner and smiled.

The first was tall, built like someone who had never skipped arm day at the gym. He had a face like rough concrete and a jaw that had clearly been broken before. His leather jacket looked expensive, but old and dirty, like its owner didn't understand how to wash things. He looked like his face had never said no to a fist.

The second one was the kind of guy you could tell was dumb just by looking at his face. It was like he was proud of it. Younger. Skinny. His eyes darted too much, like he was trying to play tough but hadn't figured out what to do with his hands. It looked like he had never been in a fight but wanted people to think he had.

"Yo," the dumb one said, too loud, like he thought they were about to mug someone in a movie. "Got a light?"

Thomas pulled his gun but didn't point it at them, just held it and said, "I've had a bad week. I don't mind adding two more bodies to the pile. Walk away."

"Easy, I'm walking away," said the big one.

The smaller, shifty one wasn't as graceful. He took off running, mumbling something incoherent.

Thomas wasn't even happy or proud. This was just life now; it was like going to the grocery store. Mundane.

He used a burner app that gave extra phone numbers and a couple of SIM cards to get the money he needed from the machines. Low amounts don't draw much attention. All said, he had $4,820, which was enough to buy the van he wanted. He pulled the SIM out and smashed it with the butt of his pistol. As he was walking away, he tossed it in the gutter. He had others.

He stretched his sore leg over Freedom's seat and hit the button.

"Next step, become a van guy," muttered Thomas as he headed toward the entrance ramp for the interstate.

# CHAPTER 14
## *I'm Home*

Thomas pulled Freedom into the Walmart parking lot, where he had agreed to meet the seller of the cargo van. He had driven through the night and had the luxury of a professionally prepared meal—*Burger King breakfast burrito*. At eight a.m., he called the number in the listing, and they agreed to meet in a public but anonymous place. It was a place where he could disappear into the crowd.

There it was: the white Chevy cargo van sat where the guy said it would. It was in the side lot backed up against a cinder block wall. The plates were still on, and they had a registration with eight months left. He had zoomed in on that detail before he even replied to the ad. This is a state where the license plates go with the vehicle, which means this one should be legal for several months without any issue. He wanted the cops to leave him alone, and this should do it.

The seller leaned against the front fender. He was in his mid-40s, sporting a worn ballcap and wearing the stained shirt of a man who works for a living. He smiled and seemed friendly enough. As long as there were no satyrs in the van, this would go smoothly.

For a second, Thomas thought about leaving. He spotted a work truck a couple of spots away from the van with someone inside. But he reined in his paranoia, evaluating instead of panicking. There was no logical way the cult could know he was coming here. The seller just needed a ride in case he sold the van, so he had a friend waiting.

*Everyone isn't out to get you, Thomas.*

*Don't get me wrong, a lot of people are absolutely out to get you, just not these two.*

Thomas pulled up on the Springfield, engine purring low as he backed into the spot next to the van.

He smiled and extended his hand. "I'm Rob."

The seller smiled, accepted the hand, and replied, "Bill. It works great. They don't make them like they used to. Want to take it for a spin?"

"Yeah, sounds great," responded Thomas. He didn't plan to go far; he didn't want to leave his bike alone any longer than necessary.

Thomas climbed in and fired it up. The engine rumbled with a slight shudder, normal for something that had worked hard, but wasn't dead yet. There were no warning lights except for low gas.

*Steering is tight.*

*Brakes are firm.*

*Windows are… window-y.*

He eased it down the street, turned right, then again, sticking close, just a couple of blocks total. No surprises.

He pulled back into the lot.

"Drives?" the seller asked.

Thomas cut the engine. "Drives."

The seller's ride was in a work truck with tools strapped all over it. Thomas nodded at that truck and said, "Any chance the five thousand dollars would include enough rope to strap my bike up in the back?"

The seller and friend exchanged a look, then the friend nodded. Thomas handed over an envelope with five thousand dollars in it. The seller gave it a once-over, satisfied. He handed over the keys, the rope, and a manila folder with a signed title and the old registration inside.

They shook once before the seller drove away. Then Thomas opened the van's rear doors, turned it slightly to angle against the slope of the lot, and started prepping the Springfield.

He used a busted curb and a flat crate to get leverage, then rolled the heavy motorcycle up with care and muscle, guiding it inside. There was plenty of extra rope and tie hooks for lashing it down tight against one wall. No rattling. No shifting. No loose ends.

Two weeks ago, he wouldn't have looked twice at the van. It was a basic white construction van that was used by painters and plumbers. Now it was something else. It was a home, a work lab, safety, anonymity, and a chance to plan. A chance to strike back against the cult that tried to kill him—that tried to kill Rebecca. The van he wouldn't have even noticed in his old life was his prized possession now. If he weren't so sore, he might've danced a jig around the van. Settling for a nod, he got to work.

*I'm a van guy now.*

He stepped out of his new-ish Chevy cargo van, locked the doors behind him with a quiet click, and headed into Walmart for some much-needed supplies.

Inside, the conditioned air hit his face, the fluorescent lights flickered, and it smelled like floor wax and bleach—he was back in society again. Somehow, he almost missed it. It was bright. Comfortable. Normal. The kind of place where he could vanish into the crowd. Sometimes you hide in shadows, sometimes by walking in a group.

He moved smoothly, occasionally muttering through his list:

- Bread, peanut butter, jelly: breakfast, lunch, dinner.
- Cot: in sporting goods. Lightweight, foldable, not the cheapest, but worth it.
- Case of water: 24 bottles.
- Milk: a single quart. Cold, real, something normal. He missed real food more than he expected.
- Bag of ice: to fill the cooler, he grabbed from Rob's place.
- Visa Gift Card: works like a credit card. No name attached.
- Bag of Candy Bars: reason to live.

He didn't rush, didn't linger. He kept his posture relaxed, but his eyes were scanning. He noted different people to make sure he didn't see them again. He knew that was his newfound paranoia, but it had been keeping him alive so far.

At self-checkout, he paid in cash. No ID. No cards.

He set up the cot in the back with his sleeping bag on it after putting the ice in the cooler with the milk and jelly.

*I lost everything, but now I am rebuilding and taking back my life—starting here.*

*It's not much, but… I just realized that I am now a van guy with candy.*

He started the drive back to the stashed weapons. He had been up since yesterday morning, but he didn't want those weapons sitting in the woods longer than necessary. He loved his new mobile base. Now he just needed the rest of his supplies.

The van rattled slightly as Thomas slowed and eased onto the loose gravel at the curve, his landmark. He was looking forward to retrieving the duffel bag he buried less than 24 hours ago. He pulled past the location, so anyone hiding in the woods would see the back of the van and not his face.

He eased the van to a stop, careful to make it look like nothing more than a mechanical hiccup. Anyone driving by would see a guy with engine trouble fixing his work van.

He popped the hood and got out, forcing a casual demeanor even though his heart was pounding. He had been ahead of the cultist for the past several days, but if there was anything with GPS in that bag, they could be here. He knew it was unlikely. He also knew what they did to enemies, and he had been a thorn in their side the last few days.

He leaned over the engine bay, pulled out his burner phone, and held it up like a flashlight. The beam wasn't pointing at anything worthwhile. He just wanted an excuse to check the camera he had left watching his gear.

He tapped into the signal his camera was broadcasting. It was short-range only. That was the price one paid for not having a data plan on a burner cell. He strained, listening for any sound of trouble or aggressive goats, while the camera connected. He checked the recorded library:

- 13:02 — wind moving branches.
- 15:47 — an awesome shot of a squirrel sniffing the camera. Rebecca would love that.
- 17:22 — nothing but longer shadows.

No human shapes. No footsteps. No hands disturbing the leaves.

He checked the live feed. Still there. Still untouched. For some reason, he still felt like something was wrong, but he didn't have a good reason for it. He was out, he had escaped, and now he was heading back to the area where people wanted to brutally murder him—it was disquieting.

A breath escaped him.

He killed the app and waved the light over the radiator, pretending to check the fluid level while a car drove past. As soon as the coast was clear, he quickly made his way to the cache. He left the hood up. If someone asked why he wasn't there, he would say he was answering the call of nature, which would make sense as long as they didn't see a dirty duffel bag with a gun barrel sticking out of it.

He quickly uncovered the bag and tossed the camera in. The bag was a little damp. It was from dew, not rain. Everything should still be okay.

Back to the van in thirty seconds. Doors closed. Hood down. Bag stashed in the back. The engine turned over with a low growl.

He felt eyes on him. He hoped it was the squirrel.

He rolled back onto the road like nothing had happened and headed for a truck stop, so he could finally get some sleep.

No tail. No ambush. Just a heart pounding for no reason. The solitude was starting to stack up. He knew it was because he always felt alone and outnumbered. He had trouble sleeping because he felt vulnerable with no one to stand watch. His cameras helped, but the paranoia and fear were starting to drag him down. Somehow, talking to Rob had helped. Rob was just a chair.

He missed Rebecca. He missed his brother, his friends—he even missed Jim, that annoying coworker who used to steal his pens.

*I don't want to reach out to them or put them in danger.*
*Well, maybe Jim.*

# CHAPTER 15

## *Thomas the Engineer*

It had been a week since Thomas purchased the van. He had been productive.

His mobile base now had an inverter and a deep-cycle battery scavenged from an RV in a junkyard. It was sufficient to keep his electronics charged. It had a one-way flow switch from the engine to the deep-cycle system, preventing him from accidentally draining the primary battery and stranding himself.

He had taken an inventory of the equipment he had obtained from the police officer and his car:

- Two 9mm handguns.
- Eight magazines.
- A SPAS 12 shotgun.
- Ten bean bag rounds.
- Two flashbangs.
- Twenty 00 buckshot rounds.
- Bulletproof vest with ceramic panels.
- First-aid kit.

AR-15 with six magazines and four hundred rounds of ammunition—this didn't seem like standard issue. It seemed like cult issue. Thomas did not complain.

The textbooks had been scanned, and some parts had been translated, but not all of them. The main book was titled Path of Blood, so he figured it was most likely about… the Path of Blood.

It looked like there were two ways to use the Path. One was to have the ichor of the gods. The other was to give a substitution through ritual to open the Path. His interpretation suggested one could either have a god's blood in their DNA or they could overload the lock on the portal with human blood. Once the altar's blood channel was full, the runes would light on the dais, and the person who opened it could travel to another realm.

He wondered if the entire ritual could be skipped since his body had opened the Path while he was possessed by Ometheon. If so, a small amount of blood on the altar would open it. He wasn't sure how much blood it would take.

He also wasn't a big fan of blood magic or going to other realms, but if he wanted to question Thaleia, he had to risk it. He had printed out an entire English version of the book to study when he wasn't working on other projects.

He finally got around to building his stun club from the Maglite and disposable cameras. He even incorporated a USB charging port so he could charge it from a phone or solar panel.

The cop's phone didn't have much on it. He had been careful in his texts. Thomas stashed the SIM card just in case and kept the phone as a backup smartphone for accessing cameras and Wi-Fi.

He had picked up the supplies to view Rob's hard drive as though it were an external drive. He just had to plug it into a USB port on his laptop. He found Rob's video. It showed several people and a few satyrs having a meeting in an old, abandoned warehouse. Using map programs to look around safely, he found the meeting place. Rob had notes that said they met on Thursdays. That was two days away, so he was shopping and building.

*Engineers don't have cool lines. We don't have "I'll be back," or "hasta la vista, baby."*

*If I am going to do this, I should work on something.*

*How about, "That's Ohm's law, pal!"*

*I'll keep working on it.*

Rob's surveillance showed the mayor was part of the cult, as well as at least two cops. One of them had been handled, but Thomas wondered how many more there were. He was in his element. He had a spreadsheet.

Then Thursday came.

The warehouse was secluded at the edge of town like a forgotten relic slowly being reclaimed by trees and vines. Its corrugated metal skin was dull with rust and age. Long horizontal doors stretched across the front. They comprised dented steel panels that slid open on groaning rails, wide enough to swallow trucks whole. One stood half open, gaping and twisted off its track like an unhinged maw.

At the rear, a concrete loading dock jutted from the wall, scuffed by decades of tires and truck bumpers. The dock still bore the faded outline of where a company logo used to be, but that too was being reclaimed.

Overhead hung a series of lights that had gone dark years ago. Inside, the air tasted of old concrete and dust. A few forgotten pallets still leaned in the corners, warped and brittle. The place felt like a death trap that time forgot. It was perfect.

---

The mayor walked into the warehouse and found the others already there. Six natives. Three satyrs. He liked to show up a little late to prove who was in charge. Those satyrs might be emissaries from another realm, but without Ometheon, the creatures were just muscle who had to hide in caves and wait until they were useful again. He let them think their riddles were sage-like wisdom, but he dismissed them when they spoke. Their minds didn't matter. They were relics of an old time and a different world.

"Where are we on Hank's murder? It was an ambush. Who knew he was headed to Rob's house for the hard drive?" the mayor asked.

"We don't have any leads on people capable of this. It wasn't the psycho from the other side. She wouldn't have known how to find him. We are still looking into it. The camera in the car was smashed, which shows he was probably a native. What about—"

A sound rang out across the large room in the warehouse. An echoing ring from a pipe hitting concrete.

"Go," barked the mayor, commanding them to action. They charged across the floor toward the sound.

A silhouette took off running through an opening by a large sliding metal door, the type that slides left to right instead of up and down. It swayed gently as the shadow brushed the door in its hurry to get away.

"Split up, cut him off," called one of the humans. The group split up to surround the intruder. One smaller group with two humans and a satyr charged through the opening after the silhouette. As they vanished into the darkness, a loud crash, followed by a heavy sliding sound, ripped through the building. The big door slid closed—followed by screams.

---

Thomas had arrived early. He parked the stolen reefer truck at the dock. He found a shut-down food distribution warehouse a few towns over that had been boarded up. He hotwired the old ice truck and brought it here without incident. He was ready ahead of schedule and waited while they filtered in one by one. He knew how many were coming thanks to Rob's investigation.

Once they were all there, he dropped a pipe and took off running past the big door.

Two of the humans and one satyr ran into the room after him. A large, half-torn sheet of plywood lay across the middle of the floor. It looked like normal debris. When one of the pursuers stepped on it, it compressed a spring and allowed two metal plates to connect. That connection sparked a switch, dropping a log suspended by two cables. The two large, metal sliding doors slammed shut and latched closed, pulled by ropes attached to the weight. In the room itself, he had hung a gas can with an open top. It allowed the correct mix of vapors and fluid to saturate the air. It was not like in the movies. A cigarette cannot ignite gasoline. It takes planning, but Thomas was an engineer.

The same plank that triggered the log trap also sent a spark to the next part of the trap: a starter from an old jeep, wired to a sparkplug wrapped with steel wool. Steel wool burns hot. It was hot enough to provide ignition for the gas trap hanging from the ceiling in the small, closed space. A sheet of burning liquid sprayed through the room, coating the cultists. The humans screamed and fell to the ground. The satyr bellowed and began pounding on the door as he burned.

Thomas sprinted through the office wing of the warehouse, making sure they could hear him. Two humans were trying to get ahead of him and cut off his escape. A thunderous boom vibrated his bones as the second trap sprang. Thomas smiled at how easy that one was to make.

It just took a bubbling pot of dark syrup, a sticky mix of powdered sugar and crushed stump remover. It was a hillbilly specialty, rocket candy, just like his uncle used to make. He filled a few pipes with it, packing them with nails, glass, and ball bearings. The ignition was easy. He soldered nails to the spring bar of a few mousetraps, then mounted shotgun shells where the bar would strike. When the trap was triggered, the nail hit the shell and acted as ignition for the rocket candy. Bits of shrapnel tore the humans apart.

At the far end of the office wing, a human and a satyr crashed down the hallway toward the noise. The satyr led, smashing a door from its hinges and sending it ricocheting down the hall. A string on the door was fixed to a small block of wood. That wood was in the jaws of a simple clothespin. It had one wire attached to the top and another to the bottom. The block was dislodged when the door was knocked open, which closed the circuit—more rocket candy. The satyr and the human both dropped where they stood.

Thomas crawled into a small utility room behind an old rusty water heater and checked his phone. He had cameras set by the traps. He could see that two creatures were still on their feet. The mayor was standing by the last satyr who loomed beside him as a bodyguard. The mayor was unarmed, clearly not used to handling the dirty work himself, but his nerves held as long as his satyr was at hand.

Thomas grabbed his 9mm and stepped out of the doorway into the large industrial room where the mayor and satyr stood. He raised the gun and fired three times at the mayor, hitting him twice. The slide locked back—empty. The mayor fell to the floor, but the satyr bellowed with rage and charged toward Thomas.

He saw the satyr coming and hobbled toward an open door on the loading dock. There was a truck backed up to that door. Thomas scrambled inside. He limped forward to the front of the box truck, where the side door stood open. The satyr stopped at the back of the truck.

Thomas turned to face his pursuer, drew the dagger, and smiled. "This dagger killed one of you before. He attacked me in my house about two weeks ago. I shoved him into a bathtub. Oh, sorry, you probably don't know what a bath is, do you? Anyway, he was on his back—thrashing, sniveling, whining." Thomas laughed. "He said baaa baaa baaa—like a scared child—before I pushed this dagger up through his chin."

The satyr was enraged. So few of his kind were left in this world. He bugled like an elk, but deeper, more primal. He charged into the truck at the human who dared mock him. Thomas merely hopped through the open door, triggering a small string to release. That string released a counterweight—both doors slammed shut, one after the other. A five-gallon jug of used cooking oil was left outside of a closed restaurant to be picked up for recycling. Thomas picked it up instead. It tipped over as part of the trap, coating the floor inside. He latched the door on the side and ran over to the loading dock door to get back inside, his hobble suddenly missing.

He had selected a reefer truck because the walls were reinforced and thicker to provide insulation. It should also help against an eight-foot-tall, angry goat-man trying to break out. It wouldn't be able to get a running start because of the oil. When questioned, the cop hadn't known much about the other side of the Path of Blood. Hopefully, the satyr would.

Thomas stopped to smile at the back of the truck—an angry, bellowing creature trapped inside. "This was all you, Rob. Your video showed me where to be. I just finished what you started, buddy."

**Clop clop clop.**

Thomas's eyes widened. He had missed something.

It felt like time slowed as he turned his head and saw a satyr running at him. He dove to the side, but not fast enough. His leg was clipped by the passing beast, sending Thomas into a spin, thudding into the wall. The creature's talons ripped open part of his thigh. Warm blood ran down his leg, soaking his jeans.

The satyr turned to face him, eyes filled with hate, smoke curling off its fur.

*That's the one from the fire trap—the trap worked, but it didn't finish him.*

*It looks like he got out and stopped the flames on his body.*

*He seems unhappy.*

Thomas pulled the 9mm that had a full magazine from his waistband. The other had been a ploy to trick the satyr into thinking he was out of ammo—a setup to lure him into the truck.

He looked up at this satyr and said, "Special delivery."

"Cosine this." He unloaded the magazine into the creature.

*Nope, that really didn't work. I'll keep working on action-engineer lines.*

Thomas hobbled, this time for real, to the front of the truck. He had first aid supplies and needed to stop the bleeding. He was getting used to not hobbling and was almost healed from all his other mishaps. Now he would be hobbling a little longer. He quickly wrapped the leg, then doused all the spilled blood he could find with gasoline. He burned it to prevent DNA testing. He was still playing the long game and hoped to return to his life one day.

He heard sirens in the distance. His little light show had alerted the fire department, and he didn't want to answer questions.

He hopped in the driver's seat and started driving away—nothing to see here, just a man and his goat.

# CHAPTER 16
## *The Dance*

The woods were silent, except for the ticking metal of the still-warm engine and the faint groan of the freezer truck settling into the dirt. Mist crept low across the forest floor, seeping around the tires and through the trees. Moonlight filtered through the branches overhead in cold shafts, barely touching the clearing where Thomas had parked.

He stepped around to the back of the truck, his boots crunching softly on gravel and dead leaves. He attached the three-foot cable he had scavenged off a defunct crane at a junkyard to the frame of the reefer truck. The other end he looped and clamped to the reinforced steel latch on the door itself. He paused, reached up, and released the latch with a smooth, confident flick.

With a clank, the heavy latch snapped free, and the door gave an eager jolt upward—but rose only a single foot the cable allowed before jerking to a stop. The thick braided cable would not fail; he was sure of that. It was knotted and looped through the inner rail, held firmly in place. The opening was just wide enough for light to spill in, but not escape. Just wide enough for a prisoner to see his captor—but not reach him.

From within, the dark let out a low, bestial growl. Something heavy shifted against the aluminum interior, and the sound of hooves on metal rang out like hollow war drums. It was annoyed, impatient. It wanted to play.

Thomas didn't react.

Instead, he turned away, walked a few paces across the clearing, and dragged a weathered duffel bag out of a bush. He began setting up his station, a comfortable place to work. He set up a folding camp chair and a wobbly card table. He placed them down carefully, methodically, in full view of the narrow opening and returned to his duffel. He produced a squat metal lantern, an old pump-style Coleman with a brass collar and green enamel hood.

He placed it on his wobbly table like he was preparing a picnic. No rush.

The truck shifted again with another bang against the side wall.

Thomas didn't acknowledge the sounds. He didn't even look up. He simply unscrewed the fuel cap, checked the kerosene, then sealed it with a deliberate twist. He flipped the pump handle and began working it rhythmically. *Huff-chuff-huff-chuff.* The pressure built, faintly audible. The hiss of vapor joined the night chorus.

Inside the truck, the satyr thudded against the walls—rage or desperation. It was hard to say. Thomas smiled. Sometimes ignoring someone is as effective as questioning them.

He adjusted the knob, struck a match, and lit the mantle. The lantern flared to life with a soft *whump*, casting a golden glow on the truck's scarred steel and the trees beyond. Shadows danced over the grass.

He placed the lantern on the ground to light the area without blinding himself. Then he left the view of the prisoner, walking beside the truck. A loud bang, followed by a heavy thud, indicated the satyr tried to punch the wall, but fell on the slick floor instead.

Thomas returned and placed a pack of cookies, a napkin, and a glass of milk on his wobbly table.

Then, finally, Thomas sat down. He leaned forward with elbows on his knees and stared into the darkness beneath the slightly open door. He saw two glints of light reflecting off very angry eyes… so he picked up a cookie and gently dunked it in the milk. He took his time and enjoyed his cookie.

"Well," he said, voice calm and edged with dry amusement. "Now that we're both comfortable…"

He let the words hang, like bait in the air.

"…let's talk about what you are doing in my world."

A low gravelly voice responded from the dark opening of the truck, "Because the gate was open. Because your world stinks of fear and forgetting. Because you built your temples out of numbers and meat and forgot the old songs. We came to remind you. We came to dance. We came because she let us in."

"Your dance feels like war. Is your dance supposed to destroy us?" Thomas asked.

The voice returned, "You danced too. The fire. The screams. Your dance is a grand show. A comedy. You use a truck door as a trap; that is not war, it is dance, it is comedy, it is madness."

Thomas smiled. "Hmm, it worked. I guess the joke's on you."

The darkness of the truck responded with a low, throaty chuckle: "I like you better this way. Ometheon was fun, but consistent. His hand was a dagger, but you—*you* make the world dance with you. It dances to your tune."

"Ometheon," responded Thomas, "how did he come to possess my body? Why mine?"

The satyr answered, "The daughter of wisdom lacked understanding. She chose the path, but not the destination. She needed what Ometheon knew, but he was a liquid without a vessel."

"What is her name?"

The darkness quipped back, "All this blood poured out like wine, but no answers. You don't even know who set the stage for the play?"

Thomas smiled. He knew he was being tested, too. "Thaleia, the daughter of Athena, had me possessed. When the Path of Blood was opened, she was already waiting on the other side. She came through and sent Ometheon back to his eternity. How do I find her?"

The low chuckle returned: "You have seen the play. You know the stage."

"Only in part," he responded. "I know she is on the other side of the Path, and I have an idea how to get there, but her realm is most likely vast. Like mine. How do I get to her?"

The satyr purred like a cat in the dark. "You want her? Then bleed with purpose. Walk the Path not as a hunter—but as judgment made flesh. Will you make her dance on your stage?"

A shift of hooves echoed in the metal box. "To make the Path open, it must know you. Tell it and show it with a gift of your life, but know who you are—don't voice another's truth. When the door opens, follow the wind south. Past the Wailing Trees. Past the gods that forgot their names. There, you'll find a shrine that once bore her mother's crest—but it cracked in silence."

A pause. Then:

"Someone waits there. A woman who remembers what the gods would bury. She walks alone. Scarred. Sharp. She won't lie to you, unless you give her reason. Speak her name if you reach her: Isadora."

Thomas considered his options. "Are my weapons strong enough to strike Thaleia down? It would be more fun if I won."

"Fun?" he echoed. "Oh yes, the gods haven't bled from mortal fire in centuries. Weapons have made some of them bleed before, but not often. Your weapons sing with fire. What a glorious play that could be. Let it sing and see if she listens, but kill her? No one knows because no one has killed her before. Wouldn't that be delicious? The play she started becomes her curtain call. Walk the Path and dance with her. Make her screams fill Olympus with song."

The truck started swaying back and forth while the satyr giggled inside. A massive monster dancing and giggling is an odd thing to behold.

"I will walk the Path." Thomas stood. "You know that our dance isn't finished? I can't let you live in my realm."

The satyr let out a rasping chuckle. "Of course, of course. The curtain must fall, but what a performance I have had. I have danced in the madness of two realms and been witness to the start of a new dance. New madness that will one day join us."

Shuffling came from inside as the satyr stood. "Make it hurt, mortal. Not for me—for the gods. Let them hear it and let them hear the screams of the daughter of wisdom when she follows me."

Thomas quietly respected his strange enemy. It was quite mad. Quite evil. But it had told the truth in fragments and done so without fear.

"As you wish," he responded as he tossed a lit flare into the truck. The oil ignited with a muffled *whump*. The smell of deep-fried chicken and burning fur filled the air, while the satyr screamed into the night.

He walked calmly to the front of the truck and placed a gas can underneath the fuel tank, a second flare taped to its side. When the flare burned down far enough, it would melt the plastic and ignite the fuel. No loose ends.

Thomas picked up his gear, loaded his van, and drove away from the burning truck—the satyr's bellows still echoing behind him.

# CHAPTER 17
## Duct Tape and Missiles

Thomas sat on the cot in the back of his cargo van across from Freedom, his motorcycle. A small LED, powered by the deep-cycle battery that powered his mobile base, lit the space. No light could get in or out of the van's blacked-out windows, which was perfect since he was in a Walmart parking lot and didn't want to draw attention.

*All right, Thomas, all you have to do now is open an interdimensional portal called the Path of Blood to a realm ruled by Greek gods and magic.*

*Breakfast first?*

He popped open Rob's cooler and grabbed a cookie ice cream sandwich. Big jobs call for brain food.

The sandwich was a small luxury, out of place in a world of traps, blood, and gods. But for the moment, sitting in the back of a van lit by a single LED, the taste grounded him. It was proof that the world still had sweetness in it.

*There is nothing like a private breakfast in the... the uh...*

*Nerd-van-a?*

*Vantheon?*

*Myth-Machine?*

*I'll keep working on it.*

He had translated the texts he found in the cave. It wasn't due to his own linguistic abilities, but due to software.

He flipped through his notes. Some were on his computer. Some were in his notebook with scribbled notes, smudged from handling, margins crammed with observations and sketchy symbols copied from cultist tomes. This wasn't random research anymore. It was focused. He had narrowed down what he needed.

He exhaled through his nose, rubbed his temple, and finally grabbed his mechanical pencil and wrote it down:

- The Path of Blood is a divine construct. It is meant only for those born of godly essence.
- True immortals (gods, demigods) can walk it freely.
- Mortals with divine blood (or divine favor) can pass with ease.
- Humans can force it open—but only through sacrifice. Enough blood to simulate divinity.
- The Corrupted (like satyrs) are rejected as an insult. They can walk through, but only if someone else opens the door.

He paused. His pencil hovered, then underlined the human point twice.

Outside, something clanged. Thomas glanced up, instinctively checking the motion-triggered camera near the rear bumper. Nothing out there.

He turned back to the notebook and added one more line at the bottom:

The door will open, but it needs enough blood to simulate the divinity. It didn't say how much it takes to do that. He couldn't find a conversion chart. He was an engineer. He liked numbers, not guesses.

His face stayed neutral, but the pencil tapped against the paper, steady and thoughtful. His vision had shown a single person sacrificed, but he found several wallets and phones. Possibly not all of them. He didn't know exactly how many people were needed, but it didn't matter. He would not pay that price.

No innocents die. He wasn't like them, and he wouldn't become one of them.

Blood was the price. The only question left was where to get it? He had planned to grab a cultist back at the warehouse the night he ambushed them, but one of the satyrs blindsided him, injuring his leg. Between that and the sirens from the approaching fire trucks, he was convinced to leave quickly without any spare cultists.

Thomas sat on the cot in the back of his cargo van, a travel mug of cold coffee beside him and his laptop balanced on a folded blanket. The coffee wasn't cold because it had been sitting for so long—it was one of those caramel mocha latte things with chocolate swirled on top. He took on the cult, wiped out the local chapter, captured and questioned a satyr from another realm, learned how to open the Path of Blood, or hoped he knew. He deserved a caramel mocha latte with extra drizzle.

He opened a VPN and private browser window and searched for local bloodmobile routes and locations. Several of the links were outdated or broken. However, he found that the local hospital had a Facebook page that listed the current schedule.

Monday: Meadow Market Shopping Center – 9 a.m. to 1 p.m.
Wednesday: High School Gym – 9 a.m. to 1 p.m.
Friday: County Fairgrounds – 12 p.m. to 5 p.m.

Today was Friday. He had lost some blood when the satyr sliced his leg yesterday, but he was sure his activities had drawn attention. He needed to move quickly.

Suddenly, it occurred to him that Rebecca was probably curious about what was happening in this town. News of the police force and the mayor being found at a burning warehouse had spread. She must have seen it and recognized the name of the town where he had suddenly reappeared a couple of weeks ago. Did she suspect that he did it, or that it was more of the cultists' shenanigans? He hoped she knew it was him, setting things right, but she probably didn't think he would go as far as he did. She didn't know how bad things were up here.

Thomas put the idea out of his head. He might be leaving this world soon, and there was a decent chance he would not be coming back. He needed to focus on the task ahead. He wasn't dismissing her or leaving her. He was protecting her. He was protecting this world. He was giving her a life that wasn't open to him at the time, and if he didn't return, he hoped she lived it to the fullest.

Back to the task—local auto shops. He looked for ones that advertised fleet services.

A few links down into the local listings, he found something promising:

**Stanley's Automotive & Fleet Repair**

The site was cheap, slapped together like someone's nephew built it after one YouTube tutorial, but it had a gallery. Thomas clicked through the images.

He smiled when he found what he was looking for: a black-and-white police cruiser, hood propped open, damage to the front fender.

Caption: *"Fleet maintenance — local PD front-end rebuild, quick turnaround!"*

He clicked again. Another cruiser. Another angle.

Same building. He found the shop that handled the local police department. It was easier to steal a car there than from the police station. The police that were left were going to be on full alert, but with luck, a car would be in the shop.

He switched to satellite view in another tab and typed in the address.

The shop was off a service road, tucked behind a grain supply and a shuttered feed store. The parking lot was gravel, surrounded by a chain-link fence. He could defeat a fence.

He leaned back and exhaled, rubbing his eyes.

This was probably it.

The cruiser he'd driven into the woods a week ago—it could be there. If it still drove and they were patching it up, it'd be sitting somewhere behind that fence, maybe waiting for a part. He clicked and dragged the satellite image, zooming closer. He decided it was time for an outing.

He drove by slowly on the service road while looking through the fence into the lot. There it was, a black and white cruiser. He wasn't sure if it was the same one, but if it ran, he wanted it. He made another loop and went past the front of the shop. It was after hours, so it was locked up for the night. That was what he wanted. He needed to see how they secured the gate.

Using his trusted excuse of engine trouble, he pulled up by the sidewalk at the entrance of the business. He popped the hood and looked inside. He made sure the coast was clear, then walked over to the entrance and snapped a picture of the lock and chain holding the gate closed. Then he pretended to fiddle with something under the hood, closed it up, and drove away.

It was time for another shopping trip. He always felt like they just didn't show enough shopping in action movies, but most of his time was spent preparing supplies. The only montage he could remember from an action movie was an old Schwarzenegger film. The hero walked into a supply store, pressed a button under the counter, and then walked into a backroom with rocket launchers and grenades. He wished he knew of one of those stores. This would go a lot smoother if he had missile launchers. Next stop: Walmart again. He wouldn't ask to see the secret back room. Instead, he decided to build everything himself.

It was a short list:

- Two remote control cars.
- Vaseline.
- Electrical tape.
- Steel wool.
- Cotton balls.
- Bolt cutters.
- And one of those chain repair loops.

With any luck, come Monday, he would leave this realm and continue his journey on the other side. Nothing had stopped him yet, but he was concerned there wouldn't be a Walmart on the other side. For now, he had a lot to plan and a short window to do it. He knew where the blood would be. He knew where a cop car was parked. It might not run. He could make do without it, but it would be harder.

He started packing his old camping backpack. He needed to be ready and have everything packed, just in case he actually succeeded. If any cult members were left, a blood heist would draw them in—and tell them exactly where Thomas was headed.

# CHAPTER 18
## *Goodbye*

The night was damp with mist and quiet in the way only small towns could manage at two in the morning. Thomas wore a mask and gloves as he made his way past the closed buildings. He was sticking to the backs of businesses where he could. The town was empty, but he was cautious, especially when the stakes were this high. Finally, he rounded the last building and saw his target: the repair shop.

A single sodium vapor light buzzed and flickered over the gravel lot of Stanley's Automotive & Fleet Repair, casting long shadows through the chain-link fence like bars on a prison yard.

He crouched by the gate, leg throbbing, bolt cutters in hand. The metal links were rusted but still sturdy. He fed the chain around the post to expose a link farther from the lock. He placed the head of the bolt cutters on the furthest link he could find, then snapped it clean through. The severed end swung back and forth with a faint metallic rattle, but nothing loud enough to carry beyond the empty street behind him.

He slipped inside, sticking to shadows, his boots crunching softly over the gravel. The shop itself was dark—no light from the windows, no movement inside. He eyed the front door, already planning.

*I need to get into the shop, hopefully, without leaving a trace.*

*I'll try the lockpicking set I got from the cop, but if it doesn't work, I'll try to remove the frame around a window to get in.*

*I didn't see any cameras, but they could be hidden.*

*There could be an alarm too, but I have my tools and bypass wires.*

*Once inside, there should be a lockbox or something with keys.*

*Maybe a desk drawer will have the keys. I'll have to look around, but I should make sure the car isn't totaled first.*

He moved toward the parked vehicle slowly. It sat at an angle, its front end exposed by an unfinished repair. There were scratches along the passenger side, and the bumper sagged slightly. Still, the tires looked solid, the body unbent. It looked drivable.

He reached for the door handle, expecting it to be locked, like it should be.

It opened with a soft click.

Thomas blinked. He leaned in and looked inside—the keys were in the ignition, just waiting to be used. He laughed. Apparently, he was an excellent car thief.

Sliding into the driver's seat, he turned the key. The engine grumbled and caught. He looked at the driver-facing camera—smashed by the butt of a pistol. He smiled again. This was his second time stealing the same cop car. That had to be a record.

Thomas eased it into gear and rolled forward, lights off. He guided the cruiser out the same way he came in, pulling through the opened gate before stopping. He left it idling, grabbed the chain link repair loop he'd brought with him, closed the gate, and wrapped the chain back through. It looked like it did before, with one replaced link on the backside. It could be noticed if someone looked, but hopefully, it wouldn't be enough reason to interfere with his plan. Humans tend to take the easy path, and as long as their lock was still on the chain, hopefully, they wouldn't think to look for missing cars.

Back in the driver's seat, he pulled away to set up the next step of his plan.

The next morning, Thomas watched the bloodmobile pull into the parking lot. It was parked at the far side of the asphalt by the woods. He didn't know where it would park, so he wasn't in position yet. He needed more donations to take place first, so he took his time setting things in motion. He hobbled through the trees, out of sight, and placed the remote-controlled car on the ground.

It was highly modified. The camera was small. It was a cheap Wi-Fi model he'd dismantled and gutted for weight. With the lens barely larger than a pencil eraser, it could stream live video to his phone. He fixed it to the hood of the RC car with a thick loop of duct tape, pressing it down until it was snug. He tilted it slightly upward, aiming just above the front bumper. Perfect for navigation.

He turned on the phone and tapped the screen to load the camera app. The feed blinked to life and showed the view a squirrel might have, right on the ground, looking slightly up.

He grabbed the small soup can that he'd doctored to contain the smoke device. It had some leftover ingredients from the rocket candy, but the mixture was slightly different. It had a little oil added for a greasier, smokier look. A Vaseline-soaked cotton ball sat on top like a fuse, and it was wrapped in steel wool. It was a basic setup. When the time came, he would send current through the steel wool. It would burn hot enough to ignite the cotton ball. Steel wool and Vaseline together burn hot enough and long enough to ignite his sugar-fueled smoke bomb. Now, it just needed a remote way to turn it on.

He took the igniter wires, rigged from the second remote car's receiver, and soldered them to the steel. Then he sealed the box, leaving just the leads protruding from the can. A fresh 9V battery was needed to provide the power to ignite the steel wool. The RC battery lacked the current to be certain it would work. So, he set up a second rig—a springy copper tab on a hinge, tied to the second car's motor system. He clipped the negative battery terminal, leaving the circuit open, and tied the copper tab to the motor pulley via a fishing line.

The trigger system was crude, but elegant: press the second remote's forward stick, the motor that would normally spin the wheels pulls the string, the copper tab snaps to the battery terminal—and the steel wool ignites. Mechanical simplicity. No risk of overloading the electronics.

He mounted the sealed smoke tin to the back of the RC car with zip ties and another loop of duct tape. It sat snug over the rear axle like a makeshift delivery pod. The 9V battery and the spring-loaded igniter tab were tucked just beside it, safe from jostling.

The quick version of this setup: one RC car drives, while the second flips a switch to send current through the steel wool. The wool would burn, which would trigger the smoke device. Each step was simple, but if one thing went wrong, the whole plan would fall apart.

He flipped the power switch on the RC car, then the second switch on the controller. The wheels gave a short whine. "Operation squirrel-view under way."

He drove the car with its payload under the bloodmobile. He had seen 16 people go in so far, so he was hoping it was enough. He left the remote car where it was under the engine compartment and walked back through the woods to his waiting police car. When the time came, a simple flip of a switch would deploy the smoke bomb.

---

The bloodmobile rocked gently on its suspension every time someone climbed aboard, a constant, subtle sway like a boat tethered in shallow water. Inside, fluorescent lights buzzed overhead, casting a sterile glow across vinyl seats, laminated posters, and a coffee machine that was overworked by the staff.

Darlene stood in the narrow aisle, gloved hands on her hips, her name badge situated beneath a sticker that read "I Make Vampires Jealous" in glittery red font.

"Welcome to the blood bus!" she chirped, waving the next donor in with a clipboard. "I'll take good care of you and give you a cookie afterwards."

A man in cargo shorts shuffled forward, eyeing the chair like it might bite.

"You'll be fine, honey," Darlene said, patting the armrest. "Worst thing that happens is you leave here with a cookie, and a smile—because we're that friendly."

She worked with the practiced ease of someone who was good at their job. Tourniquet. Alcohol swab. Needle. Friendly chatter.

"Wow, you have great veins," she said as she got to work.

"Three more minutes," she called out to the donor, glancing at the stopwatch on the wall. "You're bleeding beautifully, by the way. Gold star bleeder."

The man chuckled nervously. Darlene grinned.

Two seats down, a college student winced as Darlene slid the needle in.

"Don't look at it," Darlene said gently. "Just think of puppies. Or tax refunds. Whatever gets your heart rate up without raising your blood pressure."

A beep from the collection monitor drew her back. She pulled out the needle and slapped on gauze and tape like a pro.

Suddenly, shouts broke—"Fire! There's a fire!"

Darlene saw the smoke and quickly exited the bloodmobile. It was pouring out from under the engine compartment.

She ran back inside and unhooked the blood donor. She ushered him out as she started giving directions. "Everybody, get back. Someone call 911—stay back, stay back."

Fortunately, a police car happened to be passing through the parking lot and saw the smoke. The car whipped over and came to a halt as the officer stepped out. He didn't have on a full uniform, but he was wearing a police vest, black gloves, a cheap hospital mask, sunglasses, and a police ball cap. He stepped up to Darlene and said, "The vehicle is too close to the woods. It could start a forest fire! Do you have the keys? I need to move it to the other side of the parking lot."

"The keys are in it," Darlene responded, "but are you sure it's safe?"

The officer called back as he climbed inside: "I have to keep the town safe. I'll be okay."

The officer started the engine and drove across the lot, but the smoke didn't go with him. The smoke was coming from something that had been under the bloodmobile. Darlene looked down at the smoke, then at the bloodmobile driving away.

She started running across the parking lot, waving her arms. "Officer, wait, it was something else. It looks like a toy or something. Wait."

A couple of the donors and another technician jogged after her for a few steps, but they knew they couldn't catch it. They stood in the parking lot. Standing in shock, watching the bloodmobile as it sped away.

The second technician asked, "What is he doing?"

Darlene responded, "I guess he thinks he's saving us. He didn't know about the smoking toy."

"Yeah, it was probably just kids or something."

"When the officer gets back, let's not tease him—his heart was in the right place. He'll probably pull over, see no smoke, and bring it back."

---

Thomas drove away in the bloodmobile, laughing when he saw the technicians waving their arms. It was a little mean, but funny. They were good people and didn't deserve this, but what he was doing was going to save their lives. He needed to stop the cult, and that meant he needed blood to get to the other side. That blood wouldn't be from a sacrifice that ended a life, unless it was a cultist and he was fresh out of cultists.

Ahead, stretched across the narrow dirt road, the flutter of yellow police tape blocked the entrance. It was his own handiwork, strung between two reflector posts hours earlier. He didn't want any company to interrupt his heist. Thomas turned the oversized steering wheel of the bloodmobile as the old diesel engine growled up the dusty incline. The tape snapped across the windshield like a spiderweb. It caught on the side mirror and fluttered away as he swung the vehicle hard around the bend. The narrow trail dropped into a shallow cut between two ridges, boxed in by low brush and rock. It was the perfect choke point.

He saw his cargo van waiting right where he left it. He cranked the bloodmobile's steering wheel to the left. With a grinding hiss of brakes, the bloodmobile angled across the road, its bulky white frame now wedged diagonally between the trees and a rocky rise. There was just enough space for him to climb out, but no way a car or truck would squeeze past to continue a pursuit. He tossed the keys under the passenger seat. When they inspect the vehicle, they'll find them. Bloodmobiles are good things that help people and save lives. He didn't want to interfere with that.

Thomas moved fast. In the back, the coolers of blood were still cold and strapped tight. He checked one, twelve bags inside. He slung the carry handle over his shoulder. He was headed for the door when he saw the bags of cookies. He paused. He looked at the cookies… so many cookies…

*Of all the things I have done, stealing cop cars and a bloodmobile, I can't take the cookies. There are lines that can't be crossed.*

He stepped outside and limped down the road to the Myth

Machine. He set the cooler on the passenger seat and drove to the next site.

As he was driving to his destination, his stomach started churning. Making plans was one thing, but this suddenly felt real. His nerves were starting to get to him.

He knew it was almost time to leave this world. He wondered if he would actually do it. If he lived, then he could possibly save others. But if he died on arrival, then he would be throwing his life away for nothing. It was one thing to fight satyrs in his bedroom or blow up cultists in a warehouse. But to leave this realm—his world, and everything he knew—it was almost too much. It slipped from fear into terror.

It wasn't enough to stop him. He felt a duty to go. He wanted answers. And this was the only way he knew to get them. It was the next logical step. He just wished he were going with a few platoons or the Green Berets.

But it was just him.

He pulled into the trees that ran along the utility access road. It was the closest place he could find to the altar, and he was going to have to hoof it from there. He pulled on his backpack, the shotgun strapped along the side with its handle above his right shoulder. Then he grabbed the AR-15, slinging the strap over his neck so it would rest on his chest. Ready.

A solar panel was already strapped to the pack, with extra power packs stored in a dry bag inside. They could charge while he walked. Other various items and ammo were already in the pack, prepared in advance for this moment. His stun club rode in a holster at his side. On his left hand, he wore his fancy new glove. He had assembled it from the spare parts he had lying around after his various projects. He called it The Gauntlet of Stop-It. He wasn't great with names. He grabbed the cooler of blood and unwrapped a drumstick for the journey.

*This could be the last ice cream I ever have.*

*Caramel center, dipped in chocolate and covered in peanuts.*

*Vanilla ice cream that is impossibly creamy.*

*It's a good choice.*

Thomas nodded his head decisively and started his walk. He

thought of the things left undone and unsaid. It was a melancholy walk, but uneventful.

The altar waited in the hollow. It was quiet as stone always was. The trees stretched their limbs protectively, guarding their secret. The leaves overhead barely stirred in the breeze.

Thomas set the cooler down beside the cracked slab, unlatching the lid. The blood inside was bagged, labeled, and clean. Ten pints. Stolen without violence—but stolen all the same.

He knew the logic now. He'd translated enough of the cult's writings to see the shape of it: divine blood could open the Path because it belonged. Human blood could only open it by force, not permission. It was never intended; it was something discovered long ago by others who questioned the gods.

He took the first bag, cut it open, and poured it out slowly over the altar's center. The blood soaked into the stone like water on sand. No runes lit, no thunder cracked. Just red against gray.

One bag after another, he emptied all ten bags.

That was the blood, but now it needed alignment. It needed his blood, his essence to power it, to mark the author of the spell.

He drew the dagger he had obtained from the satyr; the handle now wrapped in paracord instead of displaying the leaves and circle of grapes. Just a tool. He sliced the back of his forearm. He never understood why people sliced their palms in the movies. He used his palms constantly. He let a few drops fall on the altar. Unlike the other blood, this time it sizzled and burned.

The stone felt warm as the runes on the altar began to glow. At first dimly, they slowly grew in intensity.

Thomas remembered the dance with the satyr. He turned and boldly called out to the forest, the stones, existence itself: "I am Thomas. I have no surname; that life is gone. I am not divine, but I will not be denied. I demand passage."

The runes on the dais sprang to life. He grabbed the gun hanging in front of the police vest on his chest and stepped up to the dais.

Thomas looked towards the east, roughly in the direction of Rebecca, his family, and his old life. He could feel his emotions building, a wave of sadness, but he was doing this for them. He was holding the powers-that-be accountable, and no one else was volunteering. He fought down the rising wave of emotions and said, "Good-bye."

He stepped on the dais, the runes flared, and Thomas was gone.

The woods were silent except for a gentle breeze rustling through the leaves overhead.

# CHAPTER 19
## *Raven and Iron*

The runes glowed white as he stepped onto the dais. The light swelled in brightness until he had to shield his eyes against it. Then, as quickly as it grew, it receded—to be replaced by a new world.

He stood on a stone dais, like the one he left behind. Its surface was etched with glowing runes, their angular forms pulsing with slow, molten light. The air was different here. Sharper. Drier. It smelled like wild thyme and ozone from distant lightning. The sky above was streaked with pink clouds as the sun peeked over the horizon. Beyond them, golden shafts of light pierced through like small windows into heaven.

The dais rose from the center of a flattened clearing, surrounded by armored women in a loose circle. Spears rested against their shoulders, and gleaming bronze plates covered their torsos. Some wore wolf pelts draped over one arm; others had sun-bleached hair tied into war braids. Some of their faces were painted, ready for violence.

They watched him with guarded expressions. Not immediately hostile, but far from friendly. One woman stepped forward, her cloak of raven feathers stirring in the wind. She spoke, but he did not understand her language.

Before Thomas could respond, a bray echoed from the hill above—low and guttural, like an elk's bugle.

He looked past the women. A narrow stone path sloped down from the dais, then curved beside a low ridge topped with gnarled olive trees and scattered brush. There, on the slope leading up the hill, stood a host of creatures. He recognized the satyr, but other creatures were unfamiliar. Creatures with horned brows and knotted limbs, half-shadowed by the brush. More armored women stood among them, but they seemed aligned with the other side.

One of the satyrs raised a wineskin in salute. Another snorted and bleated something obscene, but they were all looking at the glowing dais under his feet.

Thomas looked back at the Amazons. Their camp spread behind them. A crescent of pitched hide tents, open cookfires, and racks of weapons prepared for combat. Horses stood tied at the edge of the clearing, twitching their ears and tossing their manes as if sensing something unnatural.

Above the hill, far off in the distance, marble columns glinted in the sunlight, half-shrouded in cloud. Perhaps that was the famed Mt. Olympus, the heart of the gods. But this wasn't that. This was the borderlands. The edge. A place where myths wandered freely.

Thomas could tell there was a clear gap between the satyrs and the armored women. This was a standoff. The satyrs belonged to the cult and had held the Path of Blood until just recently. Thaleia had reclaimed it. These must be her people, guarding the threshold. His arrival must have intrigued both sides; reinforcements from the Path might shift the tide of their standoff.

The woman in the feathered cloak narrowed her eyes and spoke again, but in a sterner tone.

He replied, "I do not speak your language."

"Why are you here, outsider?" she asked in English. "No one comes through the Stone Gate by accident."

Thomas responded, "The Path of Blood was used to bring enemies into my world. Some people in my world have been attacked and killed. People close to me have been hurt. I am here to know why, to ask Thaleia why."

A tense beat passed.

"He bleeds mortal," another of the women said, eyeing the blood on his forearm, her voice low and skeptical. "But the stone accepted him."

Then the woman with the cloak smiled. "You think you have the strength to ask questions in this world? We are surrounded, and Thaleia does not know the enemy has launched an attack to reclaim the Path of Blood. The enemy has the power to take our minds if we get too close, but he fears our spears. If they come down the hill, our spears will reach the Goēs, and his mind magic will fail. If we go up the hill, his spells will make us lose who we are."

He stepped forward off the dais. "He takes minds? He forces the innocent to act against their will?" His voice edged into anger. Focus.

"That one?" He pointed. "The one bobbing… or dancing at the top of the slope?"

As he looked up the hill, he saw that the satyrs were doing unspeakable things to the women who were being controlled. Their minds were taken, and their bodies were being used—violated— against their will. He brought the AR-15 up.

*Crack, crack, crack.*

Three shots and the Goēs tumbled backward.

The women pulled their weapons, startled by the sudden sound. But they didn't attack; their minds were still processing what had happened. They followed his gaze. The mind-bender was down. Their sisters were free. But now they were behind enemy lines. They needed help.

Thomas was already moving. His leg hurt, but adrenaline is a strong medicine. He moved in a half-crouched position, rifle tight against his shoulder, finding targets.

The women were initially surprised by his actions, and he pulled ahead of them, but they saw him leading the charge, and they weren't going to be outdone. They charged past him with war cries and spears.

The freed women were in danger from the surrounding enemies. Thomas's bullets found their targets. He focused on those closest to the women—giving them space to regroup and time to fight back.

Spears suddenly filled the air as the women were in range. The enemies died in waves, unable to mount a defense after the loss of their leader. Those who lived—ran.

The warriors, their minds returned, were filled with rage and a burning hatred for their attackers. They gave chase, cutting down any they could reach until their sisters reined them in. They were too injured to continue the fight. They needed to regroup and heal, but Thomas could see the looks in their eyes. They were haunted, vacant— like a part of their soul was lost.

He knew that feeling. Seeing your own hands disobey you or

fighting as your own mind betrays you—it can break you. He spent hours crying over the mother he murdered when his body was possessed.

He also knew it wasn't his place to interfere. These were fierce warriors, that much was plain, and they wouldn't appreciate an outsider offering psychiatric help. He simply limped back down to the path, put in a fresh magazine, and waited for their leader to approach him.

He didn't want them to know the limitations of his weapon, so he reloaded as discreetly as he could and slipped the partially spent magazine into a pocket. He wasn't sure if they were friends or foes yet. It was possible there were no friends here, and he wanted to keep his options open. He had only been there for ten minutes and already, he felt lost about the people and about his path forward.

The woman in the cloak of raven feathers had already stated that Thaleia didn't know the Path of Blood was under attack and that reinforcements were needed. Which meant these women answered to Thaleia. He was here to demand answers from her. Perhaps admitting that would get him killed, but he knew this was most likely a one-way trip when he stepped on the stone. He was all-in now.

Their leader approached him, cautious but willing to listen to the newcomer. "You freed my sisters, but you do not know us."

He was looking forward, toward what he believed was Olympus. "My mind was taken." His head slowly shifted to meet her gaze. "I screamed inside my head while my hands did things against my will. Like your sisters, I couldn't stop it."

"This… cult." He waved his hand toward the corpses. "They delighted in the murder of innocents. Once I was free of Ometheon's control, I returned home. But they came after me. My girlf—mate, the woman that I shared my home with, she was attacked and nearly killed by a satyr while we slept. I do not know why Thaleia used me as a tool, just to be cast aside afterward. But I want an explanation. If it is within my power to save others from the abuse of powerful people, then I will do so. People with power need to be accountable too."

The leader of the women eyed him intensely for a moment before speaking. "Thaleia is not one to answer to others. What will you do if she chooses not to answer you?"

Thomas shifted his body to face the woman and replied, "I will get answers, or I will die trying. She did to me what that Goēs did to your people. When I arrived, you asked if I had the strength to ask questions here—I have the strength to open the Path of Blood. I had the strength to kill that Goēs. I do have the strength to ask my questions. I might not live long enough to get the answers, but with every ounce of my soul, I will push to get them. It is my right to try."

Thomas noticed the women were starting to surround him. He knew it was because they answered to Thaleia, and they were unsure of how this conversation was going to go. He acted like he didn't notice or care about their movement, but he kept his hands on the gun, glad it had a full magazine.

She took another long moment to consider his words. "Do you understand that Thaleia, the daughter of Athena, is a leader in this realm? Do you understand that it is by her request that my sisters and I are here guarding the Path?"

Thomas locked his eyes on hers. "Yes. My life is dedicated to stopping those who have power from destroying those who don't. My entire life and family are gone now. If all of your sisters were suddenly missing because of the actions of another, how hard would you push for truth? For accountability? I will ask Thaleia my questions, but I cannot control how she will answer them. Or if she will answer them. You said you need reinforcements because more of those creatures are coming. Send one of your people with me to relay your message. If I try to strike down Thaleia, your sister can strike me down. But if I ask my questions, perhaps I will get an answer that is acceptable, and we will part in peace."

"You have strong words for a man. You know that my sisters could cut you down where you stand, yet you speak plainly. That is rare," replied the leader thoughtfully.

Thomas nodded slowly. "My words are strong—and final. I speak of facing death without fear, which means my words of peace are true as well. They are not for show. If I can have peace, I will. But I want Thaleia to explain why she was willing to take my mind and sacrifice those I love."

The leader turned, her feathered cloak drifting from the movement, and looked at the bodies on the hill. "Your staff summons thunder like Zeus. Where you point it, things die. You could point it at her before she is ready."

Thomas turned to match her stance, his eyes on the hill. On the bodies. "I kill what needs to die, but that is not my purpose. I want answers more than blood. Justice more than vengeance. I will ask my questions. If she strikes, I will respond. If she is a good and honorable being, then she will explain herself. If she is not honorable, then she does not deserve your allegiance."

She turned back and looked in his eyes. "Your words are like steel. I will send a sister with you to guide you and report the enemy's movements, but I will hold you accountable to your words, to your deeds."

"As you should. I will stand by my actions as she should stand by hers."

They nodded to each other in mutual respect, and the warrior woman began issuing commands—clear the bodies, tend the wounded, rebuild the line.

She motioned to one of her sisters to come over. "I am Euryale the Raven, this is my sister Kallianeira the Iron Voice."

Thomas smiled at them and replied, "I am Thomas the Engineer."

"Kallianeira will guide you on your quest, but only as long as you keep up with her. She must relay news of our enemies. May your quest yield answers instead of violence," responded the Raven.

"May your enemies fall before you. Thank you," replied Thomas.

Kallianeira carried herself like a storm held in a human frame. Composed. Powerful. Honed by years of battle. She wasn't tall. Her head barely came to the man's chin, but she moved with a grace that conveyed power and authority.

Her auburn hair, loose and wind-tossed, spilled past her shoulders, and a single hawk feather was braided near her right temple. It fluttered with every step, a small, striking signature of her motion.

Her eyes were deep brown, steady and watchful, with the look of someone who had seen too much to be easily surprised. She wore a mix of iron and age-darkened bronze armor, dented in places, burnished in others. They were marks of survival rather than polish. Her breastplate bore faint traces of an old symbol, long worn from weather and war.

Broad leather straps wrapped her upper arms, holding tight against the muscles beneath, and her forearms were protected by well-worn bracers, scratched from use rather than neglect.

She didn't move like someone burdened by her gear. She moved like someone accustomed to it.

Kallianeira led Thomas to the horses and began preparing them. He attempted to help but was mostly in the way. "Have you never prepared your own horse before? Are you a noble?"

Thomas shrugged. "My steed is made of steel and runs on fire. My world is different."

Kallianeira's eyes widened at this revelation. "That… does not sound comfortable."

"It has a nice seat, and if you're careful with your feet, you don't burn your legs. If you ever come to my world, I could give you a ride. It's probably more pleasant than you would expect."

She shook her head. "I do not intend to go through the Path of Blood. It takes powerful magic, and my people don't trust magic. We trust steel and the strength of arms. You fight from a distance; we prefer to look our enemies in the eyes."

Thomas smiled. He liked Kallianeira, the Iron Voice. She had moxie. He replied, "The Goēs was not worthy of facing me in combat. He was a coward who hid behind the innocent, so he died like the coward he was."

She smiled to herself while tightening a strap on the horse. She liked Thomas, the Engineer. His spirit had fire.

# CHAPTER 20
## *Useful*

The women sent a vanguard ahead with the Iron Voice, and the man, wary of enemy troops still prowling nearby. They rode in numbers, ready for a fight if it came. It was a majestic sight—armor gleaming in the sun, feathers and hair streaming in the wind, spearpoints catching the light like fire. Their horses thundered forward in unison, a living wave of muscle, metal, and resolve.

The man was not as majestic. He rode awkwardly. It was partly from inexperience, partly from the clutter of gear strapped to him. A flat, reflective plate was lashed to the top of his pack, flashing in the sun. His thunder staff hung against his chest from a shoulder strap, at the ready. A metal club swung at his right hip, and a dagger with a wrapped handle was strapped below his left knee. He looked like someone had scavenged a blacksmith's scrap pile and tied it to him. Yet he moved with a quiet purpose, and nothing about his awkward load seemed accidental. Kallianeira watched him curiously as they rode. Strange, even for a man. But his words had rung like steel. And he had stood with them when it counted. She could tell he was injured, though he made no complaint. That, she respected.

Valandra rode up beside her, smirking. "What do you think of your pet man?"

Kallianeira laughed. "He speaks like a warrior. He respects our ways. I don't know what to think. I just hope I won't have to kill him."

Valandra's smile faded. "Questioning Thaleia is a quick path to death. He may be strong, but she's a goddess. He's still just a man."

"I don't want to strike anyone down, even a man, for seeking the truth," Kallianeira said. "If his words are true, if someone took his mind and forced him to do evil, then he deserves answers. Maybe even justice."

"We made a bargain with Athena," Valandra reminded her. "Our loyalty is to her and to Thaleia."

"But we saw what the Goēs did to our sisters," Kallianeira replied. "If your mind were taken, would you not want to know why it happened? Who allowed it? Who caused it?"

Valandra hesitated. "He seeks justice. That is noble. But there's also honor in loyalty, in keeping our word."

Kallianeira glanced at her. "Is it loyalty if the one we serve used mind control to force evil on the innocent?"

"Then we should hope Thaleia has an answer. And that he is wrong."

Kallianeira looked ahead. "Yes. I hope so too. It really would be a shame to kill him."

They rode until the sun dipped low and bled into the horizon, the sky deepening to a muted violet as the last light drained away. Just before nightfall, the sisters turned off the trail and entered a cluster of weather-worn ruins nestled in the arms of the hillside. Stone walls, half-collapsed and choked with moss, marked the skeleton of what might once have been a small temple or outpost. It was a place known to the sisters. The ruins were secluded, familiar, and defensible, a perfect place to rest.

They dismounted without a word, moving with the fluid efficiency of long practice. Horses were led into the central courtyard, where the crumbling walls still stood high enough to offer cover. The roof had fallen ages ago, but the stars would serve well enough tonight. The air was dry, and the breeze carried no hint of rain.

Bedrolls were laid out in the open space beneath the stars. Kallianeira crossed the clearing to where her charge stood, adjusting his gear. He was clearly stiff from the ride and still favoring an injured leg, though he didn't speak of it.

"We're stopping here for the night," she said. "You're injured and tired. Rest. My sisters will keep watch over us and the ruins. They will tend the fire and horses. I will sleep tonight as well. You and I shall ride hard tomorrow. Rest well and heavy. You will need it."

"Thank you, Kallianeira. Sleep well," the man replied. He still carried that strange calm with him. He was pleasant—for a man.

He stepped aside and knelt by the entrance, placing one of his odd little talismans in the dirt. It was probably some offering of protection to a god. Then he unrolled a strange bedroll with a metallic hiss, the seams held closed by a tooth-like metal chain that he slid open with practiced ease. He slipped inside the padded cocoon, tugged the flap shut, and was asleep within minutes. It was as if exhaustion had completely overwhelmed him, and he was only walking because of sheer force of will.

Meanwhile, Valandra and two others set to work on the fire. They built it swiftly, silently, their hands deft and sure. These motions had been drilled into them since girlhood. Build low. Shield the light. Always choose a corner with visibility. The flicker of flame danced across the stone, casting tall shadows but none that would betray their presence from a distance. The ruin's walls would hide the glow and narrow any approach, giving them a better chance if something came for them in the night.

Though they were expert fighters, the threat they faced now was less than human. Some of the creatures that followed them could see clearly in darkness and moved like whispers.

Kallianeira unrolled her own bedroll and settled near the fire. Tonight, she would sleep while her sisters stood watch. From a pouch at her hip, she drew a sliver of aged cheese, scraped away a patch of mold, and flicked it into the flames. Then came a round of hardtack and a small skin of wine. She dipped the bread to soften it and ate in silence, eyes fixed on the fire.

The crackle and heat offered a brief comfort, but her thoughts strayed—toward the man. Toward the truths he hunted, and to the questions she dared not voice aloud.

After her brief meal, she settled down on her bedroll for some much-needed sleep.

Valandra's hand gently shook Kallianeira awake.

It wasn't yet morning, and they would never wake her without cause. Kallianeira's eyes opened to darkness thick with tension. Something was wrong.

Valandra didn't speak. She only gave a slight motion toward the ruined archway and signaled for her to ready her weapon. Kallianeira nodded, heart already steadying into focus. She couldn't hear anything unusual, but her instincts flared. The night insects were oddly quiet. Maybe it was the brush of leaves too soft to be natural, or a subtle wrongness in the air. Years of training and surviving told her to prepare.

Trouble was coming.

She gave a quiet hand signal to the other sister on watch. Together, they moved to wake the rest. Silent gestures, soft touches. No voices. No metal.

She moved to the man's side last, crouched beside his strange cocoon of a bed. She placed a hand on his arm. Light, but firm. His eyes opened immediately. No flinch. No sound. He woke like a warrior. She respected that.

She motioned for him to arm himself and turned to leave, but he raised his hand, gesturing for her to wait.

From within his pack, he pulled another of his small talismans. It flared softly at his touch, casting a faint, eerie glow. Kallianeira leaned back instinctively. She had seen the destruction his thunder staff could unleash and didn't trust this thing to behave.

Then he touched it again, and it changed. It was like a pool of still water suddenly reflecting another world. An image appeared: the view from just outside the ruins—a window into the dark. Yet somehow, she could see. Everything had a green tint, but it was clear.

She leaned in.

There, lurking in the brush near the threshold, was a satyr. Beside him, two wretched Kobaloi crept forward, hunched goblin-things with flasks clutched in their gnarled hands. Tricksters who enjoy giving pain. Whether their flasks meant to blind or burn, she could not yet tell.

Kallianeira's breath slowed. She signed for the others to hold: no movement, no sound. Then she pointed to the glowing screen, still wary of its magic, but grateful for its clarity.

The man gestured for her to lean close. She did.

"I can make a light shine," he whispered, barely audible. "Right at the entrance where I left the camera."

She frowned slightly. That must be the talisman. That was where he placed the little device in the dirt before sleep. It was a scout's eye.

She gave a nod and turned to her sisters. With crisp, silent gestures, she instructed them to ready themselves. Spears drawn. Positions held. Eyes locked.

The fire they had built burned low by design. Its glow did not reach the entrance. An old tactic meant to preserve night vision and concealment. The satyr and his minions were using it against them now, creeping under the cover of darkness.

The Kobaloi would throw their flasks, sowing chaos. Then the satyr would charge amid the confusion. It was a coward's tactic, but a deadly one if uncountered.

But the Amazons were ready.

She watched. When the enemy crept into the opening of the archway, she gave the signal.

The man tapped his device.

A sudden burst of light erupted at the ruins' edge, exposing the darkness and what hid within. It was followed by a sharp, unnatural sound that cracked the air like a shout. The creatures reeled, exposed and disoriented.

In that instant, the Amazons struck.

Spears flew in silent, perfect arcs. No battle cry, no wasted motion. The only sound was the hiss of steel and the wet thud of impact.

The ambush had been reversed. Now it was their enemy caught in the trap.

Several spears struck true. One Kobaloi crumpled with a gurgle, the other let out a screech as it toppled backward. Their flasks slipped from limp hands and shattered against the stone with sharp cracks. One burst into flame immediately, splashing burning oil in a sudden gout of light that licked up the dry moss and debris. The other released a noxious plume that hissed in the air. Choking, acrid smoke designed to sting the eyes and nose. The satyr, caught between them, let out a furious bleat as fire grazed his leg and smoke burned his lungs. He stumbled back into the brush, eyes watering, hacking and snarling in rage.

Valandra didn't hesitate. The moment the jars burst, and fire roared up from the stone, she gave the signal. The warriors surged forward, flanking the flames with precision and grace. They moved low and fast, circling wide to avoid the burning patch even as the smoke curled into their path. Their eyes stayed locked on the satyr as he coughed, off-balance, a hand clutched to his scorched leg.

He tried to raise his weapon, some crude, knotted club of rootwood and stone, but Valandra was already on him. Her spear drove low, toward the hip. He twisted just enough to avoid the killing blow, but not enough to stop the second Amazon from driving hers into his shoulder. He bellowed, a sound of rage and pain, as he lashed out wild and desperate.

Kallianeira caught the backswing on her shield and slammed it forward into his chest. The satyr stumbled; his hoof caught on a flagstone. Then a final spear found his throat.

He dropped, twitched once, then lay still.

The sisters stood in a loose circle, the fire crackling behind them, weapons raised and breath even. Toxic smoke swirled low, but none of them had been touched by it. Not this time.

As the echoes of the fight faded, the ruin fell quiet again. Only the faint crackle of flame and the distant rustle of leaves remained. Blood soaked into the dry earth beneath the satyr's body, steaming faintly where it mingled with burning oil.

Kallianeira turned back toward the entrance. The man stood just inside, still barefoot, his thunder staff in hand. The eerie, glowing window he had conjured now flickered faintly in his other hand. He picked up the talisman that he had left by the arch, the one that lit when he commanded it. He held it high and slowly turned it like he was scanning the area.

Satisfied, he set it down and touched his shining window, extinguishing it. Darkness reclaimed the edges of the ruin.

He gave a slight nod and walked back inside.

Valandra stepped closer to her sister and, with a smile, whispered, "Your pet man is turning out to be useful. Maybe you should keep him."

Kallianeira didn't answer right away. She looked down at the broken jars and the curled corpses of the Kobaloi, then at the satyr's gnarled form. Her sisters could have been hurt, but because of him, they were all safe.

"A strange warrior," she said at last. "I'm not sure what I'll do with him."

Thomas had already returned to his corner and was sliding back into his bedroll. In another few seconds, he was still again, as if nothing had happened.

But Kallianeira didn't sleep. Not yet. She walked back to her bedroll and sat by the fire a little longer, thinking about the tools he carried, the quiet way he moved, and the truths he claimed to seek. He had honor. He deserved answers, but she didn't know if he would survive getting them.

# CHAPTER 21
## *She Will Never Know*

Thomas woke, refreshed after a much-needed rest. He felt like he could use another eight hours, but it was time to get under way. His guide had a task to complete, and he didn't want to slow her down.

He quickly gathered his things and went to help Kallianeira with the horses. "I need to learn how to do this since I might be here a long time. Plus, I like learning. Will you please teach me?"

Kallianeira responded, "A man who asks for help? You are full of many wonders, Thomas the Engineer. You start with a blanket. Make sure there are no burrs, or it will rub the horse raw."

She walked him through the procedure and made sure his horse was saddled correctly. She wouldn't admit it, but she was pleased to see that he wanted to help, to be a part of the team instead of demanding he lead just because he was a man.

He was a good student, listening to his instructor and asking questions when appropriate. Rather than strap his gear to his horse, he wore his backpack. He was concerned about being thrown and losing everything if the horse ran away. With his horse saddled and his gear stowed in his pack, he thanked his teacher.

Thomas approached Valandra. "Thank you for helping me in my task. You are a person who carries herself with honor. You've earned my respect."

Valandra smiled. "Thomas the Engineer, may you get the answers you seek and live long enough to use the knowledge. Safe journey." They nodded as warriors who recognized a kindred spirit.

Everyone rode out together, the horses sidestepping the burned corpses. Then they traveled around the hill until they arrived at the road. The vanguard turned back toward the Path of Blood, and Thomas's group of two continued toward Olympus.

The horses moved at a steady pace across the sloped grasslands. A gentle breeze carried the scent of crushed sage and hinted at rain to come.

The two of them trotted along for some time before boredom of the road and curiosity got the better of Kallianeira. She paced her horse alongside his. He was getting more accustomed to riding, sitting more naturally in the saddle. The man learned quickly.

She asked, "You said that Thaleia's actions nearly killed your mate. You have treated us as equals, but you own a mate?"

Thomas turned and looked at her. "No. No, I don't own her. I called her my mate because I thought your world might not understand what a girlfriend is. It is a term for people who are growing closer, but they haven't formed a permanent bond yet. Some people of my world treat women badly, like they are weaker beings. Some people treat men like they are overbearing brutes that can't be trusted. But a lot of people, including my personal group, believe that men and women complement each other. We believe men and women cover for each other's weaknesses and complement each other's strengths. I believe we are stronger together than apart."

She nodded her head, contemplating his words. "Then why isn't your mate here now? Were her injuries too great?"

"No, her injuries were not too great, but she is not a warrior. I wasn't either until this happened, but I was willing to fight back. We weren't married, but we were spending time together to see if we wanted to be married. I didn't want to risk her life, and she didn't want to fight satyrs. It was a different world, and she decided to stay behind."

Kallianeira looked at him. "So she is weak? You didn't want to risk her life?"

Thomas shook his head. "I don't want to protect her because she is weak. I want to protect her because she is special. My people are protective of family and those we care about, just as you care about your sisters. I saw the pain in your eyes when your sisters were under the Goës's power. You wanted to protect them."

She nodded in understanding. "You said you weren't married to your woman. Did her father not offer enough dowry? What did the future hold?"

Thomas smiled. "I am familiar with the term dowry, but we don't have that in my society. Marriage isn't a contract, and women can't be sold or purchased. For my people, when a man and woman meet, if they like each other's company, they spend more time together. If they think they are compatible and they love each other, then they become engaged. That is a time to start organizing both of their lives. Men and women can both have careers and property, so it takes a little planning sometimes. Then the two of them are married, they have children, and they live together and protect each other until they die."

"Because of choice? From both?" she asked quizzically.

"Because of choice. From both," he responded.

She rode on in silence for a moment. "In my society, if a man wants a woman, he thinks he can just take her."

Thomas shook his head. "If I saw a man trying to take a woman against her will, I would kill him, just as I killed the Goēs. In my group, our bodies are gifts to each other. A man doesn't take. A woman doesn't control. The two agree to share themselves. They do so for their own pleasure, but just as much for the other person's pleasure. That closeness makes the whole act much better. I believe it is the way we were intended to be together."

Her expression softened at his response. She paused to consider her next question. "What if the man marries another? Do they both have to share him?"

Thomas chuckled softly. "That would never happen among my people. My society doesn't condone that. There is a passage from an old text that says *a man shall leave his father and mother and take a wife. The two shall become one.* I like that passage. If a man and woman truly feel like they are two parts of one team, then they will both work to make the other happy. Your right arm would never attack your left arm intentionally. They are part of one being."

She shook her head in disbelief. "What you say would be hard for my society to accept."

He looked at her for a moment and asked, "Have I treated you as inferior?"

She returned his gaze. "No, Thomas the Engineer, you have not. You are not like other men."

He looked back at the road. "Then other men are wrong. They are missing out on wonderful relationships based on respect and love. True happiness for both."

They rode in silence for a few minutes before she asked, "Will you go back to your woman one day?"

"I don't know," he said, then took a deep breath as he considered his answer. "At this point, I doubt it. I miss her; she is a good person. She helps sick children as a nurse. She dedicated her life to caring for those in need, and that is wonderful. I just don't think that can be a part of my life. She would not be happy fighting, and I can't go back now that I know this war against my world is happening."

"So, you will fight alone?" she asked.

"I'm not sure of the future. Yesterday, I was in another realm." A low chuckle escaped his lips as he contemplated the massive swing in his life. "Tomorrow I might be dead. But for now, I will fight. I will fight so she can have the life she wants, even if she doesn't know what I am doing."

She considered his words. "You will fight for her to have a life raising children with another man? You will risk everything for her happiness, even if she is ignorant of your deeds?"

He smiled. "Yes. But it is more than that. I will fight what is evil. If you were attacked right now, I could ride safely away, but I wouldn't. I would fight for you, too. If a random child were in the road ahead of us, and about to be killed by a satyr, I would fight it as well. Good people need to stand up and fight back against evil. It is like weeds in a garden. If you let them flourish, you will lose the garden. If I die an unsung hero and leave my bones in a bush in a different realm, so be it. At least I tried."

She smiled and responded, "It isn't glory you seek? You fight this hard for another's peace?"

He nodded. "I did not come here seeking glory, power—pain, or blood." He paused for a deep breath. "I came for answers and justice. Just because a person has power, that doesn't mean they are correct. The powerful need to be held to account. Those without power deserve to have a voice, too. They deserve justice, and peace, and happiness."

Kallianeira responded, "I respect you, Thomas the Engineer. I hope you get your answers." But her smile faded because she feared he would be killed instead—possibly by her hand if she honored the alliance with Athena and her people.

She looked ahead again, toward the ridgeline where the sky was starting to darken with clouds. Thomas smiled but said nothing more. He rode quietly beside her, back straight, eyes forward.

She would never understand his world. But for the first time, she thought… maybe she didn't have to. Maybe it was enough to know that a man like him had walked through pain and blood and chose to keep walking anyway. And he did it, not for glory, but for others.

They rode on in silence.

# CHAPTER 22
## *Helping Hand*

The ride was uneventful, but peaceful in its own way. Kallianeira and the man rode side by side through low hills and whispering grass, the distant tree line rippling with wind. The storm that had threatened all morning still held off, gray clouds churning but not yet ready to break.

They spoke softly as they went, their voices low so as not to carry. Thomas asked about the terrain, and Kallianeira described it with a quiet pride. She pointed out the paths the native tribes once walked and the spirits rumored to still dwell in the hollows. He listened without interrupting, sometimes asking thoughtful questions, other times simply watching the land unfold as she spoke.

When hunger came, they ate in the saddle. Thomas reached into a side pouch and produced a strange, colorful, wrapped bar. He had to tear the wrapping in order to open it. It made her wonder how he wrapped it so tight.

"It's called a Clif bar. Chocolate chip," he said, peeling one open and handing it to her.

She took it with mild suspicion, turned it in her hand, then bit. Her eyes widened slightly. "This is… very good. Most road food is dry and hard, but this is chewy and sweet. Your world is full of strange wonders."

He grinned. "I like them, but I wish I could share some ice cream with you. It is food that would make the gods jealous."

She gave him a sidelong look. "Is it like Ambrosia? Mortals are not allowed to have it."

He paused to reflect. "I have never had Ambrosia. I would like to compare them, but honestly, I bet ice cream is better."

Then came the sprinkle. A soft, misty rain at first, clinging to their skin and soaking their clothes. Thomas reached behind him, dug into a side pouch again, and pulled out a weathered item he called a baseball cap. He tugged it over his head, the brim jutting forward like a strange beak. Then, after a pause, he held out a second one to her.

She took it in her hand, studied it, then eyed him as though he'd offered her a ceremonial mask. "Your head looks like the face of a bird," she said, turning the hat over in her hand.

It was soft cloth. It was not good armor.

He chuckled. "Yes, it does look a little silly, but it keeps the rain out of your eyes."

Kallianeira considered this. She slipped it on crooked at first, then she wiggled it into place. She looked around as though testing it from different angles.

"It works. It seems useful," she said after a pause.

He nodded. "It is nice in bright sunshine as well, like in a desert. It blocks the sun and the rain. It might look silly on me, but I think it suits you."

She made a snarling face, not in anger, just in disbelief. Suddenly, she wished she had a mirror, though.

They trudged through the mud puddles for hours until it was almost dusk. Kallianeira gestured and said, "There is a town just up ahead. We can stay for the night. We'll have to sleep in the barn. Amazons do not have the money that men use."

Thomas reached into a pouch, pulled out a bag of coins, and held them out. "Is this the type of coin used here?"

She took the bag and looked inside. Her eyes widened. "How did you get so much? This is enough money for an estate."

He smiled. "I took it from the cult on my side of the Path of Blood. They weren't going to need it anymore."

She took out a single coin and said, "This should be enough for the night and dinner. Although the Clif bar of chocolate chips was good, it will be nice to have a warm meal to shake the chill of the rain."

Thomas nodded and replied, "I'll follow your lead. It's your world."

Kallianeira was always reserved. She kept her emotions close, but she was happy. The man said he would follow her lead—he truly was from another world.

The rain hadn't let up by the time they reached the tavern, but the warmth inside was immediate. The air in the main room was thick with the smell of firewood, roasting lamb, and the earthy tang of wet stone. Kallianeira stepped through the door first, steam curling from her shoulders as the chill began to melt off her armor. Thomas followed, his boots squelching faintly on the rushes strewn across the floor.

The other patrons glanced up but quickly returned to their meals. Just another two weather-worn travelers. They were not a unique sight here.

They settled down at a table in the corner where they could watch the front door. Warriors don't like to have unprotected backs.

They had handed the horses off to a stableboy. He was a wide-eyed youth who didn't dare speak more than a word when Kallianeira looked at him. Now they sought the kind of comfort only fire and food could bring. They ordered a room for the night and a meal strong enough to drive the cold from their bones.

The tavernkeeper, a middle-aged woman with quick eyes and ash-gray braids, brought the food herself: two wide clay bowls, brimming with stew. Chunks of lamb nestled in a thick broth of barley, onions, and root vegetables, steam rising in fragrant waves. Olive oil shimmered on the surface, catching the firelight in golden swirls. A side of flatbread, still hot and soft, came on a wooden board, along with a plate of roasted parsnips and mushrooms charred dark at the edges.

They sat next to each other, close enough to share the warmth of the hearth. Kallianeira took her first bite in silence, her brow lifted slightly in surprise. "This is good," she said, tearing another piece of bread and dipping it into the stew.

Thomas agreed as he took a bite. "I haven't had warm, prepared food in weeks. Not like this anyway." He then took a long drink from the clay cup of mulled wine they'd been given. It was hot and sharp with cloves and orange peel. She sipped hers more cautiously, but the heat seemed to loosen her shoulders. A bit of color returned to her cheeks.

The meal was topped off with sesame-honey cakes, golden, sticky, and still warm from the fire. It felt like years since either of them had eaten warm food like this. Fighting or jumping dimensions will do that.

The tavern wasn't loud. It just had the soft hum of other travelers, the clink of pottery, and the crackle of the fire. Outside, the rain whispered against the shutters, forgotten for now. They sat together, absorbing the warmth and enjoying their full bellies.

Kallianeira tried to picture his world. A world where this was how men and women interacted. Just enjoying food and company without ownership and fear. She could get used to that. The warrior at your side could be a man or woman, and you could trust them. She allowed herself a genuinely happy smile and leaned back in her chair.

Her happiness was interrupted by the clink of a coin hitting the table. She opened her eyes to find three men standing before the table. The ugly one in the lead leered down at her. "That should cover your services for the night. I'm first." A stupid, smarmy grin spread across his face.

She flicked the coin off the table and gave a glare sharp enough to peel paint from wood.

Thomas said, "Did I miss something?"

That's right. He doesn't speak the local language, she thought before she replied, "They are attempting to purchase me."

He shook his head and replied, "That's rude. Will they understand me if I speak English?"

The stupid-looking one replied, "We understand your language. This doesn't concern you, unless you are the one who takes payment for her."

She stood with a snap. "No one owns me!"

Thomas crossed his right hand on top of his left forearm. There was a soft, almost imperceptible click before he started to stand. Before he could speak, the big one grabbed him and growled, "If you don't teach your woman respect, I will… In fact, I'll enjoy it."

Kallianeira wondered what would happen. She wasn't about to be possessed or used by these men, but there were three. By herself, it would be a hard fight. She was actually quite interested to see how her companion was going to respond. He said he would kill a man who tried to force a woman against her will. Would he risk his own safety now? He was not moving like a warrior preparing to fight against greater odds. He had stood slowly, like an old man on a rainy day.

Thomas looked down at the meaty paw gripping his shirt, then slowly raised his gloved left hand and wrapped his fingers around the dumb brute's sweaty wrist.

The big guy stiffened. His face twisted; breath caught. Stuck in a spasm. His back arched, and a raw, guttural sound tore from his throat—wet and strangled, like a man choking on his own breath. His eyes rolled back. A whimper rattled in his chest as Thomas released him, and he crashed to the floor, twitching, his hand clutching his arm.

This was the gauntlet Thomas had built from spare parts back on Earth. It was just a battery pack, some salvaged wire, and a few carefully placed metal contacts stitched into a work glove. The pinky and ring fingers carried a negative charge, the index and thumb carried a positive one. When his hand closed, the circuit completed, and the pain followed. He could make it arc between fingers for show, but tonight, subtlety served him better. No sparks. No flash. Just agony. Delivered quietly.

With a moment of preparation, he could contain a threat and immobilize it without killing it.

Thomas looked at the other two and said, "I'm not the scary one; she is. I'm trying to save your lives, but if she wants you dead—I won't stop her."

He looked at her to see how she wanted to handle it. She met his gaze, glanced at the men, and gave a dismissive shooing motion like she was sending children away. She sat back down calmly.

She didn't know what to think. What she just witnessed was both impressive and terrifying. Fortunately, the man who did it was on her side. He did what he said. He protected her. But even more impressively, he respected her honor while he did it.

Thomas watched as they dragged their leader away. His right hand rested casually on his left forearm in a relaxed pose. Once they were far enough away, he subtly flicked the hidden switch that disarmed his gauntlet.

Thomas sat down, leaned back against the wall next to Kallianeira, and sipped his mulled wine like nothing had happened. She watched him for a second, then leaned back and started sipping her wine too. Just two friends—equals, enjoying wine. She smiled and breathed in the wine.

The tavern settled. People went back to the conversations and dinners, but they kept casting sidelong glances at the strange new people sipping their wine. The tavernkeeper returned to their table. Her face was careful, neutral, but her eyes had the pinched, worried look of someone weighing risk against regret. She wiped her hands on her apron, glanced toward the back room, then finally met Kallianeira's gaze.

"I don't want trouble," she said, switching to English for Thomas's sake. "I'm not doing this because I'm mad. I just don't got a choice." She was clearly scared. She was wringing her hands and had her eyes fixed on the floor.

Thomas held up his hand. It wasn't a gesture meant to stop her, but to comfort. He said, "You are worried about retaliation. You think they will come back, and others will be hurt when they come for us?"

She bobbed her head. "Thank you for understanding. I just can't risk my family." She set a couple of coins down on the table and said, "The food's on the house. Have a safe journey."

Thomas and Kallianeira exchanged looks, nodded, and rose in unison. Thomas slid the coins across the table and into his hand.

They walked to the stables and began preparing their horses for the ride. He could have been imagining it, but Thomas would swear his horse looked mad.

Kallianeira mounted her horse and looked down at Thomas. It was the first time she spoke since the incident inside. "Thank you. For how you handled that. You showed honor... that is a respect no man has ever shown me."

"It was my pleasure," he replied. "Plus, I really enjoyed hurting that guy. His kind annoy me."

She gave a short chuckle and smiled, a true, genuine smile.

# CHAPTER 23
## *Hello Thomas*

They didn't ride far. They knew they would need shelter for the night. Soon. The enemies near the Path of Blood would do anything to stop Kallianeira from reaching Olympus, from warning Athena and Thaleia. And now, after the tavern, they'd made another enemy. Ambush was likely in the dark. They needed a defensible position, out of the rain.

Easier said than done. Especially at night, in unfamiliar terrain. Kallianeira had passed through this region before, but never stayed long.

The rain thickened, drumming against the trees, but she hoped it slowed their hunters as much as it slowed them.

Their horses trudged uphill through slick underbrush, boots and hooves squelching in the mud. The Amazon walked without complaint, her cloak soaked through, hat low to shield her eyes. Thomas followed close behind, the chill cutting through his clothes, but his spirits were oddly high. After weeks alone, being hunted and wounded, the company felt like warmth.

Ahead, it emerged from the gloom like a monument carved from shadow. A massive plane tree towered over the clearing, its trunk wide enough for three men to encircle with outstretched arms. Branches spread like twisted fingers, and rain pattered gently across its great leaves. Beneath the canopy, the ground was surprisingly dry. The vast roots curled up from the earth like ancient knuckles, rising like steps.

Thomas stepped under the shelter and exhaled.

"Seems cozy," he said, placing a hand on the bark to steady himself. It was slick, but solid. Ancient. Maybe even older than the myths they were fighting.

Kallianeira circled the tree slowly, then knelt beside one of the gnarled roots.

"Plane trees like this are sacred to river spirits," she said. "Most won't tread here after dark—not even the cult."

"That's good," Thomas replied, nodding. "It'd be nice to sleep through a night without being attacked."

He pulled out his small, two-person tent, a memento from Earth. He had used it on camping trips with Rebecca. He set it up quickly and stowed his gear inside, except for his camera and phone.

"You should climb in and get some sleep," he told her, gesturing toward the tent. "I'll take the first watch."

She eyed the structure warily.

"Does this thing… do anything?"

"All it does is keep warmth in and rain out," he said with a tired smile. "It's safe. Four hours sound good?"

She stepped toward the tent but paused at the entrance.

"You do not pray," she said quietly. "Not even under trees the gods favor?"

Thomas looked up at the leaves, wet and heavy overhead, before responding. "I mentioned an ancient text in my world. The one that described how men and women should treat each other when they are married. That text says one being created all others. That is the one I speak to. He can see into minds and into souls. He hears me when I am riding, walking, or even fighting."

"Our gods need proof, deeds. Your god looks at the soul and mind instead? How does he judge?" she asked.

He took a moment before answering. "Imagine you tried to save someone. You gave everything. Maybe even died in the attempt. Your gods would say you failed. Mine would say I succeeded, because I honored His spirit. He doesn't need me to win. He just wants me to try. Like a parent teaching a child. The parent could do everything better and faster if they didn't slow down to teach the child, but they teach anyway. They guide. That's what my God is like."

They stood there in silence for a moment, the rain muffled above them by the leaves.

"Four hours," she said at last, and slipped into the tent.

He sat there, staring for movement in the darkness, but it was too dark to see. He listened for sounds, but the rain was too loud. It felt like a futile task, but any warning of an attack would be helpful, so he watched darkness and listened to noise.

Cold crept in slowly. His muscles were starting to tighten, his soaked clothes leaching warmth. His leg, where the satyr had clawed him, throbbed with a slow, insistent pulse. He pushed the pain aside and focused on the road ahead.

He was getting closer to Olympus and hopefully closer to Thaleia. He would ask his questions, but what would he do if she didn't feel like answering? Would he really start the attack? It was one thing to demand answers and defend himself if she attacked, but what if she just dismissed him?

It would seem a waste to travel to another realm just to be dismissed and sent back without a fight.

When the time finally came to wake Kallianeira, he struggled to rise. His leg was pulsing. It had been abused for days, and riding the horse didn't help. He would see to replacing the bandages in the morning before they left.

He reached into the tent and gently placed his hand on her shoulder. Her eyes popped open—instantly awake, alert. But she did not move. Not until she was certain he wasn't alerting her to danger.

Thomas went to stand and stumbled to one side. He caught himself and then offered his hand to her to help her up. She took his hand but studied him as she stood, concern tightening her brow.

"Your injury. It's worse?" she asked.

"It's sore. I'm hoping it's just the cold causing my leg to stiffen. I should check it in the morning," he said.

"No. This could be serious. Take off your pants."

They locked eyes for a heartbeat.

Thomas burst into laughter. "Yes, ma'am."

Kallianeira blinked, then her eyes widened in horror. "I didn't mean—"

He raised his hand in a disarming gesture. "I know what you meant. It just sounded funny. We are becoming friends, and you are concerned about my safety. I thank you for your concern." He took off his pants but used his sleeping bag for modesty.

She crouched beside him, already focused, already working.

Her fingers were sure as she unwound the wet bandage, pulling it free with a quiet tug. As the cloth fell away, his leg twitched. The flesh was red and swollen. The skin felt tender to the touch.

There was a thin layer of yellowish pus clinging to the edges of the gash, still watery and fresh, but not yet thick or heavy. It wasn't as bad as it could be, but the warmth radiating from the skin beneath worried her.

She pressed gently around the edges of the wound, feeling the inflammation. His leg was swollen. Hot. But not to the point of festering.

"It is infected," she murmured, more to herself than to him. "But it is not beyond recovery. If it sits near the surface, we can still stop it."

She opened her kit, selecting clean cloth, water, and a honey-garlic mixture. "We need to clean this out. It's not bad yet, but it will get worse if we don't act fast."

She poured her water over the wound and began to scrub.

The man's jaw tightened. He wasn't about to show weakness in front of an Amazon.

"How bad is it?" he asked with a forced calm.

"Bad enough," she replied. "But you'll live. If we can keep it from spreading."

"I would appreciate living," he responded thoughtfully.

She appreciated his stoicism, but a deeper concern stirred within her. The injury would slow her mission, but it was more than that. She was starting to like her "pet man," as Valandra had called him. She had always known that his mission would likely end in death, but she wanted him to live long enough to ask his questions.

But it ran deeper. He had shown her respect. His existence challenged everything she knew about men. He was unique, and she didn't like the idea of a world without him. She pushed the thoughts aside and focused on the task—wrapping the leg.

When the wound was cleaned and the honey applied, she wrapped it in fresh cloth and stood.

"We will need to keep it clean and observe it to ensure it does not spread."

He stood, smiled at her, and said, "You should get some more sleep. You will need your strength for the journey tomorrow."

Her eyes narrowed. "It is my watch. You need rest to heal."

He held up his hands in mock surrender, then gently placed them on her shoulders. His voice was softer now.

"I won't be going with you."

She stiffened.

He continued, gently, "Your sisters' lives are on the line. You need to ride hard and fast tomorrow. Deliver your message. I'll stay here until I can travel again. You said Olympus is still days away. Once you've reached it, you can come back and check on me. Or rejoin your sisters. I am stubborn. I will be okay."

He let go and gave a small nod toward the tent.

She didn't argue. She knew he was right. But that didn't make it easy. Her duty came first. Still, she did not want to leave her ally—her friend—behind.

Thomas continued his watch, staring at the darkness, listening to the noises.

Kallianeira lay back down, but she did not sleep well.

After a fitful night, she rose and checked on her patient. His leg showed no signs of change, but it had not been long enough for real progress.

She prepared in melancholy silence. She did not want to leave him in a vulnerable state, but in all honesty, she did not want to be alone either. Normally, she enjoyed being the messenger. The Iron Voice that braves the wilds alone. But his company was different. He was an odd one, but he showed her a different way of thinking, and she liked it. He challenged her. Her thoughts. Her views. He made her see life differently than before.

Thomas pulled one of his talismans out of his bag. It was strange-looking but had a place to grip it with a hand, much like his thunder staff. "This is a gun. It works in a very similar manner to the one on my chest. It is technology, not magic. A bow fires arrows; this fires bullets. Count when you shoot. It will work 15 times before it is empty. It still has value if you find more bullets. Hopefully you won't need it, but I would feel better if you took it with you." He stretched out his hand with the thunder stick.

She took it. She was honored that such a powerful gift was bestowed upon her. He showed how it worked and pointed out the little red dot that meant it was dangerous. She attached it to her hip using the sheath that he called a holster.

She turned to him, healing kit in her outstretched hand. "You will need to use the honey when you apply a new cloth. Keep it clean."

He shook his head. "Your mission must succeed. Take the kit in case you're injured. I have some supplies in my pack. I will manage."

"You are wise and brave, Thomas the Engineer. You have the heart of a woman." The corner of her lips curled slightly with a trace of mischief.

He responded in kind. "Then you know I'll be strong enough to survive. Safe journey, my friend."

She turned quickly and mounted her horse, hiding the mist in her eyes. She did not expect him to call her a friend. It hit harder than she expected.

Thomas watched her steer her horse around the brush as she worked her way through the trees. He watched until she was gone from sight.

*It looks like it's just you and me again, Thomas.*
*Oh, good, I'm already talking to myself.*

# CHAPTER 24
## *That's Mr. Ed to You*

Thomas crawled into his tent after his new friend left. He had grown fond of her in the short time they traveled together. It was fascinating spending time with someone so different. To honor their mutual respect and similarities, he said a prayer for her under the plane tree—wishing her a safe journey.

Then he fell asleep.

His body had been badly mistreated, and he had taken both shifts the night before last. He slept for over a day, waking up the next morning with a pounding headache. He checked his watch. He had slept for twenty-six hours. A result of dehydration, loss of blood, and interdimensional travel.

*Thomas, get off your behind.*

*Your horse needs to be cared for, and you need water.*

*You're only weak, injured, trapped in a strange realm, and smell like a donkey.*

He groaned as he crawled out of the tent and stumbled to his feet, looking around for signs of trouble.

*I can't keep talking to myself. It's not normal.*

"How long do you think we should stay here, Ed?" he asked the horse.

The horse didn't respond, but that was fine. Rob never responded either. Thomas actually preferred it that way.

He walked to the tree and sat on a protruding root, using the trunk as a backrest. Then he took a slow breath.

His thigh still ached. It was a dull, persistent throb beneath the bandages, but the worst of the bleeding had stopped. Kallianeira had been gone for over a day. He was alone now, save for the occasional stamp of his horse just beyond the roots, and the hush of rain tapping on the leaves overhead.

Suddenly, he realized how much he'd taken for granted in his world. If she had a cell phone, they could text, and he would know where she was. Or she could be dead on the road, and he might never know.

*Okay, Thomas, stop that line of thought right now.*

*She would smack you so hard, your grandkids would feel it if she knew you thought she could die.*

He cleaned and bandaged the wounded leg. It was looking and feeling better, but not healed. He knew he needed to take it easy.

*Time to get to work.*

Thomas fetched water for himself and the horse, built a small fire, and prepared for a nice breakfast of jerky and hardtack. The Amazons had given him some. The jerky was good. The hardtack was not.

He reloaded his weapons, charged his batteries, inspected his gear, and then checked his watch. It had been an hour. He only needed to wait several more days.

He sat down, took a deep breath, and blew through his lips until they flapped. Ed looked at him.

"Well, Ed, I should have put a video game on the phone."

After weeks of non-stop action, just sitting was getting in his head. It was filling him with doubts and fears. He couldn't take any more.

He stood up.

He moved slowly, one hand trailing across the damp bark of the plane tree as he stepped past its outlying roots. The rain had softened to a mist now, clinging to his skin and hair like breath. Each step sent a muted ache through his injured leg, but staying still felt worse. At least this gave him something to do. Something to see.

The land sloped downward beyond the tree's shelter, revealing more of the forest's edge. A layer of fog drifted over the ground, veiling everything in a soft, eerie glow. The trees here were older than anything he'd known back home, their trunks gnarled and silvered, branches heavy with moss and time. The air smelled of wet stone and soil, heavy and rich.

And then, off through a narrow break in the trees, just where the land fell into a wide ravine—he saw it.

Across the valley, partially veiled by drifting rainclouds, rose a structure so vast it looked like it had been carved from the mountain itself. Columns the size of redwoods ringed a great open platform, each one cracked by centuries, but still upright. The stone was weathered with age, but beautiful. It was shades of white and bone, with darkness nestled in the folds of the pillars.

A massive statue stood at the temple's heart. It was impossible to tell the full height at this distance, but the scale was staggering. A figure, a powerful woman, was seated upon a throne carved with lions, her arms outstretched, and her palms turned skyward as though she were holding an invisible burden. Her face was lost to shadows from this vantage point, but her silhouette remained regal. Timeless. Watching.

Thomas narrowed his eyes, the wind catching his shirt. From here, the temple looked utterly inaccessible. The cliffs below it were steep and overgrown, and the surrounding hills offered no easy path. It might have taken a week to reach it. Maybe more.

And yet, someone had actually built it. Once, people had come here. Worshipped. Sang. Died.

It gave him a sense of peace. He may be stuck right now, but he was witnessing something that very few people from Earth would ever see. Another world. Art. Beauty. There it was: history and mystery towering in the distance. He smiled as he took in the scene, and the rain fell softly around him.

He leaned against the crooked tree and exhaled, his voice barely louder than the wind.

"Nice view, though, isn't it, Ed?"

His horse answered with a snort somewhere behind him, uninterested.

Thomas looked back at the horse. "Seen it before?"

He looked back again at the temple, lost in how big a project it would have been. It was a testament to time and skill. He stayed there a while longer, silent, watching the clouds drift across the temple's crown like even nature was admiring the view. Maybe healing here for a couple of days wouldn't be so bad after all.

And like any proper modern person, he pulled out his phone and took a picture. He enjoyed his evening, had his dinner, and went to sleep, but this time, he was more content.

Another day passed. He was feeling better but not healed, just less miserable. He handled the morning chores: rewrapped his leg, took care of Ed, made breakfast, and boiled water.

The rain had stopped, and he walked out from under the tree's protection. He wanted to bask in the warmth of the sun. It was nice to feel the heat after being wet for two days. He closed his eyes, stretched his arms, and let the rays soak into his skin.

Snap

His eyes popped open, but he didn't move. He listened. A small movement of brush, off to his right.

He knew something was there. It wasn't Kallianeira. She would have announced herself. The remaining options weren't as pleasant. He turned his head, locking eyes on the brush where the sound had escaped. Suddenly, it occurred to him that the tree's protection probably didn't cover the place where he was standing.

He wondered if it was a coincidence or if they had been waiting for him to step out.

He held his arms out, not in a gesture of friendship, but confidence, and said, "Come join me."

A group slowly stood and walked through the brush. He recognized a satyr and a human male, but the other creatures were new.

The satyr towered over Thomas. One horn was snapped, leaving a jagged edge that mirrored the long scar running down that side of his face. It twisted his lip into a permanent sneer—like he was always silently chuckling at some murderous joke only he understood. His robes matched the deep red of the one Thomas had encountered in his house, but this one carried a sword, not a dagger.

Two women with golden hair walked forward on either side of the human male. Their hair was not a dull glint of metal, but the warm, soft look of strands of silk flowing over their shoulders. It was long, loose, and tumbled down their backs to their waist. When they moved, it caught the light in shifting waves, a radiant halo that made it hard to look away.

Their faces were flawless. They had high cheekbones, smooth skin kissed by some unnatural glow. Their mouths curved into knowing smiles. Kind. Disarming. But it was their eyes that showed they weren't human. They were large and slanted, their pupils drawn into vertical slits, like those of a predator. They smiled, but the smile didn't touch their eyes. They watched the world intently—waiting for it to flinch.

They were possibly the most beautiful women Thomas had ever seen. They were pure evil.

But despite the appearance of the other creatures, the strangest one was the human. He was a little shorter than Thomas, with long blonde hair and a scruffy appearance. But it was the clothes that stood out. He wore a t-shirt, blue jeans, and work boots, and he had a gun on his hip.

Thomas had his handgun, but the rifle and shotgun were under the tree. He calmly faced the group of approaching creatures. They weren't coming fast, but they were coming with purpose. They were enjoying the anticipation, the slow walk of a predator stalking prey.

He didn't think he could shoot them all before they got to him.

"I've been waiting for you," Thomas said, stretching out his hands in welcome. "The Amazon managed to injure me before escaping, but we can still complete our plan."

That made them pause. The human responded, "You aren't one of my people. How did you get here?"

Thomas smiled, raised his hands in the gesture Ometheon had made in the memory fragment, and said, "With blood. I slit her stomach and covered myself in her life's essence so I could force the Path of Blood to open for me. Why? Don't you know how to get here?"

He locked eyes with the human. "Don't you know how to dance on the stage? Don't you know? Don't you know?" He poked himself in the temple each time he said the word know.

"You don't know how to dance." Thomas pointed accusingly. The other creatures turned their heads toward their old human.

Thomas became animated, and with each word, he jabbed his finger in the air at the other human. "You. Don't. Know. How. To. Dance."

He snapped his head to the satyr and said, "He doesn't know

how to dance!"

The satyr's mouth dropped open—part grin, part shock. He hunched forward. "He doesn't know how to dance?"

The two beautiful women were slowly changing. Their mouths were stretching open farther than should be possible, like a snake unhinging its jaw. Their fingers lengthened into talons. Growing. Sharpening. Their golden hair turned stringy and black. They looked like they'd crawled out of a swamp, dripping with rot and decay. From their mouths came a hiss, but beneath it, a high-pitched whine. Barely perceptible, but it could be felt. It built pressure on his ears. He fought the urge to yawn.

The human placed his hand on his gun but knew better than to pull it out. "I can dance. I know how to dance," he said desperately.

Thomas responded, "No! I am the one who knows how to dance. I came to dance with Thaleia. I need to find the one that can deliver her to me, or me to her." He leaned in, eyes as wide as he could make them. His tone dropped—from manic shouting to a harsh whisper. "The one past the Wailing Trees where the gods forgot their names. Do you know her name? Or are you an imposter?"

The satyr was becoming animated with excitement, bouncing from hoof to hoof and watching his old human for his response. "Do you know her name? Do you know her name?"

The human said, "There is no name. You don't know the name."

Thomas looked him in the eye and said, "Isadora." He then opened his arms out as though encompassing the whole strange party and said, "Teach the imposter to dance."

The creatures fell upon the human as one, ripping, biting, and tearing him into pieces as his scream turned into a gurgle.

Thomas laughed madly, clapping his hands. The satyr danced and hummed. The women were now cats, feasting on their lunch.

The satyr suddenly stopped and pointed at the horse, his bloodlust rising. "We can dance with the horse."

"No," Thomas responded. "That horse is Ed. Well, she is Ed to me because we are friends. Others need to call her Mr. Ed until they get to know her better."

The satyr laughed and clapped, then abruptly stopped. He

looked into Thomas's eyes, panting. "Your song tastes like copper in my mouth."

He responded, "Yes, but I want to sing with Thaleia. I want her to dance to my song. I want her to know my words." He gestured at the scene before them. "This is a comedy, but I want my words to create a tragedy. I must find Isadora and travel to Thaleia. Where is my guide?"

There was a long moment of silence while they stared at each other. Weighing. Thomas wanted to grab his gun, but he held the stare.

The satyr responded by pointing to the temple in the distance. "Go toward the temple until you find the pit. Look to the sun until you stand in water. That is where the fury lives."

Thomas nodded. "I will sing to Thaleia, but you must stop the Amazon woman. She will warn Thaleia, and I can't catch her in time. The stage is set, but she could ruin the play."

The satyr grinned and took off in the direction Kallianeira had gone. The two cats were now dog-like creatures with long legs. They bolted after the satyr.

Thomas knew they couldn't catch her. She had too much of a head start, but this tactic kept him alive and got rid of them.

Once they were out of sight, he breathed out deeply, his heart pounding.

"Alright, Ed, injury or not, it's time to go."

# CHAPTER 25
## *Reminds Me of Home*

Thomas moved quickly, just in case they changed their minds and came back. The satyrs were brutes, but those new things didn't just promise death—they promised teeth, claws, and nightmares. They were some kind of shapeshifter that his engineer brain was having trouble processing. Even after everything else he had seen, shapeshifting was just wrong.

He crouched beside the cultist's body, careful not to step in the pooled blood. Most of the man's armor was shredded, and whatever dignity he'd had was scattered across the clearing in strips, dark with blood, and some other black ichor that smelled like old oil.

He pulled the backpack, sticky with blood, off the pieces of cultist. One strap was torn, and several of the pockets were ripped open. It was unusable but might have treasures inside.

He found something heavy strapped in a side pouch. He unsnapped the straps and pulled out a long, narrow oilcloth bag, sealed tight and streaked with mud. He carefully unwrapped it, revealing a .45-70 lever-action brush gun with a short barrel. The steel was clean and well-maintained, the deep blue finish still gleaming faintly despite weeks of hard travel. He worked the lever. The action clicked cleanly. He counted five rounds nestled in the tubular magazine beneath the barrel and another seven in the sling.

At the man's hip hung a heavy-frame revolver. A Smith & Wesson Model 629, chambered in .44 Magnum—it was Dirty Harry's caliber. Six rounds loaded, ready for close quarters, and a pouch with twenty-three extra rounds. The revolver's finish was scratched but well cared for. The grip was a smooth walnut.

Beneath the revolver, tucked into a leather sheath, was a sturdy fixed-blade knife. Its blade was scratched from hard use, but sharp, the kind of tool made for survival and combat alike. A folding knife peeked out of the cultist's cargo pants pocket, its utility clear.

Nestled in a side pouch was a small first-aid kit, its contents modest: bandages, antiseptic wipes, and a few painkillers. A compact flashlight with spare batteries lay nearby, alongside a multi-tool and a coil of paracord. A hard metal case held three cigars and a cigar punch inside. The kind of thing a military person might carry to celebrate the end of a successful mission.

In a small food storage bag, he found packs of instant coffee.
*Coffee! Why didn't I think of coffee?*
*Freakin' jackpot.*

In a pocket, Thomas found a folded map and a broken compass, the paper creased and marked with faint, careful annotations. A small, battered notebook lay beside them, filled with coded notes and cryptic scribbles.

Thomas packed up his camp and stowed his new gear in his pack, except the magnum. He wore that on his hip.

"Well, Ed, we are cowboys now. We both need to look for proper hats."

He wrote a note for Kallianeira, tucked it into a crevasse in the tree, and paused with his hand on the bark. "Safe travels, friend." And with that, he carefully climbed onto his horse.

Thomas guided Ed with a gentle hand, his other resting near the rifle slung across his chest. The ground under hoof was soft from recent rain, and the brush crowded close to the narrow game trail they followed. Every snapping twig or shift of leaves made him tighten his grip. He didn't speak. The forest felt like it was listening.

His injured leg ached with every bounce, so he leaned slightly to one side in the saddle, teeth clenched against the pain. The pack on his back jostled with every step Ed took, and he could hear the faint rattle of the rifle shells he'd scavenged. The satyr and his dogs were long gone, but paranoia clung to him like a wet cloth.

As the trees thinned and the dirt gave way to crushed gravel, a road came into view. It was ancient stonework, cracked by time but still solid. He pulled Ed to a slow stop at the edge of the brush, peering down its length in both directions. Empty.

Thomas let out a slow breath and muttered, "Alright, Ed, we have to go say hi to something named a Fury. It's kind of ominous, and I'm injured. You'll have to do the fighting."

Then he gave a light nudge, and together they rode out of the trees and onto the forgotten road, careful but committed.

The road wound through the hills like a serpent. It reminded him of some of the roads back home in the hills. They too felt unnecessarily winding and doubled back too often. This road, however, was half-swallowed by roots and creeping vines. Thomas rode slowly, letting Ed pick his footing while he kept his eyes on the tree line. The sun had dipped low, casting long shadows across the moss-covered stones. It wasn't dark yet, but the light was dying, and he knew he didn't want to be caught in the dark unprepared.

Another mile passed before the forest thinned near a bend in the road. Just off the path, half-hidden by overgrowth, stood the skeleton of a building. The stone walls were blackened by fire, its roof long since collapsed. Charred timbers lay scattered, broken. It might have been a farmhouse once, maybe a watch post. Now it was little more than a hollow memory.

Thomas dismounted with a grunt and limped toward the burned-out husk, leading Ed by the reins. The air smelled faintly of ash and damp stone. Vines crawled through the gaps in the walls, but there was shelter to be had. One corner still stood firm, roofed by a half-tilted slab of stone. It was just enough to keep the rain off, if it rained, just enough to not feel like prey in the open.

He brought Ed with him and tied her to a broken timber. He knelt down in the ashes, brushed away some scorched leaves, and set his pack down. The silence here was heavy. No birds, no insects. Just the creak of the wind through the broken frame and the occasional snort of his horse.

*Rubble sweet rubble, eh Thomas?*

He didn't build a fire. He didn't want to draw attention. But he did gather a few leaves and twigs, just in case. He didn't bother with a tent either. He wanted to be able to move fast if he had to do so. He just tossed his sleeping bag on the ground and checked his bandages.

*It's nice to have new supplies from the other Earthling.*

*Earthling? Has my life become that odd?*

He settled into his bag and went to sleep.

He dreamed of his grandfather. It was an old memory from his childhood in the Appalachian Mountains. He was always told the mountains were ancient, the oldest in the world, and that the hills hid secrets older than man. His grandfather passed down the stories of their Shawnee ancestors. Creatures walked the woods at night and deserved respect.

His grandfather's stories told of dangerous voices in the woods. If you hear a woman crying, laughing, or screaming—don't answer. Don't go outside. He always locked the door at night and wouldn't step outside without a gun after dark.

The stories from his area never said what it was in the woods. It was never said to be evil necessarily, just as a wolf or a waterfall isn't evil, but either one can kill you. It was just a force of nature that would take you in a second if you followed it into the woods.

As a child, he believed in the stories. He even thought he heard a woman's voice calling him once. He pulled the blanket over his head and waited for daylight. He was scared, but his grandpa was close by, and he knew nothing would get past him. His grandpa was a powerful man. Nothing scared him, except those voices. As Thomas got older, he dismissed his grandfather's stories as the superstitions of hill folk, but as a kid, he was all in. He didn't go into the woods at night.

He was dreaming of that moment, that memory. He heard the laughter, the giggling voices in the woods outside.

Thomas's eyes snapped open, heart pounding. The voices were here. That must be why he dreamed it. His subconscious remembered the story when he heard the sound. It pulled the memory back to him while he slept, but now he was awake—and the sounds were real.

There was a woman giggling in the woods outside the burned-out hovel where he was currently sheltered. Thomas pulled his new hand cannon and watched the darkness. He saw two faint pinpoints of light. He watched them—they blinked and giggled. A few minutes later, someone on the other side of the wall behind him let out a shrill scream.

Ed was not pleased. She began neighing and pulling against her reins. Thomas lit the fire and wished he would have gathered more twigs. Drawing attention didn't matter now. He was surrounded.

He put on his headlamp, but didn't activate it. He didn't know if it would anger them or scare them. As long as they stayed back, he didn't want to find out.

He stood by Ed, comforting her. Yes, Ed was a her, but Thomas didn't know any girl horse names.

*I'm sorry, Grandpa. Assuming you can hear me up there.*

*I believe you now.*

He spent the night watching the pinpoints of light come and go, but at least they didn't come close to the fire.

# CHAPTER 26
### *Forgotten Gods*

Thomas was thankful to see the horizon beginning to lighten. It had been a rough night. He stood watch for hours, leaning against the wall with a gun in hand, tending the fire. He worked to keep a balance between enough light to keep them away and enough fuel to last the night. All while trying to keep Ed calm.

He had favored his injured leg by leaning on the good one. One leg was tired, the other sore. His back ached, and he was sleepy. Now it was time to travel.

He considered trying to go back to the tree where he and Kallianeira had spent the night. She said it would keep the spirits at bay. Perhaps these were the spirits she had meant. But the cult knew he had been there, and they might come back. He would watch for another big plane tree and hope it was protected, but he knew that going back wouldn't help his mission.

He holstered his gun, his fingers stiff from holding it for hours. He flexed them to get the blood flowing, then rolled up his sleeping bag and strapped it to his pack.

Before leaving, he took a moment to walk around the burned-out hovel, looking for signs of what had been out there the night before. He wasn't a tracker, but he thought he would see something in the grass. He didn't. There was no trace, and he didn't want to waste any more time before leaving this area.

He crawled up on Ed and got a head rush from the exertion. He knew he was too injured for travel, but staying still would kill him. He survived one night here, but another night would be suicide.

He and Ed started walking back along the path toward the temple in the distance. That was when Thomas suddenly noticed the trees. There had been trees along his route the whole time, but they were scattered or back from the path. Now, he was deep in the woods, and they looked like home—his grandpa's land. It was a deep, dark forest… with creatures that wail at night.

*Thanks for the warning about the Wailing Trees, satyr—jerk.*

*Then again, I did set him on fire afterwards.*

*Anyway, it looks like I am on the right track.*

Thomas continued his journey to Isadora. Before this, he was concerned he wouldn't be able to find her. Now, he was concerned he would. But he just didn't feel he had a reasonable alternative. Life was becoming less about fear and more about certainty. There was danger in every direction, but at least this direction had purpose. He pressed on.

The trees thinned, and he welcomed the sunlight and warmth. He stopped and took a moment to check his bandage and have breakfast. He grabbed a few twigs and started a fire. He filled his metal cup with water and set it next to the fire to warm. Then he looked at his leg. It was getting better. The edges were no longer as red, and the flesh was much less sensitive. Now it was just a horrible, painful wound. It was progress.

He cleaned it, applied ointment, and dressed it with a new bandage. He pulled out a Clif bar and dumped the instant coffee into his cup of boiling water.

He held the cup by its handle. His free hand was close to the cup, but not quite touching it. It was too hot to touch directly, but he could feel the warmth. The smell rose up like a memory of comfort. It spoke of mornings that weren't haunted by fear or cold. The bitterness hit his tongue and spread warmth through his chest. It was weak, grainy, and far from fresh, but it was perfect.

He enjoyed that coffee and Clif bar. He warmed up. Ed had breakfast but turned down the coffee. Life was almost good again.

It was a bad night, but a good morning.

He pressed on. He traveled along the road past an open field, with trees in the distance to either side. He watched the tall grass, looking for movement. He was tired of being surprised, and he didn't want some kind of angry half-sheep, half-rabbit with fangs, or whatever other monstrosity this place had to offer, jumping up out of nowhere.

Then he noticed that some of the stones to his left weren't actually stones. They were statues. He stopped to take a closer look at one of the bigger ones.

It had once been a man, or at least resembled one. He was tall and proud, his head crowned in laurels. The face was broken, jagged, as though it had cracked and snapped off. The name at its base was unreadable.  It looked crumbled, whether from age or intent was uncertain.

Thomas swept his gaze over the tall grass.

Dozens of them. Maybe more. Scattered through the field like the last memories of a forgotten pantheon. Some stood proud but broken, arms missing, and torsos cracked. Others lay in pieces, shattered and half-sunken into the earth like it was trying to reclaim them.

He rode past a toppled woman's form, robes frozen in mid-billow, one stone hand raised in what might have once been kindness. Her face was missing. Cleanly sheared away, leaving only a hollow curve where identity should live.

He stopped.

*"Past the gods that forgot their names."*

He double-checked his AR-15, making sure it had a full magazine and one in the chamber. He already knew it did. Maybe it was a leftover from gun safety lessons his grandfather taught. Never assume you know the state of your gun; always check. Or maybe last night put a fear that traveled all the way to his bones, and he wanted to make sure he was ready. The satyr he questioned wasn't an ally. He was helping because he wanted to cause trouble for Olympus, but he might also enjoy causing trouble for Thomas.

He could picture that satyr laughing his horns off at Thomas, standing all night with a gun in hand, while the wailing echoed through the trees. So, what else was in store?

He pressed forward, passing the stone remains of a forgotten time.

Far at the edge, he spotted a wide basin carved from obsidian, black volcanic glass. A place of worship, perhaps, or a reflecting pool long dried up. Moss crawled across its sides. At the center stood one last statue, larger than the rest.

Unlike the others, it hadn't toppled. It had been disfigured.

The statue stood tall, a figure of once-imposing grace now worn by time and desecration. Her body was still intact. Her cloak was carved in sweeping folds of weathered marble. The breastplate bore the faint outline of the aegis, where the ghost of a Gorgon's face lingered in eroded relief. Her spear was broken at the shaft, and a cracked owl perched on her arm.

Around her feet, wildflowers grew in the cracks, and vines had begun to climb her legs as if the earth was slowly taking back its stone.

But her face wasn't just cracked or broken off. It was scratched and slashed. There were deep gouges forced into the face and breasts. It was intentional, personal.

Thomas stood before it, one hand on the reins, the other on the handgrip of his gun.

*"There, you'll find a shrine that once bore her mother's crest—but it cracked in silence."*

*This is where he said Isadora would be found. The place where the fury was sitting around, being all furious and stuff.*

He looked past the statue, following the path of the road, as it stretched forward, its worn stones slick with moss and mud, thinning as the earth softened beneath them. On either side, the air grew heavy with moisture, and tall reeds swayed gently, their slender stems bending over pools of dark, still water. Willow trees lined the edges, their long, leafy branches dipping low, brushing the surface, sending small ripples through the still water.

*"Look to the sun until you find water."*

He was there.

He urged Ed forward towards the marsh. Ed was a strong horse of the Amazon women, but she did not like this. As Thomas approached the swamp, she began to stomp and sidestep. She let out a distressed squeal and started to back up.

Thomas subtly steered Ed to turn sideways to the swamp. He made it look like it was the horse showing discomfort, but it was so he could point his weapon at the water without looking threatening. He flipped the safety off but kept his finger off the trigger.

He calmly said her name. "Isadora."

There was no response. He looked at the swamp, the grass, the trees, but he didn't see anyone. However, it was obvious that someone or something was there. Ed continued to complain and whinny.

"It's okay, Ed," muttered Thomas, patting her neck.

"Isadora, I am Thomas. I seek to make Thaleia, the daughter of Athena, answer for her actions against me and the people of my realm. I was told to visit you by a satyr that wants me to disrupt the comfort of the beings on Olympus. I need a guide to help me reach her."

The wind shifted, and the leaves and grass fluttered as if agitated—or excited. He had Isadora's attention.

# CHAPTER 27
## *Interview With a Fury*

There was no cry, no warning. Just a heavy, wet thud, flesh meeting earth, and a splash that hissed through the quiet. He didn't see where she had been, but Ed knew. Her black wings were outstretched at her sides, whether in threat or embrace, he was unsure. Her bare feet sank beneath the calf-deep mire at the swamp's edge, the mud parting before her will.

Ripples spilled outward in widening circles, soft and slow, despite her hard landing, as though the water itself obeyed her.

She stood motionless, completely naked, for a long, dragging breath.

Then, with the jagged elegance of a puppet half-remembering its strings, she raised her hands. Poised like a cat about to strike. Fingers bent like claws. Thin, tense, crooked with the promise of violence. Her arms remained aloft, frozen in that moment before the pounce, held high by an invisible tension. Not trembling. Not waiting.

Anticipating.

Her hair, long, wild, hung down in thick strands, wet with swamp water. It clung to her face like a veil of night. Behind it, her mouth was already open. It wasn't natural. It stretched past the edges of familiarity, grinning without motion, without breath, like a Jack-O-Lantern, exaggerated beyond human. Her teeth were wrong. There were too many. They were too sharp. Her smile wasn't happy. It was the fixed shape of hunger made still.

Her eyes were wide, black. They didn't look directly at him. They gazed at a spot on the ground between them, just before him. Somehow it was worse that she looked just before him instead of at him.

They didn't blink.

Her face was frozen, like a mask. Eyes, unshifting. No breath escaped her. Her hair itself, unmoving—she approached.

The water curled like fingers around her ankles. She moved effortlessly, slowly, but was unstoppable. The water moved before her almost without sound.

Her limbs flowed with a rhythmic sway, hips rolling too fluidly, back arching too far. But her head… it did not move.

It stayed locked in place, staring. Her hands didn't waver, still outstretched in their clawed gesture, still held in that moment before the trap springs. Her eyes stayed fixed—unblinking, unchanging—as her body moved beneath them, shifting, swaying like a snake, unnatural and smooth.

Thomas had once seen a cute video of an owl on someone's finger. As they moved their hand up, down, left, or right, the owl's head never moved. It was cute at the time. This wasn't.

As she continued forward, her foot must have stepped on something beneath the surface. Her leg didn't straighten all the way to compensate. That knee simply stayed partly bent to avoid moving her head or hands. The slow, perfect movement forward was hypnotic. She almost seemed to be different bodies, somehow moving together.

She did not speak.

She did not acknowledge his presence as her feet touched dry ground. She continued until she was just feet away. Her gaze was still slightly lowered as her head had never adjusted. She stopped, no breath, no sound. She waited.

*This is a test, Thomas. No fear.*

*I just wish she would look up so I could read her eyes.*

Thomas waited too. He had said his piece. It was her turn to speak or attack.

A moment passed. Ed tried to move, drawing a brief glance from Thomas. But when his eyes returned to Isadora, she was looking at him—her mouth still open, claws still poised, eyes as black as night and unreadable.

Thomas no longer wanted to read her eyes.

She tilted her head. For the first time, he saw it move.

She locked her eyes with his and asked, "Do you have the strength to kill a god or will you be my food, Thomas?"

"I'm certainly willing to try. But more than that, I plan to make her answer, not just for what she did, but why she did it. The powerful aren't above judgment. She acted without honor. She discarded the code of any noble being for her own selfish quest and chance for valor. She will tell me why, or I will make her."

The thing's smile got bigger, even less human. Whether excitement at punishing Thaleia and Athena, or at dinner, Thomas couldn't tell. She tilted her head slowly—too far, past what any human neck could allow, as she said, "Do you have that power, Thomas?"

He shifted in the saddle. His movements were slow. Not fear. Precision. One hand kept the reins loose as the other reached back over his shoulder to the .45-70 lever-action brush gun he'd taken off the cultist. He could have used a different gun, but this had to send a message. His life depended on it.

The rifle came free with a dry, heavy sound. It was wood and blued steel, ready to be useful. It was too thick to be elegant, too short to be ceremonial. The kind of weapon built to kill something, no matter how big.

He levered a round into the chamber—*click-clack*—and the sound echoed over the swamp.

Isadora's head didn't move. But her body had stopped that hypnotic sway. She was utterly still now, watching. Listening. Deciding.

Thomas didn't look at her. His horse stirred beneath him, sensing the moment. He gave it a small nudge with his heel, pivoting in place, and sighted the idol standing crooked at the water's edge. A weathered statue of some long-forgotten demigod. Moss-covered, but still intact. Still whole.

The .45-70 barked like thunder.

A single, staggering crack that made the trees flinch.

Stone exploded. A hole opened in the statue's chest, like a heart torn free. Dust and fragments peppered the stillness of the swamp. The sound echoed in a place of silence. This area was claimed by the fury. There were no birds, no insects. No life. His horse danced beneath him but didn't bolt. Thomas kept her steady with one hand, calm as breath.

He worked the lever again—*click-clack*—and fired a second shot.

This time, the statue split down the middle. A deep fracture ran from shoulder to hip, and the upper half listed sideways, then collapsed into the water with a slow-motion splash. The ripples crawled toward her feet and died there, as if they too knew not to touch her.

He lowered the rifle across the saddle horn, still watching the ruined statue.

He looked down at her and replied, "My chances are better than most."

She straightened. Her grin softened, lips closing around teeth that no longer seemed unnatural. Her eyes, once all black, shifted. The whites appeared slowly, like a cat's pupils dilating in reverse.

She lifted her arms, ran her fingers through her hair, pulled it out of her face, then let it fall over her shoulders and down her back. Her wings slipped down and around her body. Sections from the tops of her wings draped over her shoulders while one wing tucked under the other, wrapping around her body. She shimmied as they tightened, shaping her wings into a loose, pleated toga.

Suddenly, she was one of the most beautiful women Thomas had ever seen. The transformation didn't seem to involve shape-shifting or magic, just applying a different tone with what was already there.

She stepped close, rested her head lightly on his thigh, and traced a single finger along the arm holding the reins. It was like a high-school girlfriend flirting with her quarterback boyfriend before the big game.

She looked up at him, smiled, and said, "How can I help?"

# CHAPTER 28
## *Where It Hurts*

Thomas replied, "At the moment, she is beyond my reach. I come from another realm. I traveled here through the Path of Blood. I must find a way to reach her before I can accuse her."

"Oh, I can get you close," Isadora said lightly. "But I can't go into Olympus. They don't like me."

She looked up at him and rested her chin gently on his thigh—Thomas flinched. Not much, just a twitch.

Her eyes darkened immediately, turning into bottomless black pits. Her fingers tensed around his leg.

Through forced calm, Thomas said, "Oh, sorry—a satyr sliced my leg open right there. I'm still healing."

Then he added with a grin, "It's okay. I set him on fire."

He placed his hand on hers, gently, non-threateningly.

*Do not scorn this woman, Thomas.*

*Don't lead her on either... because it might work.*

She studied him a moment longer, then eased her grip.

"I'll have to be gentle," she said, slowly running her tongue along her upper lip.

Thomas smiled, unsure how to handle this new development, but he decided that hate might work.

"Unfortunately, someone is running ahead to warn Thaleia that I'm coming."

Her eyes didn't go black this time. She gave an unmistakable human look of annoyance. It was progress.

Thomas continued, "When I came through the Path of Blood, a battle was already underway. An Amazon scout went ahead of me. I do not know what she'll tell Thaleia."

Isadora's smile returned, lighter again.

"Thaleia is arrogant. She won't run from you. She will want to see you for herself." Her eyes traced him now—not like a threat, but like a possibility. "You seem powerful… for a mortal."

She tilted her head, watching him with that slow, deliberate curiosity of a cat circling a birdcage.

"Are you mortal," she purred, "… or something else?"

Thomas held her gaze. "I am mortal. But I am powerful. And I intend to make her answer for what she did. This isn't just about violence. I want her to admit her shame. There needs to be an accounting."

She began to sway as she slid a hand across his stomach, fingertips tracing slow lines.

"I want to watch," she said. "I want Athena to see what a failure her daughter has become. Not just that she can die. Not just that she can lose. But that she failed. Failed in her nobility. In her code. Just like her mother did."

She gasped, delighted.

"Can you kill a god, Thomas? Could you kill Athena herself?"

Isadora wandered a few steps, graceful and childlike, spinning in a circle.

"I don't know," he admitted. "But I can make stronger weapons than the one I showed you." He paused. "Will Athena try to stop me?"

Isadora snapped, trembling with rage, "Athena is an arrogant fool. The goddess of *stupidity*! Who knows what she will do? I thought I knew, but I was wrong!"

Thomas watched her carefully, unmoving in the saddle. He let the moment stretch—long enough for her words to land, and her anger to breathe.

Then he said, "So, she's clever instead of noble. Thaleia was clever instead of noble, too. Maybe she learned it from her mother."

He paused again, but this time, just enough for her to look back at him.

"Did Athena hurt you the way Thaleia hurt me?"

Isadora walked toward him quickly, her face twisted in anger, but still the face of a woman, not a creature.

"You want my secrets?" she snapped.

"Only if you want to give them," Thomas said. "We're allies. Maybe we'll be friends. If someone hurt you, then it matters to me."

His voice didn't rise. It didn't need to. "I want to make Thaleia answer for her sins. If Athena has sins of her own, I understand why you'd want her to answer, too."

She smiled. "I like you, Thomas. We're going to kill them all."

Isadora spun like a dancer in an evening gown, but instead of fabric flaring, her wings unfurled, black and vast, revealing her body before rewrapping around her with perfect precision. The motion was fluid, beautiful even—if she were not so utterly terrifying.

*Close call, Thomas.*

*You're cuddling with a polar bear and hoping for the best.*

*Don't make promises. Don't show fear.*

*Definitely don't meet her family.*

Thomas chuckled, pretending to be at ease. "We have to get there first. Then, we can talk about justice. If Athena and Thaleia have acted like cowards before, they might again. How do we reach them?"

"We will have to travel quickly." She winked, unfurled her wings, and launched into the sky with a rush of wind.

Ed neighed in protest to the sudden movement, fidgeting sideways. Thomas patted Ed's neck. "Easy, girl."

He turned Ed to follow Isadora, but she soared out over the swamp. He watched her fly farther away and weakly said, "Ed isn't a boat."

Although he needed her help, Thomas gave a sigh of relief. He hadn't realized his chest was so tight. He felt like every muscle had been braced in defense, like a man preparing for a punch.

He debated his options. His first option: leave, hopefully get past the Wailing Trees before nightfall, and find a safe place to sleep. Then, possibly return to the sacred tree and wait for Kallianeira to come back. She might not even come back, though. Her sisters were at war. They needed her.

The other option: wait for the winged terror to return. At that point, she might ask him why he didn't have Ed fly after her. One other point to consider is that if he tries to leave before she returns, she might take offense. She seemed to think of him as a new friend… or toy. She might break her toys when she gets mad.

"It looks like you're having lunch, Ed."

Thomas steered Ed over to some especially delicious-looking grass and looped the reins around a statue. Then he lay down in the middle of the path, pulled out his ball cap, and placed it over his face like a cowboy in a western. He didn't sleep much last night, so he was just going to rest his eyes for a minute.

*Thump.*

Thomas felt the jolt in the earth beneath him. His eyes snapped open. He had fallen asleep, but only for a few minutes.

He heard Isadora's voice: "Aww, you are probably tired because of your leg. I'm going to help."

He reached up and moved the hat to see her looking down at him. He held it at an angle to shield his eyes and said, "Welcome back. I wondered where you went."

She rolled her eyes, shook her head, and let out a small giggle. "How silly of me. I wasn't even thinking about that. I haven't had a friend visit me in so long that I forgot my manners. I was getting Lethebloom. It is a plant that grows along the Lethe River. I used to sit there and look at the river when I lived there. I loved the Lethebloom. It's so beautiful. So fragile." Her words drifted off in silence. She was lost in her memories. Thinking of better times.

Then her fingers tightened, her voice went to a deeper, angrier tone. Something primordial. Unnatural.

"But then I was cast out! My home was taken, and I was told that I was a failure. I was sent to the world to live without friends. I lost my home."

She clenched her fists and leaned forward, looking off toward Olympus as a low, guttural scream clawed its way up from deep in her throat—rising into a shrill caterwaul.

Thomas remembered something from high school about the Lethe River. It was a river that made people forget. He could tell she was losing control again, and he wanted to redirect her.

"Lethe River? That is the river that causes people to forget, if I remember correctly. You took something from the Lethe River to help you remember your home?"

She looked down at him. Her eyes were slightly shifted past human toward the creature she appeared to be when he first saw her. Dark and angry. Then she burst out laughing as they returned to normal. "Yes, I took something from the river of forgetting to remember." She started laughing harder and wrapped her wings around her body.

"We need to leave in the morning. If we leave now, we will have to deal with the Dendralyktis tonight." She motioned for him to follow her as she continued talking, "They giggle like idiots when someone is in their woods after dark. They don't taste very good."

"Dendralyktis?" questioned Thomas. "My people call them Treewitches."

He stood, gathered his things, and hobbled after her toward a willow at the mire's edge. A small stone statue stood beside it with a basin at its base. Another forgotten god.

Isadora gestured for him to sit. "Treewitches? Do your creatures cast spells? Ours use their voices to lure people into the dark so they can eat them—or dismember them for fun. It depends on whether they are hungry."

Thomas let out a small chuckle as they sat down beneath the tree. "No, but my people aren't good with names. We have a monster called a Not-deer."

She started laughing again, gently placing her hand on his shoulder. It was a musical, lilting laugh. It was actually quite endearing.

*Whoa there, Thomas. You are starting to like her company a bit too much.*

*Do you remember the first thing she said to you? She asked if you were food.*

Thomas's heart raced; a thin layer of sweat gathered on his brow. Her company was so disconcerting that he could not tell where the line fell between new friend and dinner.

She placed the leaves from her plant in the basin of the statue. Then a single claw extended on her hand, and she pricked her skin to draw blood. Not much, she just needed a few drops. They sprinkled over the leaves.

Thomas reached over when he saw her draw blood and gently grabbed the offending hand. Her eyes snapped in his direction, but nothing else moved. She seemed uncertain about his intent, but her eyes stayed human.

"You're bleeding," he said, concerned.

Her face visibly brightened. "Just a little. My blood is immortal. It activates the Lethebloom. It will help your leg heal much more quickly. That way, we can travel faster tomorrow after the Dendralyktis go back to sleep."

"Take off your pants."

*Why are so many women saying that to me these days?*

He took off his pants, but he was wearing undergarments. Boxer briefs. The undies of champions.

He thought about covering himself further, but her open display of her body showed no fear. If he were too discreet, it might cause her to feel he was rejecting her or didn't trust her. He kept his hand cannon close by, though, just in case.

While he was stripping, she picked up a rock and ground her blood into the Lethebloom and worked it into a paste. She spread the paste on his wound and worked it into the opening.

He was determined not to show pain. He fought every urge to flinch while she worked the wound. Then it seemed to shift.

He gritted his teeth and shifted uncomfortably. "Wow, this stuff burns a bit, doesn't it?"

His breath became rapid. His hands trembled.

*Did you just fall for a trick, Thomas?*

*No, I don't think so. She could have killed you if she wanted.*

*Or maybe she is doing what Thaleia did.*

*Taking over your body with a drug or spell.*

His leg felt like it was on fire. His heart was pounding. Sweat was running down his back. He slumped back against the tree as darkness overcame his vision.

Isadora laid her head on his arm and nuzzled against his neck as she whispered, "Don't worry. I'll take care of you."

# CHAPTER 29

## *Something Sweet*

Thomas woke with a start. He was in his bed, but something startled him awake—a sound from the hallway.

Rebecca crashed through the door, slamming into the dresser. Splinters of furniture cascaded through the room as the wood was destroyed. The light from the hallway faded as it was blocked by a massive monster. Some kind of half-goat, half-man walked into the room.

———

Thomas woke with a start, heart pounding. It was a dream. It was just a dream. He was lying on his back, and he could feel Rebecca resting on his shoulder. His blanket pulled up to his chin, warm and comforting.

But he couldn't move. Why could he feel a breeze? Why could he see stars?

He wasn't in his bed…

Isadora nuzzled her nose along his cheek toward his ear and whispered, "You're awake?" She made a warm, throaty sound that started as a laugh but melted into something more intimate as she continued, "You're strong. You don't need to be strong right now. Just heal. Just sleep."

His "blanket" shifted across his body as she shifted to snuggle closer. He realized he was wrapped in her wing as he slipped back into the darkness.

———

Thomas woke when a hand was placed gently on his chest. His head pounded like he had a hangover.

Isadora was standing over him, smiling. "Greetings, my fluffy little Fury." She ran a finger through his beard. "Even your dreams are violent. You were killing things for hours."

Thomas blinked while he tried to get his head to stop spinning. He sat up and took stock of himself and his surroundings.

*One arm, two arms.*

*Two legs.*

*Five, five, five, five, one.*

*No board wedged between my ankles.*

He was not wearing pants, but that wasn't a surprise. It was midday when he passed out, but now dawn's first light peeked over the horizon.

Isadora started unwrapping his leg while continuing, "You started shivering, so I kept you warm. The Lethebloom can be powerful for mortals. Come to think of it, you might have been shivering from fever, but I held you tight either way."

She was on her knees working on his leg, but then turned and leaned close to his face while she whispered, "I think you liked it. My wings are warm, and they kept you safe."

Thomas smiled weakly. "I am having trouble remembering it, but thank you for keeping me safe. That was very nice of you."

She beamed with happiness and hugged Thomas. "We're going to have so much fun together."

She went back to his leg and finished pulling off the last of the bandages. Thomas was impressed. It wasn't healed, but it was drastically better. This was not normal healing.

*Neosporin, eat your heart out.*

"That's amazing," muttered Thomas as he reached down and felt his leg. It was still a little tender, but he could ride much harder without risking opening his leg again.

He looked up at Isadora, who was gazing at him adoringly. She reached over and used a finger to boop his nose. "Told you I would take care of you. But now we must move. The sun rises to shine its light on us, and we have a long path ahead before we reach Olympus."

He was happy to be underway. He was worried about how quickly she might shift back to predator if he shattered her play time.

He didn't want to mislead her. Truthfully, he was starting to like her. She reminded him of a cat. But she was a hurricane in a bottle: even the smallest crack would unleash something he couldn't control.

He packed his gear and mounted Ed. His leg felt much better.

Isadora stepped up to Ed and gave Thomas's leg a hug. "Ready to go?"

He responded, "I am concerned about something. If other people see you flying, they might know you are coming, and it might scare Thaleia and Athena. We should be sneaky. I think we should keep your wings hidden to keep you a secret, and I shouldn't use my strange weapons."

She crossed her arms and pushed her lower lip out. "But I like flying."

He reached down and placed his hand on her shoulder. "I agree, flying looks amazing, but I just think we should hide when we see people. If you see a town or farm, we should travel past them secretly. The rest of the time, you should fly, and I should use my abilities if we need protection."

She smiled up at him. "Okay, plus, no one should see my body except you." She unfurled her wings and stood in front of him, as though for inspection.

Thomas paused, unsure how to answer that safely. He simply replied, "The sun is up. We should start our journey—Olympus awaits."

She winked and, with a whoosh of her wings, launched into the air. She moved along the road so he could keep up.

He urged Ed forward with his knees, following her shadow.

*Hey satyr. If you can hear me DOWN there—Jerk!*

He followed the shadow for hours. She would occasionally land up ahead and wait for the horse to catch up. They finally made it back to the main road that was close to the town where Kallianeira and Thomas had stayed.

He wanted to check the tree and see if she had returned, but he knew it was too soon and needed to keep Isadora focused on moving forward. Any side projects would turn her back to affection mode instead of revenge mode. So, he pressed on.

She did a great job of avoiding notice. Whenever they neared a house or traveler, she dipped low behind the trees and re-emerged farther along the road.

A few times, she buzzed right over Thomas, which he had to admit was kind of fun. If she were actually his girlfriend, he would have thought it was fantastic and playful. As it was, he always had a small worry that she was going to grab him and fly off like a hawk with a rabbit.

It was close to dusk, and Thomas hadn't seen his guide in a while. He trudged along the road waiting for her to reappear when a barefoot woman in a leather gown stepped out of the trees, beaming with joy. "Thomas."

"Hello, Isadora," he replied with a smile.

She pointed ahead. "I waited for you because there is a town down the road. I haven't been in a town in hundreds of years. People are evil, hateful creatures that lie and steal from each other. They are so strange. Should we avoid the town?"

"I think we should stay there for the night," he replied as he offered his hand to her. She took his hand, and he pulled her up on the horse to ride with him.

"They will have food, and we can spend the night in safety. The gods hate you, and the cult is searching for me. This will also give you a chance to try different food if you like that idea."

"Ooooo," she cooed with delight, her tone high and lilting. "We can get something sweet."

"Remember, though, we have to be sneaky. No wings, none of my weapons, and we try to be noticed as little as possible. Is that okay?"

Isadora nodded. "I am just a normal mortal. I won't eat anyone, and I won't invoke justice on evil."

Thomas steered Ed toward the stable. He tossed a coin to the stable boy and helped Isadora to the ground.

As they walked into the tavern, there was a hush, and everyone looked to the newcomers. The sound of multiple sliding chairs filled the room as men moved positions to see the woman in the leather gown.

Isadora was scared. She didn't know how to act around so many people.

She wrapped her hands around Thomas's arm and pulled herself close, not meeting anyone's gaze. She whispered, "I didn't invoke justice on anyone. I promise."

He patted her hand reassuringly and leaned over to whisper back, "They are surprised at your beauty. Let's get a table in the corner."

She squeezed his arm happily because of the compliment, but still nervously.

He steered them to the corner and gestured for her to sit down before taking his own seat. As she settled, her dress shimmied back and forth. He knew people were watching and hoped they didn't notice that her dress was alive.

The tavernkeeper approached to take their order. Thomas skipped normal food and went straight to the treats.

The tavernkeeper returned with a small clay dish, warm from the hearth. Upon it rested a round cake, rustic and golden, its edges just beginning to crisp and darken. It was no showpiece, cracked slightly across the top, with a rough, hand-shaped look. But it carried the rich, comforting scent of baked grain and honey.

A thin ribbon of wildflower honey had been drizzled across it, still glistening, pooling slightly at the base. A few sesame seeds clung where the glaze had cooled, scattered like sand on a sunlit path. Steam rose gently from the cake, mingling with the tavern's earthy air of olive oil, ash, and wine.

It was simple fare, but for Thomas, it was fantastic. It was even more special for Isadora. She hadn't eaten a treat in hundreds of years.

Isadora cooed and moaned as she ate the delicious dessert, which drew more attention from the men in the tavern. Thomas knew what they were thinking and hoped these men had better manners than those at the last tavern he visited.

They passed some time sipping wine and watching the people, until Thomas suggested they go to their room. He was concerned about what she might do there, but his reason for choosing the town over the woods was the hope she would be more reserved with so many people nearby.

They entered the room. She walked over to the bed and sat down. She patted the spot next to her for him to join her.

# CHAPTER 30
## *I Was So Good*

Isadora had pushed aside the linen curtain when she stepped into the small room. The air was close and humid, carrying a faint smell of straw. A single clay lamp flickered on a low, three-legged stool beside the bed, casting long, wavering shadows across the flaking plaster walls.

She had paused to look around. She had not been in a mortal building, or any building, in hundreds of years. The bed itself was plain. A simple wooden frame with leather straps crisscrossed beneath a thin mattress, lumpy and misshapen from years of use. A coarse wool blanket was folded neatly at one end, its edges worn to threads. The floor beneath her feet was hard-packed earth, cool to the touch and uneven in places. There was nothing else in the room. There were no decorations, no ornaments, or paintings. Just the bed, the stool, and a jug of water standing in a shallow clay basin.

She decided to tell him, but she was scared. She had never told anyone before, but Thomas was so good. So noble. He wanted to fix what was broken in Olympus, in the realm of the gods. She used to be strong like him, brave like him. She had forgotten how, but he was showing her again.

At first, she thought he wanted revenge, but she listened to what he said. He kept saying he wanted to make Thaleia admit what she did. He wanted her to admit it and answer for it, but he wasn't consumed like she was. He was willing to fight, but it wasn't his first thought.

She sat on the lumpy bed. She looked at him with sad eyes, scared of facing his judgment. She patted the bed next to her.

He sat next to her. He looked nervous, but it was probably because he was so kind. He could sense her discomfort.

"You said that if someone hurt me… then it mattered to you. You asked why I was mad at Athena. You have been so good to me… I was afraid before, but now I want to tell you."

He responded, "You don't have to tell me if you aren't ready."

He was so good.

She placed her hand on his. "I want to tell you." Her voice dropped to a whisper before continuing, "I know I am scary to people. I know some call me a monster, but I used to be good." Her eyes were pleading, "I did. I was so good."

Her voice was unsteady as she continued, "I was like you. I stopped bad people because it helped good people. I tried to stop the wrong person. His name was Agrios the Red."

She turned her head slightly away from him, not to avoid him, but lost in her memory, in the past.

Agrios the Red stood over a table with his maps spread out before him. He was in his war tent. It had been in this location for two weeks while he was fighting and planning, but he was ready to move again. He looked at the possible paths to reach his goal.

One path would take him behind the enemies, a good strategic choice, but with less bloodshed. Agrios the Red was the champion of Ares; he did not avoid bloodshed.

The other path he could take would face opposition, but it would also pass by the Sophiaion, an institute of learning for young women. Nobles would send their daughters there to learn how to be proper ladies, to learn decorum and grace. Agrios let out a low growl and grinned; his men would have a good time.

He had carved a path of blood through his enemies in the name of Ares, but he went beyond bloodlust. He didn't just want battle and glory; he reveled in pain. The pain of his enemies fed him, gave him purpose.

Athena watched from above. She detested the brute, but he had purpose. She was not working with Ares, but his war would be useful for her as well. She saw the long-term implications, and Agrios was a necessary pawn to get what she wanted. Ares didn't know that, but he didn't need to know. She knew, and that was what mattered.

She watched as Agrios began to march toward the city. She smiled, knowing it would finally fall, her plan coming to fruition. The whispered strategies to Ares, the hints at the city's lack of faith, were finally paying off. Ares did as was expected and sent his dog. And the dog was hungry.

Athena watched as Agrios gave the order to pack the camp and prepare to move. The army didn't take the strategic path as it should have. They took the path of most resistance so they could bathe in the blood of their enemies.

She was not happy to see Ares's dog turn to the Sophiaion, but she was not surprised either. She did not enjoy what would happen, but it was a small delay of her plan. It was acceptable.

Ares's champion had his army surround the institute. The Paideiarches, the headmaster, stood at the entrance. He raised his hands as he spoke. "This building is a library of learning. The people inside are children who are taught the ways of culture and the ways of the gods. Please go in peace. We do not stand against you."

Agrios the Red motioned with his hand. His men grabbed the Paideiarches, dragged him down the steps, and kicked his knee to force him to kneel.

The Red looked down at the headmaster. With a wave of his hand and the dismissive tone of a man addressing a chore, he said, "Remove his tongue. He shouldn't presume to speak to me without permission."

The man struggled but could not fight the people holding him. His scream became a gurgle as Agrios looked on and smiled. This was his favorite part—almost his favorite part.

He walked past the crying headmaster towards the institute so he and his men could have some fun. He would select his trophies first, then the others could have what they wanted.

A shadow passed overhead right before a *thump* on the steps before him. A terrifying creature landed, blocking his path. Her black wings outstretched. Her hands made into claws. A jagged smile that was beyond human. A Fury. They were almost gone from the world, but one yet remained.

Fire surrounded the Fury's right arm, ran down to her hand like liquid, and then dripped into a whip of flaming judgment. She let out a scream and started to move on the human, to stop his reign of terror on this land. Agrios stepped back with a rare look of fear on his face.

Just as she raised her whip, dripping with flame and smoke, the sky opened—not rain or lightning, but a brilliant golden beam of light. It slammed into the ground with the pound of a sounding cymbal, a brass reverberation.

Athena struck the earth like a spear.

She was not—and then she was. Her bronze sandals stepped with finality. The ground rang with every step. She raised her hand. The Fury stopped, frozen. It was not from fear, but respect. The gods and Furies had an understanding.

Her eyes, gray as steel, looked at the Fury. "Enough."

The Fury met her gaze. She was confident in her judgment. This man was wrong. This man was evil. This man would die.

She responded to the goddess, "He has crossed too many lines. He intends to use the children of this institute as toys for his army. I cannot allow—"

Athena moved in a flash and spun her spear's haft into the Fury. She flew through the air like an arrow, crashing through two trees before coming to a stop, covered in splinters and dust—her wings broken, gasping for air. She tried to stand, but her bones were shattered by the goddess.

Athena vanished, her job was done, and her plan continued.

Agrios the Red walked slowly past the fallen trees and debris from Athena's attack. He looked down at the now powerless Fury lying on the ground, coughing and gasping for breath. He began to take off his armor while resuming his sick grin.

The Fury could not stop him.

Even Athena looked away, but she did not intervene. "The fool should not have questioned a god."

When Agrios was finished, he looked down at her and said, "In your thousands of years of immortality, remember what a mortal took." He spat in her face and walked away.

She slowly crawled away, through the trees.

Athena appeared over her, looking down, and said, "The time of the Erinyes is over. Do not return, or face worse." With that, Athena was gone.

Isadora cowered in fear, afraid of more mortals coming for her or Agrios coming back. She crawled as fast as her broken bones would allow—an outcast from her life. Everything she had left, including her dignity, was destroyed by the goddess of wisdom. She would not forget.

As she healed and the days turned into centuries, she withdrew from the world. When she tried to reach out, the men wanted her as Agrios had wanted her. The women were jealous of her beauty. The children were afraid. She had no one.

She sneaked back into the underworld and took Lethebloom back to her new world. She cared for it—her only friend.

Isadora fought back the tears as she sat next to Thomas. She didn't show weakness, and it was weakness to cry. He was strong, and she would be strong just like him.

She turned to look at him, to see his reaction to her story—to face his judgment. But he was fighting tears, too. He placed his arm around her and whispered, "Tears are pain leaving your body so you can heal. Let them out."

She twisted and wrapped her arms around him as she sobbed into his shoulder. He gave her what she had not had in her eight hundred years of isolation: permission to cry. Permission to heal.

She cried for everything lost, for every pain, for every moment of loneliness and fear.

Thomas twisted them around until he was lying on his back, her head nestled on his shoulder, and his arm around her. She covered them with her wing, and she cried until sleep took her. She could finally start to release the pain.

# CHAPTER 31
## *Good Morning*

Isadora woke up slowly, leisurely. She stretched her hand across the bed and found it empty. Her eyes crept open. The light from the small clay lamp made her want to squeeze them shut again for a few more hours. She was having a good day.

She squinted, a compromise she could handle. Thomas was playing with one of his trinkets and didn't know she was awake. Her night had started badly, but it was so freeing to share her past with him and get that pain out in the open. It was nice to have a friend again. She had held that vengeance and hate so tightly, but it leaked out with the tears. Now, she had permission to be happy.

She slowly stretched a wing across the room towards him and poked his shoulder.

He smiled as he patted her wing. "Good morning. How are you feeling?"

She stretched out her arm and took in a deep breath before responding, "Fantastic. Last night was hard. I carried centuries of hate. I didn't know how to move past it. It's still there, but it's not like it was. Now, I want to have treats and play. I want to explore. I'm afraid to be alone with mortals, but you make it fun."

She slid out of bed and stood up, stretching her arms over her head. She wanted to stretch her wings. There was nothing like a nice morning wing stretch, but this room was too small. She would have to wait until they were on the road again. Then she could fly.

*I wish Thomas could fly.*

*We could fly around and stretch our wings together.*

*Can someone get wings…?*

She gasped with excitement as she bent forward quickly beside Thomas. "Can you make wings? You make stuff, right? Can you fly with me?"

He whispered back, "Remember, we don't want them to know you have wings, and our door is just a cloth. They might hear you."

Her wings quickly coiled around her body, and she shimmied to wrap them tight. "You're right, no wings," she whispered. "But can you fly? Or could you?"

He answered her in a quiet voice, but not a whisper: "My realm has a thing called a hang glider. It's called that because it glides… and you hang from it… anyway, it doesn't flap, but it does glide for long distances. We could jump off a mountain together and float along, riding air currents."

She clapped and pulled her arms close to her body as she wiggled happily. "Let's go get one. I want to fly. I want to remember being happy and flying in the sun."

She started twirling around in the tiny room.

Thomas smiled as he watched her spin. "I would like to do that someday, but I still have to find Thaleia."

Isadora took a step back as her fingers began to fidget nervously. She thought for a moment and said, "I don't think you should. No, no, it's a bad idea. It just won't do. I know, I said something else before. I know I said I wanted revenge against Athena, but it isn't worth it."

She paced back and forth with nervous energy. "I know. I know. I know. I was all angry and wanted it, but it's dangerous."

She dropped to her knees in front of him and placed her hands on his legs, looking deep into his eyes. "We can be happy without revenge."

Thomas placed his hands on hers soothingly. "It's not about revenge. It's about justice and protecting people. The people in my realm were murdered because of Thaleia. She had my body possessed by a powerful spirit. Then she lost my body. That person murdered people with my hands. I saw them die, by my hands. She also caused several satyrs to enter my realm and kill people. She has to be stopped to save others."

Isadora looked down as she responded, "Does it have to be you? You're special. You shouldn't die."

He reached forward and lifted her chin to look into her eyes. "If

I put someone else in danger—if I let them take my place—I wouldn't be special. I wouldn't be who I am. Last night, you said you used to be good, an honorable being that wanted to stop evil. I want to do that too. Like you."

She nodded her head. "I want to be good again, too. Okay, but we should get some more cakes first."

Thomas chuckled and replied, "If we do go back to my world one day, I'll give you ice cream. It's like someone made a cake out of snow, but impossibly creamy."

"Very well," she replied. "First, we find Thaleia, then we save your realm from destruction, then we get ice cream and go flying."

She nodded again with finality. It was decided.

The morning air was cool as they stepped out of their room, the smell of the tavern's hearth still lingering in the hallway. Thomas went first to make sure Isadora felt safe stepping into the world of humans. The sun was just beginning to stretch its rays over the horizon, casting a warm glow that seemed to settle softly on her skin. But her eyes were already focused elsewhere, scanning the small tavern with an eager, almost childlike curiosity.

"Do you think they'll have more honey cake?" she asked, her voice low but hopeful as she stepped closer to Thomas.

Thomas couldn't help but smile at the enthusiasm. "Probably not," he replied. "It takes a while to make cakes, but I'm sure they'll have something good."

Isadora raised her eyebrows, intrigued by the idea. She was just so happy to have new tastes and someone to share them with. She followed him down the narrow hallway to the main dining area, where the first light of dawn slanted through the wooden beams above. The tavern was quiet at this hour. The tables were mostly empty, save for a few early risers or people nursing mugs of ale or wine because they were too drunk to leave their table.

Thomas stepped up to the bar where the grizzled tavern owner was wiping down the counter. A rough-looking man, his apron stained with various food remnants, grunted in greeting.

"We'd like breakfast," Thomas said, his voice light and easy. "Something quick. Something sweet. Something special. We are celebrating," he added, turning to Isadora with a warm smile.

The tavern owner raised an eyebrow, clearly sizing Thomas up, then glanced at Isadora—his gaze lingering just a bit too long at her revealing leather dress, before he nodded slowly.

"We don't normally have much in the way of sweets aside from barley porridge. At least not at this hour. I could add some honey to it."

"I'll pay for it," Thomas said, placing two coins on the counter. He was getting the hang of the currency in this area, and he knew that was more than enough for twenty meals for two people. He was overpaying a lot, but he couldn't take it with him, and confronting a god might not go well. He decided they deserved something good.

Isadora looked at him, her curiosity piqued. "And what exactly are you getting me?"

He looked at the tavern owner and asked, "What can you do for us?"

The tavern owner picked up the coins, smiled, and said, "For this money? I'll celebrate with you. Fried dough with honey and sesame seeds. A little sweetened wine, maybe? I'll even pack some up for the road for you two. I know the kind of breakfast that's going to make this morning great."

Isadora couldn't help but grin, her eyes dancing with excitement. "Fried dough?" she asked, her voice soft but full of anticipation. "What's that like?"

"Crispy outside, soft on the inside. Warm and dripping with honey," Thomas answered.

She smiled and hugged his arm. She didn't like being around people. She didn't dislike them, either. The tavern owner seemed mostly nice, but she saw how he looked at her. He looked at her like she was fried dough with honey. She hugged Thomas's arm tighter.

They took a seat at a clean table in the corner. The tavern owner returned with a small jug of wine in hand, pouring it into two mugs, the amber liquid gleaming in the morning light. He didn't speak as he set them down on the table, his gaze flickering between them.

"Drink while you wait. My wife is working on the dough," he said gruffly before retreating to the kitchen.

Isadora picked up the mug and took a tentative sip, her eyes widening at the sweetness of the wine. It was smooth, with just the right balance of honey and fruit. She closed her eyes for a moment, savoring the taste, her fingers wrapped around the warm mug.

They didn't have to wait long before the tavern owner returned, carrying a large plate stacked high with golden, crispy fried dough, drizzled generously with honey and sprinkled with sesame seeds. The scent alone was a treat.

She looked at Thomas. This was her happiest day in hundreds of years.

"Eat," said the tavern keeper, setting the plate down between them. "It's hot. I just had one in the kitchen. This is one of my wife's specialties."

Isadora's eyes sparkled as she reached for a piece, her fingers trembling slightly in anticipation. She bit into it, and her face lit up in immediate pleasure. "Oh," she breathed, her voice thick with wonder. "This… this is amazing."

Thomas watched her, his smile soft and approving as he picked up a piece for himself.

The tavern keeper smiled and headed back to the kitchen to report the success.

Isadora took another bite, more slowly this time, savoring every moment. "Thank you for showing me a new world," she said quietly, almost to herself. "This kind of happiness… It's been so long since I could just… be happy."

They ate their treats and sipped their wine to a series of moans from Isadora that made Thomas smile. She liked it when he smiled.

Before they finished, the tavern owner walked over with a cloth-covered basket. "We had some leftovers, and the Lady of the House wanted to give thanks and congratulations on your celebration. Also, you mentioned you wanted something fast, so I went ahead and had my son saddle up your horse. You can stay as long as you want or come back anytime."

Thomas answered his generosity with a smile. "Thank you so much. We really appreciate it. And the food was amazing. Please thank the Lady of the House for us."

Isadora nodded her head but was too shy to say anything

directly. She still remembered how he looked at her when he thought she wouldn't notice.

He smiled and bobbed his head as he left.

After the owner walked away, Thomas slid another coin under an empty plate. Isadora saw the gesture. She looked at him, smiling, then placed her head on his shoulder for a moment. He was the best man ever.

They walked toward the door, Isadora holding his left arm with a gentle grip, happy and full.

A man who looked like he hadn't learned about soap had been watching closely as Isadora enjoyed her food. He said, "Hey, a beauty like you must have known more than the touch of silk. Perhaps you'll teach me how to enjoy a night worthy of your charms." His buddies laughed.

They were hard men. Adventurers or mercenaries. Men used to talking big but not used to big words.

She frowned and looked away. She could feel the panic welling up inside. She knew she was safe, but she hadn't been surrounded by mortals since what Agrios did to her.

The man stood and said, "Hey now, woman, you could at least say 'No thank you, I don't like real men' instead of just turning the shoulder."

Thomas steered her around to his right arm and whispered, "Don't touch my left hand right now. It's a weapon."

Hearing his voice helped. She clung to his right arm but wondered how his left hand was a weapon.

"Whoa, hold on there. Are you whispering about me?" stammered the man. He walked forward, sticking a finger in Thomas's face as he continued, "Show some manners or I'll—"

He didn't finish the sentence. Thomas grabbed the man's throat with his left hand. The stranger froze in place, twitching.

Thomas looked at the others and said, "No need for anything rash. Your friend just needs to calm down." He looked back at the owner and said, "Sorry for any trouble."

He released the man's throat, causing him to collapse on the floor, still twitching and backing away. Thomas worked the latch to the door, and they stepped outside.

Isadora's heart was pounding. Thomas protected her. He was so powerful. She didn't even know what he did, but he showed what a real man could do. It didn't help much, though; the fear was coursing through her body.

*Just make it to Ed. Just make it to Ed.*

*Once we are on Ed, Thomas will take us away from here, and I'll be able to fly.*

Ed was so close. He was just feet away when the two men ran up behind them. One stepped in front of Thomas, and the other grabbed her arm.

She heard Thomas say, "Easy," before the pounding blood in her ears blocked out the world. She could see Agrios standing over her. She felt that fear again.

Her eyes became black pits; her mouth opened in a primal scream. She twisted, grabbed the man's hand, and used the talons of her other hand to rip his arm off. In one deft move, she reached up, grabbed his face, and ripped his jaw off. Blood sprayed over her face. She didn't care. Like a scared cat, she was feral, surviving in panic mode.

Over the pulsing blood in her ears, she thought she heard "Isadora" somewhere off in the distance. The other man was coming up on her side. She unfurled her wings with a powerful whoosh of wind, knocking the other man through the air into a building. Another hand touched her left shoulder from behind. She whipped her wing and arm in that direction, throwing the offender backwards into the stable door. His body crashed through, landing in a pile of wood and splinters. She turned to look at the threat.

It was Thomas. Her mind started to register what had happened. He called her name. He touched her shoulder.

He was trying to stop her. He was trying to protect her.

Now he was lying on the ground, motionless. She looked at her hands and saw the blood—she could feel it on her face. She looked around and saw everyone cowering—afraid of the monster.

She looked back at Thomas's body, unmoving. She quietly said, "Thomas." She killed her only friend. The only man who had ever shown kindness in her entire immortal life was now gone because of her. He gave her this beautiful morning, and she broke it.

She wailed. It was not a scream. It was not a yell. It was the wail of an emotion that doesn't have a name. The feeling of complete loss and failure. Of utter pain.

The people in the town fell to the ground or ran behind buildings. The pain in her voice rattled the ground and was even heard in Olympus. An immortal's scream. The scream of a Fury so desperate it drew the gods' attention.

She launched into the sky, flew over the rooftops, and skimmed the tops of the trees—a monster fleeing the villagers.

# CHAPTER 32
## *Messages*

Kallianeira was tired. She had been riding hard for days, only stopping for sleep.

She had just left the road and started pushing through the underbrush. The terrain was too rough to ride, and her horse could use the rest, so she dismounted.

She reflected on her arrival at the base of Olympus. No matter how many times she had approached the gate, it always impressed her. The sheer magnitude of the construction always filled her with awe.

The wind carried the scent of old stone, cooking meat, and incense. The smells shifted back and forth as she rode past the outskirts of the area. A rough half-circle of tents and low wooden structures had been pitched in the lee of a slope. Smoke curled lazily from cooking fires. Cloth banners flapped on poles. Each bore the symbol of a different god: olive branches, suns, thunderbolts, and grain. A handful of vendors peddled food, charms, and incense, while others tended to horses or knelt in prayer before makeshift shrines.

Some were petitioners, dressed in white, waiting for an audience or opportunity. Others were just hopeful travelers, pilgrims who had heard the rumors of miracles, of visions, of gods answering the desperate. She felt for them. They wanted miracles, but would most likely not be answered. The gods didn't offer assistance unless they stood to gain something in return. And the people here were out of options.

She wasn't here for them. She was here to deliver a message to Thaleia, the daughter of Athena. Her people, the Amazons, had an agreement with Thaleia to hold the Path of Blood while the group known as The Agitators was being investigated. The group was not deemed worthy of a name, just the term Agitators, so it stuck. It turned out the group was more dangerous than initially thought.

She headed directly toward the massive stone dais, half-sunken in the earth, its surface etched with curling runes that glowed dimly beneath the fading light. The platform was wide enough for ten men to stand abreast and high enough that even from horseback, she had to tilt her head to take in the arch that crowned it. Though it was wide enough for a giant to walk through without stooping, no one could cross unless the Gate permitted it.

The great arch shimmered with unseen power—the door to the gods. Thaleia was on the other side of that door.

Two figures stood at its base, still as statues. Their garments stirred slightly in the wind. One held a staff capped with a dull crystal; the other carried a scroll tucked into a leather strap across his chest. They weren't guardians. The gate didn't need to be guarded. They were attendants, messengers to the gods.

The horse snorted uneasily as she dismounted. After days of riding to get there, she felt anxious to deliver her message. She hastened to the Sentinel of the Gate of Ascent. Mortals cannot travel the Path without permission. The door simply won't recognize them. She had to relay her message to the Sentinel, the gatekeeper.

She explained to him that it was an urgent message for Thaleia, the daughter of Athena, concerning the Path of Blood and the forces that were fighting to take control of it. Despite the message of urgency, the attendant seemed to be taking his time.

"Men," she sighed dismissively before realizing what she was saying. Thomas was a man, too. She respected him, but here she was insulting all males because of one.

"Sentinels," she muttered with a slight smile.

The attendant slowly began walking toward the arch. He would carry the message to the other side himself. Kallianeira paced back and forth while he slowly walked forward. Thomas's life could be in danger. Her sisters could be in danger. She was getting angry. Angrier than she should be, but she carried the weight of others' lives on her shoulders.

She snapped, "The lives of thousands lie in the balance."

The sentinel paused and slowly turned to face her, locking eyes. He waited. She stomped and huffed in exasperation, throwing her hands in the air. He waited. "Fine. My message is delivered. I return to my sisters to fight." She turned to go.

"No," he replied. "You will wait for your god or her messenger."

She waited, staring at him. She responded with a mock curtsy before approaching a vendor to get food. He turned and began slowly walking toward the arch again.

Kallianeira bit into some charred meat on a stick. She didn't really care what it was. It was warm. It was fuel. She paced anxiously while she ate, waiting for word so she could leave.

After what felt like an eternity, she saw her answer—Thaleia herself walked through the arch. She quickened her step across the dais in search of the messenger. She stopped at the edge of the stone platform, poised like a statue half-carved from the mountain itself. A warrior shaped into something sharper than steel.

Her armor gleamed under the fading sun: bronze and silver, etched with curling patterns of waves and flame, and fitted close to her body with the precision of a master-smith. Her left arm bore a manica of overlapping metal plates, running from neck to elbow. Each plate curved and layered like the scales of a serpent, catching the light as she moved. Beneath the plates, a second skin of black leather clung to her form, oiled and tight, outlining every contour of her muscles and grace. The bracer on her forearm was a matching extension of her manica, but one solid piece, not overlapping plates. Intended for taking the abuse of direct strikes.

At her left hip hung a xiphos, short and leaf-shaped, the blade tucked close to her thigh in a sheath. People spoke of its power in combat. Most who saw the blade died before they could take the time to admire it. On her right, coiled like a serpent, a length of translucent rope shimmered faintly, as if it were made not of fiber but woven starlight and smoke.

Her face was ageless, untouched by time or mortal concerns. She had the majesty and beauty of a master craftsman's marble statue—complemented by the unyielding strength of its stone. Her long black hair flowed down her back in waves, unbound, stirred by a breeze that gave the impression of action even when she stood idle. Her eyes were gray-blue. Her gaze was clear, cold, and deep, like the sea under a gathering storm. There was something watchful in them, something waiting. The kind of gaze that didn't just see, but weighed.

There were not many who could withstand the gaze of the daughter of Athena.

Kallianeira stepped forward, happy to be dealing with a warrior instead of the attendant, someone who understood urgency. "I am Kallianeira the Iron Voice of the Amazon. We battle for the entrance to the Path of Blood."

Thaleia stepped off the dais, landing in front of the messenger. "We have met before, have we not? When your sisters agreed to watch the Path? How fierce is the battle?"

"We were trapped," answered the Iron Voice. "Surrounded. We might have been overrun had unexpected help not arrived. A great warrior from the other side of the Path. He seeks an audience with you as well, but was delayed."

The daughter of Athena raised an eyebrow. "Someone from the other side came through? An ally? Who is he?"

Kallianeira hated to give details about Thomas. He had earned her trust and, more than that, her friendship. His questions were his to ask. She responded honestly, but simply, "His name is Thomas. An honorable man. I am not impressed easily, but he has earned my respect."

Again, Thaleia showed surprise. "A man—earned the respect of the Daughters of War?"

The Amazon nodded. "Yes. He was coming with me to relay a message to you, but he was injured during the fighting in his realm. It became infected, and he chose to stay behind so I could finish my mission. He waits in the wilds for my return."

"I am interested in meeting this warrior," replied the daughter of Athena. "You seem anxious to return to him. I will prepare my warriors and come to the Path of Blood to ensure it does not fall to the enemy. If you find your ally, bring him with you. Tell him I will speak with him there."

The women saluted each other by placing a closed fist across their hearts. Kallianeira walked back to her horse, conflicted. She respected Thaleia, and this interaction had gone well. She was surprised that she had been remembered by someone such as the half-goddess. But Thomas had proven his value as well. Perhaps this was all due to some misunderstanding, and Thaleia would explain that he was mistaken. Then, they will join forces and crush the enemy.

That was what she longed for, but she feared, deep inside, that their meeting would not go well for one of them. She didn't know which side was correct, but she knew Thomas was alone and injured. She needed to fulfill the oath she made to herself: to find him alive or avenge his death.

She had been pushing through the brush when, with relief, she saw the plane tree peek over the top of the leaves in front of her. Her days of riding were at an end, and she would finally know if he was unharmed.

With her arm, she pushed a branch out of the way as the last of the brush opened to the clearing around the tree. She stepped through carefully, watching for any signs of trouble. Her heart dropped when she saw the bloodstained ground and shredded articles of clothing.

She froze. She wanted to investigate the remains to prove it wasn't him, but she was afraid to look in case it was.

She blinked back the water in her eyes, pulled her sword, and walked to the remains. They were surrounded by the prints of hooves, cats, humans, dogs, and something else. A whole host of creatures had circled the body. She studied the bloodstained remains. It was a human, male. He had strange items like Thomas. The pack wasn't a simple leather item, like her people would use. It had the strange metal teeth that made a hissing sound when the bag opened. Her breath caught in her throat as she turned away. She walked toward the tree, seeking comfort in its shelter, her horse in tow.

Then she noticed that his strange shelter wasn't there. Even if animals had torn it apart, it would still be here. She looked back at the body. The bag was similar, but it didn't have the strange, flashy panel on the top flap. She walked the area looking for more clues when she noticed something white jutting out of a crack in the tree.

She hesitated, then pulled the paper out and unfolded it.

*Kallianeira,*

*The cultist found me. No big deal, they are stupid. I killed one. He was from my side, which means he had weapons like mine. There could be more. Be careful and don't assume you are safe because of distance.*

*There were two things that seemed able to shapeshift, and a satyr. They are still looking for you.*

*I'm going to try to find someone named Isadora. I don't know much about her, but I was told that she can get me to Olympus. Protect your sisters. I'll find you and help if I can.*

*Thomas*

As she read the words, her breath left her in a single strangled gasp, something between a cough and a sob. She didn't cry, but her body was preparing to mourn and found joy instead. It had to escape.

She placed her hand on the tree for support and laughed. The dread of not knowing for days of riding had taken its toll, but now she had hope. She read the note again and laughed. It carried warnings, yes—but it was still in Thomas's voice. He still found a way to slip in an insult about his enemy while delivering the facts.

She folded the note and tucked it in her pack. She didn't expect him to come back, but she wished she had writing implements so she could give a response. To warn him that Thaleia knew he was looking for her. To let him know she was safe as well. She smiled as she pulled the feather from her hair and placed it into the crack in the tree. If he did return, he would know she was safe, too.

# CHAPTER 33
## *The Wail*

Athena felt the wail more than heard it. It shook her bones. She knew it was a Fury, one of the Erinyes. A being more ancient than the gods themselves, but she didn't know why it wailed. That bothered her.

Athena concluded her court and gave orders to her daughter. Then she began walking toward the Upper Terrace. She knew the others would want to speak about this. One Fury could mean more, and that could mean they were waking up. If the three had returned, then the gods could have trouble. They were powerful beings when they were focused. There had already been strange tidings in recent times. She needed to watch the moving pieces and plan for them.

She reached out her hand and moved a vine aside as she walked up to the low-burning fire in the brazier. It was a serene, elevated plateau nestled high among the divine peaks. It offered sweeping views of the mortal world below and the celestial realms above. Marble colonnades lined its edges, and lush gardens grew with plants not found anywhere else, remnants of a world forgotten to history. It was a quiet place of reflection and council meetings. A place where gods meet in private, away from the main halls, and where Athena found the others.

Zeus was waiting for her to join them before speaking. "The Erinyes have been missing for centuries. Is this one of your works?"

Athena shook her head. "The three have been missing for a millennium. The lessers," she said, dismissively waving her hand as though shooing away flies, "have been missing for centuries."

"We never knew what happened," interjected Apollo. "My oracles couldn't find the three, but they tell of the others going to sleep. Some in the underworld, some in temples. But at least one of them is awake now."

Athena turned to Hermes. "You've walked the edges of the

underworld. Do they still dwell there?"

"Some do. They aren't all sleeping, but they keep to the underworld," he said, as he began slowly floating above the ground, as though standing had become too boring. "After the three vanished, they continued to answer their nature, using vengeance as justice. Another one of them went missing a few hundred years after the three. The others simply faded away, perhaps searching for their sisters. They are all but gone now."

"One of them has obviously returned," Apollo responded as he stroked his beard. "Why is it back now? And why did it scream so loud the bones of the world shook? Vengeance?"

"Perhaps dying?" Zeus asked. "Or wounded?"

"No," Hermes said at last, his voice quiet. "Not dying. Mourning."

That silenced them again.

Zeus slowly shook his head, jaw flexing. "They do not mourn."

"They don't scream either," Apollo added. "Not like that. That wasn't rage. I have heard their anger. This was… new."

Athena's voice was like tempered steel. "Do we know which one? Or what it mourned?"

"No," Hermes answered. "But I can guess where she lives."

Zeus folded his arms, lightning whispering between his knuckles. "What would break a Fury's voice like that?"

Apollo replied, "Betrayal, or perhaps it discovered the fate of the three, and it wasn't good news."

Zeus looked at Athena, studying her.

Athena arched an eyebrow as she responded, "I do not know what happened to the three, if that is what you think. Even my wisdom has limits."

Hermes chuckled as he said, "I looked for the three. I found nothing. If this Fury learned something about the three in this town, I would be surprised. Especially so close to Olympus. The three would not be here and unknown."

Apollo stepped forward. "My oracles are not completely silent about the three. They believe they live—or did as of the last time I checked."

Zeus uncrossed his arms, his motion declaring annoyance. "We are guessing. We need facts, not supposition."

Athena hesitated, but spoke. "There is another matter."

Zeus looked sternly at her. He didn't like her surprises. She always withheld what she could until it was necessary, but it led to delays and corrections later.

Athena continued, "There is a mortal with a message for my daughter. He crossed the Path of Blood. The group we call the Agitators managed to open the Path and travel to the mortals' realm. He fought them in his realm, then came to ours."

Zeus's voice boomed, "And you delayed in telling us?"

Athena put her hands up as a sign of submission to the king of the gods. "I only just learned. One of my Amazons just delivered the message. The wail came shortly after."

The room fell silent.

Finally, Hermes spoke, "Do you think the three are on his side of the Path of Blood? Maybe he had news."

Apollo nodded slowly. "It makes sense. How could a mortal traverse the Path unaided?"

Athena replied, "If the Furies are awakening, we need to know. They are too powerful to be taken lightly. I will send Thaleia to investigate."

Zeus shook his head. "No, your daughter battles the Agitators for the Path of Blood. We must contain them. Others can handle the Fury."

Apollo volunteered. "I will consult the oracles."

Hermes drifted to the ground. "I will go to the town and search for answers."

Athena turned her head and looked into Hermes's eyes. "You must not speak to her. Learn her name if you can, but we must not reveal our bronze before the battle is joined."

Zeus's gaze swept over them. "Act with discretion. Do not underestimate the Erinyes."

He motioned for Athena to remain behind as the others left. He didn't speak. The king of the gods simply stared.

Athena said, "I spoke the truth. I did not know of the mortal passing to this realm until just before our meeting."

"I know you," responded Zeus. "You know, or you suspect—something. And you are withholding it. Do you know the cause of this Fury's scream?"

Athena locked eyes with her father as she replied, "I do not."

"Do you know this Fury?" he asked.

Athena broke her gaze. "I do not know, but I may. I have heard rumors of one of their kind. The last of the stubborn ones that didn't have the sense to fade away. She stood against me once. She was punished for it. I thought she died or slept."

Zeus arched his eyebrow as he responded, "If you thought she died, why do you suspect it is her now?"

Athena walked past her father with a sigh. Not a sigh of disrespect, the sigh of a daughter that doesn't want to admit something to her father. She spoke without looking at him. "I saw her shame, her abuse. I could have stopped it, but my plans required otherwise. My strategy was correct, but I can still feel a degree of empathy even for a lesser being."

"Empathy does not become you, daughter."

She smiled as she replied, "No, it does not. But I didn't have the heart to finish her. I cast her out. I have heard a rumor or two over the centuries of a winged creature hunting in the edge of a swamp. Based on the power of the creature, I suspected a Fury. It was an anomaly, not a threat."

Zeus sighed the sigh of a father who has to clean up after his child—again. "You hoped to send your daughter to discover if it was actually your Fury. If this is your Fury, will she want vengeance? It is what they do after all."

She looked into his eyes. A father's concern was looking back, but also a king who was disappointed with his subject, who made a mess. "I do not know. My Fury was shattered. She should know her place, but it would be best contained discreetly."

Zeus did not show any signs of an answer. He simply turned and walked away. His silence was his answer—fix it.

Athena walked back to her hall to consider the next step.

Hermes smiled, thankful that he had had need of the Cap of

Hades. He was doing a favor for the god of the underworld, which meant he could borrow it. It allowed concealment even from other gods, including Zeus. He listened to the conversation, and he now knew: Athena attacked a Fury and covered it up. Watching gods was always fun.

# CHAPTER 34
## *Little Zeus*

The traveler came down the winding road as the sun climbed toward its peak, casting shadows behind olive trees and broken stone walls. Dust clung to the hem of his chiton and sandals as he trudged forward. The morning had shaken off the cool of night and was starting to warm.

He had expected more sound by now. A town should have clanging hammers, voices calling to one another, and the clomps of horses, but the town ahead was hushed. Not silent, just reserved. It was as if the whole town had risen late or didn't care to greet the day.

He walked through the gate and paused, leaning on his staff as he took in the scene. Two men were working on the door to their stable. The other townsfolk were casting nervous sidelong glances at the new stranger.

The traveler approached the stables to ask why the town was solemn today. The older man working on the door stopped to pick up a hammer. The man glanced at the traveler's staff.

"It is just for walking," said the stranger as he noticed the suspicion. "I'm no danger. At least not to people, but I am a great danger to porridge. I am simply seeking breakfast."

"I own the tavern," replied the man with the hammer. "I can help with that. My apologies for the greeting. We've had a strange morning."

The stranger glanced down at the blood-soaked ground in front of the stable, then looked back questioningly at the tavern owner.

"Yes." He nodded grimly. "That's the strange part of our morning, but I assure you, this town doesn't have troubles. It's normally a good community; we just had a little excitement earlier, but that's over now."

"I'm glad it's over," replied the stranger. "But I am concerned about my safety. Am I safer leaving immediately or getting a room?

What caused this?"

The owner sighed. This newcomer did have a valid reason for concern, but he didn't want to say what happened. It didn't feel real, and he didn't want to speak the horror into words. He also couldn't bring himself to lie. He looked the stranger in the eye and said, "It was the Swampbat. It came into town this morning. I wouldn't have believed it if I didn't see it myself."

"Swampbat?" replied the stranger.

The owner nodded his head. "Yes, it's a creature that resembles a bat, and it lives in the swamp, south of us. It's not a great name, but we are simple people. The stories have existed for generations. All children are told to avoid going south, especially at night."

The stranger narrowed his eyes as he said, "You let your children travel in swamps at night under normal conditions? Just not this swamp?"

"Well… no," said the owner with a slight nervous chuckle. "It's just something we say so they know when they are older. There are things in the trees and swamp south of here, and everyone avoids them."

The stranger nodded. "That makes sense. So, this creature, it's just a big bat?"

The owner shifted his eyes around, leaned forward, and whispered as though afraid the creature would hear. "No, it was always described as bat-like. But this was a beautiful woman who turned into a bat." He resumed his normal tone as he continued. "A nice couple spent the night here. The man said they were celebrating something. I assumed they were just married, or found out she was with child. I'm not sure, but they were good people. They came out for breakfast and paid a little extra to get some special food made for their celebration. I was happy for them. I hoped they would come back someday."

The stranger looked skeptical. "They don't seem so nice if they did this."

"That happened after," replied the owner as he paced a few steps. It was nervous energy. He needed to move his body to keep his mind calm. "The woman was beautiful. One of the locals tried to speak with her, but she ignored him. Myron—that was the local; his name was

Myron. He took offense and went after her. He's an idiot, er, I shouldn't speak ill of the dead. I apologize for that. I just feel it is important to know that he was not a threat to her. At least, I don't think he was. He was the type of person who would slap a woman's… well, her, uh, rear portion and then get punched in the face. But I don't think he would do more than that."

The traveler nodded. "Some people would do more than punch a man for that."

"And they did," replied the owner. "When Myron reached out, the man protected her by touching Myron. I've never seen anything like it. He didn't strain or stress. He didn't cast a spell or use a weapon. He just touched Myron, and Myron shuddered and fell. It knocked the wind out of him. The couple continued on their way—the man was even polite about it. He looked back at me and waved."

The stranger nodded thoughtfully before asking, "So, the man turned into a bat?"

"No, no. It was the woman. I saw Myron get helped back up by his brothers, and he stumbled out after the couple. I ran over to help put things at ease and calm everyone down. They all had a few words outside, and Myron stumbled over and grabbed the woman. She turned into a bat, tore off his arm, ripped off his face, and threw him on the ground. Everyone around her was knocked back by her wings. They just came out of nowhere and threw the townsfolk into the buildings—including her man. She flew off over the rooftops." The tavern owner gestured to the south.

The owner wiped the sweat from his brow and continued his story. "I expected the man to sprout wings and fly off, too, but he didn't. I think the poor wretch actually thought they were going to have a life together."

"So, the man was just a hapless victim, tricked by the creature?"

The owner shrugged as he shook his head. "I don't know. If he hadn't put Myron on the ground just by touching him, maybe. But it was more than that. The people were about to rip the man apart, but he pointed at the ground… and he summoned lightning and thunder." He shook his hands back and forth for emphasis. "Everyone saw it, not just me. I didn't have a fit or something. Well, after that, most people ran. He just mounted his horse and left town."

"Lightning and thunder?" exclaimed the traveler. He looked around to see signs of the lightning strike. "Were any buildings destroyed?"

"Well… no." The owner twisted the hammer nervously in his hands. "He didn't exactly summon normal lightning. It was small lightning. It was just a little flash in his hand, but it struck the ground over in the road. Dirt flew up in the air. I went back inside, and I'm not ashamed to admit it. I have heard tales of Zeus looking for pretty women. I don't know, it wasn't my place to interfere in affairs that involve lightning or thunder. I went in and I latched the door."

"So, then the man left? Do you know where he was headed? I don't want to meet either one of them on the road."

The owner nodded as he continued, "Yes, he left on a horse. Not like you would think Zeus would leave. And he did get knocked down. I don't think it was Zeus at all, but who else can summon thunder? As for the direction, I don't know. I was inside at that time. Some of the townsfolk said he headed west. They talked about going after him, but I don't think anyone did. It would be the task of a fool to mess with that man. Or with his woman."

The traveler bobbed his head in thanks as he said, "I appreciate your story, but I don't feel safe here. I need to put this town behind me before nightfall. I don't need this kind of trouble. I will head east, and I will travel fast. I wish you fortune with your troubles, but I want no part."

The owner understood and wished the traveler a safe journey.

The traveler increased his pace. But he walked with the slight hobble of a man who had walked more than he should have lately, and his feet just didn't understand why. His staff was working overtime to balance the load. As he turned a corner in the road, he looked back but could no longer see the town. He smiled and floated off the ground. Hermes needed to report back to Zeus that someone was impersonating him. Flashing lightning, creating thunder, and bedding attractive women.

# CHAPTER 35
## *I Won't*

Thomas clopped along on Ed's back as he headed west away from the village and back in the direction he had travelled yesterday. He couldn't reach Olympus on his own. He hadn't come in this direction with a plan in mind. He did so because he was being chased.

Earlier this morning, after an excellent breakfast, some villagers got out of line. Isadora reacted badly and threw several people, himself included, through a wall. His back was sore now, but he was getting used to having everything ache. He took it in stride.

He must have been knocked out for a moment, because when he stood up, there was a body on the ground. Isadora was gone, and a lot of people were looking at him like he was dinner. He pulled out his trusty hand cannon and fired a single warning shot into the ground before climbing on Ed and leaving. He saw the tavern owner running inside as he passed. He felt bad about everything that happened. He liked the town, but the man who grabbed Isadora was in the wrong. Maybe not lose-your-face wrong, but wrong.

He hoped she was okay.

*Well, Thomas, here we are again in your head.*

*I'm starting to feel like Frankenstein since villagers keep chasing me.*

He looked back. No torches yet. He reached down and patted Ed on the neck. "I'm going to install mirrors on you, Ed. You'll love them."

He returned to his planning.

*I could go back to the Path of Blood and ask for another guide.*

*I could go back to the tree and wait for Kallianeira, but she might not return.*

*I could go check on Isadora, the woman who almost killed me this morning.*

He sighed. He knew what he was going to do. Yesterday morning, he would have gone back to the tree to see if his friend was there and, hopefully, get her to help. But after last night, after hearing Isadora's story… he couldn't leave her alone again. In his mind, he kept hearing her say, *"But I used to be good. I did. I was so good."*

It broke his heart every time he thought about it. She had been good, once. She tried to stop a horrible man from doing a horrible thing. She stood up for innocent, defenseless children—and a god destroyed her for it. A being of great power abused that power for her own selfish goals. That had happened to him, as well. After several hundred years of isolation, would he be a little crazy, too? His grievances were fresh. Hers had festered. She deserved better than this.

His complaints could wait. They would wait.

It was not about him needing her to help reach Olympus. It was about her needing him. She deserved to have her voice heard, too. She deserved to have a friend listen.

He turned around. In his haste to leave the town, he had passed the road to the swamp. At the time, he was just trying to live, but now he had the chance to decide what to do. He knew from yesterday that the route could be traveled within a day, but it was a long ride. He also knew that if it was dark when he passed the Wailing Trees… there would be wailing in the trees. He would be careful, but if he could reach the swamp, he should be safe. There were no animals or insects around the swamp. They kept their distance because of the Fury. He picked up his speed.

When he arrived at the turn to go to the swamp, he slowed to make sure there was no mob with pitchforks. There weren't. But there was a group of men on horses. They were different. So far, his time here had been with small towns, scattered travelers, and the Amazon. These men stood out. There were five of them, mounted on their horses and waiting in the road.

A man at the front, possibly the leader, turned his head and locked eyes with Thomas. That was when Thomas heard something behind him.

*I wish I had those mirrors.*

He pulled Ed to a stop and looked back. Five more. He turned his gaze back to the one that appeared to be leading them and nodded.

The other man smirked. He rode at the front with confidence that comes from power and experience. A man used to getting what he wanted.

His bronze cuirass gleamed dully beneath the high sun, embossed with subtle reliefs of snarling beasts and interwoven serpents. Symbols of ferocity and unyielding strength. Over his broad shoulders fell a crimson cloak, fastened by a heavy, wrought-gold brooch shaped like a spearhead, its edges worn smooth by years of battle. His greaves, polished and snug, rose to guard his shins, and on his forearms, leather bracers laced tightly, their surface scarred from old strikes.

In his left hand, he bore a round shield, painted with the blood-red visage of a raging boar with an open mouth. It was worn but proud, bearing the dents of countless clashes. At his hip hung a sword with a hilt wrapped in dark leather, its blade keen and well-maintained. Slung across his back, a long spear tapered to a razor point, its shaft carved with knotwork that whispered of battle blessings.

His horse was no mere beast of burden but a war stallion, powerful and lithe. Its coat was the color of midnight, sleek and unyielding, muscles rippling beneath its short hair. Leather barding covered its flanks, reinforced with bronze plates etched with the same motifs as its rider's armor. Symbols meant to intimidate foes and celebrate war.

Together, man and beast cut a striking silhouette. An embodiment of destruction, of war's unrelenting will, poised on the edge between calculated command and chaos of battle.

The man said something that Thomas couldn't understand as the group closed around him.

Thomas knew to show no fear. He didn't have to show confidence or arrogance, just no fear. He responded, "I don't understand your language."

The man tilted his head in amusement. "You do not speak the language of the people in this area? You must have traveled far. Why are you here?"

"In my realm, I met Thaleia, daughter of Athena," responded Thomas. He decided that bluffing had been useful to him in previous encounters. This was a half-bluff. He had actually met Thaleia. It just didn't go well. "My realm is fighting her enemies, and we need more details."

The leader was unimpressed. "Which enemies? What war? My god is the god of war. What does Athena's daughter know of real war?"

His men chuckled.

Thomas replied, "The enemies are unknown to us. That is why we seek an audience. On my side, we call them cultists. Most of them are now dead, but more are trying to cross. It is my understanding that Thaleia leads a fight against them on this side. I wish to know why they are coming to my realm."

The leader's expression shifted from disdain to calculation. The casual laughter from his men faded into a thick silence, taut with the tension of warriors reevaluating a man they had just written off.

He leaned forward in the saddle, his eyes narrowing as he studied Thomas like a battlefield from a hilltop. Searching for weak points.

"You speak of crossing." His voice was harder now. "What gate did they use? What road do these cultists travel?"

One of the others, a younger man with a scar down the side of his face, added, "The Path of Blood?" The name had weight on his tongue, like he didn't want to say it too loudly.

The leader raised a gauntleted hand, silencing him, never breaking eye contact with Thomas. "Thaleia does lead battles. You know this. That is more than most mortals should know. So, tell me— how do you know of the Path? Did one of her Amazons tell you? Or did something else whisper it to you in the dark?"

The men began to slowly form a tighter circle. Not openly hostile, but less room to breathe.

"Choose your next words with care, stranger. I have no patience for liars who meddle in the gods' roads."

"Something dark whispered it to me," Thomas replied. "Thaleia used the Path to come to my side and fight Ometheon. After he was defeated, she left, but she did not stop them all. A group of satyrs on the other side was hunting me. I killed all but one. The last one—I trapped. I questioned it, and I translated a book called The Path of Blood. It told me the Path needs the ichor of gods to travel, but they had opened it through other means. I came through because I intend to destroy my enemies. That means learning how. Thaleia might have those answers."

The leader watched Thomas in silence for several breaths, eyes narrowing not in suspicion, but in thought. Around him, the warriors' postures eased slightly. They were no longer crowding, but they were still coiled like hounds held at heel. The mention of Thaleia and Ometheon had struck a nerve. So had the name, Path of Blood.

Finally, he spoke.

"You have slain satyrs, faced Ometheon, and claim to have forced truth from one of his ilk. That would make you either a liar… or a warrior of uncommon resolve."

He shifted in the saddle, and the horse snorted beneath him. "And you speak of ichor and divine rites like a priest, but your hands rest like a soldier's." He glanced at the way Thomas was holding the gun.

He leaned slightly forward, his voice low and even. "You came through the Path. Then you are a trespasser. But you fight the enemies of Olympus… so you are not necessarily an enemy. If you seek Thaleia, then continue along this road east or return from whence you came. But the marsh has no value to you, only death."

He let that hang before asking, "Yet you ride toward the marsh? You know someone there. Say the name."

Thomas shifted in his saddle as he responded, "I seek my guide. An Amazon woman. Three nights ago, we were attacked by a group that followed us from the Path of the Blood. The satyrs I have seen before, but the other things were new. They were women at first, then they turned into cats during the attack. When they were driven off, they became dogs. I don't know what to call them. On my side, we would just say shapeshifter. My guide and I were separated, but before we were separated, she headed in this direction."

The warband stirred.

A few exchanged looks. One crossed himself with two fingers. Another muttered something in the old tongue. Something like a curse or a ward. The leader remained still, but a flicker of recognition passed through his features. The name wasn't given, but the shape of the threat was enough.

"Empusa," he said at last. "Perhaps you are stronger than you look."

He turned to his men and gave a sharp nod. One of them rode off eastward without a word, a messenger, likely. The rest stayed, watching Thomas more closely, not as an enemy, but as a thread tangled in something far larger.

"You follow your guide into foul ground," the leader continued, returning his eyes to Thomas. "The marsh is not safe, not even for those who call it home. But if your guide lives, and if she passed this way, then she passed under our gaze."

He paused. "Describe her."

Thomas responded, cautiously, "Amazon. Amber hair. A feather braided into it at her right temple. She's stubborn. She seemed to feel I was beneath her, wouldn't tell me a name, and only called me male."

The men all started laughing.

The leader nodded knowingly and responded, "Amazons are good women. Most women break too easily, but if you capture an Amazon, you can pass her around for days. They don't break. They scream and threaten all the way to the end."

Thomas sighed. If these men lived, they would spend their lives raping and murdering. He was done with this. With one deft move, he brought the AR-15 up. The leader still had that stupid grin on his face. Thomas pulled the trigger. The horses all jumped except Ed. She was used to Thomas's shenanigans. He quickly dropped five of them before they could respond.

Then came a sound through the brush on his right. Ed jumped and moved sideways as nine feet of solid muscle carved in the shape of rage burst into view, wearing the same tunic as the humans. Its frame was thick and powerful, each movement radiating brutal force, like an avalanche of power. Dark, leathery skin stretched taut over corded arms and a barrel chest, marked by scars both fresh and ancient. Some wounds had the jagged look of blades; others, the unmistakable gouges of claws—proof that even monsters were tested.

Its head was unmistakable: the broad skull of a bull, horns sweeping outward like crescent blades, ivory dulled from age and war. It bellowed as its nostrils flared, and its breath came in huffs, hot and steady. The eyes were not those of cattle, but of a thinking, hunting being, deep-set and cold.

Around its waist hung a crude iron belt, from which dangled broken blades and rusted chains, trophies or warnings. In its right hand, it gripped a greataxe forged from dark metal, its edge nicked from use but no less deadly. The weapon was longer than a man and almost as heavy, yet the Minotaur carried it like a carpenter's tool.

The beast slammed into the horse to Ed's right, knocking both horses down. Thomas could not bring the long gun to bear on his right side from this position on the ground. His leg was pinned while the horses thrashed. He pulled the hand cannon and shot the Minotaur in the head. It didn't kill it, but it caused the beast to recoil.

The other rider, who had been knocked over, had fallen on top of Ed. He grabbed Thomas's hand, fighting for control of the gun. Thomas was able to twist his stun gauntlet around and grip his enemy's wrist, causing him to convulse and release him.

The top horse managed to get up, but Ed was still struggling. Four enemy humans still remained, and one Minotaur. A human jumped down from his horse and spun his spear around. He raised it to finish Thomas, who was still pinned. Thomas, still holding one soldier's wrist, twisted to take the spear directly in the chest while bringing his cannon to bear. The spear was blocked by the ceramic plate in his pilfered police vest. The enemy's armor did not fare as well against the .44 Magnum.

Ed managed to twist and partially stand, but the Minotaur brought its axe down hard before she could move out of the way. It was still enough for Thomas to free his leg. He released the wrist of the soldier. In the confusion, jostling, and Minotaur's thrashing, the enemies were having trouble controlling their horses and managing their weapons at the same time.

Thomas stepped behind an enemy's horse, putting that soldier between him and the Minotaur. The Minotaur was lost in rage from being shot in the face, and it didn't care who was in its way. It swung the axe at Thomas, who was now behind the enemy. The axe hit the Minotaur's ally, cleaving the human and horse into pieces.

Two humans were left, one still recovering from the shock.

The remaining human on a horse pulled to one side and threw his spear, catching Thomas in the leg. He yelled as he fell back. He dropped the revolver, but reached back to the shotgun strapped to his back. The human and Minotaur were converging on him. He fired into the face of the beast. It snarled in pain, but it was buckshot, not a slug. The creature's skull deflected the worst of the damage. It still staggered him, causing it to turn its back to protect its eyes.

Thomas twisted to the human, firing two shots, blowing the human off his horse. Thomas grabbed the spear sticking out of his leg. He ripped it out and tossed it aside. Normally, a person shouldn't remove a blade as it is blocking the wound, holding the blood. But he needed to move, and it would cause more damage if it stayed in.

Thomas stood, discarded the shotgun, and retrieved his dropped revolver. The Minotaur opened its arms and yelled in rage. Not fear. Not even anger. A war cry of bloodlust. Thomas yelled the same war cry back as he kicked off a dead horse and punched the .44 Magnum into the creature's mouth—then pulled the trigger while still in the air. The war cry ended in a gurgle as Thomas slammed into it, and both bodies crashed to the ground.

The last human was the one he shocked, struggling to stand.

Thomas twisted and shot him in the knee, almost removing his leg with the powerful gun. Then he struggled to his feet and looked down at his own leg. He quickly cut a strip of cloth from the enemy's banner and tied it around his leg.

He holstered the pistol, not wanting to use any more of its limited ammo, and picked up a sword. He stumbled to the last enemy alive as he demanded answers. "Why are you shutting off access to the swamp?"

The enemy smiled. "I am a warrior. I die in glory to my god."

Thomas laughed mockingly, angrily. His voice became all but a yell as he responded, "All of you and a Minotaur died to one mortal. You think your god is impressed? I will cut off your hands and leave you alive in the care of some old women at a monastery. For the rest of your life, they will clean you like a baby after you soil yourself. Will that get you into Ares's good graces? Will that make you his favorite?"

They were rapists and murderers who killed Ed. He had no

mercy left for this one, just judgment.

The man's eyes widened with fear. "No. No. Kill me. You can't let me live like that!"

Thomas's voice was as cold and hard as steel when he responded, "Answer or suffer. Why are you exploring the swamp?"

"Ares wants the Fury," came the panicked response. "He said Athena wants her too, but he was going to get her first."

Thomas snapped back, "How do they know she's in the swamp?"

The soldier managed a half-shrug while trying to hold his leg in one piece. "The gods heard it scream or something. Some ancient primal thing. They could feel, but we couldn't."

Thomas stabbed the enemy through the throat so hard that the sword stuck in the ground behind him.

He knelt down by Ed. She died fast. She didn't suffer. He placed his hand on her neck, where she liked to be petted. She was still warm—almost felt alive—but he knew she wasn't. "I'm sorry, Ed," He said as he choked back tears. "You deserved better than this. You were a good companion. A good friend. I didn't see the Minotaur."

"I failed you."

A few tears got past his defenses. Then he yelled. It was not a wail, but a roar of rage. He was getting tired of finding so many evil creatures and humans in apparently every realm. The yell helped. It let the emotions explode out until they built up again.

As he stood, he heard the sound of a horse galloping behind him. He looked to the east. It was the messenger who had been sent back when they learned about the Empusa. He must have heard the shots and returned to fight. Thomas used the AR-15. It had weaker bullets—human bullets. The rider dropped his spear, lurched backward, and then fell from the horse. The horse trotted to a stop, trained not to run.

There were three dead horses, three still alive that hadn't run, and two pack mules tied to a horse. He didn't have time to sort things or search bodies. He was bleeding, and help could be coming for his enemies. He grabbed the saddlebags from the dead horses and tossed them on his new fleet of mounts. He picked up the spear that had injured him and used it as a staff as he hobbled to the enemy commander.

He looted a satchel, sword, and shield. They were the implements of war, and he would run out of ammunition at some point. Thomas cut a strap off Ed's saddle—a memento to remember a friend. He grabbed his own gear and then climbed on a new horse. He looked down at Ed, a final goodbye.

"I'm sorry. I don't have time to bury you, Ed, but I have to live, and I have to fight. You are a warrior of the Amazons. You understand."

He looked at the paths ahead of him.

He couldn't ride hard enough now, not with this injury. He would either bleed out on the way or end up stuck in the Wailing Trees at night. The plane tree was closer. He could handle his wound, rest, and move in the morning.

Isadora was at least safe for now.

The world failed her.

The gods failed her.

People failed her.

*I won't.*

# CHAPTER 36
## *Warriors*

Thomas steered his new horse through the brush and weeds toward the plane tree. Normally, he would be on foot leading the horse through terrain this rough, but he couldn't walk and needed to get there quickly to tend his wound.

He was slumped over the horse's neck when he finally saw the tree. Seeing the tree gave him hope and enough energy to sit upright in the saddle. He held the AR-15 at the ready as the horse stepped into the clearing at the base of the tree. He looked around and saw the remains of the corpse he had left there, but nothing else of import from this angle.

He urged the horse under the tree, the other horses in tow. He swung his injured leg over the horse and lowered himself to the ground. He could see his blood had run down the horse's side, showing just how much blood he had lost.

He grabbed a couple of saddlebags from the pack mules and dropped them on the ground as he sat, hoping for medical supplies. His were running low. He rifled through the bags and was relieved to find what he needed in the third one he checked.

He scooped together some leaves, tossed twigs on top, and built a quick but small fire. Then he placed a shallow cooking pan in the edge of the fire. He poured water from his canteen into the pan to boil, so he could sterilize his new equipment. He didn't want another infection.

While it was warming, he pulled off his makeshift bandage and pants, revealing a deep, bleeding wound on his leg. His hands were shaking from blood loss and fatigue. He knew he needed to act quickly. He re-tied the wound to slow the blood until he was ready. He threaded a needle with a waxy thread from the kit, then tossed it into the pot.

He didn't have time to be efficient or methodical. He poured a little vinegar directly on the gaping cut, the sharp smell stinging the air. He gritted his teeth against the sting, but also thought of his grandpa's collard greens. Of all the silly things to think at a moment like this, he thought of a vegetable. But his grandpa really liked vinegar in his collard greens. Now, Thomas was getting hungry. He was probably just homesick instead of hungry, but the feeling was still there.

Next, he poured a little honey on a leaf and coated the injury, its sticky sweetness contrasting with the sour vinegar, hoping it would help keep infection away.

He used his knife to fish the thread and needle from the boiling water. It cooled quickly as he blew on it. With trembling hands, he began stitching the torn flesh together, his fingers moving slowly, painfully precise, controlling the shaking by force of will.

He looked at the neatly sliced wound with its jagged stitches. The blood was mostly stopped. He soaked a clean cloth in the boiled water and gently cleaned the area around the wound. His flesh was very cold, and the warm water sent a shiver down his spine. It was almost refreshing using the warm cloth in spite of the pain.

The cloth made his body feel the cold even more. He wasn't expecting it, but he started shivering. Hard. He picked up a clean cloth and began wrapping his leg while his body seemed to shake and spasm—shock, hypothermia?

His mind had just enough energy and clarity left to get him off the dirt.

He pulled his sleeping bag out and rolled into it before passing out.

---

Thomas's eyes snapped open. It was dark and everything hurt, but he didn't move. He always woke like an alarm system. Scanning. Listening.

He couldn't hear anything, and the horses weren't spooked. He rolled onto his back and reached down to feel his leg. It wasn't wet, which he took as a good sign.

---

He didn't remember falling asleep. He remembered blinking, but the sun was up now. He looked at his horses and managed to croak out, "Good morning. I think."

He wanted to go back to sleep, but Athena was hunting Isadora. He believed Isadora thought he was dead. That would affect how hard she fought to stay alive. He needed to get to her first and keep her safe, but based on the sun's position and his weakness, he couldn't make it today. He would eat, drink, and care for the horses. At first light tomorrow, he would leave.

If he could.

He was concerned about his wound. His first leg wound had been shallow, but jagged. The claws of a satyr. This wound was deep, but clean. The head of a spear. He didn't know which was actually worse to have, but he hoped the clean slice would heal faster.

*It's a clean slice and I sewed it shut. It should just zip back together.*
*Yeah, that's right, Thomas.*
*Use your extensive experience of being stabbed with spears to draw a conclusion.*

He slowly and carefully got up and hobbled over to his lead horse. He took a spear from the saddle and used it to hold himself upright. He looked through the bags to see if there was anything helpful. There were more medical supplies, spears, coins, clothes, rope, items for repairing weapons and armor—the stuff one would expect from a war party. He also had the leader's sword and shield; they were the nicest in the bunch.

But the most interesting thing was the food. He had been rationing his supplies since he arrived. A Clif bar counted as a whole meal, sometimes a day's worth of meals. Now he had the food for ten men for a week on the pack mule: hardtack, dried meat, nuts, honey, and wine. He put some food in a small satchel and tossed it by the tree. The horses were first.

They had been standing there overnight, saddled and burdened.

He led the horses down to the pool's edge, leaning on the lead horse for support. Although it wasn't far, it felt like a journey. When they arrived, he set his spear against a low branch, close at hand, just in case. First, he loosened each girth, lifting the saddle in one smooth motion, draping it over a fallen log. He unclipped the bridles and slid the bits free, speaking softly as he worked, describing what he was doing so they could hear a voice, following the steps Kallianeira had taught him.

1.  **Hoof Inspection:** Crouching beside the stallion, he pulled the hoofpick from his belt pouch and scraped away gravel and mud from the frog and sole. He tapped the hoof heel-to-toe, listening for any uneven echo that might hint at a crack or bruise.

2.  **Limb Check & Massage:** Rising, he ran both hands down the horse's cannon bone, feeling for heat or swelling. Where a tendon felt tight, he kneaded the muscle in gentle circles, coaxing warmth away.

3.  **Coat Brushing:** With a stiff brush, he swept from withers to flank, lifting dried sweat and dust. Then, switching to the softer brush, he skimmed along the horse's mane and tail, loosening tangles and letting the animal feel the careful strokes.

4.  **Cool-Down Rub:** He dipped a cloth in the shallow water and wrung it out, then wiped the horse's chest and shoulders in long downward strokes. Kallianeira said it was for drawing heat out after a hard ride. It hadn't been a hard ride, but he suspected Ares's men didn't show their horses this level of care. He did.

5.  **Hydration & Feeding:** He found feed on one of the mules. He spread a little on the ground to make sure they would eat. He ran a rope between two trees, giving them room to move back and forth to get food and water. This wasn't from Kallianeira. It was from Clint Eastwood, some old western he saw years ago. He didn't know if this was the best way, but he saw it in a movie, so it had to be good.

When every horse seemed quiet and content, he stepped back and ran his hand over his own wound. He was breathing hard and dizzy, but still standing.

He walked around to the front of his fleet of horses, leaned on his spear, and addressed them. "You are no longer warhorses," he said with the authority of a general addressing his troops, but with the softness befitting new recruits.

"You are now—warrior horses. It's different." One of the horses shook his head. "I see you have your doubts. That's okay. But Ed was a warrior horse. A horse of the Amazon people. I don't know you guys well enough to give you names yet—unless you already have names. Can you guys speak? I just killed a Minotaur yesterday, so you wouldn't shock me if you could talk. Go ahead. Say your piece."

Silence.

Thomas knew his words were gibberish, but talking to the horses made them get used to his voice. It calmed them. So, he continued, "I'm going to be honest. I'm glad no one spoke up. That would have been weird. You guys go ahead and eat some grass; we ride in the morning."

Thinking of Kallianeira's lessons about horse care made him smile. He wondered if she was okay and if she had ever delivered her message. He glanced toward the tree as he recalled his note. He hobbled over and found his paper was missing, but in its place, he found a feather with a small leather braid.

Thomas smiled again as he picked up the feather.

*She made it. She is probably on her way back to her people.*

He looked west. "Godspeed, Kallianeira. Be safe, my friend."

After the event with the Minotaur, he decided it was time to move his gear around to more strategic places. His hand cannon on his hip had saved his life. It stayed. The AR-15 on a sling on his chest was also useful. His shotgun was attached to his backpack over his right shoulder. If his pack had been strapped to Ed instead of his back, he would be dead right now. He couldn't go anywhere today, so he used his supplies to rig a holster for the shotgun on his back. Easier to reach. Faster to draw.

But the main thing he wanted when that Minotaur had him on the ground was his brush gun. The beast had shrugged off most of the bullets that hit it, but the brush gun might have been able to put it down. At the very least, Thomas wanted the option to try if it happened again. He made a holster for it that he tied to his right leg, the trigger in line with his knee. When he bent that leg, the butt of the gun stuck up. It was the perfect height and easy to reach when he was on his back.

The whole time he was working, he was snacking. It was nice putting his hands to work and snacking without rationing. He was still dealing with all of his fears, pains, and losses, but this was something he could do. He could darn socks—so he darned socks.

He set up his tent, reloaded his guns, and stowed his gear. He drank wine, and he planned.

*One friend made it past here safely. Tomorrow, I look for Isadora. I just need to keep her safe from Ares and Athena.*

*I wonder if my guns can hurt a god.*

# CHAPTER 37
## *Silence the Scream*

Thaleia walked forward with confidence. Her gait was swift and hinted at an unnatural strength. When most people walk, there is some effort, muscle pushing forward, but her steps almost seemed to float.

She glided up the stairs, taking two at a time, though she gave no impression of rushing. She was simply not slowed down by trivial things like gravity. She walked by the attendants as they placed their fists over their hearts in salute, but she didn't notice. She had war on her mind and was anxious to get to the front lines. She strode forward into the hall.

The hall rose from the mountain stone as if Olympus itself had shaped it for Athena, or perhaps a power older than gods gave it purpose. It was a sanctuary of balance, strength, and quiet thought. Pale marble formed the walls, veined with silver and blue. They looked like ice, locked in motion. Each pillar stood tall and steady, not crafted and placed, but shaped out of the mountain itself. Their fluted sides caught the light, casting long, solemn shadows across the floor.

The majesty of the hall commanded a certain sense of quiet respect, a desire to maintain the beauty of its peace. The roof arched high above, lined with reliefs of constellations and battlefields. Moments of mortal and divine resolve.

Lamps hung in suspended stillness, fed by no flame, yet lit by a cool white glow that had no mortal explanation. Their light softened the air, giving a calming effect to those willing to receive it.

At the center stood a long table of dark wood polished to a mirror sheen. A scroll lay open on it, a wax seal broken cleanly in half. Around the edges of the hall, suits of armor stood in recesses like sentinels at rest: Amazon, Hellenic, and strange patterns from far-off lands and old wars that even Thaleia did not recognize.

There were no thrones or banners. The hall did not enforce obedience or respect. It earned it. And it rewarded presence with a kind of stillness that let one think clearly. It was not a place of comfort. It was a place of purpose.

Thaleia was not there for peace or reflection. She was there with urgency. The Amazons were under attack at the Path of Blood, and they needed their allies; they needed Thaleia. She swiftly crossed the hall to her mother, who stood at the table.

"Goddess," said Thaleia as she placed her fist over her heart in salute. Athena was her mother, but also a goddess. In her hall, she demanded respect.

Athena turned her gaze to her daughter. "Speak, child," she replied without emotion.

Thaleia relayed her message. "Kallianeira the Iron Voice of the Amazons has delivered a message. The Agitators have pushed back and threaten to take the Path. The Amazons were trapped by superior numbers, but she broke through."

Athena weighed the information before replying, "Soon, but not yet. There is another matter, a greater matter. It demands my attention and therefore yours. A Fury has screamed in a town not far from Olympus. The Furies have been missing for centuries, and their return could destabilize the gods."

Thaleia looked into her mother's eyes as she responded, "The Amazons hold the Path of Blood at our request. We swore to give them support if the Agitators returned. We must honor—"

"You forget yourself, daughter," snapped Athena. "We will honor our obligation, but the Fury must be silenced before its wail wakes the others. Very few have the power to contain one of their kind, and fewer still have the wit to be discreet and avoid causing panic."

"Yes, goddess," replied Thaleia as she averted her gaze.

Athena turned dismissively as she said, "Speak with the Servitor. She knows the name of the town. Go quickly and take whatever you need. We will speak when you return."

Thaleia hesitated. "What terms, goddess? Do you wish to offer help in her vengeance? To appease her?"

"No, she is to go away. Remind her to keep silent and do not believe her lies. If she will not listen, enforce the silence."

Thaleia turned to leave. "Yes, goddess."

Athena did love her daughter, but she was a goddess of strategy and plans, not emotion. She knew her coldness could be considered harsh by a daughter who longed for her mother's respect. She knew that some beings needed that extra encouragement.

"Wait," the goddess said softly. "You are noble for wanting to honor your word. But the Amazons won't need your help if the foundation of our world is shattered by the return of outdated beings with outdated systems of vengeance. Once the Fury is contained, I will help you protect the Path and the women who hold it. I know they are special to you."

Thaleia smiled as she turned back. "Thank you, mother," she said softly so as not to disrespect the goddess in her hall. "I will make you proud."

Athena nodded. "I must speak to Zeus of this matter. Swift journeys daughter." Thaleia turned and walked from the hall.

The Servitor stepped forward to meet Thaleia. She did not salute. She did not bow. The Servitor was in a position of some standing. She relayed information with the authority of her goddess, but she did show respect, as though to an equal. Thaleia was Athena's most favored servant.

She held forth a piece of paper. "The town's name is within the letter, as is the swamp the creature has been rumored to inhabit. A primal scream was felt by the gods. They say it was a Fury, but they have not heard such a sound before. Not from one of them. They are vengeance with wings, not things that can know love. Your mother wishes it to remain silent, no matter the means. If you return it, your mother can make it go to sleep."

Thaleia opened the letter and read the names. "They are close. Send a messenger owl to my people. I will leave immediately."

The Servitor replied, "Your mother requires discretion."

"I understand, but she also requires success. I will bring my men to help with the search, but I will handle the creature myself."

Thaleia jogged across the courtyard to the residential hallway. She would get her equipment and then join her phalanx at the base of

Olympus.

She was excited by the prospect of fighting a Fury, a creature from before her time. She was an immortal, but the Furies had gone to sleep before she was born. They felt almost mythical, made up. Not like the idea of gods or Medusa—this was a creature of ancient legend she had heard about as a child. And now, she could fight one for glory. For Olympus.

Thaleia smiled as she met her people at the base of the mountain. They were prepared for her, in uniform and mounted except for the commander, Leandros. He stood by the dais that allowed access to Olympus, holding the reins of two horses. When he saw her approach, he saluted.

She smiled; she liked her troops. She felt awkward in halls and courts, even though she grew up in them. They lacked the simple honor of fighting. She destroyed evil so good could flourish. And these were the men and women of valor who followed her into combat against creatures of legend and armies of evil. They were the best warriors in the kingdom.

She returned the salute and hopped onto her horse. She did not put her foot in a stirrup and climb up. She didn't even notice her ease of movement; she had it her whole life. She simply hopped and was in the saddle.

She turned her horse to face them. These men and women were not her army. They were her personal guard, not that she needed them. But she trusted them. They had faced many horrors together, and now they faced another.

"We face a creature of legend today. Tell no one unless I say to do so. We ride." And with that, she led the group. The town was days away, but her horses were enhanced by her mother, able to move beyond the speed of mortal mounts. They made the journey in half a day before the spell broke. It lasted as long as needed, just as her mother had calculated. Had they gone much longer, the horses would have died from the strain.

Her presence commanded respect and attention. As she rode into town, the people stared in awe and backed out of the street. She didn't give commands. She simply made eye contact with her soldiers and nodded. They understood and began questioning villagers. She gracefully brought her right leg up and over the neck of her mount with such speed and control that she seemed to float sideways, landing on the ground already walking.

She walked toward the man rebuilding the stable door. She looked at two of her men and motioned to the door. They sprang into action, repairing it for the tavern owner.

He stepped back nervously. He was thankful for the help, but their overwhelming presence made him uncomfortable. He fidgeted with his hammer as the daughter of a god approached to question him. He looked around at the soldiers and then at the hammer in his hands.

He leaned down and placed it on the ground.

Thaleia spoke, "You may hold your hammer, good citizen. This is your town and your building. My people are no threat to you. We are here to help you. I am Thaleia, Bearer of the Threads of Ruin, Vanquisher of the Emissary of Apophis, and Destroyer of the Shadow Gate of Lem. I am on the business of my mother, Athena. Please continue about your business. We are going to search the area."

As she walked past him, she gave a subtle nod, and one of her men began questioning the tavern owner.

She inspected the scene: stable door shattered, bloodstains on the ground, roof shingles cracked. Then she looked at the body. It had been moved into the barn and covered with a blanket. It was the work of a powerful beast. The arm was ripped in two, and the jaw torn clean off. It took great strength to hurt a body that precisely. Normally, she would expect either more damage or less. Usually, the bodies were either shredded entirely or killed by surgical precision. But this was the work of something that could tear a human into pieces with no effort. It did not take pleasure in this killing. It didn't linger. It was efficient.

After her inspection concluded, she walked back to her horse, where her men were gathering. They quickly relayed reports of their interviews with the people of the town. Stories of a winged demon that killed and shrieked before flying south. Stories of a powerful man who could hurt and disable with even less effort than the demon. He could control thunder with his hand. He rode west. From the description, it was hard to say which of the two was more dangerous.

This was unexpected. She came to find a Fury.

Now she had a second mystery. A man who could defeat with a touch was an ally of a Fury. And from the testimony of the tavern owner, it was the man who directed her. Was it possible that this man compelled it?

This was bigger than her mother knew.

# CHAPTER 38
## *Two Roads Diverged*

Thaleia gave a hand gesture, her index finger pointing up and swirling in a circle. Her men returned to their horses. She tossed a leg over her saddle with casual grace, an almost nonchalant motion that showed her poise matched her strength. She rode to the middle of the street and turned to face the townsfolk who had gathered to see the strangers.

In a clear voice that carried down the street, she said, "My goddess Athena has dispatched me to help with your troubles. You are a good people and don't deserve to live in fear. I will investigate who these beings are and see to it they are judged. I am sorry for your grief. I am sorry for your losses. Have faith in the goddess of wisdom to protect you. She is my mother. But she is a mother to us all. May her wisdom bless your lives."

With that, she turned and rode out of town. She meant what she said to them. She was a mighty warrior, but she had a heart and didn't like seeing their suffering. This was why she hunted mighty beasts. There was glory and the excitement of combat, but she loved her people and wanted them to live their lives to the fullest, to have children that were safe from these monsters.

She had never had children herself. She liked the excitement of travel and exploration. Her mother was the goddess of wisdom, but also of strategy and war. She wanted to prove herself worthy of her mother's name, so she didn't have time for other interests. She was the goddess's right hand.

As her troops emptied from the town, she looked at Commander Leandros and gave a single nod. He called out, "Point, flankers, rearguard."

Three horsemen galloped ahead, three dropped behind, and two groups of two pulled off to the right and left. She had trained them to send scouts all around the main group to give warning of potential traps or to look for signs of their prey.

They did not have to ride very far before one of the point scouts returned. As he approached, he turned his horse sideways so he could give his report and quickly speed back ahead of the party.

The commander reined his horse to a stop before the scout. "Report."

The scout gestured along the road and replied, "Trouble ahead. Dead war party. It looks like Ares's men found something they didn't expect."

Thaleia made a clicking sound to calm her horse as it fidgeted sideways before asking, "How big is the party?"

"Ten men and a Minotaur."

The men normally held their tongues and acted as soldiers, but this news caused a stir. The men murmured while the horses, sensing their rider's discomfort, fidgeted. A Minotaur did not die easily.

She let out a low whistle. "Any signs of who or what they fought?"

"No, Strategis Thaleia. It is a well-traveled road. Tracks were difficult to determine, but there were very few that were fresh. It appeared to be a small party. Doros rode on ahead to look for more tracks."

Thaleia nodded.

Commander Leandros called out, "Forward." The scout galloped ahead, and the rest resumed their pace.

Leandros rode abreast of his Strategis, his general, and asked, "It is not my place to presume your mother's business, but it would be helpful to know what we hunt. Did it kill the Minotaur?"

He was loyal. They all were. They would ride into Tartarus itself if she commanded it, and they would do so without complaint. But she respected her soldiers, and they deserved to know what was at stake.

She looked over at her commander and responded, "A Fury of old. This mission is of great import to Olympus. It also requires great discretion. The relics of ancient times can't be allowed to wake, or they risk shaking the foundations of the world. As for the man who was with her, I don't know what he is. The group we fought at the Path of Blood has returned, and the Amazons are sore pressed, but the Fury must be handled first. I suspect they might have found a way to enrage this one, but that is just a guess."

He shook his head slowly, weighing the implications of the Furies' awakening. They were beings older than gods but had been asleep since the time of his distant ancestors. They were just fairy tales for children now—except one just attacked a town.

"If the Agitators can awaken the Furies, our armies would be overwhelmed. The gods themselves would have to fight them."

Thaleia nodded. "And that is why we will find this man who commands it."

As they spoke, they saw the scouts ahead, on foot, inspecting the scene.

The scout who spoke before gestured to the Minotaur, "I've never seen damage like that. Some of the others, too. There are holes punched right through armor like they weren't wearing it. The beast is missing the back of its head. It is as though he were hit from the inside out. This is dark magic."

Thaleia whipped a leg over her horse's head and dropped to the ground, but barely made a sound, just a small puff of dust at her landing. She walked through the carnage, looking at tracks, reading the battle.

"The tracks do indicate a small group left to the west, but I believe it was just a group of horses with one rider. There are more dead men here than horses, and it looks like one horse came this direction and was killed. That one has no emblem of Ares on it. The style of the saddle indicates it was once of the Amazon women. If I read this correctly, one man did this, then took the horses with him."

The commander knew her tracking skills were far beyond his. He was an excellent tracker, but her sense of sight was magnitudes better than his. One of the gifts of being the daughter of a goddess. She had also been tracking since before his grandfather was born. He trusted her assessment.

Leandros gestured west. "Do you think that's the man we hunt?"

Thaleia walked back to her horse and sprang onto its back. She looked west along the road and then south toward the swamp. "I must hunt the Fury. Commander split the company into two. Clean this mess, then go west. Look for the man. He is dangerous, but I will not act without knowledge. Speak with him if he will hear you. Try peace and reason first. Only kill him if your life is threatened."

The commander placed his fist over his heart in salute. "Yes, Strategis."

As he dismounted, he called out, "Hammer and Anvil."

The soldiers separated into two groups as they had drilled for years. It was a simple but effective tactic. Thaleia led the hammer. In a tactical situation, the anvil group would use shields and either hold a position, braced against a charge, or directly attack an enemy. The tactic was meant only to mire the enemy, not overextend. Then the hammer would charge into an unprotected flank or rear, crushing them between the hammer and anvil.

The anvil group had larger shields and were prepared to fight on foot. The hammer group had longer spears to drive the charge through the enemy. In this case, it was an easy way to separate the phalanx even if they weren't planning to use the maneuver.

Thaleia turned toward the anvil. "Take care of yourselves and each other. May the goddess give you wisdom and strength."

They saluted in response as she rode away.

The commander began the grisly task of burying the bodies. He inspected things as he went, but there were very few details of importance. The dead horse appeared to be of Amazon origin. He respected them. They were a strong warrior caste who worked with Thaleia on several occasions, but he could not believe a single female warrior could have done this damage—except for Thaleia. He had seen her do this kind of damage. But the Amazons were mortals.

It took hours for them to dig a hole, drag the bodies, and bury them. Normally, he would prefer setting the bodies in a pile and burning them, but the grass and brush along both sides of the road were tall and dry. It could destroy the town if a fire spread.

So they dug. Like a true leader, he took his turn with the shovel. He led by example, and his men worked all the harder for him, not because of fear or discipline, but because he earned their respect.

The scout who had gone further west to watch for tracks returned, drawing his horse to the edge of the road.

Commander Leandros walked up the bank to meet him. "Report."

"The tracks from the horses curve off the road to the north. They appear to be crossing country."

Leandros made the twirling finger gesture which meant to mount up. It was a shallow grave, but it was more than men of Ares deserved. He led the anvil west until they found the tracks the scout reported. They had already had a full day, and he didn't want to get caught in the wilds in the dark. It wasn't safe to leave the road too far behind.

"Make camp," called out their leader. "Low profile. Let's go back into the brush off the south side. I want people to walk past and not know we are here. We'll pick up the trail in the morning."

He was a commander under Thaleia. It was one of the most prestigious commands in all of Olympus. He had earned it through grit and valor. But for the first time in a long while, he was worried.

He didn't want to face a Minotaur, much less whatever had blown that one apart. But fear had no place in front of his crew.

He looked north, where the tracks disappeared into the brush.

He would find this man. No matter the cost.

# CHAPTER 39
## *Three Facts*

Thomas's alarm buzzed softly. It was all he needed. He had set it to wake him before the sun was in the sky. Enough time to get the warriors ready.

He didn't actually know what time it was. He used his watch and smartphone to track time's passing, but he had never gotten around to changing anything when he arrived. So although he didn't know the current time in Olympus, he knew it was four in the afternoon back home.

Head pounding, leg throbbing, he crawled out of his tent.

He broke down the camp quickly and loaded the horses. Although he had killed Ares's party, he knew that Athena had sent her own people. They were actually more dangerous. Even if they didn't attack, Isadora would not react kindly to the name Athena.

Thomas stood in front of his new warrior horses and crossed his arms. "Okay. We have a big day ahead. We need to ride as hard as my leg will allow until we reach the swamp. If we don't make it, we will be stuck in the giggling forest, also known as the Wailing Trees. It's not as nice as it sounds, especially after dark. I need your best today, warrior horses. Make Ed proud."

With that, he hobbled to his lead horse, gripped the saddle horn, and slowly hoisted himself up. His body was in bad shape, but his friend needed him, and he would not let her down.

He moved slowly through the brush on his way back to the road. Carefully. It was tricky enough in the light, and the sun was not up yet. He wanted to give himself as much daylight as possible for his journey. He couldn't lead on foot like he would normally, at least not until he healed.

The sun started to peek over the horizon to the east, casting long shadows along the road. He smiled when he heard the clops of his horse's hooves on stone. Now he could travel faster. He steered his horse to the east, toward the sun and toward the road that led to the swamp.

A group of men emerged on horseback from the brush in front of him. He heard sounds behind.

He and Kallianeira had used this spot to enter the road because it had a flat landing to the north, but the south was rugged with dips and walls of rock, even rugged enough to hide an ambush.

Thomas took a deep breath and flipped the safety off on his AR-15.

*You just walked into another ambush, Thomas.*

*How many people are you going to have to kill today?*

The lead man raised his right hand, a universal sign of peace, meant to show he was not holding a weapon.

It was not a universal sign of friendship to lie in wait for unsuspecting travelers.

The man spoke, but Thomas did not understand him.

"I do not understand your language. I am a traveler passing through."

The man responded in English, "My name is Leandros. I am the commander of these men. A man who does not speak the local language is an oddity this far from the ocean. Where do you call home?"

"Nowhere," responded Thomas. It was honest. "My name is Thomas, and I no longer have a home. It was destroyed by enemies. However, the region was called Appalachia."

Leandros nodded knowingly. As a soldier, he had seen many places destroyed. He had destroyed a few himself. "I am sorry for your losses, traveler. But perhaps you can assist with my investigation. I am searching for a man who destroyed a war party that belonged to Ares. It was just a short way east of where we are now."

Thomas arched an eyebrow. "That was me. They had a Minotaur too. Are you here to avenge them?"

"No. But I am curious. How did you manage that by yourself? Did you have an ambush that caught them off guard?"

He shook his head. "No, those men had me surrounded, much

like yours now. Do you have a Minotaur in the bushes?"

The commander stiffened. "I do not like being threatened."

Thomas looked to his left and then to his right in an obvious manner, then responded, "It looks like we have that in common."

They locked eyes for several seconds, waiting for the other to blink. Finally, the commander motioned with his hand for his men to back away from the newcomer.

He nodded as a sign of acquiescence. "We mean you no threat. We are not friends of Ares. Our god dispatches us to fight against him often. You may have saved a few lives by killing that group. I thank you. If I may ask, what led to the attack? Ares should not be working in this area."

"They stopped me to chat. It was going well enough until they started talking about how much fun they have with Amazon women. They described how they treat them. One of them is my friend, so I killed the group to keep others safe. It wasn't hatred or vengeance. It was justice. It was needed."

The commander chuckled. Then his eyes narrowed as he replied, "Now, I know you are new, stranger, but that was not a good lie. The Amazons do not make friends with men."

Thomas clenched his teeth. This man was wasting his time. "I'm special. Is this conversation turning back into a threat now, or are we still friends?"

Leandros nudged his horse forward, not threateningly, just to instill a sense of closeness. "I am just confused. Perhaps you misspoke. I have lived here my whole life. I have fought side by side with Amazons, but I have never befriended one. How did you do it?"

Thomas responded with a sigh, "I mean no disrespect. This is turning into such a pleasant conversation, but a friend of mine is in trouble, and I stand by my friends. I have a long way to go and a short time to get there. I would be happy to discuss this at a later date. Is there anything else you need before I leave?"

The commander's countenance dropped. "I'm afraid you cannot leave. I am also investigating a murder in the town, aside from the investigation of the war party of Ares. Do you know anything about that murder?"

"No. I know of a woman who was attacked and defended herself. There was no murder."

Leandros nodded. His soldiers began to move closer, cutting off escape. "How did you know that woman?"

Thomas locked eyes with the commander. He shifted slightly in the saddle, making it look like he was just getting comfortable, but he subtly pointed the gun at him, in case it was needed. "I will give three facts. One: she is my friend. Two: I don't want to kill you. Three: I will kill every last one of you if you force me."

The commander raised his hand slowly. He didn't know how, but he knew the strange man meant it. He was so convincing that the commander believed he could do it. The description from the town, the dead Minotaur—this man was a whirlwind of death.

"Give him some space," called the commander. The soldiers backed up. One of the warrior horses gave a snort of relief. "You seem a civilized man, Thomas. You understand we have to investigate murders?"

"I do. Did you investigate the nature of the murdered man? Did you ask the tavern owner what that man did to the woman? He was upset that she turned down his advances, so he grabbed her. She stopped him—I'm proud of her."

The commander turned and looked at one of his men. The man nodded, agreeing that the dead man had grabbed her. It matched the interview.

He turned back to Thomas. "My apologies. I don't mean to impugn your friend, but the stories are a little more detailed. Did she sprout wings and fly away?"

A couple of heartbeats passed as they weighed each other. Thomas responded, "Do your stories say that I had nothing to do with the death? If so, I would like to be on my way. Peacefully."

Leandros sighed. He didn't want to push this man. He didn't feel he had a right. Although the stranger was powerful, he had done nothing wrong. He had, in fact, been useful in destroying Ares's men and their pet. The tavern owner said he was nice. The commander was a warrior, not a thug.

He replied, "I ask a moment more of your time. You claim

friendship with both an Amazon and a Fury. That is unheard of. Furies do not have friends, and Amazons do not like men. Even one would be a stretch, but two seems strange. Please help me understand. What is the Amazon's name? Perhaps I know her."

"Which god do you serve?" asked Thomas. He didn't want to risk putting Kallianeira in danger by giving her name to an enemy, but if this man had truly fought by Amazon women before, perhaps he could be an ally.

The commander shifted uncomfortably at that. "I am not the one giving answers."

"You better start."

The troops shuffled, preparing for their commander's order.

Again, he raised his hand. "Hold."

"Very well, stranger. I serve the goddess Athena, and in her service, I am here to investigate what happened in town. I have answered your question. What is your friend's name?"

*Athena. She knows about Isadora; that is why he is here.*

*This isn't just about the town. Isadora is being hunted.*

"Kallianeira the Iron Voice." Thomas reached into the satchel on his side and retrieved a feather with a braid dangling from it. "She left this as a message to me at the last place we saw each other, a place we sheltered for the night. She used this to let me know she had delivered her message to Athena. Her task is complete, but I still need to deliver my message to Thaleia."

The commander's eyes went wide. "I do know that name, stranger. You impress me by knowing it. Thaleia said the Iron Voice was in a hurry to get back to her injured friend. I assumed it was another of her kind that had the leg wound." The commander looked down at Thomas's bloodstained clothing.

"If you wish to deliver your message to Thaleia, you will find her in the swamp. She is a day's ride ahead of us."

Thomas smiled. After all this time, all this pain, and all the struggle, he was about to complete his quest. He was going to meet the woman who took his life. He might not live through the next twenty-four hours, but it would be over. His message would be delivered.

He looked the commander in the eyes. "Oh, you want to come

with me? Very well, let's go."

Thomas nudged his horse forward toward Thaleia, surrounded by her troops. She had destroyed his life before, and she was now standing between him and Isadora.

# CHAPTER 40
### *Sisters*

Thaleia was up before the sun. Her warrior side wanted to battle a legend of old. She wanted to see what a Fury could do, not so she could kill, but so she could challenge herself. She respected beings so ancient that even the gods themselves feared them and called them relics. If this were truly one of them, a true creature of legend, then she would prefer to let it live.

She would try to use the Threads of Ruin if she had to fight it. It was an ancient item, forged by Hephaestus, the blacksmith god, after he learned his wife was unfaithful to him. He wove this net and set a trap over his bed. When he was away, Aphrodite and Ares joined each other in that bed. The trap was sprung.

Hephaestus didn't simply walk in and catch them. He invited the other gods to join him. The goddesses refused to come out of modesty, but the male gods gathered and stared at the lovers in their unescapable embrace.

The net's only power was that even a god couldn't break it, but that changed after the trap was triggered. The Threads absorbed the rage of Ares being trapped, the shame of Aphrodite on display, and the truth demanded by Hephaestus. Now it could be cast on an enemy, ensnaring them, tightening so they couldn't escape, and punishing them, especially if they didn't tell the truth. If it could contain two gods, it should contain a relic.

He had given it to Thaleia long ago as payment for a favor. It was a reminder of his wife's infidelity, but it was so powerful he could not bring himself to destroy it. He was a creator, and this was a unique item that could never be replicated.

She strapped on her armor, manica, and sword, but no shield. She did not like hiding behind a wall when she could simply destroy her enemy instead.

The sun was just starting to peek over the trees as Thaleia mounted her horse. The creatures in the Wailing Trees were going to sleep. Her men would be safe to travel through them. She directed them to keep their distance. She hoped to speak with the creature without the threat of her guard approaching.

She walked her horse through an open field. There were statues all around, old and damaged, forgotten gods. She rode forward past them, listening for any signs of the creature.

She stopped a short distance from the swamp and dismounted with a grace that demonstrated her experience. She rested one hand on her net, ready to launch it, but she hoped she wouldn't need to use it.

Her horse whinnied but didn't run. It was trained and loyal, but it was unhappy. Something in the swamp was screaming danger to the horse.

"Fury," Thaleia called into the swamp. "I am Thaleia, Bearer of the Threads of Ruin, Vanquisher of the Emissary of Apophis, and Destroyer of the Shadow Gate of Lem. Your people have been missing from the realm for centuries. I would like to speak with you."

She stepped forward alone.

Her boots sank into the mud immediately. It was not deep, but it was enough to remind her that this place did not welcome her. It was not her land, and it would hinder her if a fight became unavoidable. Cypress roots pushed up through the muck like twisted bones. Trees leaned in, their trunks swollen and draped in moss like sagging skin. Even the light had gone dull, filtered through branches so thick it felt like standing beneath a cloth.

She pushed deeper into the marsh where the dirt had given up completely, moving without fear of what might rise from the water. There were no ripples. No birds. No insects. There was a silence that pressed in. She hated that silence. It wasn't peaceful. It was preparing.

She started tracing her fingers along her coiled net, finding comfort in its presence.

She felt a shadow pass over what little light remained. Her heart pounded. She looked forward to challenges, but adrenaline still surged when they were close.

She stopped moving. "Fury, what is your name?"

There was no cry, no warning. Just a heavy, wet thud of flesh meeting earth, and a splash that hissed through the quiet. Her black wings outstretched, slowly pulling into her sides. The waves turned to ripples and then stopped almost immediately, as though the swamp welcomed her presence.

She looked into Thaleia's eyes, her head tilting in one direction, then the reverse, but her body didn't move. Just her head. Back and forth. Back and forth. Her eyes were pitch black holes that did not blink.

Thaleia gripped the net but did not pull it. She was ready, but didn't want to force a confrontation. It could still be peaceful. But if she had to, she was sure she could defeat it.

A sound of water cascading came from her left. Thaleia's eyes widened. She slowly turned her head and saw a second creature stand from the swamp. It had been lying in wait beneath the still water.

Now there were two.

She repeated her question, "What are your names?"

The first Fury hissed a response, "My name doesn't matter for something like you. I am ancient beyond your understanding. I have lived long enough to see the birth of gods. Do you think we answer to you?"

The second Fury made a gurgling sound as it said, "Where is my sister? She wailed in pain. We have not seen her in centuries. We felt her injuries. Something powerful is needed to hurt one of us."

Another splash from behind. Thaleia was actually afraid. She faced combat many times, but she had natural advantages because of her bloodline and tools. This fight would be beyond her, and she knew it.

The third Fury blocked her exit from the swamp. It said, "We awaken. We seek our sister. We seek the three."

Thaleia slowly backed toward a thicker concentration of trees, hoping to use them as cover if she had to flee. It was a futile gesture against these foes, but it was her only hope in a fight. "I am here because of the wail, the same as you. The gods of Olympus wished to know what happened. I do not know who was hurt."

They slowly closed around her, heads never moving up or down, just twisting left side up, right side up. The two new Furies mirrored the first, every head turning in perfect unison. They moved in a slow, mesmerizing rhythm as they closed on Thaleia. She backed through the trees.

She gripped the coiled net so tightly that her hand hurt. "Would you like me to take a message back to Olympus? If you are awake, we should coordinate. The gods will want to speak with you."

The first Fury let out a slow, high-pitched guttural sound from its throat.

The second Fury said, "The gods are children. They do not matter. Where are my sisters?"

Thaleia could feel actual panic starting to set in, yet she forced her voice to be calm. "I do not know. But I will look. If I find one, will I be able to return to this location to speak with you?"

The third Fury's voice wobbled in a low growl as it drew out the word, "Nooooooooo. We return to the underworld. But we seek our sisters. We will be watching."

With that, all three of them launched into the air with such speed that the water shot up behind them in spouts. They crashed through the canopy, sending a cascade of branches and twigs into the water. Then they were gone.

Thaleia placed her hands on her knees and took a deep breath. It felt as though she had stopped breathing. She didn't fear death, but these things had an aura of dread that radiated from them.

She walked back out to her troops, wearing a brave face. They didn't need to know what was happening, but her mother did.

She walked alongside her horse and, with a flex of her calves, landed sidesaddle. She was thinking of the implications of this new information when her thoughts were interrupted by one of her women.

"Strategis Thaleia. Commander Leandros approaches from the north. A scout came ahead of them. He found the man who directed the Fury in town."

Thaleia was tired. She spent hours walking through sludge, and now she was spattered in swamp muck. She wanted to return to Olympus with her report on the Fury threat, but the investigation of the man was important as well. She looked to the north and saw Leandros's party approaching. He had returned quickly. She expected a full report on the man the townsfolk feared, the one who could summon Furies.

With this new threat from the Furies, he could be a powerful ally—or a powerful enemy.

She nudged her horse into a trot to meet the commander.

Leandros placed his fist over his heart in salute, but before he could speak, Thaleia saw the man. Her eyes widened.

Her hand snatched the Threads of Ruin loose from its strap.

"Ometheon," she hissed.

# CHAPTER 41
## *You Again*

Thaleia swung her left leg over her horse's neck, lifting herself out of the saddle. She landed with a light step—not bending her knees from impact, but in readiness. Poised. Her hand gripped the Threads of Ruin. She ran forward, slightly crouched, ready to throw when the target presented itself.

*How many times must I vanquish this monster?*

Her mind drifted back to the atrocities Ometheon had caused.

She had been called in by her mother to investigate an especially heinous murder. Normally, this was not one of her duties. She was more accustomed to war than to solving crimes, but this was a special case.

Someone had been defiling temples. One of Athena's temples in particular had been ransacked, and the goddess was enraged.

As Thaleia had walked into the temple to investigate, she was moved to pity by the carnage left behind. As a warrior, she had seen death many times, and it was never pretty, but these people were tortured beyond anything she had witnessed before.

Organs had been pulled out while they lived. Limbs had been removed while they yet lived. Skin removed—it was a sickening scene. It wasn't just that it had been done, but that so much of it had been done.

It must have taken days for these people to die. The bodies were at different states of decay, which meant they were killed very slowly and one at a time. The Agitators intended to inflict terror as well as pain. This drove the fear deeper into the victims as they watched their friends tortured, begging for mercy.

Even Thaleia had to turn away. She needed to give her eyes and mind a moment to breathe before continuing.

She continued deeper into the temple. That was when she saw the children—the same had been done to them.

She clenched her teeth, but not in anger. She was angry. She was furious. But in that moment, she was trying to stop the tears. She had never seen this type of horror. It was beyond disgusting, beyond vile. It was the greatest evil she had seen. No word had ever been invented to describe what was done. And it was done to children.

She went into the high priest's personal chamber. There was blood everywhere. It was on the floor, the walls, even the ceiling. It was intentional. It was like it had been used to paint the room.

Her eyes scanned the room slowly, disgusted by the sheer level of hate and pain this scene held. She looked along the bloodstained walls to the third stone from the arch. The one her mother told her to use. She grimaced as she placed her hand on the bloody rock. The wall slid away.

She wiped her hand on a cloth, lit a torch, and held it out before her as she descended into the darkness of the crypt.

Her mother said this area should be untouched. Only the blood of the gods could open that door. Thaleia had just enough for it to obey.

But she was wrong. It was not untouched. She found an arm at the base of the stairs. She drew her xiphos as she continued. It was an unnecessary precaution, but it made her feel better to have it in hand.

She walked to the reliquary arca, its twin doors carved with scenes of owls carrying spears. Her heart was beating faster as she reached for the latch that could only be opened with the blood of a god. Her mother said this arca contained secrets that she kept even from the other gods. It too was covered in blood.

She opened the doors—to emptiness. The secrets were gone.

There were other temples. Other murders. She hunted the murderer for three years before finally learning his name, thanks to a single survivor. A young woman in a monastery had jumped from a window, breaking both her legs. It was a painful price, but one worth paying. She survived the horror that unfolded inside.

Four years before her monastery was visited by mysterious ritualists, she had seen a man she thought was handsome. He was a priest of a god, but she couldn't remember who. It was during a pilgrimage to the shrine of Zeus atop the Trail of Judgement. She never spoke to him, but she had attended some of his speeches. He spoke of how mortals should aspire to immortality. He said the gods favor those bold enough to let nothing stand in their way.

His name was Callistos.

He did not have the blood of a god, yet he could open things sealed with their blood. It was impossible, but there it was. He did it. It was said that he sought a way to travel the paths of power. The Path of Blood. He intended to become as great as a god, or greater.

Another year passed before Thaleia finally got ahead of him. She waited in the darkness, watching, as his followers prepared to move on another library. A place of education and enlightenment turned into a pool of suffering and death. What kind of monster could allow that to happen to children? What kind of evil stood by and did nothing while others suffered?

She would not stand by. She would act.

At her direction, she set a trap and surrounded the ritualists. Her men and women slaughtered most of them. But Callistos himself ran. He ran like the coward he truly was.

He hoped to lose her, sprinting through the darkness. He thought he could escape.

He was wrong.

She saw him glance back, afraid. She sprinted with the speed of her heritage. Easily three times his.

He looked away from her to see his path, but that was when she slammed her armored fist into his back. He pitched forward into the dirt, hard. His face smacked the ground with a satisfying thud.

She flipped him over handily as though he were a child. It was a display of her massive strength advantage to let him know that obeying was a better option than fighting.

She gripped his throat with her armored hand to punctuate the sentence as she said, "You cannot escape me, Callistos. You will lead me to the Path of Blood, or Hades will seem pleasant compared to me."

He grabbed her arm and pulled himself closer. He acted as though an indignant child, pathetic as he postured. "Callistos is dead.

I am Ometheon, the mouthpiece of god."

In disgust, she hit him, knocking him out.

Back at Olympus, she questioned him, but he never broke. He never gave anything useful. He just spoke of dancing and madness and how great his power would be when he ascended past the gods. The gods were not amused.

He was brought to a high cliff at the top of the mountain and chained. He was given a last chance for mercy: to reveal how he learned of these great secrets, but he refused.

Zeus ordered Ometheon to be dragged to the edge and covered in pitch. The gods stood witness as Zeus launched a bolt of lightning into the mad priest, setting him alight and knocking him from the heights of Olympus. He sounded as though he was laughing with joy until he was finally passed out of earshot.

It was as though he truly believed he was not defeated even in death. It turned out he was right. A year later, Thaleia was dispatched to another scene.

This temple was like the others: the same symbols, brutal butchery, walls painted with blood. And they knew where to go to find the secrets. Ancient texts, hidden from mortals and gods alike. Some of the texts were from a time even older than the gods. They had been taken, too.

She knew she had to find a way to get ahead of them, but she didn't know how. She had already cut off the head, but this was not a snake—it was a hydra. It just grew new heads and kept moving.

She would occasionally take out a cell, but she could never take out the whole.

She needed a new plan, even if it wasn't sanctioned or favored by the gods. This killing had to stop at any cost.

# CHAPTER 42
## *Here's Looking at You*

Thaleia returned to her mother's hall after the attendants had left. It wasn't unusual for her to be there in the middle of the night, but she went there tonight to avoid attention, to avoid opinions that would only slow her down.

She walked back to the private chambers behind the table, through the rooms to the smooth, unassuming wall etched with an engraved map of the land. She traced the road from the great tree to the swamp, the lock for the door.

The wall slid open silently. She wasn't actually doing anything wrong. She was simply retrieving something she had left here years ago. Her mother had said it was dangerous, unnatural, perhaps even cursed, but she needed it now.

She stepped down the stairs to the chamber her mother had set aside for her. It was a place to keep trophies, relics, and items of power that shouldn't fall into enemy hands. She kept her Khopesh, Sekhem-Ka, here when she didn't need it.

The weapon resembled a partially straightened sickle, but the metal itself looked like a Damascus blade twisted into madness. Black and silver lines shifted across the surface, slow and restless, like blood crawling beneath skin. Nothing dripped. It didn't bleed. It remembered. Every life it had ever taken was carved into the shifting lines and trapped beneath the surface. They were etched into its grain like a scar.

Whatever it was, it was thirsty.

It made her powerful. More than she already was. But there was a cost. When she wielded it, she lost her calm. Her strategy. She stopped thinking and started feeding it.

But tonight, she didn't come for the blade.

She came for another item she had picked up under the sands of that desert. It was the tomb of some ancient being that played at being a god. She had forgotten its name. It didn't matter. But those people and their pyramids were obsessed with the dead.

There was a mirror of black obsidian glass with a faint silver shimmer. Her mother told her it was a cursed relic, but powerful. A way to see across the veil, but spirits can't be trusted.

The murders continued to happen. Ometheon knew why and who was responsible. If she could find a way to get the information from him, then she could get ahead of them and stop this violence.

She took Ometheon's dagger and pricked her finger, placing a drop of blood on the mirror to attune it to her. Then she placed the dagger on the mirror to link it to her target. She looked deeply into the black surface. As an actual mirror, it was not very good. There was a slight reflective surface in the sheen of the obsidian, but when she looked deeper, a face started to form.

She closed her eyes, concentrated on the spirit of Ometheon, and held the mirror in front of her face. The dagger did not fall. It slid across the surface of the mirror, and its hilt came to rest across the top with the blade pointing to one side. It was stuck as though held by a lodestone.

She opened her eyes. It shimmered slowly; the edges of features started to take shape. A screaming face, but no sound at first. Ometheon's spirit shifted into focus, and his voice started to come through, screaming in agony.

She said, "Ometheon, it is I, Thaleia. I need to know about your people. Who is—stop screaming. Ometheon!"

His screams and sobs were incoherent gasping sounds. He managed to choke out, "sum-mon—me."

"How?"

His screams resumed. She knew he was useless in this state, but if she could summon him into the mirror, she could offer to leave him in the mirror instead of eternal suffering. He could be a continuing source of information, but still trapped.

She didn't know how to do it, but she focused, trying to pull him toward her and into the mirror. His face became more solid in the reflection. His burns and scars began to fade. He was just a spirit, but the mirror showed a representation of the power of his soul. He began to take solid shape.

His years of studying secret texts of the gods and of beings even older than the gods had given him powers beyond those of a normal Goēs. His soul moved toward the mirror, crossing through realms of existence. He fought against the pull, not so he could stay behind, but so he could choose a new location.

She realized her mistake. She couldn't send him back; she couldn't target like that. He attempted to go to one of his people; she attempted to pull him into his new prison. It was a battle of wills. His hand reached through and grabbed the hilt of his dagger. The shock broke her focus. His hand pulled away through the mirror. It took the dagger with it. She cried out in frustration, redoubling her focus. She pushed every ounce of willpower into the mirror. It was not enough to win, but it was enough to interfere.

They both lost the test of will. His soul was flung into reality randomly, like firing an arrow in the dark while surrounded by people. Someone would be hit, but neither could choose where he would land.

Her heart dropped. She had lost him and, beyond that, she had launched him into the world. She focused, forcing him to appear. It didn't work. She could see him, but he wore a new face. She could see a direction and the strange bedchamber in which he stood, but he ignored her.

She screamed a series of threats at him. Finally, she said she would destroy the mirror. It was the only anchor that kept him in the world where she could reach him, but it was also the only thing that saved him from eternal torment.

Her threat got his attention. He smiled with arrogance as he responded, "I know where the Path of Blood is. I know where they all are. The secrets I stole from your mother showed the entire network. I told my servants, and I told my god. Send me back, and they will never stop. They will collapse the weak points between realms. The worlds will bathe in blood."

"I will destroy your servants, and the gods of Olympus will not stand by while your master meddles in their affairs. The weak spots do not matter. Even if you open them, they will be closed again."

Ometheon laughed. "Do you know what the weak spots do? They allow travel, yes, but they also stop travel. If the spots are broken open, the realms will merge. My god destroyed a weak spot thousands of years ago. He wanted to see what would happen."

Thaleia waited for him to finish, but he just smiled. He wanted her to ask. She found his games annoying, but had no choice. She asked, "What happened?"

"Atlantis drowned."

Thaleia felt as though her heart had stopped. She was staggered by the sudden realization of what could come. If a weak spot were destroyed, mountains could move, oceans could shift, and entire continents could be destroyed. It wasn't just a threat to this realm. It was a threat to all realms.

She didn't know how many millions or billions might die. But it could be the single greatest attack in the history of all the realms. She couldn't allow that to happen.

But it could also be a bluff. She had to find the Path of Blood for herself, but she didn't know where to start… except for this mirror.

Ometheon continued, "The Paths have an order. They must be opened in the correct sequence. They have to be destroyed in that sequence as well. Sending me back means you learn nothing, and my god will destroy everything. He will remake the realms in his image. If I remain in the world, there is a chance to stop my god: by finding me.

"I don't care about his plan. You searched for me, you studied me. You know I only care about my legacy—my power! Let me remain free, and you will have a chance to stop him. Once I am a god, I will even help you."

He faded as her concentration slowed. It was still linked, but he was not fully drawn in. She could not destroy the mirror. She would, but not yet. Not with so much at stake.

For the next two and a half months, she used an oracle and the mirror to track Ometheon's spirit. She found the Path of Blood and took it from the Ritualists. Athena bartered with the Amazons to hold the Path on behalf of Olympus.

She passed through to the other side and shattered the mirror, sending Ometheon back to his eternity. She slew his allies on the far end of the Path. With the Path under her control, she could continue her larger mission, locating Ometheon's master.

The first weak point was safe. And if it was safe, the others were safe. But the bigger threat was still out there.

# CHAPTER 43
## *Tink*

When Thaleia had seen Leandros escorting the host of Ometheon, she had leapt into action, flinging herself from her horse and grabbing her Threads of Ruin. She advanced, positioning herself to throw them and capture the newcomer.

When Thomas saw Thaleia, he too decided to dismount. He leaned forward, almost lying on his horse's neck, and swung one of his injured legs over the saddle. Then, with both arms supporting his weight, he slowly lowered himself to the ground. His legs cracked. His back throbbed from being thrown through a door. His head pounded from loss of blood. He held onto the horse while he fought the head rush from the exertion.

Her soldiers drew their swords, but were confused. The man was not Ometheon. They, too, had hunted him and knew what he looked like. They weren't at the execution, but they were at the base of the mountain watching when his flaming body was cast from the peak. They looked on with grim satisfaction as he screamed through the sky to his final end.

She didn't have a clean throw because he was by the horse. She waited to see his next move. He slipped his strange bag off, holding it by the straps, as he limped forward and away from his horse.

Thaleia threw the net. Thomas threw his bag. The bag landed exactly where he intended in the center of the net. It snapped around it like a trap and dropped to the ground with a damp thud.

"Yeah, that's right," snapped Thomas. "I remembered that thing from the cave."

She drew Aletheia, her xiphos, pointed it at him, and spoke words he could not understand.

"I have no idea what you are saying, but everyone else seems to know English for some reason. Try again."

She smirked. "Your lies won't trick anyone, Ometheon. These soldiers helped capture you the first time. They will be happy to send you back to judgment again."

He began slowly walking toward her, limping but focused. His voice was steady but with an edge of anger. "This body once held Ometheon because of you, but I am something worse. I am the husk of the man you destroyed. I am Thomas, the tool. The tool you used and then cast aside. Why? Why did my life, my family, and my people mean so little to you?"

She paused; this was a new tactic. She did not expect the powerful Ometheon to engage in a conversation. "You claim you are not the spirit of Ometheon. Then how do you know what happened in the cave?"

Thomas pointed a thumb at himself as he replied, "Because it's my body. I was there too. A powerless witness. How did Ometheon possess me? What was the glass you broke on me in the cave?"

She eased her stance, lowering but not sheathing her sword. Her troops did the same, curious now rather than tense.

The sound of a breeze rustled through the grass and leaves as no one in the field dared disturb the silence. If she gave the order, they would overwhelm the newcomer, but it seemed his words had stopped the daughter of Athena.

Finally, she spoke: "Ometheon is a great evil. A murderer who slaughters men, women, and children alike for his own goals and power. He had to be stopped."

"And my body was the only way to stop him? What did he use before my body?"

Again, she hesitated, not sure if she believed the newcomer, but she did not want to reveal the secrets of the gods to her people.

Thomas didn't take his eyes off her as he spoke over his shoulder. "Leandros, did you fight Ometheon?"

"I defer to my Strategis. It is her place to speak, not mine."

Thomas and Thaleia, eyes unblinking, each weighed the other, but neither moved.

"You may answer him, Leandros, but be cautious. Ometheon is

a skilled liar."

The commander responded, "We fought alongside Thaleia. It was her wisdom and strength that captured Ometheon."

Thomas arched an eyebrow, but never looked away from Thaleia as he spoke: "If you were by her side, why didn't I see you in the cave on the other side of the Path of Blood?"

There were a few sharp breaths and horses fidgeting as the troops shifted. This question had surprised them.

After a short pause, Leandros said, "I have never been to the other side. I am not a god. The Path is forbidden to mortals. Aside from the Agitators, no one has traveled the Path in centuries, perhaps longer, even millennia. They were sealed."

Thomas tilted his head slightly. "No one? Is Thaleia, the daughter of Athena, a person who would lie to her people?"

"No. She may not tell us things we don't need to know, but she is the most honorable being I have ever met. She has my complete faith."

Thomas nodded. "Very well, Thaleia. Have you been to the other side of the Path of Blood? Did you attack my body there?"

"Yes." Thaleia was uncertain what this man's plan was. It was possible he was speaking the truth. These did not seem like the words of Ometheon, but he was a brilliant liar and tactician. There was also no way a normal mortal could cross from the other realm. She did not trust him, but she would not lie to her people either.

At her confession to traveling the Path of Blood without telling anyone, her people again shifted. Leandros turned from the newcomer to his leader. "Strategis? You traveled the forbidden Path without telling us to secure it? It is your right, but I was unaware."

Too much had been revealed. She knew her loyal retinue deserved an explanation.

"Ometheon was captured and executed, but the murders didn't stop. I have seen great evil and great slaughter in my hundreds of years, but as all of you know, the rituals this person performed were beyond anything else. The torture. The mutilation. They were indescribable. But he also inflicted that pain on children… it was more than I could bear… and somehow it was continuing after his death.

"I must protect my people—at any cost. I used a cursed artifact to speak to Ometheon, to learn who was continuing his work. He screamed in pain from his eternal torment and couldn't answer my questions. I tried to pull his spirit into the mirror, but he was more practiced at spirit magic.

"He fought me."

She finally broke eye contact with Thomas. The confession had tempered her fire. She was still weary, but now that she started, she wanted someone to know.

She looked around at her soldiers, people who would follow her because they trusted her. People she had kept secrets from. She spoke:

"We fought, but in the end, we both lost. He didn't get to possess the person he wanted, but he wasn't trapped in the mirror. He ended up trapped in another realm. He possessed the body in front of us.

"I used the mirror to track his spirit to our side of the Path of Blood. I could not endanger you by asking you to defy the gods and travel the Path, so I crossed alone.

"Once there, I killed Ometheon's people and broke the mirror that allowed him out of Tartarus. His soul left its host and the realms.

"I had hoped it was a final solution, but the person before us is the body he possessed."

She looked Thomas in his eyes. "But a mortal could not cross the Path of Blood easily. It was believed to be impossible before Ometheon did it. How did you?"

Thomas stepped forward. "You could have simply shattered that mirror at any time to send him back? To give me back my body? You chose to let my people suffer. To let me suffer. Your soldiers didn't know what you did—did the gods? Did your mother? Did you even try another Path?"

He was furious. To make a mistake was one thing. To lose control of the spirit because it was more powerful was understandable, but to do nothing?

"I did not seek the counsel of the gods. I wanted to resolve the issue myself. I believed I could contain you—him."

Thomas took another step forward. "So, your own ego caused all of this? Your arrogance?

"If you simply lost control of the spirit but couldn't stop, I would understand. I would say you were sloppy and should have consulted with others. But I could understand. Instead, you knew the price I was paying. The price my victims were paying. The price my family paid— and you did nothing! You didn't ask for help? You just let us die, and you claim Ometheon is the monster?"

Thaleia sheathed her sword. She was still unsure, but this man's passion was not Ometheon; it was noble. It was an honor that Ometheon did not have in him.

She shook her head, unable to find words at first. "The fate of all the realms hangs in the balance. If Ometheon's people can destroy the weak spots, the realms will collide. There was once a great city called Atlantis that was built on a weak spot. A trading hub between realms. It was destroyed in a single event when the weak spot fractured. If they all rupture, both our realms will be broken. I should have asked for help, but I had to learn where the Path of Blood to your realm was.

"I should have considered another way. I should have asked for guidance."

Thomas reached into his shirt pocket and pulled out the stack of driver's licenses he had found from the victims of the cult. He carried them on his left side, above his heart, to remember them. To remember that his body killed them. He looked at the stack and began reading names. "Sherri Smith, 32 years old, mother of two.

"My hands opened her body and pulled out her organs while she screamed. She begged for mercy so she could return to her children, and my body laughed. MY BODY!

"I remember pulling out her organs and draping them on my face. That is what you made her endure. You made me endure. I still have nightmares of her blood dripping off my hands because of you.

"I visited her house and hid outside in grief while I watched her little girls cry because mommy never came home. Her life mattered."

He tossed the ID at her breastplate. He didn't throw it like a weapon; he tossed it, relieving his burden and passing it to her. It *tinked* off the metal and fell to the ground. She stumbled back from the weight of the deed, not the laminate.

He read the next card. "Jonathan Skies, 43 years old, was a war veteran who served his people to keep them free, to keep them safe. He deserved to die with a weapon in hand or as an old man in bed. He died when my hands ended his life as he was strapped, defenseless, to a slab of stone. His life mattered."

*Tink.*

"Tanya Jenkins, 17 years old. A child! Her whole life ahead of her. She didn't have a chance to find love, to have children, or to even find a passion in life. She was murdered before she could choose. Her life mattered."

*Tink.*

Leandros wanted to stop this. He just didn't know if he had the right. It wasn't about the man; it wasn't about Thaleia. It was about justice for the victims. Somehow, they felt like victims of this new man, Thaleia, and Ometheon at the same time, and their voices needed to be heard.

He slowly dismounted and took a step forward while Thomas started reading another name. Thaleia's head was lowered under the onslaught, but she saw the movement from the corner of her eye. She made the slightest, almost imperceptible motion with her hand, a simple swipe.

Her commander knew it meant to not interfere. She felt it too. The voices of the voiceless deserved to be heard. He stopped and waited.

Thomas continued to read. With each name, he gave voice to their life. He said they mattered. He passed their license and burden to Thaleia by tossing the ID at her breastplate—*tink*.

He read the last ID. "Rob Warren, 72 years old. A hero." Thomas had been stern—loud, even yelling at points—but for Rob, his voice lowered. It felt more personal. He had to stop for a minute to calm his emotions. When he lived in Rob's house and saw the evidence on his computer, he came to know and respect him. Rob was a friend he never got to meet.

He stood for a moment looking at the ID. He flexed his jaw, took a deep breath, and continued in a low, respectful voice, "He was investigating the disappearance of his friend. They found out and captured him. He was tortured to death by my body to learn what he knew. I believe his death was probably worse than the others because they didn't want him to die; they wanted him to talk.

"Because of his bravery, he bought time, and he had records. I was able to learn who the cult members were in that area. The ones you left behind to kill my people. I learned from his notes where they had meetings, so I went there ahead of them. I waited. At the time, there were only six humans and three satyrs left. That victory is because Rob gave his life for a battle that never should have happened."

He looked at the ID for a long moment in silence. Then he slipped it back into his own pocket, unable to give it up.

"Although there are most likely more names, I only know one more. Thomas. My surname doesn't matter because I no longer have a family. I left my people and my world behind to protect them. After you shattered the mirror, I woke with no memory of what happened—at first. I returned to my home to find months had passed. As I slept, Rebecca, the woman I used to share my life with, and I thought we were safe, at least for a night. A satyr broke into my house and almost killed us both.

"I am a husk of what used to be a man. You murdered my life; you just didn't have the decency to kill my body when you did it.

"You said you had to stop Ometheon and that your actions were necessary. In one month, I found and killed the cult members on my side, learned how to travel the Path of Blood, made allies in this land, tracked you down, and demanded answers. You are the daughter of a god. With all your resources, you couldn't do better?"

Thaleia was at a true loss for words or solutions. He was correct on all counts. She had been proud of stopping Ometheon, but she never thought of the consequences of her actions. Now, facing Thomas, a man filled with righteous anger, she could not respond.

The silence hung heavily over the field. Thomas waited. He was patient. He had been searching for answers as to what type of person could do this. He was surprised that no one had struck him down yet. That at least showed she had some honor left in her.

Weakly, her voice barely audible, she answered, "I failed. I cannot bring back the dead. Their deaths are my burden, not yours. You had no choice—I did. I will help you rebuild your life in whatever way I can."

There was no fire left in his voice when he responded, "Their blood runs down my hands every night when I sleep. Their burden cannot be removed. Perhaps for you it is as simple as rebuilding a life. You are immortal. I don't have time to rebuild what I left.

"Instead, I will help others have a life worth living. Those with power cannot simply step on those without. There must be accountability. I have learned of other injustices. I will give what's left of my life for them."

Thaleia lowered her head, ashamed and weak after the confrontation. She slowly looked up and into his eyes. "I can offer you my immortality. My choices have cost you your life. I can offer the gift of mine."

Thomas narrowed his eyes in shock. He hadn't come seeking immortality, but he was surprised the monster that destroyed so many lives would actually offer it. "Did you speak the truth about the threat to all the realms?"

"On my honor, I swear it."

Thomas nodded. "Then how could I accept your offer in good conscience? You are already investigating a great threat. I would not be who I am if I let my selfish desires outweigh the danger the realms face."

"Perhaps there is another option," she replied after a pause. "You are correct that your accomplishments are impressive. Perhaps it is time I learned to ask for help. I ask, not for me, but for everyone in the realms. Let me petition my mother on your behalf. I owe you a debt, and I will accept your judgment over me, but let us meet with her first."

He was intrigued. Athena was the one who destroyed Isadora for her own selfish desires. If he could actually be given power to help others, then he could keep Isadora safe.

Perhaps it was time he learned what a god could offer.

# CHAPTER 44
## *Meeting Her Mom*

Thomas responded, "I agree. I will meet with your mother. If the fate of the realms is at stake, then I will act to help. When do we leave?"

"I will activate a token to inform the goddess Athena that I am ready to return," she answered. "We will leave within a short watch's time. While you wait, I invite you to use my physician, Lysandra. She has cared for the phalanx during several campaigns. Your horses will be cared for, and your equipment will be brought to you. Leandros will show you."

He nodded and began hobbling toward Leandros, but he looked back to see her kneel. She began collecting the licenses of the people who died because of her decision. She studied them as though committing their faces to memory. He watched her for a moment, wondering if he had misjudged her.

Lysandra welcomed him to her tent as she said, "Take off your pants."

*Why didn't I know about this place in high school?*

She went over his injuries. Most of them were older and were healing on their own, but the spear wound was fresh and deep. She applied a pain-killing ointment and wrapped his leg. As she was wrapping up, Thaleia entered the tent.

With a nod, Lysandra was dismissed. Thaleia then turned to Thomas, shuffling uncomfortably. "I wish to offer an actual apology for what you have endured. I realized that I had not said the words to you. I am sorry. My actions… they are inexcusable. I had told myself it was best not to bother others, but you are correct. It was arrogance."

Thomas reached his hand forward. "My people have a gesture. Two people extend their hands, palms open, and grasp each other. It is to symbolize two things: first, they carry no weapon; second, each will uphold the other if they fall. If we are to work together to end this threat, then we should each be willing to uphold the other. It is called a handshake and is used to show an understanding has been reached."

She tentatively reached forward and took his hand. She smiled as they shook. It was a strange gesture, but also a new start.

"There is one other matter," she said. "The townsfolk reported a murder by a creature we call a Fury. They are also known as Erinyes. It was in the company of a powerful man who controlled it. I was sent to investigate. Do you know anything of this matter?"

He nodded in response. "I am the man, but I did not control her. She was injured long ago and separated from her people. I am her friend, not her master. As for the attack, it was self-defense on her part. A man grabbed her forcefully; she stopped him. Speak with the tavern owner; he witnessed the event."

"After everything you accomplished, you also befriended a Fury? That is unheard of, even in lore."

He shrugged. "I'm friendly."

They looked at each other for a moment before she could form a response to that statement. "Our transportation has arrived. We should depart. Your supplies are waiting in the chariot."

They walked out of the tent. Thomas was immediately awed by the sight that awaited him.

A chariot of polished bronze inlaid with dark lapis stood before them. Its edges were etched in celestial script that pulsed like a heartbeat. Its wheels did not touch earth but hovered a finger's breadth above it. The script continued around the wheels as well, slowly moving along the wheel, giving the impression of motion even when still.

But the most inspiring part of their vehicle was the mechanism that powered it, two Pegasi, the mythical winged horses of legend. Each of them stood taller than any mortal steed. Their bodies looked modeled from stone, white marble, with majestic wings folded like sails at rest along their backs. They pawed the ground as though anxious to fly.

The chariot had no driver. It followed the will of Athena herself and was waiting for their charges to climb aboard.

Thomas let out a low, surprised chuckle.

Thaleia turned to him, amused. "Have you never flown before?"

"I have, but by mechanical means, never by such beautiful beings. Pegasi?"

She was surprised he knew the name, even more surprised that his people could fly without them. "Yes, you know them?"

He nodded. "My world has legends from thousands of years ago, but they were believed to be stories, nothing more. I am happy to actually see them. Shall we ride?"

He was pleased to see his backpack and a couple of bags in the chariot as well as his sword, shield, and spear. They weren't keeping his weapons from him.

*I wonder if my horses will be brought to Olympus.*

*I would hate to have to walk back here to get them.*

*Hey Thomas, you are about to ride a flying chariot pulled by winged horses.*

*Don't look a gift Pegasus in the mouth.*

The journey passed quickly and mostly in silence. It had been a heavy exchange earlier, and neither of them had anything left to say.

They landed right outside Athena's Hall, and he followed Thaleia inside. It was also awe-inspiring, but he kept that close to the vest. This world was filled with many wonders but also horrors. He knew what Athena had done to Isadora. He would not be easily swayed, but he also knew she would destroy him in a second if he got in her way. He wanted to see how the goddess of wisdom would handle this situation.

She led them to a table with maps spread across it and a tall, beautiful woman who stood over it. She wasn't beautiful in a contemporary sense. She looked as though she were modeled from bronze. Technically perfect. Impressive. But cold.

Her head turned slowly, intentionally studying him, the ragged, limping, bloody mortal who was hobbling across her great hall.

Thaleia could tell her mother wasn't pleased. She didn't like surprises, but she would want to question this mortal who crosses realms and befriends creatures of legend.

She spoke formally as she saluted, obeying the protocol appropriate for a goddess in her hall. "I am Thaleia, Bearer of the Threads of Ruin, Vanquisher of the Emissary of Apophis, and Destroyer of the Shadow Gate of Lem. I come to petition the goddess Athena for her wisdom and strength."

Thomas looked from the goddess to Thaleia, unsure of protocol. He said, "Hi, I'm Thomas."

Athena arched an eyebrow as she turned her body to face them. "I will hear your petition."

Thaleia told the story of what had happened over the past several months. She did not hold back to protect herself from her mother's wrath. She confessed her use of the cursed relic and the trip through the Path of Blood. She explained how Thomas, as a mere mortal, had the power to travel that Path and track her down. She left out one detail. She did not mention that Thomas had befriended a Fury.

He wondered if she was protecting him.

After she finished her story, Athena turned to Thomas, weighing him anew with this information about his feats. "Are these words true, Thomas? Did a mortal travel the Path of Blood without the blessing of a god?"

"Yes."

"And how did a mortal force open the door? How many did you kill?"

He looked directly into her eyes, unafraid. "I did not kill anyone to activate the Path of Blood. I used small bits of blood from several people who gave their blood freely. I used mine as well."

She smiled. She appreciated strategy.

"Very well, daughter. What is your petition?"

Thaleia looked at Thomas, a moment of fear and hesitation passing before she gave words to her request. "Thomas's life was destroyed because of my choices, my arrogance. I offered my immortality as recompense. He said he doesn't want my life. He wants accountability. When I told him of the threat to the realms, he offered to help. He is a great hero, but he is injured, and his life is broken. I ask that he be empowered. Like the heroes of legend. I submit to him and ask that he be given the power to pass judgment, regardless of the cost to me."

Athena's smile vanished. "This is no small favor you ask, daughter. If I empower him over you, he could choose to strike you down. He is mortal. He does not have the soul of a god. Mortals are fickle, easily swayed. They can be rocked like ships on the ocean by the smallest waves."

Her daughter replied, "This mortal had the drive to accomplish tasks thought impossible. He will not be swayed as easily as others. The destruction of his life is my doing. Please, goddess, help me correct my mistake."

Athena walked up to her daughter, paused to consider, then turned and walked out of the room.

Thomas looked at Thaleia, confused. "So… was that a no?"

"No. I mean 'no' it wasn't a no. Or possibly no. She is the goddess of wisdom. She sometimes takes a moment to consider, but if her answer was no, she would have said it now. We will have to wait. Are your legs able to stand, or are the injuries causing issues? I can arrange for a chair."

He shook his head. "No, but thank you. I can stand for a bit."

They stood in silence for twenty minutes—he checked his watch—before Athena returned with a servant carrying a box.

The servant placed the box on the table and opened it. Inside, something was wrapped in a blanket. At Athena's gesture, the servant carefully unwrapped a sword, taking great care not to touch it. The blade looked like Damascus steel, but instead of black and silver lines, it was black, streaked with lines that glowed like embers. They moved slowly, almost imperceptibly, as though a slow fire smoldered beneath the surface.

Once it was exposed, the servant looked to Athena. The goddess nodded, and the servant left quickly, happy to be away from the strange scene.

She looked at Thomas, motioning for him to come forward. "Mortal known as Thomas. My daughter has petitioned that you be empowered to hold even a demigod accountable. This comes with risk. Your best choice might be to return to your old life. To live what you have left in peace if you can. But I will honor her wish if you accept the risk."

"It is the realms that are at risk. If I chose the safe path, I would no longer be me. If I can help, I will. I accept the risk."

Athena looked to her daughter, holding the moment, then

looked back to the mortal. "So be it. It is your risk, your will. I shall grant the petition. I agree to empower your soul to manifest its power, but it will be your power, simply brought to the surface. But a demigod would still remain beyond the reach of a mortal, so I also grant this weapon. It is an ancient blade, the origin unknown. It has the power to challenge even gods if you will accept it."

He nodded. "I accept."

She placed her hand on his chest. A shimmer of light appeared, but it didn't seem to have an origin. It simply was.

Thomas gasped as he felt something within him. It seemed to move through him. Out of him. But not away. Like having a chill that vibrates from within. Then it returns.

He looked down at his hands. A light sheen spread across his skin, like a mist, but it slowly turned a blue, silver hue. It drifted out of his pores, over his skin, slowly covering his whole body. It began to become solid, hard, and metallic. The light suddenly snapped into place as a full suit of armor that clung to him like a second skin, forged in a shape both ancient and familiar.

Its form echoed the lines of Greek hoplite panoply with a broad chestplate and angular greaves.

The metal was a deep, smoky steel, dark as storm-touched iron. Not black, but nearly. The surface caught the light in dull, ember-like glimmers, like the last glow of a forge gone cold. Subtle veins of ashen silver traced faint, almost imperceptible patterns across its surface, like the remains of ancient threads burned into the metal.

A cloak rippled into shape, draped from his shoulders like a shadow cut from the darkest night. It flowed like silk but seemed lighter. It wasn't really cloth; it was a shadow of his soul.

He could feel powers beginning to form—manifestations of his soul, his desire for justice, and the destruction of evil. He felt the ability to see truth, to see insights into souls themselves. A resonance. He looked around with new eyes. He could still see as before, but now he also saw lines of energy, vibrations.

Athena and Thomas looked into each other's eyes, both studying the other. He saw images, thoughts, sins.

He saw that she doubted the strength of any mortal's soul. This mortal was going to be given the power to judge her daughter. She didn't like it. The goddess of strategy could not allow an empowered mortal to have the ability to challenge her bloodline. His empowerment was meant to backfire. She thought his weak mortal greed and selfishness would cause his soul to manifest in an unstable manner. She thought it would rip him apart and kill him on the spot. She thought wrong.

But that wasn't her only plan. In case he lived, she also gave him the sword without telling him what it was. It was older than the gods themselves. They did not know its origin. She didn't lie about the power. It could kill gods and had killed them, but only when they tried to use it. The few that tried had their souls consumed before they could strike. The weapon had many names: Godkiller, Eternal Flame, or simply the Sword of Eden.

He looked at the sword. Its existence had a resonance that mirrored his own. He understood it. It was meant for justice. It was meant for destroying evil. The gods who tried to use it had used it for their own selfish desires.

It called to him. It sensed a kindred spirit that sought justice. As his fingers wrapped around the hilt, coils of flame circled them and rose along his arm.

Athena's eyes narrowed as he lifted the sword. The sword flared to life, light pulsing through the ember lines. Brighter and brighter it shone, until it separated. Like fireflies gently lifting from a branch, the weapon turned into motes of energy. They lazily drifted toward him, surrounding his body. The embers absorbed into him just as his armor had shimmered out. His soul absorbed the sword.

The goddess watched the transition with mounting curiosity. This mortal was a mortal no more. He said he wished to be helpful; perhaps he could be. A new pawn for her to play with.

She looked into his eyes with the amusement of a child with a new toy—until they changed. At the corners of his eyes, liquid metal seemed to seep over the whites, slowly pooling until his eyes looked like mercury, shimmering and reflecting. Then they shifted and reflected sins instead of light. Athena saw her plan to kill him mirrored back in his gaze. He knew what she tried to do. And he showed her that he knew. The goddess of strategy was revealed.

She saw her own sins. She felt them. The goddess of wisdom and war looked away. She didn't mean to do so, but with all her planning and scheming, she did not expect this. The mortal turned into something new and powerful. Then the sword accepted him, and his power deepened. Her mind raced to formulate a new plan, but she didn't have enough details. She didn't know how strong the sword had made him.

He turned to Thaleia. She looked into his eyes. She saw all of it: Thomas waking in the woods, soaked in blood. Rebecca was injured, almost killed. Victims mutilated while they screamed. Children crying over their mother. She saw everything her choices caused. More than seeing it, she felt it. She felt the fear, the pain, the hopelessness of being lost and hunted. He didn't force it into her. His eyes simply reflected the truth.

She realized something about Thomas in contrast to her life of blessings. It is not strength to be unafraid when victory is assured. It is strength to defy fear when you have no power. He had had no power, yet he did not stop.

Thaleia dropped to her knees and sobbed. She knew what had happened, but this made it real. It made her feel it, not just know it.

She fought back the tears. Her mother instilled in her that warriors don't cry. She clenched her teeth and said, "I am ready to accept your judgment. I will not fight it."

He gently touched her cheek with his right hand and tilted her face to look up at him. His eyes had been the most horrifying things she had ever seen, but they were changed again. The reflection was gone. In their place were his normal human eyes. Weary. Brown. But kind.

"You made bad decisions, but you are not evil. You lost sight of what is important because of pride. Swear to never compel an innocent to lose their innocence again."

Thaleia took a breath, still fighting her emotions. "I swear it. I will never put my pride over an innocent life again. I will help mortals so that I might atone for the lives I destroyed."

Thomas held his left hand forward, the gauntlet absorbing back into his body, revealing his fingers. He closed his hand, and when he opened it, a sphere of black obsidian glass rested in his palm. The core of the stone held an ember bolt of lightning that pulsed the same shade as the motes from his sword. The lightning was bright at first but dimmed to a dull glow.

"It is a link, a manifestation of my soul and your oath. You are bound to me through this promise."

Thaleia took the stone. It felt warm in her hand. "I will keep it as a reminder of my failings. To make sure I do not repeat my sins."

Thomas crouched so they were eye level. "No, it is not a reminder of the past. It is a promise of the future. It is a symbol of the peace you will bring. If your oath is about to break, I will feel the resonance of your soul through the stone, and if possible, I will help you."

She closed her fingers around the stone. Somehow, holding it gave her a sense of comfort and of peace. He would hold her accountable, but he also offered to help. She smiled despite the rawness of her emotions.

They were allies now, linked by oaths and souls with a common purpose of saving the realms.

THOMAS, THE OATHWARDEN, WAS BORN.

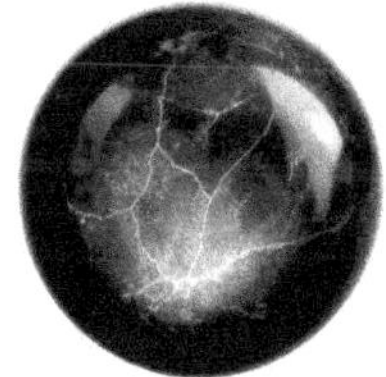

Hello Readers,

Thank you for making it all the way back here. I love building this world and I hope you will continue the journey with me.

I have a personal request: reviews help search algorithms and make it easier for others to discover my story. If you like my tale— Please leave a review.

Whether you leave a review or not, thank you for being a part of my world.

James

*Newsletter sign-up available at www.jamesdconrad.com*

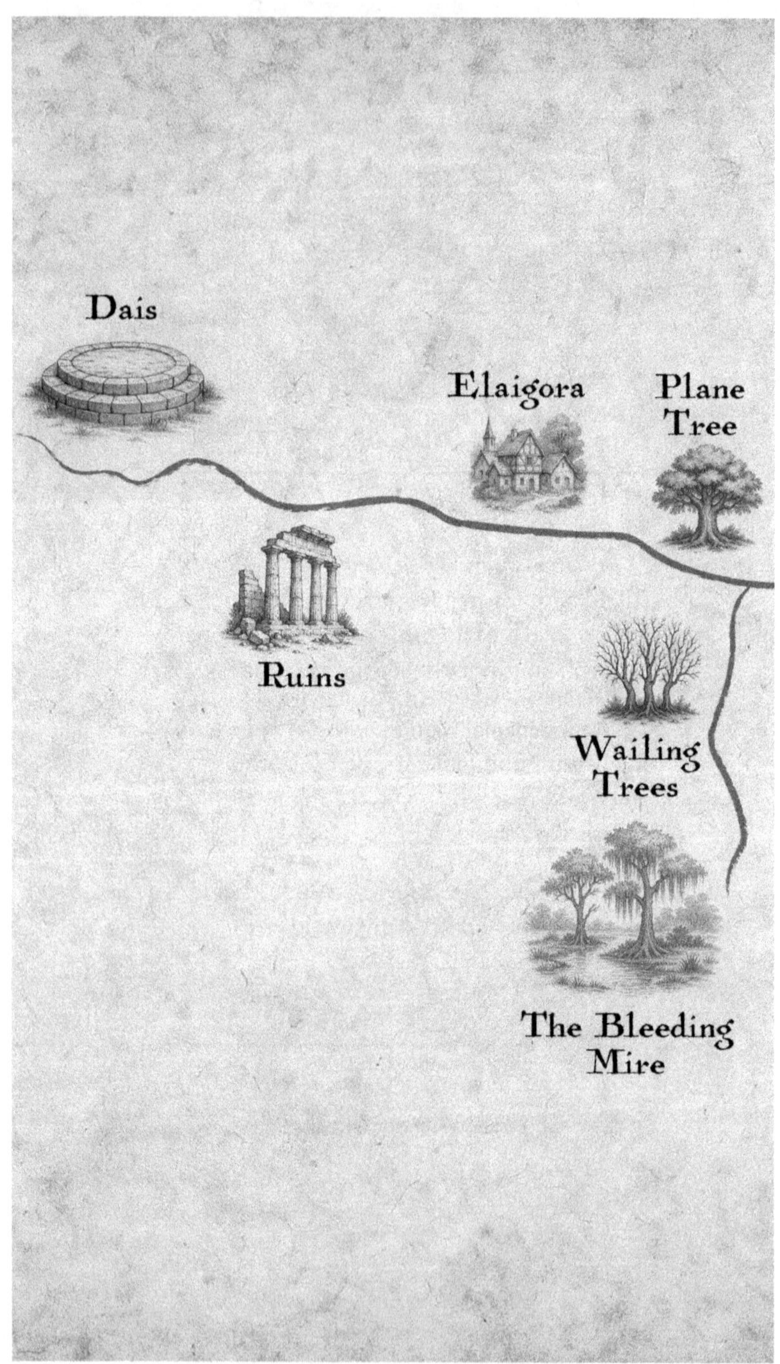

Dais
Elaigora
Plane Tree
Ruins
Wailing Trees
The Bleeding Mire

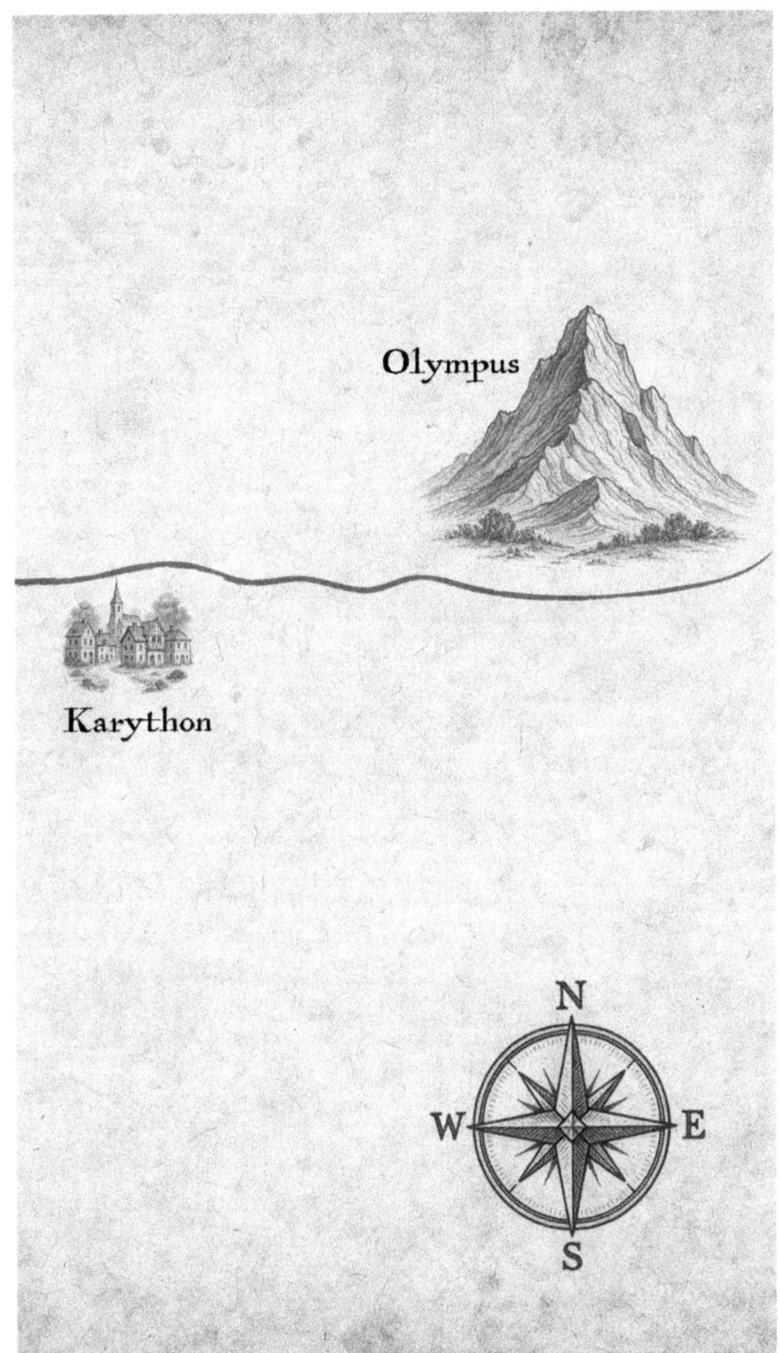
Olympus
Karython
N
W
E
S

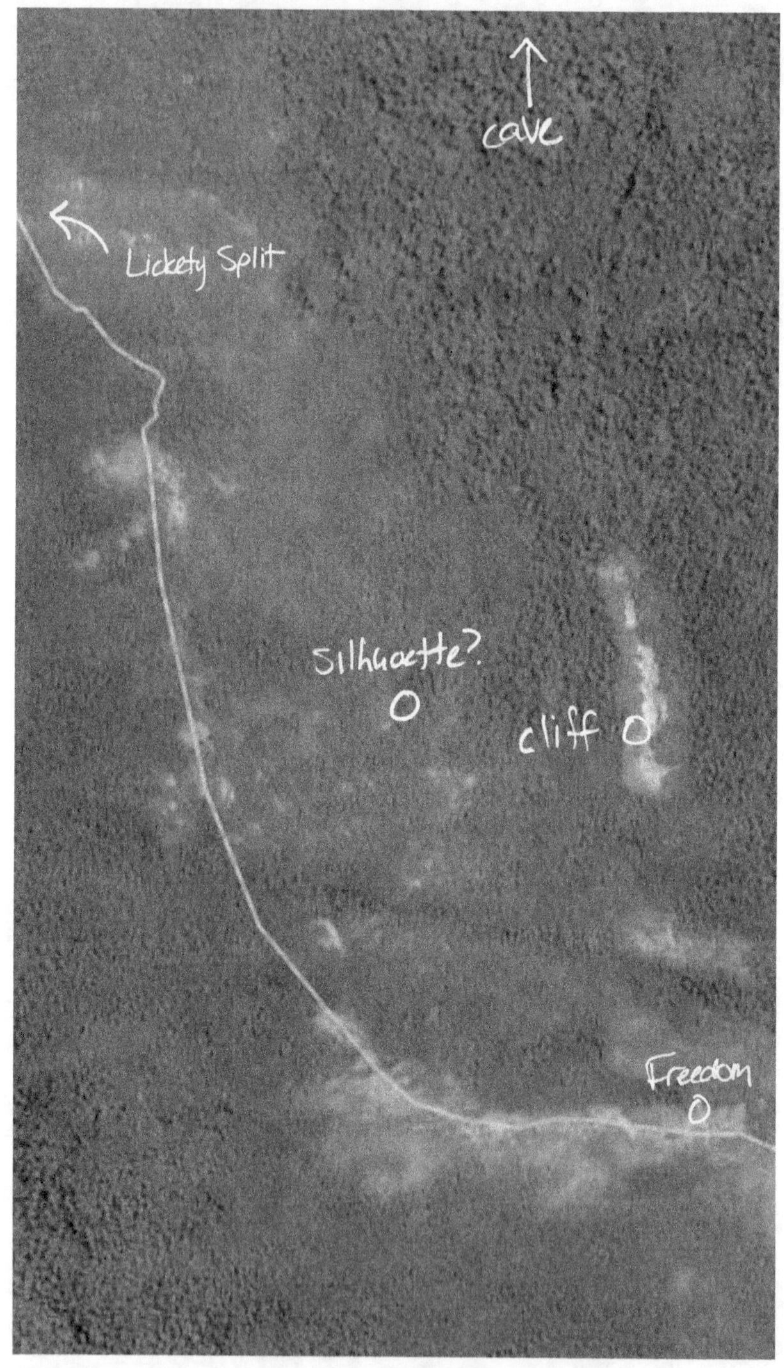
cave
Lickety Split
Silhuoette?
cliff
Freedom

# APPENDIX

## GREEK GODS

**Apollo:** In Greek mythology, Apollo is the god of the sun, music, prophecy, healing, and archery. The son of Zeus and Leto and twin brother of Artemis, Apollo is often depicted as a youthful, radiant figure representing harmony, reason, and order. He served as the patron of the Oracle of Delphi, where mortals sought divine guidance. Apollo is also associated with the lyre, the laurel tree, and the bow. Widely worshipped across the Greek world, he was seen as a bringer of both plague and healing, embodying the balance of destruction and restoration.

**Ares:** In Greek mythology, Ares is the god of war, representing the brutal, chaotic, and violent aspects of battle. He is the son of Zeus and Hera, and often portrayed as impulsive, bloodthirsty, and feared even by other gods. Unlike Athena, who embodies strategic warfare, Ares is associated with raw aggression and the frenzy of combat. Though worshipped in some regions, particularly Thrace, he was not widely revered in the same way as other Olympian gods. His symbols include the spear, helmet, warthog, and vulture.

His followers are often those who revel in the power to inflict pain or take what they want through force and domination. If Athena is a chess master, Ares is the one who flips the board and storms out.

**Athena:** In Greek mythology, Athena is the goddess of wisdom, warfare, and crafts. She was said to be born fully grown and armored from the head of Zeus, which is an actual, crazy detail from mythology. Known for her strategic mind and calm demeanor, she was a patron of heroes and the city of Athens, which was named in her honor. Her symbols include the owl, the olive tree, and the aegis—a protective shield associated with Zeus. Unlike Ares, who represents chaotic battle, Athena embodies disciplined warfare and civic order.

In this world, she is the mother of Thaleia. Her strategic mind sometimes prioritizes outcomes over individuals. Victory over morality. For instance: what is the best way to achieve peace? Kill everyone. The logic is sound. The result is peace.

**Hephaestus:** In Greek mythology, Hephaestus is the god of fire, metalworking, and craftsmanship. The son of Zeus and Hera, Hephaestus is known for his skill as a divine smith, forging powerful weapons and artifacts for the gods, including the armor of Achilles and the thunderbolts of Zeus. He is physically lame, having been cast from Olympus as a child. Despite his deformity, Hephaestus is revered for his creativity and technical mastery. His symbols include the hammer, anvil, and forge.

He forged the Threads of Ruin, Thaleia's net. He crafted it to catch his cheating wife in bed with Ares. The net was invisible and indestructible. It became a unique item when the confrontation of three gods bled into it.

**Hermes:** In Greek mythology, Hermes is the god of travel, communication, commerce, and trickery. He is also known as the messenger of the gods. The son of Zeus and the nymph Maia, Hermes is often depicted wearing winged sandals, a winged cap, and carrying the caduceus—a staff entwined with two snakes. He was believed to guide souls to the underworld and served as a protector of travelers, herdsmen, and thieves. Known for his speed, cleverness, and wit, Hermes plays a role in many myths as both a helper and a trickster.

He is trouble but not because of evil—because of mischief. He can fly thanks to his sandals, and often borrows the Cap of Hades, which grants invisibility. Even the gods don't understand his speed. He moves from one place to another quickly, whether through teleportation, acceleration, or something tricky; they are not sure.

**Zeus:** In Greek mythology, Zeus is the king of the gods and ruler of Mount Olympus. He is the god of the sky, thunder, and lightning, wielding the powerful thunderbolt as his signature weapon. Son of the Titans Cronus and Rhea, Zeus led the Olympian gods in overthrowing the Titans and established order among the gods and mortals. He is often depicted as a regal, mature man with a beard, symbolizing authority and power. Zeus presides over law, justice, and hospitality, and his numerous myths include both his roles as protector and as a figure with many human-like flaws.

He likes the ladies.

# FURIES OR ERINYES

**Furies:** They are goddesses of vengeance who pursue those guilty of crimes against family, particularly murder and oath-breaking. They are older than the Greek gods and were born from primordial beings.

Three Furies were set apart. They could call the swarm when necessary, but the Three vanished a millennium ago. Most of the swarm went to sleep over the next one hundred years when they couldn't find their sisters. They sought the safety of the underworld or old places of power, such as temples. A few remained awake afterward, continuing to do good in the world by destroying the most heinous beings.

Their number has never increased, as there are no male Furies. That is why they went to sleep. To preserve those that remained until the Three returned.

# EGYPTIAN GODS

**Apophis:** An ancient Egyptian figure representing chaos and disorder. Often depicted as a giant serpent, Apophis was said to attack the sun god Ra during his nightly journey through the underworld. Though never part of the divine order himself, Apophis symbolized the eternal struggle between stability and destruction. He is not a god, but a mythic enemy of the gods—an embodiment of cosmic threat rather than a character with personality or lineage.

None of that matters. He is simply from a different group of powerful beings that Thaleia once fought. He calls himself a god just as the Greek gods do, but for the most part, they leave each other alone to keep the peace. I picked him because my kids loved Stargate SG-1 growing up, and that is how complex lore works.

# CRITTERS

**<u>Amazons:</u>** In Greek mythology, the Amazons are a legendary tribe of warrior women renowned for their martial skill and independence. The Amazons are said to have created a society largely separate from men. They are sometimes depicted as adopting female children and only occasionally having children through unions with men from outside their society. They were known to raise their daughters as warriors, often rejecting traditional Greek gender roles. The Amazons appear in many myths, notably as opponents of heroes such as Heracles, Theseus, and Achilles.

They are proud and want to live their own lives without being possessed or controlled. They also aren't really "critters," but I didn't want to make another category. It seemed like too much work.

**<u>Empusae:</u>** In Greek mythology, the Empusae (singular Empusa) are a race of female demons or spirits often associated with the goddess Hecate. Known for their shape-shifting abilities, they frequently appear as beautiful women to seduce and deceive travelers, especially at night. Beneath their alluring façades, Empusae are said to prey on human victims, drinking their blood or life force. They embody themes of danger, deception, and the boundary between the mortal and supernatural worlds. Terrifying and malevolent, they are closely linked to witchcraft, curses, and the underworld.

**<u>Goēs:</u>** In ancient Greek tradition, a Goēs (plural Goētes) refers to a sorcerer, magician, or practitioner of the dark arts, often associated with necromancy, curses, and the summoning of spirits. The term carries connotations of secret or forbidden knowledge and was sometimes used derogatorily to describe those who sought power through occult means. While not always evil, Goētes were often viewed with suspicion or fear, occupying a liminal space between the mortal and divine, and sometimes involved in manipulating supernatural forces for personal gain or vengeance.

The Goētes associated with the cult also seem to have the power to cause others to lose themselves in bloodlust, turning on their own allies.

**<u>Kobaloi:</u>** In ancient Greek mythology, the Kobaloi (singular Kobalos) are mischievous, impish spirits known for their trickery and playful pranks. They are often associated with caves, forests, and dark places, where they amuse themselves by deceiving or startling humans. Unlike malevolent demons, Kobaloi are generally more pranksters than threats, sometimes exhibiting a crude or bawdy sense of humor. They are considered minor nature spirits and share some characteristics with satyrs and other rustic entities.

Like the satyrs, there appears to be a portion of them within the Agitators, the group Thomas calls cultists. The kobaloi in that group are more aggressive and stronger than normal. The ones Thomas has met so far are dead.

**Minotaurs:** The Minotaurs are a race of formidable, bull-headed humanoids known for their immense strength and fierce warrior culture. Said to descend from the original Minotaur—a unique offspring of divine and mortal lineage—this race is believed to have spread in isolated regions beyond the reach of the Greek world. Minotaurs possess great endurance and a primal connection to nature, often living in caves or rugged wilderness.

Known both for their physical power and tribal honor, Minotaurs value strength and loyalty above all. Though feared by many, some legends tell of Minotaurs who have allied with humans or gods, serving as guardians or fierce warriors. Their culture blends raw ferocity with a strict code, making them formidable foes.

**Satyrs:** In Greek mythology, Satyrs are male nature spirits associated with wild places, music, and revelry. Depicted with human upper bodies and the legs, tails, and horns of goats. They represent untamed natural forces that love celebration, plays, and wine.

Though all Satyrs are male, myths suggest they reproduce by fathering children with mortal women or nature spirits. In such unions, the offspring inherit the form and nature of the Satyr father, allowing the race to persist across generations despite their lack of female counterparts.

The Satyrs associated with the cult are more aggressive, stronger, and larger than normal representatives of their kin. They are crazed with bloodlust. Or plain craziness.

**Pegasi:** In Greek mythology, the most famous of the winged horses is Pegasus, born from the blood of the Gorgon Medusa when she was slain by Perseus. While ancient sources generally treat Pegasus as a unique creature, later traditions and artistic depictions expanded the idea into a race of winged horses, commonly referred to as Pegasi.

Pegasi are typically described as majestic horses with powerful feathered wings, capable of flight, and often associated with divine favor, storms, or the heavens. They are sometimes linked to Poseidon, god of horses and the sea, and were believed to dwell in remote mountainous regions or to serve celestial beings. In myth-inspired traditions, Pegasi symbolize freedom, swiftness, and the boundary between earth and sky.

# ARMOR

**Thaleia's Manica:** Thaleia wears a custom arm guard modeled after Roman manicae. It consists of overlapping metal plates from shoulder to elbow, offering protection against glancing blows and strikes during close combat. From elbow to wrist, the arm is shielded by a solid bracer, reinforcing the most exposed area. The entire assembly is mounted on a leather backing that encloses the arm, allowing for secure movement without restricting agility. Designed for her non-dominant arm, the manica serves as both armor and a substitute for a shield, balancing defense with speed.

# HOPLITE ARMOR

Hoplites were heavily armed infantry soldiers of ancient Greek city-states, equipped for close-formation combat. Their armor typically included:

**Helmet:** Usually made of bronze, with styles such as the Corinthian helmet featuring a nose guard and cheek plates.

**Breastplate (Thorax):** Crafted from bronze or layered linen (linothorax), protecting the torso.

**Pteruges:** Strips of leather or fabric hanging from the waist or shoulders, sometimes reinforced with small plates, protecting the hips and upper thighs while allowing mobility.

**Greaves:** Bronze shin guards covering the lower legs.

Hoplite armor balanced protection with flexibility, enabling soldiers to fight effectively in tight formations.

# WEAPONS

**.45-70 Lever-Action Brush Gun (Short Barrel):** The .45-70 lever-action rifle is a powerful firearm originally developed in the late 19th century for big-game hunting and military use. Chambered for the .45-70 Government cartridge, it delivers substantial stopping power and effective range. A short-barreled version, often called a "brush gun," is designed specifically for maneuverability in dense brush, thick woods, or jungle environments. Its compact size allows quick handling in tight spaces where longer rifles would be cumbersome. Despite the shorter barrel reducing muzzle velocity slightly, the heavy, slower .45-70 bullet carries enough momentum to penetrate tall grass, light brush, and other natural obstacles with minimal deflection. The lever-action mechanism allows for rapid follow-up shots, making it a favored choice for hunters and outdoorsmen operating in challenging terrain or destroying statues. Clearly, everyone should have one.

**Flame Whip:** A weapon summoned from the Fury's inner being, made of living flame. It forms and moves according to her will alone, burning with intense heat and precision. The whip can vary in length and intensity, vanishing when not needed. It leaves no ash, only the mark of judgment. The whip is not a separate entity—it acts only as an extension of the Fury herself.

It is her, so she cannot drop it any more readily than a person can drop their fingers.

**Khopeshes:** (yes, that is the plural version. I thought about writing kohopesheseseseseses) are sickle-shaped swords that originated in ancient Egypt. They feature a straight grip with a forward-curving blade that broadens and hooks outward near the tip. The outer edge of the curve is sharpened, making it ideal for slashing and hooking attacks. Unlike a typical curved sword, the khopesh combines the chopping power of an axe with the control of a short blade. It often measures between 20 and 24 inches in length and was commonly made of bronze or iron. The Sekhem-Ka is made out of nightmares or something.

**Sekhem-Ka:** : Translation: Might of the Soul. It is an ancient khopesh of Egyptian origin. The dark blade is marked by veins of deep crimson that seem to shift and pulse, giving the impression of a living weapon. Solid to the touch, it resists corrosion and the wear of time. The blade strikes with unusual weight and momentum, and it can instill growing bloodlust in those who wield it. Thaleia sometimes carries the Sekhem-Ka not out of pride but necessity; it is a weapon accepted rather than chosen. Those who have weak will find it nearly impossible to let go once they take it up.

**Smith & Wesson Model 629 (.44 Magnum)** The Smith & Wesson Model 629 is a robust, stainless steel revolver chambered for the powerful .44 Magnum cartridge. Known for its significant stopping power, it earned a reputation as a "hand cannon" due to its size, recoil, and effectiveness in both hunting and self-defense. The Model 629 features a six-round cylinder, a heavy frame to absorb recoil, and a smooth trigger pull for precision shooting. Its durability and firepower make it a favored sidearm among those needing reliability and impact in close quarters or high-threat situations like Minotaurs or door-to-door salesmen.

**SPAS-12:** The SPAS-12 (Special Purpose Automatic Shotgun) is an Italian-made combat shotgun developed by Franchi in the late 1970s. Known for its distinctive appearance, it functions as both a semi-automatic and pump-action shotgun, allowing versatility in various combat scenarios. The SPAS-12 is chambered to hold six rounds of 12-gauge shells and is favored for its durability, reliability, and powerful stopping capability at close ranges. It features a folding stock, a distinctive perforated heat shield, and a robust design suited for military, law enforcement, and tactical use.

**Threads of Ruin:** The name given to the net made by Hephaestus. He used it to trap his wife, betraying him with Ares. It is unbreakable and unescapable (yes, that's a word, so is "inescapable," but "unescapable" is older. Respect your elders.). As a result of all the gods looking on at Aphrodite's shame, Ares's anger, and Hephaestus's truth, the item was empowered with a bit of each of them. It can be coiled into a rope or cast as a net. It can inflict pain at will or when a person is dishonest.

Thaleia loves hurting people… just bad people.

**Xiphos:** The xiphos is a short, double-edged sword used by ancient Greek warriors, especially hoplites. Typically measuring 18 to 24 inches in length, it features a straight, leaf-shaped blade designed for cutting and thrusting in close combat. The blade widens slightly before tapering to a point, allowing for deep, precise strikes. It was often carried as a secondary weapon, used when the primary spear was lost or broken. The xiphos was usually crafted from bronze or iron and fitted with a simple guard and grip for efficient handling in tight phalanx formations.

Thaleia's xiphos is named Aletheia, which means truth (literally unforgetfulness or no secrets). It is special. Read book two.

## OTHER

**Dirty Harry:** You should watch it. The bad guy is hilarious.

**Grandpa:** He is real, and he told me not to answer voices at night. Things in the woods would call you, and if you answered, you wouldn't come back. They have roots in tribes from the region. They were known by many names: whistlers, callers, voices, spirits, or simply "the wood." They weren't great at naming stuff.

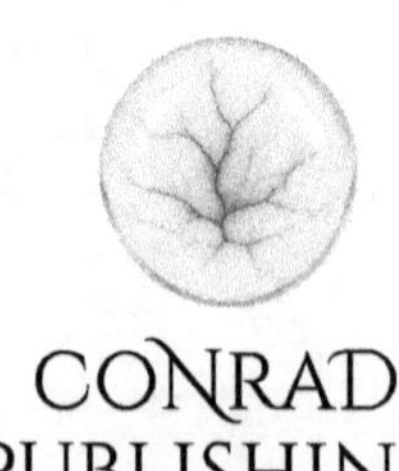

CONRAD
PUBLISHING